KARA SHIELDMAIDEN OF EIRE

THE FORERUNNER SERIES BOOK 4

JAY VELOSO BATISTA

DARVEL LLC

Copyright © 2022 by John "Jay" Veloso Batista, Jr.

US Copyright Registration: TXu 2-324-130

eBook ISBN 1078109567

Paperback ISBN 979-8837016448

Hardback ISBN 979-8837021121

Library of Congress Control Number: 2023910993

All rights reserved.

No part of this book may be reproduced in any form or by any electronic or mechanical means, including information storage and retrieval systems, without written permission from the author, except for the use of brief quotations in a book review.

For Rachael Noel
my dearheart
my inspiration
my brave shieldmaiden

"In the flush of love's light, we dare be brave. And suddenly we see that love costs all we are, and will ever be. Yet it is only love which sets us free."
-Maya Angelou

∿

In memory of Suzanne Elizabeth
Mother, Grandmother, Teacher & Friend
1933 - 2021

SPECIAL THANKS TO:

Complicated works like this novel require assistance. I want to thank those "behind the scenes" individuals who helped and supported me in the process:

—Xanxa Symanah "Sarah" Wallace and Gil Blackadore, author of the 'Donavan and Lafourche' mystery series, for their valuable synopsis input and guidance

—Cover art by the incomparable Jake Caleb of https://www.Jcalebdesigns.com

—Proofreading provided by the Hyper-Speller at https://www.wordrefiner.com

—Maps and drawings by Joe Cantrell and James Clark

—Quarantine cloister at the ITC Maurya Hotel, New Delhi for uninterrupted time to write chapter 8

—Liquid encouragement and support from my fellow author Norman Gaither

—My incredible ARC readers including the two Mikes, Hannah, Rachael, Joe, Frank, Ed, Ken, Mala, Camilla, Jill, Tonia, Susan, Lars-Ingemar, Dina, Nick and many more

—My author social media groups, the 200 Rogues of FB and Twitter Self-Publishing Group

—All the "Shieldmaidens" who I have been honored to serve beside in business and life, including Linda, Susan, Mary, Esther, Mala, Karyn, Maureen, Rachael, Sarah & MA, and my surfer-girl grand-nieces: Thank you all for enriching my life

—and for my wife Annette's continuing support: through the trying and the boring, you have been my steadfast anchor and biggest fan. Love ya!

CHAPTER 1
PREFACE: OUR STORY SO FAR...

During the mid-9th century raids of the British Isle, a Saxon witch cursed Viking invader Alf "Ironfist" before she died at his hands, damned for three generations. Conqueror Alf settled west of Jorvik in the Kingdom of Northumbria, established a homestead compound, and fathered three sons, his first-born Alf, Agne and Karl. His wife lost in childbirth, Ironfist implemented a successful trading business, extended his farming lands and attracted supporters and tenant farmers to his banner.

Good Danes, Ironfist and his sons answered the call to fight in what later became known as the "Great Horde" and assisted in the conquering of Kingdoms of Anglia and Mercia, winning fame among their peers, and the jealousy of a few rivals. After one successful battle, his second son Agne decided to return captives to Eddisbury in Northern Mercia, unwittingly releasing a local lord's eldest son Cerdic and establishing a relationship with a powerful Mercian family. Smitten with Cerdic's younger sister and her renowned sky-blue eyes, Agne married Gurid which furthered the family's influence and trade connections.

On the Jorvik highway traveling home, bandits robbed and murdered Ironfist and his eldest son. People suspected the members of the Magnus clan of the crime and hot-headed youngest son Karl fought a drunken brawl with the eldest Magnusson and slayed him before witnesses. Despite paying the wergild price for a man's death, under rumors of retaliation Karl gathered several of Ironfist's retainers and sailed north to fight as mercenaries in the kingdoms of the Northern Way. Agne grew his father's business, extended their holdings and with Gurid raised a family of seven children, Willa the eldest daughter, Ange the younger whom they nicknamed "Cub," Kara, Sorven the second son, Thorfinn the third son, Hilda and a baby girl named Neeta.

'Thorfinn and the Witch's Curse,' book one of the Forerunner Series, begins with a centuries old ghost named Raga watching over the third son from the thatch in the longhouse roof—he is a disembodied mage searching for the one foretold to release him from his miserable existence and he uses a raven as his 'mare' familiar in the lands of Midgard. Agne has arranged to apprentice his second son to a blacksmith and takes his third son to Jorvik to discuss his apprenticeship with a Nordic wood carver. Gurid's cousin, a matronly widow named Yeru retells the family legend of Ironfist and his defeat of the Saxon witch, while a on far-flung isle Karl meets a soothsayer. A newly hired laborer tells Agne's boys he knows the spot where the witch in Ironfist's story lived, and the four boys sneak out to seek treasure—the ruined shambles are a disappointment and all they find is a rusty iron bowl, giving Sorven a cut finger for his trouble.

Quickly Sorven grows ill, much too sick to be explained by natural causes. To her horror, Yeru discovers a "night" mare rides him at night, and his two brothers follow the hideous black creature back to the dilapidated ruins where Sorven's blood, spit into the sorceress's cauldron, is drawing the ghostly witch back into the physical world. While Cub attacks and defeats the mare, timid Thorfinn stumbles to hide, spills the pot of blood, and accidentally breaks the spell. Furious, the apparition attacks the young boy and rips his "hug" from his "lich," his soul from his living body. The terrified Thorfinn runs away, but... his life is changed forever, for he is changed into a vardoger, a "forerunner" who is preceded by his own ghost in Midgard during waking hours and can pass into the realm between the nine Norse realms when his body sleeps.

The ghost Raga helps Finn adjust to his forerunner existence. A marriage is arranged for Willa the eldest daughter. Karl and his Viking crew find themselves snowed into a port far to the north, face and defeat a were-bear, fortify the town defenses, and agree to leave men behind to protect the village with a promise to return with replacements come summer. Young Finn eavesdrops on a plot to murder his Uncle Karl, steals a broken sword with a mysterious magical glimmer and finds a strange blue lizard which he keeps as a pet in the Realm Between Realms. He tries to warn his family of the murder plot, but few pay attention, many ignore, fear, or shun him.

Thorfinn's odd behaviors raise suspicions, and his worried family is convinced to bring in a Siedr witch to help recover from the vardoger haunting. This elder contacts her spirit guide and is manipulated by the spectral witch seeking revenge on the Ironfist family. Uncle Karl returns with his crew and a grand wedding is held with poetry and songs, insult contests and plenty of strong bridal mead and ale. Drunk from mead, Thorfinn and his uncle are both settled into a small house at the end of the compound, where Finn awakes in the Realm Between Realms, finds the courage to face the ghostly witch and using his magic short sword, defeats her. Turning to his snoring uncle, he lifts Karl's sword in Midgard to wake him, alerts him of the threat and helps him defeat the assassins. After the battle, Uncle Karl agrees to take Thorfinn to sea.

Two weeks later 'The Vardoger Boy,' book two of the Forerunner Series begins with Cub and his father called to war in support of King Guthrum of Anglia as he faces King Alfred and the forces of Wessex. Karl recruits Gallic sailors to take north to replace the men he left behind, and Thorfinn, as he attempts to board the Viking longship, learns there is a mast troll aboard, hidden in the Realm Between, who instantly recognizes the vardoger and tosses his "hug" from the vessel.

While Cub learns coordinated attack methods in the Danish Army, the Magnus clan takes advantage of the men's absence and attacks Agne's compound seeking blood vengeance. The longhouse and barn are set afire and, in the confusion, Gurid, Yeru and the children escape. The mast troll demands a quest from young Finn in exchange for his passage, and in the Humber Estuary sends Finn to steal an enchanted pearl from an evil tangie, a "kelp-man" and his minions. Suspicious of the strange boy, one of the Gallic sailors Martine purchases an ointment to spy into the Realm Between Realms. Kara and Sorven face a fight for their lives with forest bandits, and Yeru falls to an arrow wound. The family takes shelter in a homestead where they learn hunting dogs are soon to be set upon their trail, and leaving Yeru and the baby behind, Gurid makes a deal with a farmer to cart Kara, Sorven and little Hilda to Willa's new married household on the Mercian border.

The Danish Army is defeated at the battle of Ethandun where Cub witnesses the death of his father Agne and is left unconscious on the frontline. Karl and his crew arrive at the coastal village to find it deserted, the palisade wall broken, and the buildings ransacked. Friendship won, the mast troll teaches Thorfinn to ride a bull rush and the ghost boy and his friend Raga fly to spy on the were-bear, learning details of his man-made island fortress in the center of a lake. The bear hosts a dark elf, and the creatures capture Raga, while Finn uses his enchanted sax to kill a werewolf and escape. Willa's husband returns to his home, his face brutally cauterized, and gives Gurid Agne's ancestral sword as proof of his death. His own father held as a war prisoner, he intends to take his family to Jorvik to call in debts and arrange a ransom. Sorven departs with Willa and her husband, and Gurid takes Kara and Hilda to her family in Mercia.

With the help of Martine's Siedr salve, Thorfinn convinces his Uncle Karl the mast troll is real, he actually is a vardoger, and his stories of the were-bear's island hideaway are true. Knowing spies watch from the forest, Karl makes a show of departing the small village, sails north and uses Finn's help to find a guide through the marsh to the bear's lair. In the battle that ensues, Finn surprises the dark elf and wounds him with his sword. The Vikings triumph over the bear clan and free their slaves. While Thorfinn helps his Uncle Karl from the Realm Between, the dark elf escapes... and Cub awakes in chains on a forced march, sold to the tin mines as a slave.

As 'On Viking Seas,' book three of the Forerunner Series begins, we learn the injured dark elf has other Midgardian minions he commands to take revenge on Thorfinn, Karl and his crew, providing an enchantment to control Odin's mythical Wild Hunt to do their bidding. Captured by the forces of Wessex after the Battle of Ethandun, Cub is enslaved in the tin mines of Devonshire. The second son Sorven accompanies his oldest sister and her family back to Jorvik to collect a ransom for her father-in-law. The second daughter Kara, their mother and little sister hide in Eddisbury with her Mercian uncle.

Cub inadvertently uncovers a smuggling operation and is rewarded but earns the ire of a deceitful slaver. Sorven, under Dundle's wing, falls in with a bad crowd and vows revenge on the people that burned their homestead. Turning 14 years old, Kara is groomed for an arranged marriage while her uncle is elevated to a higher position in the new Mercian puppet government under the control of Alfred of Wessex. Uncle Karl and his Vikings are shipwrecked on a mysterious floating island and attacked by evil ghosts of the wild hunt. The warriors cannot win against the supernatural foes, and despite his previous warnings, the mast troll implores Finn to release his mysterious, Jotunheim lizard into Midgard. A tiny pet between realms, once freed in Midgard the creature expands into a lindworm, a huge, winged serpent with clawed arms, who scatters and defeats the ghostly attackers. The departing ghosts drop their weapons and treasure for the crew to retrieve, Karl giving a silver flute to Thorfinn and keeping a strange rune medallion for himself.

Scattered family members rally to Kara and her mother, including their old nurse Yeru, Bjorn their blacksmith and the boy Kaelan. Bjorn arranges to have Kara continue her military training with a renowned shieldmaiden Hege. She learns to fight better, despite making no friends among the Mercian lordlings in her class. On the mysterious isle, the Vikings repair their ship and sail east. During the voyage,

Thorfinn is taught to play his magicked flute by the mast troll. As a vardoger, Thorfinn uses Siedr magic to "visit" his family and learns of his father's death and his eldest brother's capture. In Jorvik, Sorven helps waylay an innocent man and steals his short sword in preparation for his revenge.

Their Viking ship repaired, Karl and his crew sail to the shores of a petty Norwegian kingdom where they draw lots to see who will childmind the dragon and who will go ashore. Karl is seeking a brother-in-arms, a Chieftain Hamund, Son of Hothl. They find his household in disarray, his beautiful wife and oldest daughter dead, and his youngest daughter Allinor, fighting a mysterious illness. Allinor's hand is withering, and she is unable to communicate with people... but she can hear Finn's flute! Thorfinn and Raga visit her in the Realm Between Realms and in her dream state she believes her hand is whole inside a bottle where she grips a beautiful flower, making her fist too wide to pull out of the mouth of the jar, but in the Realm Between Raga recognizes the heavy, glass bottle as full of evil magic. Finn and Raga meet a "hidden folk" house spirit, an "armaour" hearth man, afraid and cowering under the fire grate. He warns Finn and Raga of the three witches and how they wait until the victim is too weak before they steal her life.

Cub is drawn into a dubious plot to save two young boys and ends captured and flogged. Kara is groomed to meet her suitors, and when the newly installed king of Mercia comes to visit Eddisbury, Kara and her mother are invited to join the royal banquet where she will be presented. Uncomfortable introductions transpire and Kara is accosted by one of the suitors, a hated boy from her weapons training, who she quickly disarms but embarrasses herself before the thegns, the landed gentry. Two suitors withdraw their offer, but a third steps forward, more determined to make her and her strength part of his family line. Thorfinn finds Cub recovering from his whipping and by eavesdropping as a forerunner ghost learns Cub is to be sent on a smuggling run as a pretext for his murder.

Thorfinn, Raga and Karl trick the witches to come early for the girl, and Karl, protected by his mysterious medallion, beheads a were-badger while Thorfinn and Raga face the other two were-creatures in Allinor's chambers. In the battle, Thorfinn cuts off the wing tips of the vulture-witch and by accident, Thorfinn smashes the jar, breaking the spell. The girl and her father recover, and an impromptu celebration is held.

The night his eldest sister gives birth to her firstborn, Sorven and his accomplice take revenge on the man behind the blood feud and steal horses to escape the city. Under the pretense of delivering firewood to a local monastery, Cub is forced to smuggle tin ingots to a remote harbor. Thorfinn the vardoger arrives to help his eldest brother from the Realm Between Realms, and together they defeat Cub's captors and Cub flees on a ship to Britany. Kara finds Kaelan, retrieves her armor and her family's ancestral sword, and takes flight.

Late one winter night, hidden under blankets and tarps, Thorfinn's dragon is snuck into a barn. Unbeknownst to the Vikings, an old woman lurks to watch them, her fingers and toes bandaged and weeping blood, all chopped off at the first knuckle....

Norse Legends

Vardøger

A vardøger, also known as vardyger or fyreferd, is a spirit predecessor in Scandinavian folklore. Stories typically include instances that are nearly déjà vu in substance, but in reverse, where a spirit with the subject's footsteps, voice, scent, or appearance and overall demeanor precedes them in a location or activity, resulting in witnesses believing they've seen or heard the actual person before the person physically arrives. This bears a subtle difference from a doppelgänger, with a less sinister connotation. It has been likened to being a phantom double.

Éire

- Northern Uí Néill
- Ulaid
- Bréifne
- Airgialla
- Connachta
- Lind Duachail
- Southern Uí Néill
- Dublinn
- Lagin
- Luimnech
- Osraige
- Loch Sanman
- Mumu
- Pont Lamse
- Concaith

- Mainister Buite
- Slaine
- Dam Liac
- Trefet
- Lusca
- Loch Gabor
- Sord
- Findglas Cainig
- Cluain Dolcain
- Dublinn
- Nas na Rig
- Cill Dara

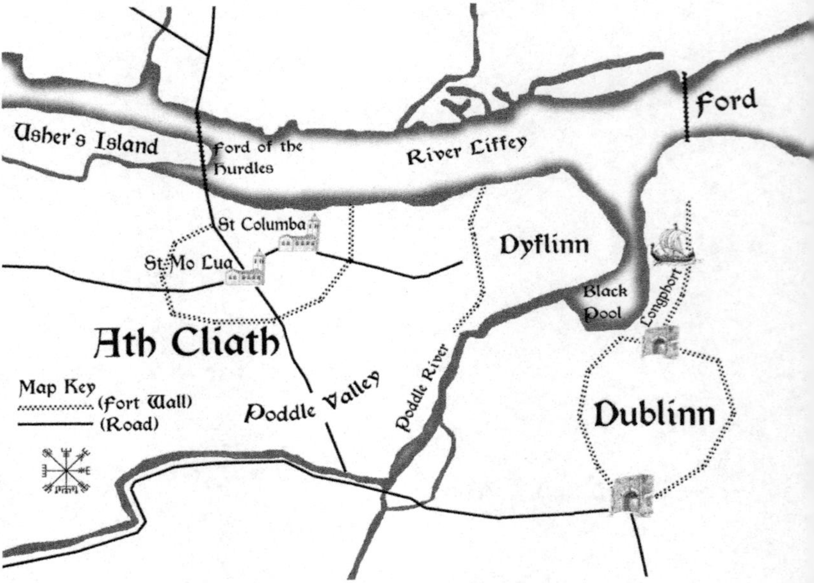

Ford
Usher's Island
Ford of the Hurdles
River Liffey
St Columba
Dyflinn
St. Mo Lua
Black Pool
Longphort
Ath Cliath
Map Key
(Fort Wall)
(Road)
Poddle Valley
Poddle River
Dublinn

The North Way

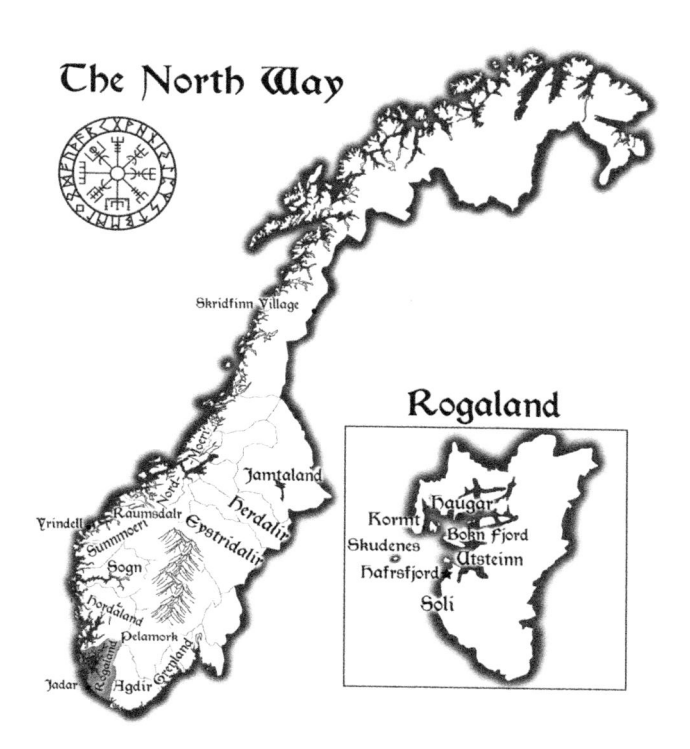

Rogaland

CHAPTER 2
ALL HAIL THE KING OF DUBLINN

KARA

"Something's awry...."

Already committed to its course, the knarr sloshed over the rapids, the empty boat riding high on the incoming tide washing up the River Liffey.

A thick pall of smoke clouded their view through the scrub and saplings on the southern shore. Glimpses of tall, wooden palings poked above the fumes, a cloud of pigeons scattered from a sudden flash of flames, and incoherent shouts peppered a rhythmic clanging, as if a soul beat a signal on an upturned pot.

"Hold the course." The captain lifted his hand to quiet his murmuring crew.

"Seems unnatural, Cap'n." The sailor next to Kara paused, his oar held dripping over the waters.

"Mayhap Dublinn's afire."

"Easy...." The captain pushed his potbelly over the bow rail and squinted into the afternoon sun. "Hold the course."

Kara slid closer to Kaelan on the bench.

When the slaver offered to ferry them on his return to Dublinn, Kaelan had tried to dissuade her, not trusting the beefy, squint-eyed trader. His price good, less than the amount they received for the sale of the nag, it left them with a pocket full of hacksilver. And while he sniffed at her ill-fitted leather armor and the long sword strapped to her back, he never questioned their motives once they showed their coin.

The boat jostled into deeper water. Kara glanced at Kaelan—despite her push to run away, he had been her anchor these past few days, and protective in his own way. He smiled at her and touched her vambrace, toying with the leather bindings.

"Swing her a port now, into the Poddle." The mouth of the tributary river churned with tidal wash. Kara listened to oars scull and splatter. The ship rocked. Kaelan placed a hand on her shoulder, and she offered him a wan smile. The ride over rough seas had left her with a heaving stomach, not much improved by the sour smell of the unwashed crew.

Rounding the promontory, the ship turned into...

Chaos!

A snarl of ships splashed and collided in the waterway before them. Vessels of all shapes and sizes jockeyed and banged, congesting the small bay. A snekke with oars beating the waters to froth crowded a slow-moving knarr overloaded with bales and a clutch of shrieking women all roped together.

Propelled by misaligned rowers, the snekke surged towards them.

"By Njord's whiskers!" The portly captain waved his fist. "What are ye at?" Wide-eyed sailors shouted back, a jumble of cries.

"Hard aport! Hard!"

The ship swung tight, the pilot heaving on his till, the deck tilting, starboard rowers lifting their paddles high to avoid the oncoming traffic. Oars clattered, the hulls scraped.

"Ahoy, ye lee born bastards!" Poles jabbed and pushed aside the collision, curses flying from all sides. A swell sloshed water through their scuppers, washing across the deck. Tackle swung loose overhead—Kara ducked the ropes and grabbed Kaelan.

Pandemonium ruled the waterway. Half-raised sails sagged across midships or dragged loose in the bay. Shouting sailors struggled with ropes, poles, and paddles, a handful climbing rope ladders, men running along the wharf, others bent over the sloshing waves, struggling to pull wayward swimmers back ashore. Skiffs overloaded with passengers poled and rocked across the bay. Coracles bobbed and twisted in the bedlam, their unheeded pilots shouting at the larger ships plowing through their midst. Deep water swirled in a dark, central pool. Kara tried to make sense of the commotion.

A Norse longphort stretched the length of the left shore, a tall paling wall parallel to it, joining a wider fortress wall that ringed an entire village. Crates and bales stacked haphazardly along its length. A quick glance across the black pool to the distant shore showed hints of a second fortress, two wooden steeples rising above its palisades.

Grumbling, the captain guided his pilot to an open berth at the end of the long dock. The knarr smacked nose first into the wooden pilings, jostling the crew and shaking Kara from her seat—she stumbled to her feet. An obscuring wall of smoke rolled across the shoreline, smarting her eyes. Kaelan coughed, steadying Kara with a hand on her back. The captain lurched out of the cloud and yanked a sailor by his collar.

"Tie us off!" He shoved the man over the gunwale. "Be quick, you bugger-brained bottom-feeder, or I'll send you to Helheim myself."

"Ho!" A shout barked out of the smoke. Kara could discern three figures jogging along the wharf to their boat. A throaty woman's voice. "What are you about?"

"We told all, cast off!"

"Listen, ye beetle brain codpiece! Flames a-ragin' on Winetavern, soon your leaky ole bark will burn a'well."

Their thick accent confused her, but Kara grasped the intent. The captain growled at the insult, and shouted back, "I come to claim my stock! Is my right. Got orders for Eire girls and field thralls..." He waved his hand in a useless attempt to clear the smoke from his face.

"Yer right be worth nay, if the Bregans afire your ship!"

"What?"

"Ye heard me." The wind shifted, blowing the smoke out of their faces to trail across the bay. Two women armed with wooden clubs stood before them, the taller waving her cudgel overhead in a threatening manner. A lanky boy with a bucket hid behind them. "Brega and Leinster joined to avenge the sack of Saint Cianán."

"Barith kicked a hornet's nest this time!"

"Turncoats let them pass the gate." The taller guard gestured with her club at the sailor on the dock, indicating he should climb back aboard, and the scrawny fellow turned his questioning face to his captain.

"Probably Dubgenti scum, stirring the pot." The shorter warrior locked eyes with the captain as she spoke. 'Dubgenti'—never having heard this word before, Kara recognized the fat slaver understood. He huffed, his mouth worked as if he had a retort ready—Kara watched his shoulders slump, his head wobble. He dropped his eyes from the warrior's gaze, set his jaw and huffed. Behind him she could see the ships had fallen into a semblance of order as they rowed and poled out of the black pool, laboring against the rush of the incoming bore.

"Bregans, eh? Thor's goats, a nasty lot—think this skirmish lasts?" Kara noted the captain avoided the blonde woman's eyes.

"The king's guards defend, numbers rally to our honor, but...." The smaller woman wiped sweaty blonde hairs from her forehead. "These Irish be fighting fiends."

"Best sail north to Lind Duachail or drop sea anchors in the deep to wait it out."

"Aye." The captain grumbled and turned to his pilot, motioning for him to turn the boat from the dock.

"Wait!"

Kara dragged Kaelan forward. "We're not with them. Let us stay." Kaelan gave her a wide-eyed, pleading expression which she chose to ignore. She leaned across the gunwale. "We've come to fight—we'll join your guard."

"Pah." The shorter woman rolled her eyes. "Young'un spoiling for a tussle, eh?"

The leader measured Kara.

"I'll nay turn away a fighter, an' ready in armor..."

Kara kicked her leg over the railing and jumped to the dock. Standing a head taller, Kara gazed up into the guard's pale blue eyes—the clear, calculating gaze reminded her of her mother. Kaelan lowered himself next to her.

"Know how to use that?" The big woman pointed to the sword hilt over her shoulder.

Kara gave a short bow. "We'd be proud to fight for King Ivar."

"Ivar... you mean I-Mar?" Her snort stifled a chuckle—the two women glanced at each other. "Old 'Imar' been dead near five years!"

"King o'Dublinn is Barith, his son, so crowned since High Lord Findliath captured Halfdan the usurper." Kara could tell the big woman watched her closely for a reaction. Behind her she could hear the knarr push from the quay, oars rattling in their sockets and thumping against the wooden planks.

"Well." Kara glanced at Kaelan. "That would explain why he brought no aid to Guthrum at Ethandun."

"Ethandun? Heard it was a rout." She squinted at Kara. "Ye fought at Ethandun?"

"No, my father and brother. They were...." She hung her head. "Lost."

"No matter, girl, we can use your Dubgenti sword and your brother." Kara started to correct her about Kaelan, but the blonde warrior pulled the bucket boy forward and drawing a brush from the pail, smeared a blot of whitewash across her chest and did the same to Kaelan. "Turn," she commanded and marked their backs.

"Watch for these marks—our guard know you by this white, and you them as well."

Kara turned back, expecting more instructions. His nose running from the smoke, Kaelan sniffed loudly, and behind him, the fleeing slaver's ship rowed around the bend.

"Get on, girl," the bigger warrior pointed with her club. "Show what yer made of."

Kara squared her shoulders and marched down the longphort, weaving between stacks of cabbages and piles of wool, tangles of rope and clumps of discarded sailcloth, Kaelan trailing close at her heels. Kara could feel the warriors' eyes on her back. Gulls squawked and hopped from their path.

Paralleled to protect the southern approach to the longphort, the paling wall intersected the fortress an arm's breadth from a gate large enough for a wagon to pass. Drawn closed and barred from the outside, a small door allowed access through the gateway, barely large enough for a single person to pass. A bull-necked man blocked the entrance, an iron helm with a thick nose guard fastened tight over his ears, and a battle ax in each hand. Fresh, the whitewash mark dribbled down his chest.

"Hey, we are here to..." With a grunt, the guard stepped aside and gestured for them to step through the portal.

Kara ducked and crossed into Dublinn.

Narrow streets led in three directions from the small, gateway courtyard, the fire smoke denser inside the fortress walls. The clanging metal continued to ring, muffled by the wattle and daub buildings leaning precariously over the roads. Cautious and unsure which way to follow, Kara inched forward, her hands open at her sides.

Kaelan stepped beside her, put his finger in his chest paint and held it high. "Guess we have the permit; didn't even question us." Kara agreed—the streets lay deserted. A cat slinked around the corner and disappeared.

"Have you heard this word, Dub-genti?"

"Never. But that old slaver knew it," Kaelan whispered. "They called us 'Dubgenti.'"

"Ja," Kara crept forward, putting her hand across her mouth to inhale a less smoke. Shouts and a high-pitched scream sounded in the distance. Kara paused—she could hear the clatter of weapons.

"This way."

Their chosen roadway rapidly tightened to an alley,

barely wide enough for two to pass abreast. Kaelan pulled his farmer's blade from his belt. "Want your sword?"

"Not yet...." She crouched and reached back to touch his arm. "These are tight quarters, hard to swing."

Kara winked at her companion. Kaelan helped her escape Eddisbury and the plans for her forced marriage, and she had learned little more about him in the few days on the run together. Aged two years older, he acted tentative and gentle when he laced her armor or helped her from the saddle. During the journey they avoided personal conversations, shy with each other despite sharing a horseback. She liked the way he watched her and sprang to protect her, despite the fact as the trained warrior she should be protecting him—clearly a farmer's son, he had never had consistent training or held a weapon in battle. She remembered her father's words to her and her brothers when she had begun training in her eighth summer—He had held up his fingers to count. "Remember, for every ten you face, five are farmer's lads, fresh from the field, handed a spear and told to fight. Disarmed, they will run. Three will have training but are easily defeated through skill. One will be crazed with Odin's battle lust—avoid berserk attacks for they are blind with the All-Father's passion. And one...." He held his finger in her face. "That one is why we practice every day, for that is the real warrior who tests our mettle and calls the Valkyries from Asgard."

Kaelan weakly returned her smile, his eyes wide, his knife tip jittering as they advanced—*he's nervous*, she thought—*ja, a farmer's lad....*

Moving as quietly as possible, Kara led them deeper into the city. Planked walls and heavy shutters hemmed in the narrow way. They stepped over a foul-smelling trench and through a series of winding turns, pushed aside curtains of laundry and entered a straight pathway. The air cleared ahead.

Kara swiveled to Kaelan—he bit his bottom lip, the way he did when he worried about her. She read concern in his face.

"I'll be careful."

The alley dumped into a square, one of a handful of side courses ending in the cobble-stoned plaza, and two broad boulevards crossed the space, one left to right and one at an angle to the other—these broader roads spaced wide enough for horses and wagons. A clatter of metal and wood sounded, and the rhythmic clanging stumbled and stopped.

Three men entered the square from the angled road, jogging with blooded swords in their hands. Out of breath, they glanced over their shoulders, paying more attention to the way they had come than what they faced. From the way one carried his arm tight to his side, he nursed a wound.

"No white," Kaelan whispered.

Kara dipped her head. She had seen it, too—here stood their enemy. "They look tired to me."

Kaelan fumbled at her back to release her sword. Nerves overcame him, his fingers slipped on the rope that snugged the blade in place for their journey. Before he could free and pull it clear of its sheath, the lead warrior shouted and raised his sword over his head, running to attack. They were discovered.

Kara pushed Kaelan back with the flat of her hand—no more time for fiddling over the longsword. "I can take them," she hissed.

Head lowered, eyes forward, she dashed across the square, ducked under her opponent's wild swing, and aimed a kick at his knee. With all the force of her momentum, it connected in a satisfying crunch. Surprised, the man crumpled, dropped his blade, and grabbed at his joint. Kara kicked the short sword aside in the general direction of Kaelan, hoping he would grab the weapon before another. Using her forearm bracer, she backhanded the prostrate man and knocked him senseless.

Across the square the wounded man pressed against the far wall as his compatriot shouted incoherently at Kara, threatening her with the point of his sword. Tan hair standing like flames from the top of his head, the Irish warrior spat a string of words at her and jabbed at her with his sword—*gobbledygook*, Kara thought, *but I know what he means.*

"You think because I am girl you can gut me with your big sword, eh?" She gave him a smirk and waggled her head, motioning him forward with her hands. He spouted more angry words, shaking his fist and making threatening motions with the sword, and despite his bluster, hung back, his eye on the groggy fellow whimpering and clutching his knee a few steps from her. His eyes measured her, and the fact she wore armor gave him pause notwithstanding she carried no weapon in her hands. Behind her she perceived the scrape of iron against the stones—Kaelan had collected the short sword from the man she had disarmed.

Wary, the Irish warrior slid his foot forward, gauging her readiness. He moved across the muddy courtyard.

Shouts and the sounds of chase echoed from the avenue behind her combatants. Her opponent never took his eyes from hers while the injured man stumbled along the buildings, calling to the man facing Kara.

Too distant to connect, the warrior thrust forward with his sword and danced on the balls of his feet. He shouted at her, waved his blade in both hands like a dowsing rod, and side-mouthed a comment to the man slinking aside.

"Missed me, you... ah, you hedgehog!" Kara chided herself—do better! "You milk-fed sow! Come and get me, you teething baby, you wetnurse...." She had never been good at mocking adversaries before a fight, and besides, this one didn't understand her language.

He understood her intent... with a sudden rush, he charged her. His blade sliced close to her side, and he grabbed to grapple with her, clutching the air as she ducked under his arm. Leading with a furious assault, his blade swung over her head, to her left and to her right, and stabbed viciously by her face. Each time Kara sidestepped, glad Hege had made her practice evading enemy strikes, finally skipping back out of his reach. She dusted off her hands in an exaggerated manner she hoped would taunt him.

"Missed me again!" She edged away.

Anger puffing his reddened cheeks, the warrior charged and swung a downward stroke she deftly dodged. He countered with a slice to connect with her midriff—his initiative announced his movement and Kara rolled with the swing, darting aside. He screamed in frustration and his wild, follow-on blow smacked his blade against the roadway, snapping off its tip. As he recovered from his overreach, Kara lunged under his defenses and pushing off with her opposite foot, drove the heel of her palm into his chin—the blow cracked his teeth together and dazed him. She pranced back and held her arms wide, watching and waiting for his next move.

Blood flowed freely from his mouth—he bit his tongue when the unexpected punch connected. Furious, his slurred words splattered flecks of blood in the air.

"It's wetnurse, isn't it?" Kara circled. "You don't like being called a wetnurse, eh?"

His face beet red, blood dripping from his chin, he glowered at her, arms spread to mimic her stance. He carefully inched closer, scrutinizing her every move.

Kara noted the change in his approach—he no longer assumed she was a girl to be easily overwhelmed, nor was he driven by a careless, assumptive bravado—he recognized he faced a trained foe and focused with murderous intent. Her murder.

"Wetnurse." She smiled at him. He slid towards her, his legs bent, his stance ready to counter.

"Wet. Nurse."

"Kara! Behind!" Kaelan shouted.

While Kara fixated on her attacker, the forgotten wounded man had moved behind her and he stumbled forward with a short knife, stabbing at her back. She rolled with the blow, feeling the sharp edge scrape across her leather armed back, and as the strike flowed through and his arm passed her side, she elbowed the off-balanced man in his jaw, his head snapping in the direction of her punch, and his body tumbling underneath her.

Seeing her distracted, the man with the sword leaped forward, his sword jabbing at her belly. Kara fell back over the prone man, the sword arcing over her, and she kicked with both feet, knocking the sword from his hands. With a shout, he fell on her, fumbling to reach her neck and raining blows on her head and shoulders.

Kara set her jaw and butted the top of her head into his face, crushing his nose and knocking him unconscious. He slumped over her, a dead weight.

"Wetnurse," she muttered. She heaved and shoved the

limp bodies, and pulled herself from the pile, quickly checking the prone figures for knives or hidden weapons.

"Bravo!"

Kara raised her head.

At the mouth of the angled lane stood a clutch of warriors, most white-marked as Dublinn guards. In the center, a tall man dressed in a velvet cap and a tooled leather vest applauded her, the warriors at his side inspecting them with a mix of reactions, a few impressed, others glowering and several inscrutable and aloof. Quickly sizing the group, she estimated about fifteen. Kara glanced at Kaelan, holding his knife and the retrieved sword from the man with the broken knee.

"Where did you learn this skill?" Parting his personal guard with a dismissive hand, the dark-haired man crossed to Kara, while his guards spread out to encircle the plaza.

"Stiggsdatter." Kara cleared her throat. "Hege Stiggsdatter was my tutor... and my father."

"I have heard of Stiggsdatter." A towheaded boy about the age of her eldest brother pointed at Kara. "Fought with my Uncle Ubba when that scum Odda stole the raven crest."

"Hmmm." Overpowering the woodfire smell of the burning city a whiff of spearmint wafted before the tall man, and she noted his sword hilt boasted a carbuncle stud and silver, filigreed handle. On his heels followed a young maid about her age, a freckled beauty with a tangle of brash, red hair falling to her waist and two daggers at her belt. Kara had never seen such a fiery mane.

"And tell me, why call your enemies 'wetnurse?'"

Kara gawped at a loss for words.

"Is this considered a flyting insult from whence you hail?"

Stepping forward, a wide shieldmaiden with a thick, blonde braid over her iron breastplate held a flat, blunt sax to intervene.

"Who be ye, strangers?"

Kara recognized her accent from the guards on the longphort.

"Kara Agnesdatter, daughter of Agne the son of Alf Ironfist, and his wife Gurid, daughter of Eanulf of Mercia. And this is my...," she hesitated and glanced over her shoulder at Kaelan.

"Sword companion." Kaelan stepped over the prone body and let his weapons drop to his side. "Kaelan, son of Ulbrecht, son of Madden."

Kara overheard the blonde warrior mumble, "More Dubgenti." The tall man smiled, placed his hand on the woman's sword arm and gently lowered her blade.

"Come, Kara of Agne and Kaelan of Ulbrecht, walk at my side." He pulled the redheaded girl close and tucked her hand into the crook of his elbow.

Kara wondered at the group, especially the young girl—despite her fine, velvet gown and silver brooches, the girl stood stiff jawed, distant, her hands stretched wide and loose at her sides.

This leader acts as if we should know him, Kara thought. *The number of women guards matches the number of men—clearly, this is a place for me to build my reputation.*

With a flippant wave, the leader directed his guards to collect the wounded invaders and fasten them together with coarse rope. Kaelan fell in at her side and the tall man and his guards led a parade along the wide avenue, the prisoners pricked along at sword point in the rear. The blonde boy who had known her teacher ducked his head to Kara, his hand resting on his hilt—she could tell he sized her as they strolled the avenue. Along the road, the buildings grew in stature, long halls and taverns replacing the hovels and narrow alleys. Scorched wooden walls indicated the trespassers' intended damage had been thwarted. Yet in the city fires threatened as intermittent clouds of smoke roiled across their path, making their eyes water and Kaelan sneeze.

This sauntering pace confused Kara, and a peek at Kaelan showed he had no better understanding… he rumpled his lips at her, his brow scrunched and eyes wary. Instead of freeing her family sword at her back, Kaelan handed the captured sax sword to Kara, and she hefted the blade and checked its balance. The avenue took a wide turn and opened into another square.

Kara stumbled on the cobbles as she gawked.

Here the city of Dublinn rivaled any great city she had seen, larger than the Mercian hilltop fortress of Eddisbury or the sprawling lanes and docks of crowded Jorvik. Two-storied buildings stacked tall over the lane. Fire had gutted one building: a swarm of soot-blackened citizens manned a bucket line, dashing water from a hidden source against cut-stone foundations and archways. The height and breadth of the remaining skeleton of beams and smoldering trusses impressed Kara. An oily smell of burned flesh hung in the air, and flocks of pigeons and laughing gulls swarmed the laborers, scattering under foot or crying from posts and rooftops. Somewhere a cow lowed. Opposite the burned-out husk, a pointed steeple thrust higher than Kara had ever seen, a wooden cross affixed to its top. She marveled at the unique style of the building and wondered at its purpose. The party meandered through the crowd to a longhouse by the fortress wall. Before the familiar, Norse-style hall, several smaller buildings near the gate had burned to piles of ash. Bodies lay discarded among the coals.

Signs of a struggle marked the carved entry, the hobnailed door hacked and splintered, the ornamental carvings chipped and defaced. Splashes of blood and lumps of sodden straw burned black marked the walls, blooded and scattered indicating the attempt to fire the building had been prevented through force of arms. The guards pushed the tall man and the redhead back into the center of the group and took charge, drawing their weapons. Trying the latch, they found the bar lifted and opened the great portal.

Inside, a dim light from guttering pitch torches lit the space, the rafters casting odd shadows. Heavy tables and benches had been knocked askew, smashed to splinters or piled indiscriminately.

As her eyes adjusted, Kara could see a battle had raged in the hall. Men and women lay gutted on the floor, a few moaning in death throes, others dismembered in pools of offal and gore. A sword hung wedged in a support post; a broken shield clutched by a headless man on the floor; a plump woman bent backward over a table, the knife that stole her life sunk deep in her chest, in her hand a tangle of hair ripped from her adversary. Like the warriors around her, Kara fell silent and paused to survey the carnage.

The tall man elbowed his way through his guards, coughing at the stench. "Where is the king?"

The towheaded lad pushed past them. "Barith?"

"Come all, let's find my cousin." One of the guards pulled a torch from its socket and the group broke apart to search, leaving Kara and Kaelan with the redhead in the center of the ruined longhouse. Kara caught a sneer creep across her face as she watched the tall leader worm his way through the piles of furniture and bodies—as quick as the expression appeared, she recovered her poise and returned to a bland, disinterested demeanor.

"Here!" The warrior with braids called, lowering her torch to a form propped against a post, sprawled in an awkward pose.

"Brother!"

The boy reached the body on the floor first, dropping to his side and tenderly attempting to correct his uncomfortable posture. He gently laid the man out on the floor as more surrounded the corpse, their torches held low. A severe gash had split open his forehead, and the boy leaned close, wiping the smear of blood with his sleeve. The face, his handsome, flecked-gray beard neatly trimmed, appeared gaunt and pale to Kara.

"Does he yet breathe?"

The boy shuddered, his back humped over the prone body. Kara gathered his crouch hid his tears—from her vantage, she could see his barely controlled sobs. Collected, they could see the dead man's wounds, a deep gouge in his belly welling dark blood, a lengthy slice on his forearm, scratches on his neck and gory hack marks on his legs—he had fought to the end. Slowly the boy straightened the stiffening legs and pulled both hands to cross them on his chest, torn fingernails already blackened with bruises. The battle had been savage and ultimately hand-to-hand. Kara scanned the area, measuring the number of bodies cast aside by the combat—by her count, this man had fought and defeated more than seven armed assailants.

"The son of Imar rides with the Valkyries this day." The tall man laid a hand on the boy's shoulder, an attempt at a comforting gesture. Kara watched the boy flinch at his touch and drop his face further to hide a grimace. *He hides his anger*, Kara thought, *like the girl who skulks at the back of this crowd.*

With a deep sigh, the blonde shieldmaiden raised her torch.

"The King is dead."

Heads hung as prayers murmured. All eyes turned to the tall leader. In slow measured actions, he removed his cap releasing a thick mane of black hair and held his palm out to each encircling him. The woman knelt beside the crying boy and gently pulled a silver ring from the dead man's forefinger. Rising, she placed the ring on her leader's outstretched palm.

"King Barith is dead." She solemnly gazed from face to face in the flickering light. "Long live Mac Ausle...."

"All hail the King of Dublinn."

CHAPTER 3
FREEDOM GAINED, FREEDOM LOST

CUB

Nothing could wipe the grin from his face as Cub dipped the canvas bucket into the sea and poured water over his head—a sailor had lent him a chunk of flower-scented, pig-fat soap and ignoring the jeers of the deckhands working the oars, he stripped naked and dowsed himself with ocean water. A few chilly splashes later, he wandered naked amidship, and spent a few hacks of his silver to buy spare clothes for himself and his fellows, especially bartering for a needle-bound, woolen cap to cover his head scraped bare by the slavers. The raw lashings on his back stung from the brine, but he felt and, more importantly, smelled clean for the first time in months. With a satisfied sigh, he squatted next to the captain, a lanky, grizzled sailor.

Free. He smiled at the clear night sky. *I am free*, he thought, *and Druce, the slave monger met Tyr's justice, may he rot in Helheim.*

The captain, a man who had carefully avoided formally

introducing himself, shared a lump of seedy bread and explained the crossing would take a few hours. They should arrive by dawn. Lifting their sail to the wind, the crew drew in the oars and the longboat skimmed across the starlit waves. Cub didn't blame the captain for being circumspect, taking care not to share his name and family with a bunch of scruffy, escaped slaves—as the old adage reminds, 'it is ill to have a thrall for a friend.' As the sailors drifted to sleep around them, the captain spoke quietly, "Do you have plans among the Franks?"

"Hadn't thought," Cub admitted.

"Guess that's the way of thralls: No future, no plans."

"I used to be a good swordsman."

"Swords?" The captain sucked his teeth, worrying at a seed caught in a tooth. "Swords are hard to come by, expensive."

"What will you do with this load?"

"We sell the ingots. Can't command a high price like in the official tin market, but sure can get fair profits on this smuggled load. Money goes to Rolf's coffers. He will share us a cut for our troubles."

"Rolf?"

"Ja, he came a'viking back a few seasons and liked the place, never left. Locals call him "Rollo." He's been assembling a Britany army ever since. He leads the Eastman here in the Holy Roman Empire." The captain chuckled. "Not much of an empire. Roads all a mess, the land lawless and the folks o'Britany chafe under the yoke of the Gauls. A minor province, far from the Frankish king and his powers. That's why it's been easy for Rolf the Ganger to take land and control..."

"Think this Rolf would have need for a good man?"

"Would need to prove yourself, I'd say. Rolf's not a trusting sort."

Cub closed his eyes and rocked by the boat, drifted into a light sleep.

Pink light tinged the horizon before dawn. Cub stretched and twisted his sore back from side to side, working the muscles and the fresh scars so they would not heal too tight. True to the captain's prediction, the coastline heaved into view with the sunrise, a rocky line to their south. The ship skirted the shoreline to the east while the captain and pilot searched for landmarks to secure their landing. About midmorning the pilot steered the craft into a small, coastal bay, a tiny hamlet tucked among a forest boasting a short dock, a simple haven in a storm. Gray stone houses with wooden shutters unlike any village Cub had seen, the morning sun sparkled off a hint of frost on the roof thatch. Split-rail racks stood on the wharf, drying fish in the sun. Long punts and skiffs tied dockside, and a few old men of the place sullenly watched their approach. Two met the landing, young sailors adept at tying the ship and propping plank ramps in place. The captain had arranged for a horse-drawn wagon, and the sailors organized to pass the ingots to the shore. A scrawny lot not much use to the working sailors, the freed slaves climbed to the wharf and one by one wandered past the villagers and into the forest. Leaning on a piling, Cub watched the operation as the wagon strained and creaked under the increasing load. The captain joined him.

"Where are you taking the load?"

"Me and a few men escort the wagon inland to the trade. You are welcome to tag along, but...." He peered at Cub from under his brow, delaying his response. He wrapped a single tin ingot in a scrap of cloth. "Don't get in my way. If anything should go awry, you could get hurt." He patted the long knife in his belt.

The wagon filled, the captain and five men led the horse into the forest. Cub hesitated in the village square, following the horse-drawn cart from a distance. A mix of trees, vines and thick brush crowded the narrow pathway out of town. Forest birds twittered and swooped from the branches overhead and the dray made steady progress, the slope of the hillside leveling on a grassy promontory. The way weaved between rolling hills and stands of hardwoods. The horse trundled past cultivated fields not yet sown for the new year, others fenced sheep wandering the pastures. They trudged over a low bridge, constructed of the same ashen stone used in the village, the stream beneath chortling with fast-flowing water. Cub stopped and drank, the water fresh and cold.

By the time the sun reached its zenith, the wagon trundled into a village, a much larger town built of the same dingy rock and straw roofs bleached bone-white by the sun. The Vikings followed the avenue to a crossroads in the center of the town, Cub lingering behind. As they passed, Cub noticed men rise to watch their passage. A few knots of bystanders formed in their wake—Cub wandered closer to a group of three, one with a thin beard, and another paunchy with an iron sword strapped across his back. Grimy, he noticed, their fingers black and their teeth brown.

To his surprise, he could understand them! Heavily accented, the words sounded unmistakably Cornish in origin, words Brother Piran had taught him during his time in the mine smithy. These Britany folk spoke a Cornish-like tongue—he chuckled to himself and edged closer.

"Wait, master said. Wait 'til theys in tavern...." Iron

sword hawked and spat in the dirt. "Listen you wretches, master say we rob 'em after the deal is struck, so's he keeps the tin rightly bought and we takes back the coin. Listen for the whistle."

The two agreed, one repeating the word whistle.

"We have enough to take 'em?"

"I hear north men fight like cornered bears..."

"Fools, we outnumber two to one." He slid his iron blade partially from its rough, canvas loop. "And I counted three knives betwixt 'em."

Cub eased back from the men, gaining distance to better observe the square ahead. Knowing what to search for, he could picture the opposing array aligned against them now, small groups of field hands and a few burly men dressed like smiths in heavy aprons, all seemingly disinterested in the wagon's arrival, slyly watching every move. The captain and his men led the wagon forward into the square, wary of the gathering crowd and clearly intent on the tavern at the crossroads, a low-roofed building with stables and horses milling about a split-rail fenced yard. As they reached their destination, the sailors maneuvered the cart, backing it into the stable yard. Two men stayed with the horse, jiggering with its yoke and bit, and nervously watching the street while the captain hefted his cloth-wrapped package and led the rest of his team inside.

Cub checked his surroundings, few options for weapons at hand, until he spied a shovel, a flat wooden scoop with a short handle, leaning against one of the houses. *This will have to do*, he thought as he grabbed it. He hunched over, tipping his head to hide his face as much as he could muster under a noonday sun. He stepped to the three men in the lane.

"Hallo!" He cleared his throat. The three eyed him suspiciously.

"Get lost." Iron sword growled.

"Who're you?"

"Master say hide!" Cub hissed through clenched teeth. "What you doing?" The three gawked at him. "You give us away! Come," Cub motioned to an alley across the lane, hoping his broken Cornish fooled them. "We hide there...." He strode confidently toward the narrow path between two buildings.

A muttered curse followed him, and at the opening of the alley as he turned, he found the three wandering toward him, iron sword lagging the others. The foremost man crept conspiratorially close. "Do I know you?"

"Here, step in." Cub motioned with his shovel. "Hide 'til the signal." He tapped his ear knowingly and pushed the first two past him into the narrow alley. The one with the iron sword confronted him in the opening, a perplexed wrinkling to his brow.

"I said, who are you? I've not...."

Cub suspected the shovel broke his jaw. The baffled aspect to his arched brow never changed; the blow connected, and he slumped in a heap.

Cub swung backward with the scoop catching an unguarded rogue in his crotch. Buckled over, Cub disabled him with a single swat to the temple. He kicked the third backward into the tight walkway, jumped back over the first unconscious man and jerked the iron blade from its canvas loops. A rip of tearing cloth accompanied his pull as he yanked the sword loose. Before he could brandish the weapon, the last man stumbled to his feet with a loud gulp, turned and ran away, disappearing into the narrow alley. Cub quirked his brow at his retreating back, bent and grasped the first assailant by his collar and dragged him deeper in the alleyway, tossing one body atop the other.

Cub peeked around the corner and mapped his opponents in his head. Two more loitered casually in the lane before him, a group of four, including the men in heavy aprons, slowly advanced on the stable grounds, and he suspected more lurked in the cross roadways. He wondered...

Leaning out of the alley, he called to the two closest, "Psst! Hey, hallo!" The men turned and he waved at them with his widest smile. "Come here!"

They hesitated and glanced at each other.

"Come! Here!" Cub insisted in a hoarse whisper, pointing to the ground with one hand, the other holding the sword behind the wall out of their view. "The master..." At the mention of this mysterious leader, their expressions grew suddenly concerned, and the two ruffians increased their pace and stepped forward into the alcove. Cub stepped back into the dim light to wait for them—as the first entered he pointed at the pile, and said, "Look!"

With a gasp of surprise, the first man dropped to his knees to inspect, his partner pushing past Cub for a better view. A simple crack to the back of the head of the passing man and a shove toppled the would-be thief on his cohort, and by the time the inept bandit extracted himself from the pile of bodies, he found the point of the iron sword at his throat.

"You want die?" Cub asked, in broken Cornish. His face pallid, the man worried his chin with nervous fingers. Cub grabbed him by the hair, wrenched him to his feet, and pressed the blade into his back. Grabbing a free wrist, he pulled his arm behind his back at an unnatural angle, holding the wriggling man secure. Pushing him forward to the lane, he forced the man's head around the corner, his mouth at his ear.

"Call."

"What?"

"You call. Names." Cub rubbed the man against the rough stonework. "Call names!"

Not such a bad idea—the man decided to call for support.

"Pierre! Max! Here, to me!"

In the lane, the four men turned to the sound of his voice. A burly one, frowning, placed his hands on his hips. Another ducked his head and turned back to watch the two sailors in the horse run. Cub clucked his tongue and pressed the point of the sword into the flesh at the small of his back.

"No, Max, come here. MAX!"

Cub could see the four holding a subdued discussion in the lane, one gesturing back towards the alley where he hid, another dramatically waving his hands in the air. The pantomime easily detailed their confusion and unwillingness to deviate from their scheme. As they viewed the street, they acknowledged, indeed, their plan had gone awry—where hid their crew? These people spoke with their hands—clear instructions assigned, the men had abandoned their posts. A pointing forefinger, a chopping motion, a dismissive flutter of fingers. Watching, Cub realized he could nearly narrate their argument, and he smiled, satisfied with his disruption. Baffled, they hesitated on the verge of a decision to investigate.

The man in his grip jerked and pulled, attempting to wriggle free of his grasp to escape—startled, Cub poked him with the blade, puncturing his back. Suddenly hurt, the man cried out, and not a low moan of pain, a bloodcurdling scream. "My death, my death! He kills me!"

"Oh, All-Father save me from such cowards!" Perturbed more than angry, Cub slapped the man's temple with the flat of the blade, dropped his arm hold and smacked the fool's forehead into the wall, knocking him senseless. As his limp form staggered, Cub kicked him out into the road, where he splayed across the dirt, inert—*that should grab Max and Pierre's attention!*

Cub hesitated—*should I leap out and confront the onrush? Or...* in the alley by his head a shutter hung loose on its jamb. Hinged from the top, Cub found it unbarred and easily lifted. Tossing the heavy sword through, he scrambled into a darkened room.

Moist, stale air assaulted his nose—*why don't these people take baths*? He fumbled in the dim light for the weapon. His eyes adjusted—a brazier of cherry-red coals festered in a corner, and the shutters let slivers of light slip through in bright stripes... an old crone sat on a straw pallet, her eyes wide with fright, her mouth a surprised "Oh!"

"Quiet," he hushed her, holding a finger to his lips. Outside he could hear a rising commotion underway, growing in force and temper, angry bellows, yells of surprise and muffled shouts. Heard through the wall words came muddled and difficult to follow. Outside, those who reconnoitered called for help. Bodies in the alley! Come quick, plan discovered. All is spoiled!

Cub unbolted the door, gave the old woman a toothy grin and repeated the Cornish phrase Brother Piran had hounded into him, "Forgive me my sins."

He swung the door open and leaped into the lane, quickly assessing the situation. Max turned out to be one of the husky smiths, and he bent over the prone body in the street, a nasty, long knife in his fist. Another man waved and shrieked from the narrow alley entrance, gesturing and, in Cub's opinion, overreacting. The big unsuspecting man on his knees—weakened from a year in the Devon mines, Cub recognized this was not a time for heroics, fair fights, and brave battles. With a grunt, he drove the dull, heavy blade into the bulky neck before him. Immediately the wound gushed blood down the smith's spark-pocked apron.

Max the unready struggled to his feet, grabbed for his neck wound and, as Cub wrenched the sword free his blood spurted across the lane, a fountain splattering the gray stone walls. The injured man twirled and croaked, his voice injured by the blow.

"Whoop!" The man in the alley entrance stumbled back from the arcing, gory stream, his eyes popping wide and his mouth slack. As far as Cub could tell, he had no better weapon than a wooden club.

"Boo!" Cub barked at him, and he dropped his club, turned, and scrambled away, running as fast as he could. Big Max staggered, dropped his dagger, and toppled forward into the dirt. Cub snapped to face the foes he figured rushed to attack his back. At least, that is what he would have done in a similar situation.

Cub had underestimated the amount of reluctance farmers possess when considering whether to engage in battle with anyone, particularly when insurmountable odds in one's favor had unaccountably crumbled. Pierre and his compatriot had retreated to the crossroads where they vacillated in indecision, and while three others arrived from the other direction, the two Norse sailors had pulled their knives and advanced through the stable gates.

"Oy, Pierre!" Cub called in broken Britany. "Time to be

dead, eh?" Cub puffed out his chest and marched forward, swinging the heavy blade loosely in his grip.

Maybe the sight of the runner hightailing it over the hills beyond, or maybe the gore that drenched Cub's sword arm—Pierre didn't wait for a better translation. He forfeited his fellow by pushing him toward Cub and turned to run in the opposite direction. Shocked at his treatment in the face of danger, the man pitched to the ground blubbered, casting aside a nastily curved fruit knife. Cub kicked it aside. The three other attackers watched two Viking sailors approach, each holding a knife at the ready, each smiling and ready for battle.

"Run now." Cub pointed his blade at them. "Run and we no make dead." The man on the ground leaped to his feet and scrambled after Pierre. The others hesitated, back-to-back.

"I say... RUN!"

Their nerve crumbled, and slowly their retreat increased in speed until they dashed out of sight. *So much for the local muscle,* thought Cub. Laughing, the two sailors crossed to Cub and grabbed his arm to shake his hand in the northern way.

"Did you see them run?"

"The sneak thieves! How did you know?"

"I speak their tongue! I overheard them talking."

"Baldr bless you!"

"What have you done?

"Taught them a lesson."

"A lesson they'll soon not forget!"

"How many did you kill, boy?"

"I think only one, but there are five more who will need time to sleep off my... instructions." The Vikings guffawed, slapping Cub on his back.

"There is a signal they said," Cub flapped his sword arm to throw off bloody droplets. "A signal to attack. A whistle."

"A whistle, eh?"

"Let's let this whistle plot play. What do you say?"

"I like the way you think, boy." The three wandered back to the paddock, leaning on the rails next to the tavern's porch. Cub hid the blood-covered blade behind a post. He brushed the dust from his tunic and reset his cap, rakishly tilted back on his forehead. Checking the empty streets, he noticed the old woman he had disturbed peeking from her door and gave her a sly wink.

Their wait did not last long—the captain and a bald elder swung open the heavy oaken door, the host clearly well-dressed and overfed, in the midst of assuring the crew, "...whatever the commotion, tis nothing to worry over...."

He stopped mid-sentence, seeing three unexpected Northerners barring his way.

"What is the meaning of this?"

Cub gave a small bow. "Watching our wagon, your honor."

Rubbing his shining pate, disdain curled his lip—he recognized a sassy reply. The captain frowned and his crew from the tavern glanced confused from face to face. Cub jutted out his jaw and held his arms akimbo, a mildly threatening stance. Unused to such rude treatment from a youth, the elder sneered and waved his hand in an imperious, commanding gesture. He sucked and puckered. A loud, distinct whistle sounded.

Everyone paused. His whistle echoed in the village streets.

Cub lifted his hand to his ear and leaned forward in an exaggerated way.

"You might try again, I don't think they heard...."

One of the sailors next to him snickered. Grunting, the Brittan huffed deep and whistled again.

This time the two sailors whistled back, holding the note until chuckles overtook their wind, and they broke into laughter. Nonplussed, the captain and the others smiled weakly, not comprehending the joke. Cub reached behind the post and drew out the iron sword. The village elder blanched as he recognized blood stains on Cub's sleeve, and he bumped into the captain trying to step aside. Cub walked steadily forward, lifting the blade, and switching to his version of the local tongue.

"They not come. They run away." He held the blade to the man's throat.

Mildly surprised at Cub's sudden switch to Cornish, the captain and the other Vikings sidestepped and let him press the man until he stopped, his back flat against the wall.

"You want tell him?" He indicated the captain with a tip of his head. "Or you want give him purse and keep tin?" Cub swung the sword tip in a slight movement to indicate the wagon. Mouth working, the local landholder shifted his eyes from Cub to the crew and back. Watching his father trade, Cub had seen this hesitation before, as men weigh options in a negotiation gone wrong. Cub chuckled at his discomfort and switched back to his native tongue.

"Decide, old man. We don't have all day." He squinted at the man, the sword point never leaving his neck. "For your deceit, we have every right to take your heart, take your gold and keep our tin...."

"In fact," one of the sailors who had witnessed Cub scare and chase the locals interjected, "we would be in our right to return with our entire crew for Tyr's compensation." Bits of truth becoming apparent from these words, his captain huffed, crossed his arms slowly and glared at the squirming elder. The old man chewed his lip and sized Cub.

Impressed he did not try to lie, toady, or beg, Cub let the old man inch back from his blade and fumble at his robe. Reluctantly he drew out a leather purse and handed it to the captain.

"Is that all you have?" Cub poked the iron sword in the man's chest. The bald man shuffled through his cloak and drew out a smaller pouch.

"Captain, our host has decided to pay a premium for the tin we have brought to sell. He should be more hospitable in the future." Several sailors laughed at the man's discomfort, and Cub withdrew his weapon, allowing the man to turn and flee back into the darkened building.

Switching to his broken Cornish, Cub spoke to the dark interior, "A warning. Try again fool us East men and we make you be dead."

The captain gathered his men, tucked the second purse into his belt and directed them back to their ship. In high spirits, the sailors recounted their version of Cub's defeat of the local ruffians, and as they passed through the town, all laughed heartily at the two bodies in the lane and the pile of groggy men jammed in the narrow alleyway.

"You should have seen that big oaf, stuck like a pig!"

"Spraying like a cat in heat!"

"You, boy, you need to tell this tale o'er a horn."

Cub chuckled along. "Sure, ale is always good."

"I see you found yourself a sword." The captain gestured at the iron blade.

"A bit unbalanced, but she should work." Cub bounced on his feet.

"The name's Colden." He held out his palm.

"Agne Agneson." Cub grasped his arm above the wrist

to shake the offered hand. "My friends call me Cub."

"Cub it is, then." Cub stooped to rub the blade face in grass alongside the lane.

"I'll not forget the favor you did me and my men this day, Cub." Colden gripped Cub by his shoulder. A sailor beside him waved in agreement. "No better way to earn trust. Honest as Tyr, and a fighter like Thor without Mjolnir. When we get back from this voyage, I will keep you by my side. Rolf can use a man like you, especially as you speak the locals' words."

SORVEN

Squatting by the smoldering fire, rain trickling down his neck, his feet sodden in his boots, Sorven suffered, miserable and cold. His stomach pinched and gurgled, weeks since a proper meal. Or a bath... *not that these mountain bandits care how I smell... gods, they reek.*

Cold, night mist crept slowly through the damp trees around their camp. Smoke wafted and smarted his eyes. A spit over the fire ill-roasted a hare, the poorly dressed carcass covered in singed bits of fur, burned dry spots and red, raw splotches. Sniffing, Dun leaned close, hiding under his meager oilcloth. The remaining Welsh brigands, all three wrapped in filthy, wool blankets, crouched around the fire, trying to keep warm and drooling over the bit of meat on the skewer. One mumbled incoherent nonsense at Dundle, who sniffed and huffed along in agreement.

This is the way they had lived for weeks.

After they had escaped Jorvik, he and Dundle rode across Northumbria into Mercia, hiding during days and traveling at night, the weather growing blustery and cold, the horses ever more tired and lame. Finally faced with starvation, they sold the horses to a farmer and hid for a fortnight in a remote wayside tavern on the route into the Welsh Highlands. A dank place filled with transients, roustabouts, and peddlers bent on passing by with haste, there Dundle found them a refuge of sorts, falling in with a group of Welsh pickpockets and sneak thieves who hid from a Mercian sheriff of renown. Dundle spoke their language well enough, using hand motions and wasting bits of coin on ales for the motley gang. When they had ultimately run out of money, the crew invited them to join their plans for a permanent escape into the mountains across the border. The way they explained, it would be a glorious life free of all constraints and restrictions, where they could come and go as they pleased, take when they had wants and rule the land with the might of their arms. Enticed by hints of outlaw danger, highwayman adventures among the high hills and pastoral valleys, Dun wheedled, cajoled, and finally begged Sorven to join the adventure. Faced with no other recourse, Sorven had yielded to his sniveling.

Nothing went as planned.

Sparsely settled, the mountain homesteads well protected by dogs and angry farmers, the easy pickings they had expected never materialized, and forest game eluded them, day after day. Supplies grew thin. A few of the rogues deserted after days, leaving the most desperate to huddle with Sorven and Dun over wretched fires in steep valley nooks. The only one who blessed with a hint of sense, Sorven insisted they move their camp each day, avoiding other camps of vagrants and the tiny villages. While the others grumbled and hissed at him, in the end, they were too lazy to argue and slogged along after him to a new spot in the thick forests. They lost track of the days.

Snow fell, melted away, followed by night cracking crisp with frost. Despite his empty, growling stomach, Sorven could not bear to eat the uncooked rabbit when his impatient companions fell on the scorched game and tore it to pieces. Dundle, his face and sparse beard smeared with grease, offered him a scrawny leg which Sorven declined, swallowing his bile.

A heated discussion bounced between the three remaining thieves. Dundle translated fragments to Sorven in a hoarse whisper.

"A'hunt, Olof say he come n'a big town, more farm than he count, and no walls." He emphasized the fact the village ranged along the hillsides, unprotected by a palisade or fortress. Sorven slumped on his haunches—he knew where this discussion led, the topic reoccurred every few days.

"They want to raid it, don't they?"

"Ja, talk 'bout a stealin'. Food, horses, neh?" Dundle leered from under his drenched hood.

Two of the thieves scratched in the mud by the fire, conspiratorially whispering and chuckling to themselves, the third sitting quietly glowering. The two pantomiming the plan could have been brothers, snouts like a hound, tiny mouths, faint chins, and beardless cheeks, while the third barrel-chested and thick necked like a farm laborer, dull-witted and nursing an unfailing angry mien unless asleep. The brute's name was Olof, and the other two had unpronounceable Welsh names, and to tell them apart Sorven called the taller one 'Bumble,' and the other one 'Bramble.' Not understanding his tongue, they did not appreciate his joke.

Lines and confused squiggles marked the dirt by the banked coals, hand signals and head wobbles led to an agreement. One of the long-nosed boys pointed at Dun and Sorven.

"Says we sneak back way, o'er fences an' such whatnot."

"That's their plan?"

"Aye, each sneak differ ways."

Sorven snorted.

"Says smells bread a'bakin." Dundle wet his bottom lip. "Bread... gotsa be a bakery."

Sorven sighed.

"That's all to it? All those words, and we just steal in and take what we want?"

"Crash n' snatch, Sorvie."

Sorven stared at the coals sizzling under the misty rain. Bumble chattered more nonsense, his twin bobbing along.

"Nobody guard a bakery...."

Burly Olof stood and stretched, muttering and growling.

"What did he say?"

"He want'a fight. If not this, then...."

"Then what?"

"Then one a'us." Dundle sighed. "He's wantin'a break somethin'."

Sorven unwrapped his oilcloth and stood. "It's decided. Where is this village we are robbing?"

Smiling, the Welsh bandits recognized Sorven had agreed to their ill-defined plan, and they all talked at once, collecting their few possessions and kicking wet leaves from the forest floor over the smoky campfire remnants. The big man grunted and stood to the side, picking at his teeth with a bone from the meal—he provided the brawn for their brains. Sorven had long decided the muscle comprised the single functioning part of this highwaymen team. Dundle bounced along, genuinely excited, ready at last for action.

After a bout of initial excitement, a somber silence fell over the group as they wound their way through the trees and brush, trying unsuccessfully to follow game paths and avoid brambles and hook vines. The rain turned to sleet, a glossy shell soon covering their hoods, caps, and shoulders.

Slippery, the trek down the mountainside triggered a few falls and Welsh curses. Sorven hung to the rear, watching Olof's hulk skate the steep path, clutching at trees and brush to hamper a pell-mell tumble. Fleet-footed Dundle hopped from tree to tree, the two twins dogging his heels. Finding a crooked branch, Sorven used it as a walking stick, supporting his weight as he stepped around the skid marks of the previous passers. A stray twig whipped his forehead. The cloudy sky spat hail, cutting their vision to an arm's length at best.

With a yelp, one of the 'not brothers' stumbled and pitched headlong down the hillside. He disappeared with a clatter, a cascade of rockfall and a series of splashes. His companion called to him, a jumble of incoherent consonants to Sorven's ear, and as he crept forward to reach the same abrupt drop, he scrambled to find a hold, ultimately tottering to fall the after his fellow. Olof held out his arms and planted his feet securely in the muddy scree, Dundle leaning around him and calling out in a hoarse whisper.

A groan sounded from below.

Olaf acting as an anchor, Sorven used his oilcloth blanket as a rope to climb the sheer drop. Reaching the end of his tether, Sorven sat on the ground and slid unceremoniously down the remainder of the hill. The shale outcropping ended in a strip of grass and a gurgling brook lined with last season's cattails. The twin bandits lay half submerged in the stream course, one holding his ankle and muttering, the other coddling his wrist. The cloudy sky broke, flashes of the moon lighting the scene.

"Dun, slide on your arse." Sorven stood and brushed the pebbles and mud from his backside. "It's not too steep."

Olof careened down the hillside and splashed into the creek with a growl. Dundle followed, following Sorven's instructions, taking care to not lose control of his slide. As Sorven and Dundle stood to the side, the three Welsh bandits whispered arguments punctuated with whimpers from the one who could no longer stand.

Sorven hung back from the angry brute. Difficult to see in the poor light, he didn't need sight to know what happened, he could imagine the rage bloating Olof's face red, and his hands flexing into fists. Dundle tried to speak and triggered a bark needing no translation—mind your own business! With a grunt, Dundle parked next to Sorven and watched the three shapes in the gloom.

The shapes spat angry words. A whine of pain, followed by pleading words. The dispute continued in a guttural and threatening way. A tussle ended in a loud cry, and Olof stumbled out of the dark to peer into Sorven and Dundle's faces.

"Come."

Sorven understood that word. He fell in after Dundle and watched the silhouette of the big man as he led them along the banks of the stream. Behind, he could hear moans and murmurs from their abandoned companions.

Olof knew where to lead—the brook widened as it reached a dell in the cleft between the mountains. Stone fences marked farmsteads and they found a winding cart trail paralleling the stream. The village straddled the mountainsides. Sorven could smell peat fires, silage and, yes, the yeasty odor of fresh-baked bread. His mouth watered.

A glimmer of fires along the lane lit the dreary night. The few flashes lit the hillsides where the stone-walled farmsteads perched on their terraced pastures. The sleet had turned to a mist. Sorven rubbed the damp from his cheeks.

Olof wrapped his arms around them and pulled them close, his stench quickly erasing Sorven's appetite. He crouched and pulled them to their knees beside him. He grumbled, insistent and conspiratorial—Dundle translated his directions.

"We'r ta stay a'hind these here, and Olof takes t'other." Dundle motioned with his flat hand to the stacked stone fences, to his right and his left. Sorven dipped his head in understanding. Olaf waited for Dundle to finish speaking, he pinched both their shoulders as he continued his explanation.

"We'r ta stay quiet." Sorven could discern the wince on Dundle's face as Olof squeezed his arm. "No noise," he hissed. Olof continued his brusque commands, shaking both boys to emphasize his points.

"Girls, wants women," Dundle explained. Sorven rolled his eyes. "...and silver, wants silver." The big man blew his fetid breath in their faces.

"Two-faced Hela, just keep his smell from me," Sorven muttered.

"He's talk 'bout sum, I don' know, sum' word 'bout...." Dundle sputtered. "Oh, All-Father's eye, jus' nod yer head. Nod yer head, like ya know what I tells ya."

Feeling the wide hand tighten on his shoulder, Sorven bobbed along with Dun. Olof chuckled in their ears.

Even in the dim light, they could see a grin split Olof's

face and he arched his back. Sorven tried to suppress a shudder. He didn't need Dundle to interpret his intent. With a snort, Olof released them and waded across the stream, pointing to the opposite bank, and making a chopping signal with his hands. In unison Sorven and Dundle bobbled their heads, and as they watched, the big man wrung his hands as if he snapped a poor soul's neck. He waved at them and directed them into the rolling fields. His glare told them they should move faster. Sorven pulled Dundle over a stone wall and settled him on the edge of a cabbage field.

"Listen, Dun." Sorven pulled the older boy close. "This is crazy. We don't know what we are getting into...."

"But Olof...."

"Olof nothing. He's bull-headed enough to run down anyone he finds. He plans to take by force. Do you think that will work for us?"

"Uhh...."

"Really? Dun, we're half starved, wet and dirty. These farmers, there's no taking them by force. We're not Welsh mountain men who kill with bare hands, are we?"

"We gots yer sword and me knife...."

Sorven pushed him against the wall. "You ready to battle?"

Dun dropped his face and fumbled with his belt, his knife tangled in his cloak. Sorven listened to him sniff.

"Let's follow this pasture line and get a better view, eh?" Dun muttered—Sorven couldn't hear. "Listen, I am not going with you unless you act with care. This is no game, we could get hurt...."

Not waiting for Dundle's reply, Sorven crawled up the slope, digging his feet into the turned loam and holding tight to the wall with his right hand.

The hill rose at a steady slope. Sorven reached a gate at the top, split planks set in channels. Dundle crept to his side and helped quietly slide the beams into their pockets. The upper field terraced flatter than the lower, a pile of stones and rocks in the corner and a low wide building at the far end, a black bulk barely discernable against the dark sky. Sorven hushed Dundle and stumbled across the turf—the ground here lay untilled, a grazing arena.

"Stay close."

"Sure as... oof!"

A ram hurtled out of the dark! The beast surprised them both, swooping across from the darkened end of the lot and bowling Sorven over to skid along the close-cropped lawn. Rolled head over heels, he stumbled back to his feet. Less agile, Dundle found himself under the hooves of the animal. In the dark ewes bleated, and their protective sire stomped and danced and butted, hectoring Dundle across the pasture. As soon as he scrambled to his feet, the ram knocked him prone.

Sorven ran forward into the deep shadow of the barn. The commotion behind him grew in volume as the sheep raised an alarm. A dog nearby growled. Dundle blurted "Yip!" as his horned attacker found him again.

"Dundle, stop fooling around...." He banged his shin against a low-slung beam, tripped over a knee-high wall, and fell with a splash. Deep mud, wet, grimy, and smelling of...

Pigs! A beast snorted next to his ear, snuffled, and nosed his face with a slobbery snout.

Spitting dirt Sorven tried to stand and slipped in the muck, his legs flipped out from underneath him, and he landed on his back with a smack, squirming animals on all sides. He thrashed and rolled and pushed himself to a sitting position. A squalling creature wiggled from under his legs—piglets, squealing and racing around the dark pen. As he struggled to stand, the sow banged him hindmost into the muck, chuffing at her babies, turning them aside. The big animal backed away, mud sucking at her feet.

As Sorven struggled to his knees, Dundle, running from the angry ram, collided with the same hidden pigpen wall, and tipped over to land on Sorven, both tumbling back into the pigsty. They flailed in the slop, Dundle coughing from a mouthful.

"Loki's whiskers!"

"Hush, you fool, we've raised the alarm." Sorven grabbed Dundle's arm and led him across the pen, each step sinking to their knees in the muck. Dundle blubbered.

"Thinks it broke a rib..."

"Hush." Sorven hiked a leg over the enclosing stone wall and jerked the whimpering Dundle alongside him. The ground on the other side hard packed, he climbed to his feet, the dog sounding closer, his barks angry and clear.

"O'er there." Dundle pulled free and ran.

"No, wait!"

Dundle groaned as he smacked into a split-rail fence in the dark. Sorven scrambled to his side and seized him.

"Hold!" He hissed in his ear. "You can't see. I can't see. Don't go running in the dark, you'll make it worse." Panting, he pushed Dundle's head the way he wanted him to examine.

"See there?"

A few shutters flew open, the warm glow of firelight outlining shapes in the windows. Below by the lane, torches rallied, reflecting light on the clutch of houses in the village center. Despite the dark, they could discern a few shapes moving between the houses on the mountainside. A crowd formed. Men shouted and answered. A roll call echoed around the narrow vale. Dogs barked and added to the confusion. Sorven crawled forward, yanking Dundle along behind him.

"What a disaster," he grumbled, his oilcloth wrap lost, dropped in the field.

"Sorvie, thinks I'm a bad way. Am I bleedin'?"

"Loki's balls! Bleeding? You're covered in pig muck!"

"Oh Sorvie, we gots t'a run."

"Hush." Sorven pulled the whining boy by his collar—*I can't believe he fought at Ethandun*, he thought, shaking his head.

"This way." He shuffled Dundle over another stone wall and climbed slowly after him. "Keep your head low. We can climb from here and escape back into the woods...." The field had been terraced flat, a narrow run planted with... onions, he could smell them, recently harvested and pungent. The gang of torches moved below, a meandering line following the stream course through the valley. Calling and shouts had stopped, the dogs reigned. A quiet settled over the gorge as the searchers fanned out and sought trespassers.

Dundle sneezed.

Sorven swallowed, turned, and glared. "Shhh."

Dundle sneezed again, followed by a loud sniff. "Tis onions...."

Sorven tried to clap his hand across Dundle's mouth to stifle the next blast, his reaction too late. Louder than his first two, the sneeze echoed from the far gorge wall. Below, the searchers turned towards them.

"Loki plague us!" Pulling Dundle by his arm, Sorven dashed across the onion field, Dundle buckled over baying a string of noisy sneezes, each more violent than the last.

Reaching the upper wall, Sorven lifted Dundle over and scrambled close behind him.

Short, bushy trees, spread in line, a type of orchard blocked their path.

"Duck!" Sorven warned and dragged Dundle through the boles. Dundle grunted and swore as he banged his head against branches in Sorven's wake. One last sneeze, and they fell silent, the rustle of dead leaves marking their passage.

As torches climbed the hill, Sorven could see silhouettes with pitch forks and rakes. A mob chased them, and ahead he could see more men moving to block their way. At the edge of the orchard, a narrow path led to a homestead, the thatched roof a hulking shadow against the sky.

Sorven pulled a wheezing Dundle along the path, stumbling across a narrow courtyard. Moonlight shone through a break in the clouds and rain-damp leaves sparkled—beyond this farmhouse, the forest grew thick and inviting.

"This way." He turned into the yard and rushed forward.

The farmhouse door swung wide, a matronly woman in a linen gown waving a smoky torch in their faces. Two plump girls in the same linen wraps peeked around her sides. At the sight of Dundle and Sorven, the threesome shrieked and backpedaled. Sorven glanced at Dundle—*no wonder they are frightened*, he thought, *he's a fright, covered in mud, sticks and leaves, the whites of his eyes peering from the tarry mess*. He checked himself—not much better. With a yelp, the woman flung the torch at them and slammed the door shut. Tossed with no aim, it whizzed past and smacked the ground throwing sparks.

The distraction caused by the women gave the mob enough time to catch Sorven and Dundle and they jabbered in their tongue, spreading out in a half-circle to surround them. The farm tools menaced. Dundle sneezed and slumped against the farmhouse wall. Sorven growled and in a show of desperate bravery, jerked his mud-covered sword from his belt and brandished it.

A somber, grizzled farmer stepped forward and unwrapped his heavy cloak from his shoulders. Approaching Sorven, he swung the wrap like a net and neatly tangled sword arm and weapon in the folds. Sorven fell back a step, surprised he could be disarmed that quickly. The men pressed forward, pitchforks, poles and rakes all held at waist height and aimed at the boys' chests.

One man pushed to the forefront and bellowed words in Welsh.

Sorven side glanced at Dundle.

Face blanched white, Dundle dropped to the dirt in a faint.

Hanging his head, Sorven raised his hands to surrender. The mob surged forward and tossed a ratty blanket over his head, and, as luck would have it, the first blows connected with his temple. Enduring the beating no longer mattered, for Sorven fell unconscious at their feet.

KARA

"Clean this mess."

The King who they called Mac Ausle waved at his gathered warriors. At his feet, the boy silently hunched over his dead brother. Brushing his thick hair back from his forehead, the King pointed at a man. "Take my betrothed to the storehouse beyond and set a guard to protect her." The selected soldier motioned to the reluctant, redheaded girl.

"And you...." He snapped his finger and motioned, trying to remember.

"Kaelan."

"Ah, yes, son of Ulbrecht, you go with Gunna and Asta, and clear the rioters from the streets."

Kaelan squinted at Kara. She gave him a side-eye indicating her consent, shifting her gaze to the short sword in her hand.

Noticing his hesitation, broad-chested Gunna ducked her head to the king in a rough bow, her blonde braid swinging. "Come boy, we won't eat you and there's little fight left in these rebels."

Asta clucked her tongue, "I don't know, Gun, I may take a bite." She gave Kaelan a wicked smile, drawing chuckles from the king's guard. Her thick, straw-colored hair matted with a heavy oil, the shield maid winked at Kaelan and wiggled provocatively. Kaelan's eyes widened. Asta bowed to the king and stepping past him, she elbowed Kara aside as she followed Gunna and Kaelan to the door. Kara made a move to join them, and the new king held out his hand to stop her.

Surprised and unsure, Kara watched the three leave. Her voice caught in her throat—*what just happened?*

"Sichfrith, off your knees. Your brother is gone, there is nothing to do now." The boy climbed slowly to his feet. Kara could see his red-rimmed eyes and a drip clung to the point of his nose.

"We must give my brother the high burial due his rank."

"Of course, you make the arrangements, and we shall bear the costs." The king peered distractedly at the rafters and his warriors dragging the dead from the hall. Sichfrith, Kara thought, is a son of Ivar. Not much older than she and Kaelan, he stood a hand taller than she, his nose sharp and pointed, his face slack and eyes vacant. His hands trembled at his sides. The king ignored him, gesturing to the door. "Go, gather your brethren and settle the details."

Sichfrith sucked in a lungful as if he prepared to speak, and as Kara watched his shoulders collapsed and he slumped out the open door. Rough tables scraped and banged as they resettled in their places. Shutters propped open to air the room.

Carrying the remnants of a broken shield, a man whispered with the king, who mumbled in agreement and sent him away. During the afternoon's excitement, Kara had not given the tall man much thought... as her new liege lord, she studied him closer—Mac Ausle stood taller than most, at least three hands taller than she, with broad shoulders and a square forehead. Strong and muscular, his hands broad and chipped with scars. His black hair hung on his back like a mane, his cheeks shaved clean, a dark stubble shading each blue. He smoothed his tunic of pressed white linen, a soft, tight weave that highlighted a golden chain around his neck. Each finger held a ring, bands of silver and gold, and his wide belt, tooled leather inset with tin rivets, snugged tight around his waist. A heavy, utilitarian knife buckled to his girdle, and a leather frog hung loose at his belt, his jeweled blade tucked through it. As she examined him, his eyes found hers and the corners of his mouth quirked in a smile.

"And you, my wet-nurse warrior...." He beckoned her forward with an open palm.

"Yes, King Mac?"

The sovereign chuckled.

"You are fresh off the boat, aren't you?"

"Ahh...?" Kara stuttered, at a loss.

"The Eire word 'mac' means 'son of.'" The newly

crowned king smoothed his cloak. "My father was as famous as old Imar, his boon companion. They ruled together for many years. You may call me King Ausle." He measured her with his brown eyes and offered her a smile both charming and unnerving.

"You can fight, I saw you. Even unarmed, Kara Agnesdatter, you stand your own—I saw Gunna, chief of my guard, wonder at your skill. You impressed us, maid. You are young and fresh...." He unabashedly studied her figure. "Such a beauty and uncorrupted by... well, no matter. We have need of a warrior, one we can trust...." He pulled a silver band from his finger—a squiggle shaped like a bird, pressed into the ring. He offered the bauble to her.

"It's the Ragnarson sigil, the raven, like the banner Ubba lost."

Kara admired the ring and moved to return it. The king waved her away. "No, tis a gift for you, a token of friendship and welcome." Tipping his head forward, he peered at her from under his brow, his grin knowing and practiced. He stepped nearer and placed his hand on her forearm. Kara glanced around the hall, and the guards paused, watching her with their new lord. A few of the men smirked.

"I thank you, Your Highness..." She made to curtsey as she had been taught in the Mercian Court.

"No, thank you, young maid." He lifted her from the bow, and stroking her arm, the king took her hands in his. His eyes held hers, she held her breath as he inched uncomfortably closer. She smelled his odor, strong and not unpleasant. Releasing her hands, he took her by the shoulders, purposefully gazing into her eyes, his words blowing across her cheeks.

Kara dropped her eyes. A sudden flush trickled up her neck. *Why would he act this way? Is this the way of Eire? Is this right? No man has ever acted this familiar with me, even Kaelan in our hurried rush to escape Eddisbury kept me at arm's length, as any proper gentleman would.*

"May I count on you?" The king murmured. "May I call you to my service? Will you come to my aid?"

Perplexed and flustered, Kara touched her forehead in agreement and barely whispered a response, "Of course, yes, my lord."

The king released her arms, stepping back. He motioned to one of his guards, a round woman with an iron helmet.

"Kara joins my household guards, Tordis. Show her the maids' dormitory, the armory, the gatehouse and guard stations, offer her a bath and fresh clothes as befits my chosen guards, and let her join us here for supper."

"As you command." Tordis glumly took Kara by the arm, giving her a yank and breaking the King's spell. Kara stumbled after her into the late afternoon sun.

Pulling her arm, Tordis led her around the struggling fire brigade and across the square. Try as she might to slow their progress and gain composure, the woman marched Kara awkwardly across the stones. As they reached the main avenue back into Dublinn, she pushed her against the wall and grabbed her chin, peering into her eyes.

"Listen, little muttonhead." Tordis worried her chin. "You watch out, little country girl. Do you hear me? He saw you coming. Don't be falling into a kingly stupor, all breathless and wet—that's what he wants! Don't let his charms ruin you—women fall for Ausle, and now he holds the throne, more will fight to bed him and carry his brood."

"What?"

"Listen, lassie, Bradon Ausle has good traits I warrant, and he takes care of his own, but he is a woman chaser through and through. As the skalds proclaim, 'Ill it is when men, with smooth talk, sidestep what is just and good.' Young maids like you are his meat and butter."

"I... but, I...." Kara blushed at the frank words and dipped her eyes away. Tordis cocked her head, jutted out her jaw and glared into Kara's face.

"You need to know Bradon is betrothed to Muirgel, daughter of the King of Mide, that redheaded witch we bow and scrape to, and let me tell you, she's not above bitter revenge for interfering in her games. Sweet as a rose outside, nasty as a toad beneath. Poisonous bitch. We know not her plans... she bristles, none too happy about the union, but I tell you, girlie, steer clear of the both of them." Tordis released Kara and brushed her hands on her vest, pulling the iron helmet off her head and smoothing her sweat-tangled, salt and pepper hair. Kara saw one of her ears had been savagely crushed and healed scrunched like a budding flower. None in the square paid them attention. Smoke from the fires blew across the roadway.

"Your name is Tor...?"

"Tordis," she offered. "That's right. Been in the King's guard for seven years, old Imar himself brought me in." She beamed when she mentioned the old king's name. Short like her Aunt Yeru, this woman had puffed, rosy cheeks and a spiderweb of wrinkles around her eyes. Her hair had sprouted prematurely gray, like a winter sky before the rain, and it stuck to her ears and forehead. "Sorry to see Barith go, a great fighter he was, I am sure the Valkyries ride with him to Odin's banquet this day. A fair one, as far as kings go. Always treated us good, whether Findgenti or Dubgenti."

That word. "Dub-genti?"

"Oh, you are unschooled, child!" Tordis chuckled and took Kara by the arm. "Come with me, I'll show you the city and try to help you ken the madness of Eire and our Dublinn on the River Liffey." Drawing a short, sax-like blade, she led Kara across the wide avenue.

"There are four roads you need to know. We are walking north now, away from the south gate behind us. This is the Great Ship Street. We will cross Werburgh Street, there, and head right to the longphort. Parallel to this is the Fishamble Street and markets, and cutting across it is our soldiers' haunt, Winetavern Street," she winked and continued, "You came in from Mercia, yes?"

Kara agreed.

"Means you probably Dane blood, eh? An 'Eastman?'"

"Ja."

"Makes you a 'dark foreigner,' or a 'Dubgaill' in the local tongue." Tordis tugged her hair. "Before this turned, tis like yours. Makes me 'Dubgenti' just as you. You a Dubgaill, we are Dubgenti, Saxons, Danes, we all are dark foreigners, get it? So is King Ausle." Windows and doors opened, people venturing outside because the battle had passed. Kara noticed how sullen they appeared, heads tipped low, faces stern and unhappy. An old woman swept the stoop before her wattle shack, and a group of small children jumped about in a game of tag. They skittered aside as Tordis swaggered through the lane.

"Years before the dark foreigners came a'viking, a gang came from the Northern Way, most fair-haired and blue-eyed, and these the locals called fair foreigners, 'Findgenti' or a single 'Fingaill.' These Vikingr tried to settle but the old high kings of Eire fought like savages and nearly drove them out—Dubgenti reinforcements let the foreigners establish six kingdom cities, Dublinn, Lind Duachail, Lock Sanman, you know the rest... Yet, those crafty, old Irish kings, they found ways to divide the fair and the dark and caused us to fight among ourselves. Bloody, back-stabbing mess, I tell you." As they walked no one challenged them—the crowds slunk aside to stare as they passed.

Tordis waved to the gate watch and pulled Kara through the northern gate doorway where she had entered earlier in the day. The battle over, ships jostled and maneuvered, tying back to the wharf. Sailors, slavers, and fishermen crowded the shore.

Standing on the teeming dock, Tordis continued, "There across the Black Pool in the River Poddle, that marshy bit and those shanties, we call that Dyflinn—see, there's a wooden post wall running north to south across the promontory, that's to slow the Irish armies if they come to attack the longphort. The Poddle valley, a wash below those trees there, that's where we grow our vegetables.

"Behind Dyflinn wall, you can see them spires in the distance, tis the twin city to this Dublinn called Ath Cliath, another walled fortress under the protection of the King o' Dublinn. To the north of the city is a spit of rocky land, which we can't see from here, called Usher's Island, and we have another longphort there for trading. The king also protects one more fortress at Clondalkin, about two leagues to the west of Ath Cliath."

Kara repeated the funny-sounding Eire names, trying to commit them to memory. Tordis clapped her hands to chase seagulls from a crate and take their perch. "These are Vintrsetl, old wintering camps—originally pirate bases we fortified and claimed as our own." She squirmed back on top of the box and set her sword across her knees.

"You know what we do here, eh lass?" Kara glanced along the wharf. Men had tied children together with ropes around their necks, most young girls near her age. Shouting and banging the planks with hammers and poles, the gang pressed the tethered group forward onto a waiting ship.

"Thralls." Kara watched the children being shoved and kicked.

"Aye, lassie, we round slaves up in raids and carry them back to send to Mercia and Devon and Northumbria. Mercians want kids, easy to control, others want men of fighting age, women proven fertile. Big money in thralls. King o' Dublinn takes tax on every head. Tis why the king is so sporting rich."

"Don't the Irish fight you? I mean, for their children."

"Ja, they fight. Savages. Like beasts, crazy, drunken beasts. Seem to not need a reason, just like to drink and fight, nigh unstoppable. The Eire, they are shrewd, wily in their own way and with their own kind, and lots of quarrels and grudges lead them agin each other as much as agin us. Makes me wonder they won't all kill each other off." She snorted, leaned closer to Kara and lowered her voice. "Makes them weak."

"Doesn't the King of the Eire rally them against us?"

"King?" Tordis chuckled. "You mean kings. There be more kings of the Eire than you can count on your hands! King of Osraige, king of Brega, king of Leinster. The Eire call their kingdoms 'tuatha.' High kings of the Ui Neill and old kings, lords and barons, clans and brotherhoods, and add them holy warriors and those monks in their abbeys, and everyone with a different claim, a special treaty of this here place or that there stone, the 'fifths,' a different pact for each day of the week." She flicked her fingers as if chasing gnats. "All them Eire, they be a foolish lot. Fight one day, sell their mothers the next, even sell their bairns."

Kara leaned against the crate. "Is that all, fighting and slaves?"

"Trade more than thralls here." Tordis pointed to the piles of uncarded wool and wooden crates. "Wool and sheepskins, cabbages, mutton and cured beef when we can get it. Salt from the coast. Up Usher's Island, we load timber, wheat and millet in season, all bound across the narrow sea to Mercia. All good coin." Kara noticed a missing tooth in her smile. "Aye, tis a good life if you like the rough and tumble. What brings a young'un like you to our Dublinn?"

"I am hoping to..." Kara straightened her shoulders, lifted the short sword, and pointed at the dark swirl in the middle of the river. "I am here to sell my sword arm, ready to follow in my father's footsteps. I... I want to fight, to hone my skills. I want to make my name."

Tordis sighed and her smile hardened, the crinkles around her eyes softening as the humor left them. "Yeah, plenty o' need for a strong arm. King o' Dublinn forever needs more soldiers. I seen many... they come and go." She gazed out over the water and tapped her blade absent-mindedly against her knees. Kara noted liver spots on the backs of her hands. After a moment of silence between them, Tordis cleared her throat.

"Listen, girlie. You seem like a good kid, like a colt new to its feet and ready to run." Tordis gave Kara's shoulder a squeeze. "This ain't the place to run, little lass. Eire is a place o' deep danger, far more treacherous than you'd ever believe. All the fury and fighting, peril and risk, it raises the blood—we're on the edge of a blade every day, every hour. Passions run high. Crazy devotion to the gods, wild gambles, fights and bawdy conduct, the likes of which I wager you've never seen. 'Twas me, knowing what I know, I'd peg that boy you came with and climb back aboard a ship bound for home. I hear daydreams in your voice, and yes, I remember the ambitions o' being young. Listen closely now, there's not a trusty one in the batch, from the kings on to foot soldiers. Not the Eire, not the Findgenti, not the Dublinn guard and not even your Dubgenti mates.

"Not one can be trusted. You remember that." Tordis held Kara's gaze. "If you forget, you won't be sorry…

"You'll be dead."

RAGA

Hamund, son of Hothl's longhouse. Such a glorious place!

The warmth of the hearth, carefully tended by boys dedicated to our comfort and kept furiously flaming by the fiery hands of the little armaour troll beneath the grate, the young maidens plying their sumptuous banquet, the merry songs and poetry. A grand, carved barnstoker pillar raising the roof high, and woven tapestries hung from the walls, capturing and storing the body heat from these freshly bathed and perfumed people. A beak of mead, a dip of ale, a slice of bacon, seeds and porridge and venison stewed in its own juice. Delectable. A room full of cheerful men, women, children, and a few newborns at the breast, and here in the Realm Between Realms, in the corners where I can spy them, a few more of the hidden folk, partners watchful over this tiny wedge of Midgardian peace and contentment. Not only the hearth-man, that strange silver tree in its corner and those tiny gnomes who chase the mice along the joists above.

Never have I known a more hospitable and welcoming abode! Even in my time in Constantinople at the beck and call of the emperor, I never experienced such deference, respect, and acclaim. These northern men give my mare full rein, a roost in the rafters, a place at each table, and invited by the chief himself to sit upon his chair—not at all like Finn's home, where his fat, old aunt oft threatened to cook my mare and chased me with a broomstick. For the life of me, I can't understand young Finn's reluctance to climb the high ridge and join the festivities here in the seat of Hothlson power, Unlahdil, secure under the banner of the titular jarl of Lade.

"Watch it, bird, you're getting fat." Jormander clucked his tongue and offered my mare a thin slice. I cocked my head to give him my disapproving eye, snatched the morsel and with a simple flit, soared to the rafter above to peck and tear at the sinewy sliver of deer. Satisfying, and yes, well, he has a point about the extra weight, yet none could not feign to notice the sleek, healthy glow of my mare's fledges, the brightness of its eyes, full of health and vigor. It is not my fault these spoil me, proffering affection for my raven mare in memory of their Odin All-Father and his pets, Huginn and Muninn, godly thought and mind.

From my perch, I watched Karl Alfenson and his shipmates at the long table, across the hall from Chief Hamund's family and retainers, yet placed in a position of honor. Martine and Havar sat to each side, facing the skald Jormander and his nephew Thorfinn. They joked and passed a pitcher of ale. Havar kept his kindly eye on the boy; as his weapons trainer spending hours each day with him, he has grown fond of the skinny child. Finn has grown these few months, sprouting a hand taller betwixt the time of heavy snows and now, as the ice melts and the first tufts of green sprout in the slush and mud. He braided his silver-white hair, a long tail pulled over his shoulder, the end tied with a leather cinch and a faceted red bead. A lad soon to number twelve years of age, he remains a boy, no hairs on his chin, his eyes owlish in his heart-shaped face, his shoulders narrow and juvenile. Finishing my snack with a gulp, I dropped to his shoulder and joined their merriment.

A tipsy Martine grinned and leaned across Karl to finish speaking to Havar. Whatever flytings insult she cast his way, the big man laughed and clutched for her in mock hostility, both spilling their beer on Karl in the middle. He sputtered and slammed a palm on the table, tumbling the wooden platters and sending his crew scrambling for their horns and wooden mugs.

"Raga, nice of you to join us!" Karl slopped ale from his horn as he gestured at my mare. "Ah, leave the bird, mon capitan." Bleary-eyed Martine ruffled Karl's beard. "Ici, Raga est celebritie." I have noticed the more Martine drinks, the heavier her Frankish accent becomes until she loses all Dane words in blather and mumbles.

Havar found her comment hilarious and rubbed his captain's hair. "Ee-cee, ee-cee!" Karl growled like a bear and good-naturedly shoved them both away, the bench beneath them tottering. Under me, Finn trembled with laughter. A good poet, ever attentive to his audience, Jormander filled every cup again, sloshing the brown beer over fists and the remnants of the meal. Behind us, a man strummed a tagelharpa, the notes in a joyful key. Karl wrapped his arms around Martine and Havar and sang along with the tune. The table joined the melody, loud and raucous. As Thorfinn joined the song, he stiffened—tipping my mare's head to peep, I saw Allinor had pushed onto the bench between Thorfinn and the skald.

"There you are, Thorfinn Agneson." *Allinor snuggled into the boy, pushing her rosy cheeks close to his with a wide grin— It's easy to tell she's been at her father's mead herself.* "I wondered when my hero would come sit with me."

Finn reared back from her, his shoulder jerked and tipped my roost, his cheeks blotched rosy, and he sputtered, unable to answer. My mare squawked as it dropped unceremoniously to the tabletop, landing in congealed gravy. Taking control of my mount, I shuddered to toss off any debris and cocked my head at the girl, and I am not alone—surprised by her sudden appearance, Havar, Karl and Martine stifled their jocularity and leaned forward across the roughhewn table. Martine raised an eyebrow, and swallowing hard to maintain a serious demeanor while in her cups, she asked Finn, "Have we forgotten our hostess?"

"Now, Thorfinn, we are here by the grace of Hamund." *Karl glanced at Havar for support.* "I think you need to..."

"Dedicate?" *Jormander offered.*

"Yes, dedicate time and attention to our dear hostess." *From my position on the table, I saw Allinor Hamundsdatter bat her eyes and beam, gazing into Thorfinn's eyes barely a handsbreadth from his nose. She placed her hands on his chest and toyed with the bead on his braid tip.*

Over her shoulder, Finn gave us a pleading stare. His uncle burbled and nearly choked in his attempt to hold back laughter. Allinor had been smitten with Thorfinn since the defeat of the three volva who attempted to steal her life. The besotted girl dogged his steps, trying to hold his hand or give him small tokens, calling him "her hero." She had cut a length of her hair and braided it into a keepsake for him, embarrassing the boy when she gave it to him in front of the crew. Harmless and childish, nothing to cause worry, a childhood crush. Martine waved him away.

"Go sit with Hamund." *Karl said.* "Keep the girl company— after all, she's your age." *He bit his lip to hold his serious expression.*

Finn hung his head and pushed back from his bench, allowing Allinor to take his hand and drag him to the head of the table.

"I hope he doesn't die from elsk!" *Jormander said.*

"Tres jolie, 'love sickness.'"

Unable to hold his amusement any longer, Havar burst into gales and slapped the table. Karl and his companions joined him in the laughter. Karl turned to me.

"Old ghost, go keep your eye on the boy."

"She may try to kiss him!" *Martine scrunched her nose in mock dismay, resting her hand on Karl's forearm.*

"No doubt little Allinor already plans their wedding!"

"And children!" *They guffawed as Karl shooed me.*

The table ran the length of the hall, making it easier for me to leap into the rafters and hop beam to beam through the cook fire haze nestling in the crook under the shingles. The girl pulled her unwilling paramour through the crowd of merrymakers and settled at the dais at the end of the long table where her father sat on his raised, carved chair. Allinor had planned for Finn—she had set a small tableau with fancy, carved cups and a plate of sweetened breads to share. Tenderly touching his braid Allinor chattered at the boy, recounting her day, her needle-binding and embroidery, and other household duties, explaining how she practiced her skills to be a good wife. Her emphasis on the word 'wife' not lost, Finn hunched his head lower. She lifted her mother's wooden key to the house, a ceremonial token indicating her rule of all things domestic, looped around her neck with a length of twine. With a sigh Finn slumped to her side on the floor, leaning back against the platform and picking at the biscuits. I dropped to his shoulder. With a grumble, he waved me off, so I swooped to perch on Hamund's great chair where I could watch the boy.

The son of Hothl offered me a piece of salted fish—He liked for me to hang over his shoulder, suggesting to his followers I honored him like Odin's pets, bringing him news of the world. Truthfully, I learned more from listening to his men than he ever absorbed from me, since only Thorfinn could hear my whispers in Midgard. Hamund recovered, much better than when we had first met—the months since we had defeated the witches and saved his last daughter from their spell had been good to him, his improved appetite had filled out his cheeks and his belly, his groomed hair and beard cleaned, combed and sparkling with beads. Polished brass and silver armbands marked his popularity with the jarl and flaunted the rewards of battles won at his side. And his deportment had improved, his humor returned and his sly, plotting mind—I must say I grew in admiration for this northern chieftain as I eavesdropped over his shoulder, week after week.

The elder Alsvid sat next to his liege. "...after a two-day slog, we found the fort abandoned. Holjan, son of Garm, had taken flight, his hearth cold, his hall emptied."

"No justice for his crimes."

"We waited too long."

"Black frosts of Porri moon held back our passage."

"As the skalds counsel, slow and sure."

"No matter, the warlock has played his hand and now it is merely a game of Hnefatafl."

"I suspect this is no game of chase," *Regin, who sat on a stool to Hamund's other side suggested. Hamund turned to his cousin.*

"Harald Tanglehair calls for his shields. Holjan toadies to the coins of Agder."

"Holjan is a coward."

"He may not face you in battle man to man, but he has been consorting with nether powers and rumors are he treaties with Vanaheim...." *Alsvid made a sign against the evil eye as he mentioned the realm of the dark elves.*

"More likely, he heads south. Kjotve the Rich has bought his loyalty for years. That viper king of Agder and his son Haklang, they build a force to oppose Harald."

"More the reason we should tighten our alliances." *Hamund partially rose from his throne and raised his hand to catch the attention of one of his men. With an understanding nod, the guard ducked around the dais to the room at the end of the longhouse, Hamund's private chamber.*

"Allinor, my snowbird." *Hamund gestured to his daughter.* "Send young Thorfinn back to his uncle's men and stand you, here, by my side. It is time." *He stood, pulling a wolf fur stole from the seat to throw across his shoulders. At his side, Alsvid and Regin slowly rose to their feet, brushing crumbs from their tunics and smoothing their beards.*

Finn climbed to his feet, glancing from the chief to the girl. With a motion, he called me to his shoulder.

"What's this about?" *Finn whispered to me.*

"No idea."

We wormed our way through the crowd. As we passed, more of the household appreciated their chieftain had stood and one by one they stood to join him. Thorfinn pushed in next to his uncle and his shieldmaiden Martine, climbing on top of the bench for a better view. My mare, disturbed by the press of the crowd, pitched, and grasped the boy tight, fluttering wings to maintain a perch.

At the head of the room, the guard returned with Regin's brother, Otr, leading a figure draped in an ermine hood and cloak. I craned my neck for a glimpse around the hulking Havar. Her face hidden, clearly this was a woman to be presented to the gathering, not as tall as those around her, dressed in a fine, emerald gown glimpsed in flashes beneath her wrap. Allinor beamed at Hamund's side, bouncing slightly on the balls of her feet. The bulging-eyed Otr aided the woman's climb to the dais and moved her close to his cousin.

"My friends and allies," *Hamund addressed the assembly.* "As the days shortened to the Skammdegi of winter, we of Unlahdil faced an unknown blight, no ken of its purpose or design. Distraught over the deaths of those nearest me, I admit to you my brethren, I had lost the tread of my skeins,

I knew not what to do, how to lift the curse. Unprepared and unguided, our slaughter month brought none of the usual bounties, the volva curse hung over us... still, we faced our terrors together. None faltered, none shirked their duty. Each of you I have thanked for your loyalty during my dark hours." *He held his palm out and gestured around the hall, men and women smiling in return as his eyes found theirs.*

"Yet, the All-Father blessed us with the return of my companion in arms, my banner friend, Karl Alfenson." *A spontaneous cheer lifted from the crowd. Hamund quieted them with open arms.* "The bold succeed where soever they go, and so it is with our hero who uncovered the wicked plot and defeated the witches of Holjan. And beyond his valiant effort, the son of Ironfist has continued to provide for us, his snekke drawing the sea's bounties to our hall even in the deepest of the bone-sucking month, when snow clogged our byways, and our fjords froze solid." *Another cheer raised.*

"Good we have a lindworm who fishes the rough, winter seas," I whispered to Finn.

"As you all heard me declare on the night he broke the curse, I intend to make Karl my brother." *He reached out and took the woman's hand, holding it high. A hush fell over the crowd—on tip toes, Finn peeked around Martine for a clearer view.*

Otr pulled the cape from the woman's shoulders, unveiling a mass of thick, blonde hair.

I will tell you: I have seen many a beauty, from the palaces of the Holy Roman Empire to the rough courts of the Danes, Saxons and Britons. The harems of an emperor, slender Gaul queens with lengthy tresses, the rugged, sun-kissed splendor of Visigoth women. This Nordic maid rivaled them all. A ribbon tied her hair back from her wide, smooth forehead, a single ruby bead glittering over her smooth brow. High cheekbones and a backward tilt to her head gave her a haughty cast, softened by a broad smile of strong, white teeth, lips the color of her bangle and snowy, pale skin. A scattering of freckles crossed her nose beneath penetrating, green eyes. While her gown covered her in a modest way, her doeskin belt hung jauntily at her hips and accentuated her figure. A slight blush bloomed on her neck. She relished the attention, offering a shy wave to those close by.

"Signy." *Her name whispered on all sides.*

"My cousin," *Hamund continued.* "Beautiful child of Unlahdil, playmate of my daughters and my beloved niece, Signy. Our light in winter, kept hidden, far from our curse and..." *he indicated his attendants,* "kept from our hall all these moons by treacherous weather. We welcome you back to our hall and hearth." *Mutters about the room confirmed agreement. A guard in the back hefted his horn and called out,* "To Signy, welcome home!" *All joined in the toast.*

Hamund called for quiet. "Karl, son of Ironfist, come forward."

Turning to his captain, Havar quirked his eyebrow. Karl tried to catch Martine's eye—she studied the tabletop, one arm around Thorfinn—I walked across the boy's back and settled, one claw on Finn and the other on Martine. The crowd parted to let Karl pass.

"My Signy is past 16 summers, past the time we should have settled a bride price for her. Your valor has proven more valuable to me and mine than gold or silver. On the night of the curse's fall, I promised to make you my brother, and thus I give to you my niece, our Signy, with her brothers' support and concurrence." *As the crowd applauded this announcement, Otr and Regin stepped forward to hug Karl and pound his back good-naturedly.*

Karl mumbled words of thanks, the girl cheerful at his side.

"We will settle the wedding for an auspicious month, perhaps Solmanudur at the sun's highest zenith," *Regin announced.*

"No matter, brother." *Hamund emphasized the word 'brother,' and pulled Karl and Signy forward by their wrists to hold their hands high.* "Such a hallowed event will be the official wedding in the sight of the gods, but as we all know Freja loves to see a couple wedded in the first bloom of family, yes?" *A bawdy salute shouted from around the room, a few laughing coarsely. A blush made Signy's ear tips scarlet—the tip of her tongue touched her upper lip and she gazed at Karl. Under my claw Martine jerked.* "In my hall, I am lord, and I declare you married this night." *Karl's mouth gaped open, and he froze with his arm in the air.*

"What's happening?" *Finn asked.*

Martine dropped her head slowly, stone-faced and peering from under her lowered brow.

Hamund put Signy's hand in Karl's and called, "Skol to the new couple."

Karl gazed at us, his face a mask—while he cast his eyes over all of us, to me he focused on Martine. She would not meet his eyes. For the first time in all my travels with him, the great sea lord dithered at a loss, studying his men and glancing back at the yearning girl holding his hand.

"As they say...," *Jormander leaned across the table.* "A gift always seeks to be repaid."

"Ja," *Havar agreed.*

Martine huffed, brushed me from her shoulder, turned heel and stomped out of the longhouse.

"What?" *Thorfinn squinted at the departing shieldmaiden, and back to Havar frowning at his uncle. Stretching my wings to balance on the boy's scrawny arm, I glimpsed Jormander roll his eyes.*

"What? Will someone tell me what is going on?"

KNETTI

A few chips of hacksilver was all it cost to camp in a fisherman's shed and tend a fire to dry his catch. Warmed by meager flames, after a while she had grown accustomed to the stale odor of woodsmoke and dried fish. White strips of shriveled flesh hung from the racks overhead. Head wrapped in old rags, her hook nose masked by a filthy scarf, she had hidden here on the edge of the tiny fishing village. No one gave her a thought, flitting through the evening shadows, or awake before dawn to peep in hall windows, counting the swords, measuring the snekke and supplies. Through the slats in the ill-fitted plank walls, she could spy on the entire village. For moons she had secreted here, watching, waiting.

From her frost-rimed shutter, she watched the Dane sell-swords troop back to their longhouse on the bay. Stomping through the slush, the warrior woman led the way. She kicked at the piles of snow, head unbound, an angry swagger to her pace. The skald followed her, eyes on his feet, working his way carefully over the slippery course. On this return trip, their captain did not accompany them back from Unlahdil—*probably scheming with the pretender Hamund*, she thought, tucking her mutilated hands under her armpits for warmth.

There.

The vardoger.

He skips along by that big oaf, she thought, *the great, wide one who is his minder, sword master and teacher, always with an eye on the boy. They all protect him, but this one watchs him the most.*

This one and the ghost, the old ghost who rides that raven mare. And... the lindworm. Dyr Nisse had not warned them of the dragon.

As she expected, she found the bird circling overhead, a blot against the stars. She watched the black animal circle, fly lower and as the warriors entered the longhouse, it swooped through the open door. The heavy door banged closed, and a loud clunk sounded as the locking bar slid in place. *Home for the night.*

She had learned much, biding her time, nursing her wounds. Her fingers and toes ached—to stem blood loss, she had burned each joint with a glowing charcoal, one by one, biting a wooden stave to hold cries of agony that would have drawn nosy neighbors. Despite her drastic treatment and her Siedr healing salves, the pain remained, a lingering soreness in her lost digits, a pain in the missing parts. She welcomed this pain, a reminder of the revenge she sought, the vengeance she craved. For her lost sister, for her displaced lover and his lost hall, and for the mutilation that had ruined her dearest coveted magical skill: Her fingers and toes chopped off, her "wings" were clipped— she would never transform into a vulture again.

Stirring the ashes in her hearth, she added a few sticks and blew on the coals to rebuild the flames. The ache of the aged had settled in her bones, the chill of the shed adding a stiff twinge to her maimed knuckles and a deep throb in her legs.

Ja, she grudgingly admitted to herself, *we had been warned by our Vanaheim master. The dark elf had told us, but me and my sisters underestimated what we thought a simple boy. This creature is no boy—he is vardoger, able to pass through the Realm Between to gain entrance to the nine realms beyond Midgard.* With the utmost care and enchantments to hide her Siedr spells, she had watched him move across realms, the boy and his ghost and dragon. A formidable trio, awake in the daylight, and in a different way watchful at night, and sensitive to Siedr curses. The cursed boy possessed a magicked blade, deadly in the Realm Between Realms. And guarded by his uncle and battle-tested warriors, this 'boy' dwelt secured from harm: no quick chance here for revenge. These warriors had fought and escaped the Oskorei, Odin's Wild Hunt—they would easily overcome her. The night of their defeat, the uncle had overcome her sister's incantations—even with all her spying she had no understanding of how he had managed that feat. She murmured a prayer to the trickster god Loki.

Knetti numbered the warriors and counted their arms and shields. She knew the early morning hours the lindworm slipped away to hunt in the sea, the times to expect its return. She knew a protective troll lurked on the snekke longship, hiding from the crew in the astral realm.

Knetti huddled over her miserable fire, pulling a ragged shawl around her. A moon past she had smuggled word to Holjan and Rind—they knew the real danger faced and to plan accordingly. She must wait... and she would wait, wait for the moment when these guardians grew lax and the vardoger wandered far from his lich. She whispered to the flames.

"We can wait, ja, we can wait. Vengeance comes to the patient. No simple death for this boy. We will capture, we will torture, his pain he will howl across the realms, and all will know he has submitted before he dies.

"When the fyreferd is weakest, when his hug travels afar, that is when we will strike, and woe to this vardoger boy, Thorfinn Agneson."

CHAPTER 4
SEPARATE WAYS

THORFINN

Sitting on the edge of the short dock, dangling his legs over the turgid, slushy water, Finn watched a flock of gulls circle the bay. He tooted on his silver flute, not playing or practicing, merely making noise. Long winter nights grew shorter and the cold, white orb of the sun shone through a gap in the eastern mountains, yet they couldn't leave—the seas remained too rough and unpredictable for sailing, at least so their pilot warned.

"Wanton minx...."

Bangs and scrapes sounded as Martine freed a tangle from the mast, shaking the stiff ropes violently to knock off ice. Studiously focusing on the black-capped birds, Finn tried to pretend he didn't hear her mutters and snorts. In a foul mood, she rose early to stomp from the longhouse, quick to her chores—she existed in a constant bad mood of late. Kol, the pilot, worked on a rig to lift the bow from the waters to scrape clean the barnacles, and he also kept his head low, intent on his work. Berthed on the single, rickety wharf in the bay, no ship-house in this tiny village, nowhere to port the boat and let it dry for the winter, Kol worried over his charge.

This is no fun, Finn thought, scratching at the frosty rime with a stick. Little village with nothing to do, no children near his age, a bunch of smelly, old fishermen and their fat wives bunched in knitting circles every dark afternoon. They all dressed the same, smelled the same, in fact looked the same—nothing to do here. He tossed the stick into the bay.

Once the weather had broken, Uncle Karl's crew worked each day to haul stones from a nearby mountain creek and rebuild the sea-walled fields. Heavy, back-breaking work in the cold slush and ice, resulting in tired, grumpy evenings staring into hearth fires. Gone were the nights of song and ale, Jormander's poetry and sagas, and long, boastful tales from Jorn. The crew of the *Verdandi Smiles* barely fitted in the longhouse Karl had been gifted by Hamund. Everyone slept wrapped in thin blankets, stretched out near the hearth or on the benches set like shelves into the walls, uncomfortable and tight for the largest sailors like Havar. His uncle had commandeered the small back room when he returned with Signy under his arm, declaring privacy his reason. Finn didn't like her—*ja*, he admitted, *she was pretty* —Raga used big words to describe her, like 'haughty' and 'self-absorbed.' Finn thought her cruel. She treated him as her personal thrall, ordering him to bring her things or do her chores. His uncle ignored the way she treated him and the other sailors. He avoided her. *Another reason to sit on the dock in the morning cold....*

Only Goorm, his lindworm seemed happy. Each morning before dawn, the dragon would sneak out of the barn and slink over the dunes to the waves, hunting for cod and an occasional seal. He kept their larder stocked and helped Uncle Karl sail a boatful of smelt and haddock upriver to Unlahdil fortress each week. If the villagers knew of the beast, they kept awareness to themselves.

Raga fluttered next to him.

"Where you been?"

"Well, what a manner you have."

Finn grumbled. "You wouldn't understand."

"Hum, unhappy with your lot?" Martine cursed and banged the benches on the boat. "And I see you're not alone."

"This place is no fun. A block of ice. I want out."

"Out? Where would you go? Fancy a visit to Unlahdil? Little Allinor would be excited to see you..."

Finn snorted.

"Aye, I thought not."

"It's just... there's nothing to do. Everybody's busy, too busy for me. And at night they're all too tired to sing and dance like we used to. Uncle Karl spends all his time with that prissy girl. I wish we could get away, you know, set sail." He swooped his arm and pointed off to the horizon.

"Where would you go?"

"I don't know." Finn climbed and offered his arm to the mage that rode the black bird. Raga hopped to his perch. "Maybe we could visit Jorvik, or go see... well, see if Cub is safe."

"And see your mother... and your brother and sisters, and your old homestead?"

"At least there would be something to do."

"Finn, my dear boy, you suffer from the great malady known to plague all who travel wide and far." The bird clicked in his ear. "You are homesick again."

"You've said that before..."

"Aye, you yearn for your place and people, despite the passage of time and the knowledge all places and people change... it's a longing, a wistfulness for a time you hold dear to your heart. Nostalgia, if you will. Jormander would warn you to steer clear of the Norn Urd's honeyed song of the past, but I've seen this disease in men across the centuries, and there is little cure save a return to the place that haunts them." The bird hopped to the longship's railing and lifted one wing. "So, Thorfinn Agneson, my vardoger companion, why don't you go visit them?"

"I would but..." Finn hung his head.

"But what?"

"I used my last bullrush to help Cub with those slavers."

"Why didn't you say? I can fly and find you more..."

"Won't the snows have pressed them flat?"

"Not all reeds fall under the weight of winter's cape. We need to go seek them out." The raven hopped from one foot to the other. "We could ask Goorm to ferry us about the bay so you can make your cuttings."

"Really?"

"Cheer up, boy. I will take a tour and find us a likely bayside rush bed, and you go prepare. This eve we will cut you new rushes and you can magic them to visit whosoever you please."

Finn stroked the raven mare and lifted it to fly into the clear sky. He returned to the longhouse with a spring in his step. *Ja, I can visit my family*—seeing his mother, his brothers and sisters would help him feel better. He spent the remainder of the afternoon preoccupied with the decision of who best to visit first.

Even Signy's imperious demands at dinner couldn't break his renewed spirit—Finn happily served her meal, collected the used plates, and filled his uncle's horn at her command. Finn noted how his uncle brooded in an uncommon way, using his finger to draw in ale splashes on the tabletop, silently watching his fatigued crew lounge on their benches, avoiding Martine and Jormander at the other end of the room. While Finn noticed the change in his uncle, the girl did not—Signy clung to his arm, chattered in his ear, and twirled her fingers in his beard. After night settled, Gudrun tended the fire and blew out the whale fat candles, and the tired men quietly stumbled to their beds. Excited, Finn had trouble falling asleep, twisting on his mat, adjusting the broken sax hilt he carried at his belt, his leg bouncing with pent excitement....

Thorfinn awoke in the Realm Between. Dim light rose from the fading coals in the hearth. The winter chilled hall echoed with snores.

The raven mare roosted in the rafters, its beak tucked into a shoulder. He gathered Gunhild, his magical sax short sword and fitted it into his belt.

Raga's ghost waited across the room. His natural form revealed an exotic figure, his eyes, like his skin, nut-brown, his strange silken garb, bejeweled turban and curl-toed slippers. Short in stature, the top of his head would not have reached Uncle Karl's chest and his big words and peculiar manner often stumped Thorfinn, yet Raga has been his friend and teacher for years, and Finn had grown fond of the old ghost, full of arcane secrets and weird tales of faraway lands. He could find no better guide for the realms beyond Midgard.

"Let's be on our way, young Thorfinn." With a flourish, the mage indicated a shutter propped narrowly open to allow a draft to circulate the hall. "You can slip your shattered sword through here."

Finn slipped Gunhild through the crack in the window and

they both passed into the courtyard. A quiet incantation from the elder mage slipped the bolt from the barndoor. The lindworm waited for them, wiggling in excitement. Grasping the dragon by the ruff at his neck, the vardoger Finn and his mentor climbed aboard the beast, and Goorm leaped into the night sky.

Raga directed the sinuous wyrm across the waters to a sheltered cove on the far side of the river. There, along the banks a stand of dried bullrushes stood, mired in the snow and ice. Thorfinn used his sword to cut the stems as the mast troll had taught him, using the Siedr magic to pay homage to the power in the stalks. He took five magicked reeds, grasping them hard and concentrating to hold physical objects from the Realm Between, and asked Goorm to take them back to the barn, where he carefully stored the stalks in a back corner. He selected one, a strong, straight stem and set it by the door. Before he departed, Finn stopped to scratch his dragon underneath his chin and thank Raga for his help.

Raga straightened his tunic and brushed imaginary dirt from his sleeves. "Be careful, little fyreferd. More dangerous things than spirits fly the night skies." Finn agreed, impatient to leave. He whispered the spell to breathe life into the rush.

"Hupp Horse Handocks, ride, ride on bulmints! Away!" The bullrush quivered with enchantment, and Thorfinn soared towards the glittering stars.

Worried about his eldest brother, he commanded his mount to carry him to Agne Agneson. He had left him sailing from the shores of Devon in a strange ship. The whirling flight carried him southward, a long, winding journey over two oceans and great expanses of land. His reed settled him in a fortified village on a nondescript lane before a wide hall.

Finn recognized Eastman handicraft in the door carving and posts, and the building resounded, alive with rowdy cheers and singing. He slipped his ghostly face through a wall and took measure of the place.

Filled to capacity, he found a party well underway. A raucous, loud, joyful celebration.

Wider than longhouses he knew, the hall mixed the design of a Nordic longhall with a continental tavern, a serving bar and casks of ale along one wall and lengthy roughhewn tables lined in parallel. Across the room a stone fireplace roared with flames, logs piled high on its hearth and iron cauldrons swung close to the fire. Hams, ducks, pheasants, and woven strings of onions hung from the beams, one scrawny mallard dangling close to his nose. Crowded with happy revelers, singers with tambourines and scantily clad women serving from leather pitchers, while Thorfinn had trouble understanding their accent, clearly this festive occasion celebrated a grand event. The food smelled delicious. He distinguished the leaders from the chaos of the room, three big men at a middle table, one spouting poetry like a skald, the others laughing at his side, and men and women harkening to them with expressions of admiration and respect.

Behind one of the riant chiefs he spied his brother—a woolen cap on his head, his beard scruffy, sprouting anew with a sprinkle of gray hairs. With a grin on his face and a horn in his hand, Cub chuckled along with the poet and his hecklers. Thorfinn watched him speak to his neighbors and take a bite of brown bread from the table. His comment raised a hearty guffaw from the men surrounding him. Finn smiled to himself—Cub acted recovered, healthy, and well fed. He had found a safe place.

He watched the festivities for a while, enjoying the crowd and their fun. Such a difference from life with Uncle Karl far to the north, he thought. Here, the binds of comradeship made all a family—he could see it evident on their faces and easy manner and longed for it as he watched from a hidden corner.

With a sigh, Finn decided to continue his journey, retrieved his magicked bullrush and called on the charmed steed to carry him to visit his mother. The long reed bent and flew him into the night sky.

The Mercian fortress of Eddisbury bustled with late evening activity. Torches and braziers lit the streets and, uninterrupted by the settling darkness, work on expanding the palisades continued—men shaped paling posts with axes and draw knives, others winched long beams into place, and more chipped and fitted stone foundations, hammering the rocks to square the groundworks. Smoke from cookfires lingered over the hilltop city. Pigeons cooed and clustered in the eaves. Guards stood along the walls where the construction had opened the fortress, a few wary and alert, others drowsy and uninterested. Unnoticed, Finn landed in their midst in a broad plaza before a church and a manor house.

He glanced around—why did the reed bring me here? He listened to the racket of the construction, the grunts and calls of the laborers over the pounding hammers. Shouts, whistles, and the boom of a post dumped into a hole. There... his mother's voice, recognizable but unintelligible—he could hear the anger in her words. He followed the sound and wandered past two slouching guards into the manor house.

Gurid stood in the ornate promenade that ringed a house garden, Hilda clinging to one hand and Neeta straining to escape the other. His glowering Uncle Cerdic blocked his mother's way, his arms crossed, and legs braced wide. A few men gathered behind him, their faces stony and grim.

"...lost for all we know," *his mother said, as he approached.* "It's been weeks. Weeks! and nothing."

"Now, not yet a fortnight, and you can't say nothing...." *Cerdic motioned with his palms as he tried to calm her.*

"I don't care you found she passed through Chester.

Young, unmarried, and hot-blooded, it's a dangerous combination."

"A bit like her mother at her age…"

Gurid chose to ignore his snipe. "If you won't… should I leave Yeru to care for the babes and go search myself?"

"Now, dear sister."

"Don't 'dear sister' me!" *Gurid stooped to lift struggling Neeta.* "Just like your nephew who rots in a Wessex slave camp, you are content to let them die, out of sight, out of mind."

"Gurid, calm down, you know we have…" *Finn's mother turned away.*

The state of his mother worried Finn, her head uncovered, her blonde hair loose, snarled, and disheveled. A spot of spilled food marked her breast, her boots scuffed and muddy. Upsetting to him, her eyes loomed dark and sunken, ringed with fresh wrinkles. Worry lines etched into her formerly smooth forehead, his mother appeared much older. She didn't have a coat.

"I must get these to bed."

"You're not helping," *Cerdic continued, blood reddening his cheeks over his bushy, black beard.* "Barging into my meetings, assaulting the aldermen, making demands. You know Aethelflaed, daughter of the King of Wessex, has ordered us to fortify this burgh, we cannot spare a man effort…"

Gurid turned back. "Their blood, brother, it's on your hands. Yours!" *She turned heel and nearly walked through Finn's wandering vardoger. He watched his uncle sigh at her departing back, a man close to him laying a hand on his shoulder.*

Finn trailed his mother and sisters through the manor gate, across the square a short walk to a place he had never visited in his prior visits. Built into a row of houses, each had a high-pitched roof and an inset doorway. Gurid pushed the door open and shuffled the girls inside. As she reached to pull the door closed, Hildie tugged on her arm.

"Wait, Mama," *Hildie advised.* "Let Thorfinn in."

Gurid froze in the opening.

Finn smiled to himself—From the beginning of his curse, his sister had been able to see his vardoger. Gurid hesitated, the door held wide, the warmth of the room escaping in steam.

"Thorfinn?" *She stepped back into the lane.*

Finn slipped in beside her as she checked the alleyway.

"Close the door." *Yeru pushed back from her bench. She had set it by the fire pit in the center of the floor. Hilda smiled at her mother and gently pulled the door shut.*

Gurid paused in the doorway. Yeru took Neeta from her, wrapping the toddler in a blanket and returning to rock her by the fire.

Better accommodations than their last place, planks covered the floor, and a ring of bricks circled the firepit, an iron tripod over the coals holding a blackened porridge pot. A ham hock hung from a ceiling beam and a ladder at the back of the room led to a narrow sleeping loft tucked in the roof joists. Thorfinn crossed to an empty bench and sat, his hug rocking the seat faintly.

Watching for signs of his forerunner ghost, Gurid caught the movement and held her hand to her mouth. "Oh."

Hilda moved across the room and sat at her brother's feet, smiling at him.

"You can see him?" *Gurid hoarsely whispered.*

"Oh yes, mother, Finn is here."

"What?" *Yeru scowled.*

"Thorfinn..."

"Here?" *She made the hand sign to ward the evil eye.*

"Ja, so says Hildie."

"Ja, mama, he's right here." *Hilda indicated the bench.*

"He's taller and his hair is long. He has a braid. He's smiling at me."

Gurid rushed to the space, moving her arms ineffectually around, cautiously trying to feel for his shape. "Oh Thorfinn, Thorfinn, my baby. Are you well?"

"He nods ja."

"And your uncle?"

"Ja." *Hildie agreed.* "He nods."

"When can they come home?"

"He does this," *she held her palms open and made an exaggerated shrugging motion for her mother.*

"Thorfinn," *Gurid sat on the other end of the bench and spoke to the air.* "Do you know of Cub? I mean..." *she glanced at Yeru and back at Hilda.* "Have you seen Cub?"

"Ja, Mama, he says ja, and he smiles."

"Is my Cub alive?"

"Ja, mama."

"He has seen him?"

"He nods again, ja."

"And is he..." *she hesitated.* "Is he safe and whole?"

"He nods ja, mama."

Thorfinn watched his mother lean forward and draw a deep breath, tears forming in her eyes. "Oh, little Finn, you have lifted a weight from my heart." *She silently sobbed for a moment, wiping her eyes with her sleeve.*

Hildie rose to hold her hand. "No crying, mama, Finn says Cub is fine." *Her shoulders juddered as she tried to compose herself.*

"One less to worry over." *Yeru hummed from her spot by the fire. Finn noted how her shoulders drooped and the skins sagged at her throat. She held his littlest sister awkwardly, favoring one shoulder. Her hustrulinet sat askew on her head, stray gray hairs dangling loose over her forehead.*

Gurid acknowledged Yeru's comment with a deep sigh and blinked her eyes to clear her tears. She scrutinized Hilda who watched an empty space where the vardoger sat.

"He is..."

"What?"

"He points at me, points at himself, and Neeta and holds his hands, like this." *She stood and marked a high spot in the air, a lower level and another....*

"What do you think he means?" *Yeru asked.*

"I am not...." *Gurid rolled her eyes at the rafters in worried confusion. Hildie pointed to Neeta and pantomimed.*

Thorfinn chewed his lip—talking in hand signals through a seven-year-old remained more difficult than he had expected. He stepped through his movements once more, slower, trying to emphasize his sisters....

"Oh, I know! Our family!" *Hildie smiled, pleased with herself—Thorfinn bowed to his little sister and prompted her to tell his mother.* "Thorfinn asks about the rest of our family," *She held her hand high.* "You know, Willa is tall, and Cub is here, and Kara and Sorven...."

"Of course," *Gurid smiled.* "Willa should have had her baby by now—we have no news yet. Sorven is safe with her in Jorvik. Espen and his family watch over them both."

"Tell him about Kara," *Yeru muttered, and studied the dozy child swaddled in her arms.*

"Kara." *Finn watched emotions play across his mother's face, her brows knitted, and her bottom lip trembled.* "Kara... ran away. She took your father's sword. Your Uncle Cerdic intended to pay a Mercian dowry and had settled on a suitor when she disappeared. We think she left with Kaelan Ulbrechtson—you wouldn't know the boy, but they were... friends, I'd say. Nothing more, as far as we knew. So angry over the wedding plans, and I pushed..."

"Don't go blaming yourself again." *Yeru adjusted her shawl.* "We've been over this before. 'Twas a grown girl, able to choose her own mind."

"Kara did not want to wed—she had a crazy notion to join her father and brother as a warrior."

"Wanted to be a shieldmaiden." *Yeru twitched her head in Thorfinn's general direction, an angry moue on her lips.*

"We...." *His mother faltered, struggling for words. Finn sympathized with her—he knew the pain, to be separated without any news.*

"You don't think...?" *Yeru peered knowingly at Gurid.*

"Eh?"

"Well, the boy has seen Cub, perhaps...?" *Gurid understood what Yeru suggested.*

"Thorfinn, can you find Kara?"

"Ja, mama." *Hildie beamed.* "Finn says ja." *Hildie brushed off her dress and stepped back from her mother. Gurid glanced at her cousin, a tentative smile easing her fearful bearing. Hildie waved with her hand, motioning her mother to lean forward.*

"He gave you a hug, mama." *She giggled.* "No, I'm too big for that..." *and she pushed at her brother's specter, crossed to the door, and slid the lock aside. Finn waved goodbye to the room and stepped back outside to retrieve his magic bullrush.*

Time remained this night, he could find his sister Kara.

KARA

Soldiering for the King of Dublinn.

Kara paused to wipe the sweat from her eyes. Not exactly what she had dreamed... Not much soldiering, mostly hard labor, barely better than slave chores.

A team of guards had been assigned to repair the fortress wall damaged by the recent arson. New posts had been ax-felled, dragged to the Poddle and floated downriver, sharpened and prepared in a pile, ready to set. The wet, slippery weight of the boles required five individuals to carry each from the riverside to the palisade. Another set of men and women dug at the foundation with short, wooden shovels until their hands blistered and the spades split under pressure. Two men rigged a rope harness to lift posts into place, and once settled in their new holes, the laborers scrambled to pack dirt back around the base and lash the poles against the section of wall to be fortified.

"Don't see the goddess Gunna breaking her back."

"Nor any of her findgenti cronies."

"Damned cream of the Findgaill."

Not one to complain, Kara held her tongue. This her second week in the city, she kept to herself as Tordis suggested. And listened.

"Bradon King pays no mind to us grunts here in the dirt."

"I thought he'd be better," a lanky boy offered.

"Nay, these kings, they all be the same."

"At least our ale is good."

"I hear the Eire have a 'water o' life,' a powerful spirit."

"Ja, tasted once—burns all the way down, but hmmm." The woman rolled her eyes and wiggled her head. "Warms the belly and frees your cares...."

"Loosens your tongue, you mean."

"And spreads your legs?"

Work paused as men guffawed at the joke. Over the laughter, the woman called out, "Runa, don't go confusing yer motives for mine!" Kara smiled and dug deeper in her hole, flipping a load of the sandy soil onto the pile. The banter continued all afternoon, the team enjoying the camaraderie of shared labor. By the time the sun settled behind the trees, voices stilled, fatigue overriding good humor.

Sore and filthy, Kara followed the team as they entered the southern gate, swung it in place and rammed the bolt home. They wandered the main avenue to the barracks, men stripping off their muddy tunics, a line forming for the baths. Tordis waved to her from the doorway of the pit shed she shared with a few elder guardswomen. The younger shieldmaidens stayed in a barracks, separated from their commanding officers, jammed together in a long room with a small brazier to chase the chill away. Kara took her place in line for the baths—men would go first, followed by the women.

Waiting her turn, she noticed Kaelan returned from his duties. He had been sent to hunt, and from the deer carcass hanging from the stave he carried on one shoulder, the trip had been successful. His companions laughed and joked with him, and he didn't notice her in the evening shadows, pushed against the wall and covered in muck. On the other end of his spit, Helka shouldered her share of the weight, a high-cheek-boned woman a few years older than them both. A bow slung over her back, and a clutch of arrows hung at her belt. Slinking along by his side, Asta hung on his free arm, her hair braided in a complicated bun behind her ear, a handful of sparkling beads woven into the tresses. All three chatted, smiles on their faces, their clothes clean and no worse for a day in the forest.

Asta glanced her way. If she saw her, she ignored Kara —instead, as she told her companions goodbye, she leaned close to Kaelan, grabbed his cheeks between her hands and gave him a kiss on the mouth!

"Thanks for a great hunt, Kay."

Surprised, Kaelan nearly dropped his load.

Asta called to her friend, "I tell you, this little hunter is all mine." Helka barked a laugh, her retort a hoarse whisper, with a hip wiggle to indicate her vulgar intent. A few of the bathers in line chuckled as Kaelan's mouth fell ajar, his blush rising to his ears. Asta patted his cheek and strode off to the barracks, Helka tugging in the opposite direction to carry the dressed hart to the kitchens. Stumbling, Kaelan followed her.

Kara stood dumbfounded. She flexed her fists, watching Kaelan led by the older girl, her throaty laugh ringing in the lane making Kara wince. Her head spun with questions and her heart throbbed in a funny way. *What had happened on their hunt? Why was Asta so familiar with Kaelan? Why would she kiss him, so brazen and in front of so many witnesses? And why hadn't he stopped her? Had he given her reason to believe he welcomed a kiss? They had spent the day together, close in the thicket, all alone...* Kara imagined them in the forest, talking to pass the time, flirting and teasing like she did when she had time alone with Kaelan. She swallowed and brushed at the dirt on her arms and hands—not merely experienced warriors, those Findgenti stood taller than her dirt-covered mess, acted more worldly, more regal in bearing, and... well, so blonde and pretty. Everyone could see... *no wonder Kaelan took liberties with them, wanted to be with them, wanted....*

The woman behind her gave her a light shove. "Move along." The line had moved on while she stared after Kaelan.

Throughout her bath, Kara moved in a haze of her own doubts. Around her, the women stripped and rinsed in the wooden tubs, ladling warm water over their heads and backs. Gossip, laughter, and light-hearted singing accompanied the bathers. Kara paid little attention. Head lowered, she washed the mud from her work clothes and hung them to dry, buffed the dirt from her boots, dunked herself in the tub and pulled a clean linen smock from the pile at the door. Barefoot, she rushed from the crowd to the barracks. Her burlap bag lay where she left it, tucked under her sleeping pallet, her armor stacked neatly inside with a few clean dresses. Rummaging through the sack, she dressed quickly, ran a comb through her damp hair, pulled on her boots and tied her father's ancestral sword to her belt, long and awkward, its heavy pressure a comfort nonetheless.

"Good old Wolftongue." She patted the hilt at her shoulder blade. Not waiting for her work companions to rejoin her, she rushed to the planned feast at the Dublinn longhouse. Glancing about the room, she didn't find Kaelan in the assembly and she noticed Gunna watched her enter. The blonde warrior shared a side table with several maiden guards, Asta and Helka among them. As Kara passed, they laughed together at a private joke. Kara stomped past them, pretending she didn't hear.

Reaching the head of the table and finding no Kaelan, Kara turned to retrace her steps.

"Ah, Kara Agnesdatter, tarry a moment."

Kara recognized the King called her name—at Tordis's suggestion, she had avoided the King for days, staying a distance from him and his entourage. She turned to his voice and bowed her head.

King Ausle lounged on a heavy chair, his betrothed Muirgel at his side. He acted drunk, his eyes red-rimmed and a dash of froth on his upper lip. He motioned at her with his horn. "Sit, sit, child. You can alleviate our stodgy company. Where have you been hiding?"

Muirgel sat stiff at his side, her fair face rigid, her gaze on the untouched food on the wooden plate before her. A feast spread across their table, too much for them and their few guests, roasts and root vegetables, tiny, jellied birds and dried fruit, savory and sweet pies, strange bowls of spoon bread and hearty porridge, and pitchers of beer. A few cowed thralls stepped lightly around the guests, refilling every horn and mug before being asked. A few of the city elders sat next to the king and his future bride, drinking as heavily at the regent himself, and not happy drunks, a somber, brooding lot.

"My lord, I work to repair the burned section of our fortress wall."

"Truly? A beautiful child like you is set to the manual labors?"

"Someone's got to fix it." A man next to the king snorted. "Don't see your lordship doing it."

The king made a noise, part growl and part chuckle. Kara noticed the future queen jump at the sound. "Are you suggesting I put my hands in the filth? Perchance you need to show me loyalty and go dig in the trenches yourself."

The elders all shifted, one taking a swig from his horn and answering, "Probably do us good, the fresh air, the exercise, the show of loyalty...."

At this, the king of Dublinn laughed, passed his horn to his personal thrall, and pointed to the bench opposite. "Sit, girl. I command it."

Kara took one last scan around the hall and settled into place across from the king and Muirgel.

"See?" He waved at his retainers. "See, she doesn't question; she obeys her lord's commands."

"As well she should, Your Highness." A man hissed at his side.

"Best loyalty my coin can buy...." The laughter rang humorless. Muirgel tipped her chin higher and studied the twirls of smoke in the rafters. The king raised a hunk of beef from the platter in front of him and took a sloppy bite, waving the meat at Kara to prompt her to help herself. Kara chose a carrot and took a nibble.

"Are you betrothed, young Kara Agnesdatter?"

"No, King Ausle." She filled her mouth and reached for a slice of venison. A young girl, probably six years of age, brought her a mug and filled it with watery beer.

"Well, a beautiful girl like you can take her time—you are entering the cusp of maidenhood and have years before you settle to whelp a litter." The casual way he uttered these words embarrassed Kara and she dropped her eyes to the table, feeling the back of her neck warm. The king leaned across the mass of stacked platters and placed his hand on hers. She glanced to Muirgel, hoping for support against this bold talk—the princess rolled her eyes and turned away. The men around her liege leered at her, and the king himself smiled with all his teeth, arching his brows in an invitation. He stroked a finger the length of her forefinger. Kara froze, a crunch of carrot half chewed in her open mouth. Such brazenness triggered a twist in her belly, unbidden, uncomfortable, and confusing.

A hand gripped her shoulder, the surprise giving her a scare.

Gunna stood behind her. She squeezed her arm in a painful way.

"My lord king, please excuse my interruption. I must remind this one of her assignments. She is new and forgetful in your presence." One of the elders snorted at this comment, and King Ausle curled his lip.

"What better duty than to entertain her king?"

"Why none, of course, my lord, but our guards are tired,

and I have assigned this one to the Clondalkin watch tonight."

"The watch?" One of the elders stabbed at a pie with his knife. "Heard the Irish grow daring on the road to Clondalkin fort...."

"More vengeance for Barith's raids."

"Night watch?" The king puffed. Muirgel contemplated Kara with an odd glare.

"Take her then." King Ausle dismissed Kara from his table and turned to the men beside him. "We shall play with her another eve." This comment drew more stilted laughter from the old men.

Gunna roughly pulled Kara to her feet, and with a simpering smirk plastered on her face, bowed to the king. Twisting her tunic and kicking the longsword aside, she dragged Kara from the table. As soon as they distanced themselves, she hissed in Kara's ear. "Didn't Tordis warn you to steer clear of our lord lecher?" She hustled Kara through the crowded room, bumping into strangers and barging through discussions with an impunity secured as the chief of the king's guards.

"Yes, but...."

"Are ye seeking royal favors, after a roll or two?" Gunna pushed her face into Kara's, her breath hot on her cheeks. "The empty-headed girls before ye got nothing but a bastard for their tumble with Bradon Mac Ausle. Foolish and young, like ye."

"No, I didn't...."

Gunna growled, her lecture at an end, and pressed Kara into a bench seat. Kara faced a group of warriors, the ones her workmates called the 'cream of Findgenti,' four, tall, blonde maidens, Asta and Helka in the middle, their mouths drawn, brows creased, squinting at her.

"What is she doing here?"

"Pulled from the jaws of Mac Ausle." Gunna rolled her eyes at her cronies. "He offered her a snack before he devoured his own." The girls sniggered at the joke.

"Or passed her off to one of his aldermen for a coin...."

"Or on a bet." They cackled like hens in the millet.

Kara regarded the remnants of the meal before her, scraps and chewed apple cores.

"May I...?"

Gunna took a half-eaten apple and pressed it into her hand. "T'weren't no joke about tonight." She gave her a shove, "Get up and go. Meet at the south gate and take yer place in the night watch."

"But I worked all day at the wall."

"Aw, poor, frail babe..." one of the girls joked. Kara glanced around—none in the packed room paid attention to this group of warriors in the corner—in fact, soldiers consciously held apart from this gang. Gunna clapped her hands and pointed at her. Two of the women stood, as if to force her to leave.

"Don't want to hear it, newbie. Ye have two leagues to patrol this night, tween here and Clondalkin fort." Kara rose to her feet and turned to leave.

Behind her, Helka muttered, "Good riddance."

"Ah, ye only want her out of the way so ye can move on her Kay." Kara whirled around to glare at the Findgenti crew. Asta smirked at her, fists on her hips in a taunting pose, and Helka formed a moue with her lips.

Gunna glared at her. "Ignore them, girl. Get your armor and get to the gate, the patrol leaves soon enough."

"Ye don't want to know what happens to those who shirk their duties."

"I bet Kay doesn't shirk his *manly* duties...." One of the

women gestured to her hips in a crass way, and Kara took a step back, her fists balling. Gunna stopped her with a palm to her chest.

"Go child, before these bait ye to a fight ye can't win." Kara hesitated. "Go!"

Kara stomped out the hall. Outside she saw a small group of soldiers collecting at the gate—she rushed to the barracks and pulled out her breastplate and bracers, struggling with the ties as she hurried to join the patrol.

"Hurry now!" A gaunt man took control of the squad. "We march to Clondalkin and spell the garrison there. Single file, spread by five paces, give yourself room to swing —these Irish bastards charge in close to hamper swords. You, new girl, you hold the rear and watch our back." Walking Kara to her spot, he organized the crew, passed out a few torches, and encouraged them to draw their weapons. He signaled the gatekeepers to open the small passage through the great gate.

"I heard Bregans hide in our forest."

"Ja, last night Clondalkin watch fought off a band of twenty or more."

"Hush, we got a job to do...."

The leader waved his firebrand. One by one they stepped over the high threshold and left the fortress of Dublinn.

"Don't fall behind and don't get distracted. A quick march through the wood will carry us to the fortress."

Outside Dublinn, the evening settled into a half-moon night, clear and cloudless, and bright enough to see, stars beginning to peek through the darkened sky. Kara fell into her place, finally tightening her bracers properly and drawing her father's longsword. Last in line, she warily scanned the brush along the lane. Lush with greenery, the shadows deepened in the flickering torch light. Glow worms flashed under the trees. A bug swooped about her head, and she shooed it.

"Spread out and stay watchful."

The lane tracked the river. They passed over a small bridge spanning a tributary that emptied into the Poddle and marched through a marshy stand of reeds and squeaking night birds. The squad spread out on the roadway. The steady, silent march gave her time to think.

Kara didn't like this new king. Thinking back on his advances, she grew annoyed with herself for not being more assertive, and she wondered at his flattery... was she truthfully 'a beauty?' No man had ever been permitted to touch her like that, and her feelings grew muddled. The situation perplexed her because, despite knowing good maidens never entertained such impiety, a part of her appreciated his royal interest. *Is he harboring serious intent... or is his interest feigned, merely to toy with me? No, Gunna and Tordis were right.* With a frown, she vowed to steer clear of this King of Dublinn. And those Findgenti girls—Gunna's squad—Kara had never experienced people who purposefully goaded comrades. *Why push me to lose my temper, why push me to fight? Weren't we all on the same team? They are all so familiar with each other, speaking of the privacies between men and women openly and with no embarrassment.* They acted like the king in this way— *Would the goddess Sjofn, who turns the minds of men and women to lovemaking, be behind all this talk? Such a strange place, this Eire.* Her conflicted feelings jumbled her thoughts, and she grew more upset, bewilderment leading to irritation. She huffed and stomped, her mood distracting her from watch duties.

As the patrol rounded a bend and turned to the west, a

voice called her name. Kara paused to peer into the darkness.

"Kara." Kaelan rushed out of the darkness.

"Oh, it's you."

She returned to her march, following the file who moved through the forest. She had wanted to see him all afternoon... but now, after the king's mistreatment, the hazing by Findgenti warriors, and... that kiss.

"I didn't see you at dinner and...." He paused between pants. "I helped the cooks with the roast."

"Hmm."

"I didn't see you... I watched for you."

"I saw you well enough."

Her tone made him hesitate before he answered. "What do you mean?"

"What I said."

Kaelan stumbled along beside her, quiet for a moment, watching her profile. Kara kept her eyes forward, watching the soldier before her. She tried her best to ignore him.

"Kara?"

She cleared her throat.

"Kara, what's wrong?"

"Nothing." She thrust out her chin and kept her pace.

"Kara?" Kaelan reached out to touch her arm.

"Don't." She jerked her arm away.

"What's wrong?"

She stopped and turned to face him. "I saw you today."

"But I didn't see you."

"Obviously." She turned and strode from him.

"Kara, what's wrong?" He scurried to catch her. "Have I done something?"

"You?" She poked him in his chest with her free hand, waving the sword in her other. "You, no, not you. While I dug trenches in the mud and moved great, hulking trees, Freja save me from blisters and bruises, you went hunting with those, those... Findgenti," she spat the word.

"Wha...?"

"Don't try to deny it, 'Kay.' I saw you, I saw you kiss Asta."

Sputtering, Kaelan jumped to defend himself. "I never! *She* kissed me!"

"You spent the day with her, you and Asta, away in the wood. Together. And with lewd Helka, too. I know what those want, those..." Kara sputtered, unable to find an insult worthy of her anger.

"No, Kara, it was not like that, we separated, I swear. Apart in the trees, I ...."

"Hey!" A sharp bark from the patrol leader chopped off Kaelan's pleading. "What did I say? What did I say? QUIET! I swear on Mjolnir, I will slap you both until you can't stand."

The squad, strung out in their line, broke apart into clumps of soldiers, and a few turned on Kara, dropping their defensive poses and clustering to hear their leader's rebuke. "Gods protect us! Be quiet, you two, this is hostile forest." He pointed his torch at Kaelan. "I don't know who you are, but it's time you..."

Hidden enemies had waited to exploit a mistake in discipline. Bursting from the trees with battle shrieks, a disorganized swarm of warriors attacked.

"For Saint Cianán!"

"For Brega!"

Kara's leader tossed his torch at the advancing attackers as they scrambled out of the brush.

"Defend! For the All-Father!"

A brawl erupted. Armed with heavy, short spears and

wooden clubs, the wild Irish warriors jabbered and shouted as they struck. Surprised, Kara and Kaelan stumbled back from the surge.

Kara recovered her wits and shuffled in front of Kaelan, her sword held ready. A disheveled warrior with leaves and sticks in his beard stabbed at her with his spearpoint, aiming at her belly. As she parried his blow, another leaped at her from the darkness swinging a heavy mallet. He bellowed, lifting his shoulders to increase his intimidating size, and shaking his war hammer over his head. Young men barely older than Kaelan, they reeked of strong liquor. Both warriors closed to grapple with her, the first enemy slammed her sword arm with the stock of his spear, the second lifted his hammer over his head to strike a killing blow.

Kaelan dived into the fray. In an unplanned rush, he drove his knife into the armpit of the warrior with the raised club, surprising his opponent and diverting his attack from Kara. Inside the man's reach and too close for a club strike, the fighter fell back with Kaelan clinging to him. Screaming, Kaelan plunged his blade over and over, chipping ribs, seeking to bite deep. All around them battle cries had quieted, replaced by a determined struggle, a clatter of wood, steel, and grunts of exertion.

Kara glimpsed Kaelan's assault out of the corner of her eye. While the smack to her forearm caused a sharp pain, despite the blow, Kara managed to maintain her grip on her sword. Her foe drew back his spear for another attack and she dodged aside, leading his thrust. He followed through and jumped close where her weapon would have little room to maneuver. Sensing his move, Kara dropped the blade and clipped his thigh as he threw his bulk at her—she struck his leg, her sword slicing deep. His battle rage overwhelmed any pain and he grabbed her in a clinch, lifting her off her feet and throwing her to the ground, her sword knocked loose from her grasp. Dropping his heavy weight on her chest, he reached for her throat.

Punches to his gut had no effect—sweaty fingers scratched and dug to find her neck. She thrashed beneath him and kicked, arching her back. His hands found purchase and he began to squeeze.

Leading with his knife, Kaelan tackled from the Bregan's blindside. The two tumbled off Kara, leaving her struggling to catch her wind. She fumbled for her longsword, torches dowsed, the path dark. Unrecognizable fighters careened about the lane. Kaelan and the Irish fighter rolled next to her, neither staying on top of the other for long.

She found her sword. Shapes lurched in the darkness, toppling over each other... she could no longer discern her friend from the Irish warrior. One kicked the other and fell on top, beating the body underneath.

"Kaelan!"

His voice grunted from the ground. Kara swung her sword at the shape on top, putting all her weight behind the blow.

Sharp steel connected nearly decapitating the soldier. She kicked the flailing body aside and pulled Kaelan free. Covered in slippery gore, he hugged her and dragged her quickly into the brush, hushing her with a hand across her mouth.

Torch-blind, the sudden darkness made it impossible to tell which side gained the upper hand. Kaelan held Kara by the shoulders as they watched the silhouetted combat. As their eyes adjusted to the night, clearly a number of the Dublinn squad had run away, leaving the remaining forces to fight hand-to-hand with the Brega forces. Fierce and brutal attacks—Kara wondered at the violence, victors savaging the bodies of the defeated, pounding, pulping broken bodies. Under the tree shadows, Kara had no way to tell who fought who—anyone speaking drew an attack from the opposite side, and each had fallen silent. Whimpers and groans lifted from the wounded in the lane. The combat slowed—fighters faltered, unable to distinguish friend from rival. Two of the attackers stumbled into the forest and crashed off through the underbrush. Kara moved, rising from her crouch.

"Wait," Kaelan whispered in her ear. "Let them go." More drew away, and the rivals separated, some immediately dashing into the brush, others standing defiantly in the road. An eerie quiet returned to the wood.

Kara watched as three remaining individuals moved, checking the bodies. A small cry sounded as one dispatched a wounded opponent. Groans accompanied the lifting of a shape from the ground, and four shadows continued toward the fortress, one limping badly and clinging to another. Remains lay scattered and humped in the roadway, by Kara's count more than twelve lay dead or dying. Tucked under low-slung branches, Kara held Kaelan and waited until certain the danger had passed.

"What was that about?" Kara whispered, her head close to his.

"No idea."

"Those savages."

"Out for blood revenge."

"Oh Kaelan." Kara hung her head—the emotions of the battle passed, leaving her shaking. "What have I done? This place..."

"What do you mean?"

"I brought us here and..." She paused, trying to collect her thoughts. "Kaelan, I don't know who to trust."

"What do you mean?"

"Everyone hates newcomers like us. The Dublinn guards don't respect the new king. The local people hate all us foreigners. And from what I have learned, there are lots of minor kingdoms and each wars with the other. And... everyone wants to kill everyone."

Kaelan knelt at her side and offered, "You wanted to test your skills, to become a shieldmaiden."

"Ja, but I didn't expect this...."

"Hush." Kaelan pulled her deeper into the foliage. "Someone comes."

A single torch wound through the forest from the south, the light slowly working its way closer. They could discern a small sheaf of reeds, smoky and not extremely bright. The figure, wrapped in a hooded cloak, wandered in and out of the tree line, calling a name in a low-pitched voice.

"Otir?"

Kara gathered a woman stood before her, unarmed save for a kitchen knife at her belt. The hood hid her identity.

"Otir?" She moved close, hesitating as she came to the bloody bodies. She shuffled back from the fresh corpses.

"Otir...?"

Across the road, the bushes parted, and a man stepped into the dim light. His clothes marked him as royalty, his chain mail vest buffed to sparkle in the torchlight, his velvet cloak edged with ermine, and his doeskin boots rising above his knees. Tall and slender with wide shoulders, he had a handsome face with dark, wavy hair and a well-trimmed beard. The grin spread across his face revealed relief.

"Muirgel."

They rushed to each other and embraced, her hood falling aside spilling her thick, red hair. Kara lurched, unsure—the king's queen to be here, meeting a stranger in the wood. At night.

As they kissed, Kara realized this man was no stranger to her. Muirgel smiled warmly, gazing into the eyes of the man—was this the same haughty woman who ignored her in the hall and left her to be embarrassed by her betrothed? They spoke, whispering in the tongue of Eire, strange vowels beyond Kara's understanding. Clearly, these two had much to share—they spoke over each other, kissed several times, and continued their dialogue. At points, Muirgel became animated, shaking her fist and waving the torch, and the man Otir stroked her hair and whispered to her, calming her. Kara may have caught the name Ausle, she couldn't be sure.

Kara and Kaelan lay next to each other, controlling their breathing and watching the couple in their earnest exchange. The dim light did not seem to scare the glow worms, and the air swarmed with night flies and bugs. Sparkles and flashes danced in the shadows. Ignoring the bugs, the couple grew silent, held a long embrace, and the tall man bowed to Muirgel and slipped back into the forest. The red-headed woman sighed, arranged her hood, and returned the way she had come, a tiny flock of glow worms flowing in her wake.

Kara spoke first.

"I wonder what that was? I wish I understood..."

Kaelan rolled onto his side, his face next to hers. "They're in love."

"But she's promised to the king." She turned to him.

"You can tell by the way they gazed at each other... the way they kissed."

His breath caressed her cheek. Her breath snagged in her chest.

"Kara, I didn't kiss Asta... that wasn't my kiss." He leaned closer to her face, and a funny feeling rippled through her stomach.

"Kara, this is my kiss...."

Kara stiffened as Kaelan brought his mouth to hers. At first, she expected a fast peck like she had seen Asta take... Kaelan lingered. Wrapping an arm around her, he prolonged the embrace, pressing his lips against hers. She relaxed and closed her eyes, letting the feeling in her stomach spread, a warm rush up her neck. She could hear her heart patter in her ears, the pace quickening.

When he ended the kiss, she tucked her face in his neck, inhaling his smell amidst the scent of fresh blood. Her heart surging, she clung to him, dizzy and excited and despite the dirt and the smell of death, happy in his arms. The night flies and glow worms found them, and Kara carelessly waved them away.

THORFINN

Riding the bullrush to find his sister, the reed guided Finn west across a narrow sea to a land he had never visited. He followed a river and passed camps and fortresses. Trusting the Siedr magic to take him directly to his runaway sister, he let the staff land on a winding road bisecting a heavy forest.

In Midgard, a battle had recently taken place in this wooded thicket— Bodies lay strewn across the roadway, from their positions clearly near death or already gone. There, under bracken and bushes, lay his sister Kara, scandalously close to a boy he did not know. Dressed in armor, she held his father's ancestral sword Wolftongue, bloody from the recent fight—both splattered and dirtied, the boy drenched in blood—they had taken a side in the battle. He could see she rested unhurt and for an unknown reason remained hidden.

Across the road in a small glen, a man and a woman embraced. He wore fancy clothes, and she had a mass of curly, red hair—Finn couldn't understand a word of their speech, and Kara and the boy watched them intently.

But... what a forest! Finn had traveled the Realm Between for years since the witch had separated his hug from his lich, yet this place emerged completely unique. Expecting a few will-o-the-wisps or glowing fungi, the nightscape that unfolded before him amazed him. In the Realm Between, dancing between his eyes and the physical world, he witnessed a remarkable panoply of creatures. Everything came alive, moving, swimming through the air, and to his amazement, they danced to an intricate rhythm! Lines of hidden folk paraded across the lane, moving with coordinated steps. A throng of hidden creatures swarmed the air, hung in the trees, and crept along the forest floor, more mystical beings than he had ever seen in one place, more than when he ventured under the Humber Estuary. All sizes and shapes, and to his surprise, the tiniest immediately rushed to swarm him! The excited and curious crowd dazzled his eyes, and he waved his hands to chase them away.

Finn wished Raga had accompanied him—the old ghost probably knew where he was, what he had stumbled upon, and how to best deal with this strange parade. Multicolored, people-shaped sprites, barely the length of his fingers, with gossamer wings like a dragon fly flocked to the couple as they embraced, swirling around them in a synchronized dance. Tiny men with salamander heads and speckled skin rode beetles through the air. Frogs the size of his fist with stilt legs as long as his arm and bloated, yellow eyes marched in formation, and flat-faced, furry balls with humanlike eyes hung from long, prehensile tails in the surrounding trees. Bats with tiny riders dressed in green leaf armor carried needles as weapons. Odd, floating balls hummed and shivered, and cats with sparkling, brindle-striped fur slinked by. Little, bug-headed men stretched and snapped their mandibles. And ominously, scaly spiders of diverse sizes, with faceted eyes, proboscis, claws and tentacles, congregated over the dead bodies in the roadway, and a few warily circled him. Numbering more than he could count, squads carrying phosphorescent mushrooms, or waving flower sprigs, others carrying sharp sticks or tiny weapons. And the noise, above the voices of the couple, the chittering and snaps, whistles and chirps lifted in a cacophony.

Shaking his head to clear his astonishment, Finn recognized to gain any understanding of this wild place, he would need to learn their languages first. Calling the spell Raga had taught him, he turned the words as they passed him into small, magicked birds and plucked them from the air to swallow. The words of the hidden folk became clear, and he grasped the words passing between the redheaded woman and her dark-haired lover.

"...timing will never be right!" *She threw her hands in the air in a sign of surrender.*

"Muirgel, our love will outlast this fool, make certain of it."

"He presses forward his wedding, now Barith lies moldering, and he has ascended the usurped crown."

"My men inside Dublinn caution patience. In time we will drive all the foreigners back across the sea, the dark and the light."

"Why could we not elope now?" *Finn listened to the sprites cheer at her suggestion.*

"And risk our fathers' wrath? Kings of the Ui Neill do not suffer headstrong children. What is done is done—your father settled the war with your hand, and we cannot risk a breech. You know it pains me to be separated from you, but there is nothing we can do won't risk war afresh. We must delay the wedding until we can engineer Ausle's fall."

"You don't know what he's like."

"I can imagine."

"No, you can't. You are a decent and worthy man—Mac Ausle is a lech, not an honorable bone in his body. Treats me with contempt; forces me to attend while he seduces his willing bed slaves. I hate him." *He consoled her by stroking her hair and planted a kiss on her forehead, on her cheek and on her mouth.*

"Darling, every moment I am separated from you is painful. I love you so much, my heart is ready to break. I yearn for our times together, these briefest of instants hidden away from prying eyes." *When the man uttered the word love, the hidden folk echoed, love, love, love.*

As Thorfinn watched the couple, a sudden change occurred in the sprites and beetle riders circling his head. The frenetic activity settled, the dancers and parade halted, and the flyers all landed. Turning from him and the people in Midgard, each creature bowed in their own way, turning to face the west.

From the deep forest, a golden elf entered the glade.

Thorfinn had seen elves before, the dark Vanir, taller than men, with sunken, hollow cheeks and coal-black hair. This being stood as different from the dark elves as night is to day. The trees, brush and vines parted to allow the elegant creature passage. Childlike in stature, the slender elf stood a hand taller than Finn himself, his fingers unusually long, his blonde hair thick, cascading past his shoulders in waves. While his dress marked him as a warrior, his beautiful, high cheekbones and delicate, aquiline nose would have been the envy of countless Midgardian women. His bearing regal, his movements fluid, in his left hand he carried an ebony staff with an inlaid, golden blade set like a finely wrought ax at its tip. Speaking in gentle tones, he waved the rod over his minions, and they settled at his feet. Finn quickly swallowed the magicked words to ken the creature's language.

"Rest, children, after such a journey, we have so much to prepare."

"Love, love..." the multitude of creatures chanted, lifting to the air to circle the embracing couple.

The elf laughed, a melodious sound, and continued cooing to the assembly. Turning to Thorfinn, he stepped forward and pointed his staff.

"Ho, Fyreferd, well met." Nervous, Thorfinn gave a stiff nod of his head, wondering to himself, should I bow?

"We had not expected a fyreferd loose here in our forests. The children want to play with you." He motioned with an open palm at the forest. "Neither did we imagine we would find lovers in our wood." Closer, Finn could see the elf's eyes, wrinkles around them providing a hint he aged much older than he first appeared. "My vanguard is drawn to human lovers like moths to a flame. Powerful emotions draw them, love..." he gestured to the slumped bodies on the road, "...hate and anger. Tis love rightly lures them, like iron to a lodestone."

"Who are you?"

"Do you not recognize us, spirit boy? We are the vanguard of the Summer Court. We clear the path and prepare the way for the king and queen, our princes and princesses, dukes and duchesses, the entire glorious Seelie Court of Fae. We travel from Alfheim, now the Winter Court has returned to Vanaheim."

The elf paused.

Finn grasped the couple had finished their clandestine meeting and departed, the woman pulling her hood tight and wandering back toward the river, and the man slinking into the forest. The multitude gathered at the elf's feet chattered and flit-

tered, their lively and energetic natures overcoming his commanding presence. He smiled at them. Behind him, Kara whispered.

"...I wish I understood."

Her companion moved closer to his sister. Finn heard him say "They're in love."

"But she's promised...." *Straining to hear her murmurs, Thorfinn and the elf stepped closer to listen.*

"You can tell by the way they gazed at each other... the way they kissed."

At the word "kiss," the sprites took to the air, swooping across the ground toward Kara.

"Kara, I didn't kiss Asta... that wasn't my kiss." *The boy moved his arm and touched his sister.* "Kara, this is my kiss...."

The hidden folk jolted into the air to their dance again, this time circling Kara and the boy who held her.

"Call them back," *Finn begged.*

The golden elf chuckled. "Not likely, see how they act? She must be a maid, and this is her first love." *The tiny fae creatures piped and sang, chanting,* "love, love." *Kara, tight in Kae's embrace, absently swatted at the tiny sprites swooping and dancing around their heads.*

"My Summer Court hunts these young loves, those who find loves' first kiss in our wood." *The elf turned to face Thorfinn, calmly explaining.* "Their fruit is marked for us now, so perfect, the sprites wait to steal the newborn and carry the child to our court, leaving a changeling behind in its place. Human children make the best jesters."

Loves' first kiss? Steal the newborn? Changeling? Finn understood the elf meant these hidden folk would claim Kara's baby from here in the Realm Between! He stumbled back from the golden elf child, unsure whether he was more horrified fae creatures would steal his future niece or nephew, or his unwed sister would soon lose her honor... and how could he warn his mother?

"No! Not my sister!" He swatted at sprites near him, the fleet fae easily dodging his awkward swings. Stepping back from the elf, the tug of dawn pulled on Thorfinn, his waking lich calling his vardoger back in the north, and despite his desperate desire to stay and aid his sister, his Midgard body compelled him to return.

Attempting to sound threatening, he bleated, "Leave my sister alone!"

Undisturbed, the elf smiled at him.

"No doubt we shall see you again, little Fyreferd. The Summer Court awaits...."

KARL

"Enough."

Karl stood and brushed the sand from his hands. The seawall repaired, his farmers could plant with no fear of a breach overrunning their fields with salt water. The moon of Einmanudur had nearly changed to Harpa, snows melted from the lowlands and fragments of stubborn ice clung to the mountain roads and highlands. River ice had melted and its tributaries, bright turquoise with mountain runoff, rushed to the sea.

"Havar, send word to Hamund and his men. Time we meet the jarl and answer this summons of Tanglehair."

"Thank the gods." Jormander wiped mud from his cheek. "This thrall work kills my back!"

Enough, he thought as he marched his crew back through the village to their longhouse. *Enough of this stinking village, enough of hard labor to keep my men tough, enough of the waiting, enough of*—he glanced at Martine, her neck stiff and head purposefully turned from him—*well, enough of all of it*. He clapped his hands.

"Everyone, bathe and don your best travel vestments. Dress to face our jarl and his future king, the son of Yngling. Wear your armbands, especially those Harald awarded us. Sharpen your weapons, prepare your shields, we leave on the morrow." A collective sigh of relief lifted from his crew, and while not an enthusiastic reaction, good humor and playfulness returned to the sailors. Earnest packing started on all sides.

"Gudrun and Thorfinn, to me." He led the sailor and his nephew to the back room where his bride Signy lounged on a pallet of fur pelts and pillows. These past months she had grown plump, sometimes nauseous in the morn. He suspected she carried a child. He had quietly paid a young woman from the village to watch and act as a midwife when her time arrived.

Finn bounced into the room on his feet, a silly grin on his face, and Gudrun stooped next to him, head trembling slightly, gripping his hands to hide any tell-tale tremor.

"Gudrun, Harald means to wage war. While by my side in battle is obviously the best place for you, instead I must task you with a most important duty. You must stay here and guard my nephew and my new bride."

"Uncle Karl!"

"Do not pester me to join this voyage, Finn." Karl leaned close. "I promised your parents I would protect you. Taking you into battle would certainly break my oath." He glowered at the boy. "Besides, I don't trust another Siedr curse will creep in and try to take Signy, so your skills in the beyond can guard her from such enchantment, ja?" He watched as the boy's shoulders slumped and he bit his lower lip, scowling at the girl on her bed. "And what of your wyrm? Who will take care of Goorm if you leave?"

Finn scuffed his boots. "I guess...."

"So, you agree...?"

The disappointed boy would not meet his eyes. He dipped his head to indicate agreement.

"Gudrun, I do not want her or my nephew at Hamund's longhouse." Karl took the old man by his forearm. "I don't trust Hamund's retainers, especially the ones he leaves behind, but I trust you. Stay here and guard the boy and my wife."

"I will guard them with my life."

"I expect nothing less." He patted the man's arm. "While I am gone, the village will need to plant and watch for the herring run. To a man, they need guidance. You, in my name, will need to remind them to fish and plow to secure a bountiful harvest. I shall rely on you to make it so."

"Ja, Captain, you can count on me."

"Good." Karl pointed to the door. "Now, go help Kol ready the ship—we will be loaded with extra men Hamund and Regin bring."

Gudrun moved quickly. The boy kicked his boots against the rug and dallied. Karl closed the door slowly behind Thorfinn, slotted the bolt in place, and turned to face his bride. Anticipating his desire, she unclasped her tunic and opened her arms to welcome him.

~

THEY SET SAIL AT DAWN, the day clear and the water calm. Seals cavorted in the bay and a flock of puffins swam past their bow as they rowed into the open ocean and lifted the sails. Happy to be once more upon the sea, the crew of the

Verdandi Smiles sang shanties and sprawled along the deck playing Hnefatafl, capture the king, wagering on the outcome. The pilot Kol grinned like a boy at the Ylir festival, steering the snekke through the rollers, spray in their faces and seafoam rolling across the deck.

The voyage south took a few hours. As the sun passed its zenith overhead, Hamund called "This is the river."

"Trondheimsfjord." Jormander pointed up the river. "This way to the Lade Gard." They navigated the longship into the bay and rowed upstream, chanting with each stroke. Rurik plumbed the depth for the pilot, dropping his weighted rope and calling out measurements. The fjord cut deep and winding through sheer mountainsides and under craggy cliffs. At the base of a massive granite mound the river widened, and as they rounded the bend they came upon a fleet of ships, the Lade armada. Hamund stood on the bow and brandished his blue banner—men cheered and waved at him, pointing toward the shore and a wide longphort. Taking command, the pilot carefully threaded the ship through the crowded waterway and moored to the side of a broad knarr roped to the wharf itself. Sailors on both vessels reached to tie the ships together.

"Come cross, Hamund Holthlson!" a brawny blond sailor called, as catwalks settled in place. "Jarl Hakon waits for you in his hall."

"Havar, Jormander and Martine with me." Karl turned to Kol and Sorli looping the sail ropes in the stern. "Keep her shipshape and ready to leave." Hamund led the way with Regin and Alsvid as his bodyguards, Karl and his men behind, Martine at the rear. Karl paused on the walkway— under his breath, he cautioned them to keep their ears and eyes open, especially Martine who spoke a different set of languages. She squinted at him. Karl wondered at her difficult to read expression. She appeared healthy, her close-cropped hair freshly cleaned, her cheeks scrubbed rosy, her leather vest tooled with embroidery and bright pieces of abalone shell, a long knife at her belt and hammered copper armbands on her forearms. Tall, lithe, and athletic, imposing even. One of the Lindenwood shields hung from a strap across her shoulders.

"More than forty ships in this bay," Havar offered, stretching his neck.

"I count forty-two plus ours, that's forty-three," Jormander whispered to Karl.

"Quite a navy."

"Ja, I bet that's twenty more than Harald has...."

"We shall see..."

The long dock led past warehouses and drying racks, boathouses, and extended sheds for twining ropes. Hamund knew his way, stepping around groups of surly seamen and avoiding the packed entrances of wharf-side hovels, the lower-class taverns and brothels. An occasional shout of recognition and swap of bearhugs slowed their progress—many here knew Hamund or his cousins by sight. Beyond the longphort, a wide valley parted the mountains, green with sprouts of winter wheat. The Lade Gard, the farm stretched across the cultivated fields, fruit and nut orchards lining the pathway to a palisade which fortified the homestead on the knoll.

The heavy, oaken gate stood propped open with tree stumps, a group of warriors milling about the entry, one of which challenged the group, recognized Hamund and gripped his forearm in the northern way of welcome. A man in leather armor stepped forward.

"Karl Alfenson."

"Ja?"

"Do you remember me?" His wide grin revealed a missing front tooth, his blond hair braided in a loop at his neck, a splash of gray hairs striped his beard. His arm boasted three gold rings, gifts of honor from his liege. "We fought together at Harald's side on the fields of Trondelag, when we defeated Gryting of Orkdal, near six years ago."

Karl remembered. "Dag, you old bandit!" They embraced, Dag pounding Karl on his back. The men loitering about the gateway visibly relaxed.

"The gods have treated you well, Son of Ironfist."

"And you, Son of Dag, you've not missed many meals!" Karl poked his friend's belly.

"And you bring big Havar and your skald!" The man shook both men's hands in turn. "You keeping your old captain out of trouble?"

"Barely," Jormander answered.

"And who is this?" Dag extended his hand to Martine.

"Martine La Fontaine, hired sword." Karl did not miss the subtle way she emphasized 'hired.'

"I don't know your accent... but I like it." Dag measured her, noting the knife at her belt, her tight leather breeches, and her polished bracers. "You must be a fine fighter, to be one of Alfenson's deputies. If you weren't armed with a shield on your back, I'd have thought you were something a little more..." Dag winked at Karl. "Personal. An exotic beauty like you, you're definitely that old rogue's type...."

"Martine is..." Karl paused as Martine met his gaze, nostrils flared, her eyebrows prompting him to finish his thought. "Valuable and...." Staring into her eyes, he lost his words.

"Better than most men." Jormander pulled Dag from the shieldmaiden. "And she drinks less, so there's more left for us." He chuckled and wrapped his arm around the man's shoulders. "Come, lead the way, it's time we make our way to the jarl." Martine fell in behind Dag and the poet. Havar tipped his head at Karl's hesitant response and gave him a playful shove forward into the yard.

Woolen sailcloth, wooden blocks and tackle, and great coils of hemp rope crowded the courtyard. Men bent over the gear, assembling purchases for the fleet, sizing the sheets and poking eyelets with awls. Banners dyed forest green hung from strings, drying in the chill air. The operation appeared organized and thorough, ship wrights stepping through the laborers with a word of guidance, serious instruction, or a rebuke.

Beyond the busy yard, the immense longhouse had doors twice the size of man, each postern carved with runes and curled wyrms. Its shutters thrown wide, smoke curled from the fire holes in the clinker-fitted, plank roof, and the smell of tar and canvas wax mixed with an odor of roast beef. Inside, whale oil lamps and a roaring fire in the central hearth lit the hall. The tables had been carried away, leaving a single, square table at the head of the room, the remaining space filled with long benches and a crowd of warriors, relaxing or sitting to the side in muted conversation while newcomers queued to meet the jarl. Hamund and Regin motioned for Karl and his team to join them in line.

Jarl Hakon, the son of Grjotgard, reminded Karl of a work horse—big, brawny and bald, his long face, drooping ear lobes and a wide nose with flared nostrils dominated his thin beard. More a grimace than a grin, his mirthless sneer displayed flat, shovel teeth. Karl sensed hidden strength in his grasp as they gripped arms over his introduction by Hamund. Dag mentioned he and Karl had fought by Harald's side at Trondelag. A small group of wizened and experienced warriors, including a solemn shieldmaiden, stood close to the jarl, warily watching the new soldiers greet their lord.

"You know Gryting then?" The jarl pointed across the hall to a group of scarred warriors with wolfskin capes and iron helms under their arms. With a scar across his forehead and one mangled ear, Karl recognized grizzled King Gryting standing amid his men. "Since his defeat at your hands, he has been a staunch ally of Tanglehair."

A roughly drawn map spread on the table, small carved ships lined across it, a handful marked with a green dot and stacked in a bay—Trondheimsfjord Karl assumed, where they currently anchored. A group of eight more green tokens marked ships located to the south of the fjord. And far to the south, a larger collection of ships marked with red—a cursory count indicated the reds outnumbered the greens. Set aside, off the map itself, lay tokens from Hnefetafl games, and one singular king piece—Karl assumed this would be Harald's armies, their location hidden from those in the room. *Smart,* Karl thought, *for who knows where loyalties lie in this crowd of strangers, outsiders, and mercenaries.*

The jarl handed Hamund and Karl each one of the forest-green banners. The dye had made the felted cloth stiff. "Hamund, Son of Hothl, long have you been a loyal and trusted lord in my lands. Now Harald has promised to make me a true jarl in his kingdom, you shall reap the benefits of your faithful allegiance. You and your cousin Regin will take command of my ship, *War Eagle* under the direction of my admiral Uffe."

He turned to Karl. "You, lawful brother to Hamund of Unlahdil, you shall remain in command of your vessel. You are assigned to Egil and will fight under his command." The jarl motioned a man forward, a squat fellow with shaved cheeks and a long mustache, a tooled, leather tunic and a golden armband. Egil clutched Karl's hand in the Norse way, evaluating his grip. "Egil is my cousin by marriage and has commanded my fleet in a sea battle off the coast of Rogaland. He will set your place in the array and relay my commands." He waggled his head to indicate the interview had ended, and Egil motioned Karl to the side. A new group of fighters stepped to the table.

"Son of Ironfist, well met." Short of stature, Egil pushed close to Karl and spoke with his brow tipped back. "This evening we will gather the captains of my command together and discuss strategies and tactics. Jarl Hakon is dividing the fleet into four navies, each with a purpose and goal. We will meet there." He pointed to the corner by the great door. "Tables will be returned, and we can sup together, the ships of my team."

"And Tanglehair?"

"Hakon plots with Harald to join us, proper time, proper place." Egil tugged his mustache. "Until we meet this evening, you and your team are free to rest, gather supplies or whatever you need. One word of warning...." He squeezed one eye shut in a lopsided squint. "No strong drink when we are at sea, I'll not allow it. We all depend on each, man to man, ship to ship. Any weak links I will toss to Nord myself. Are we in agreement?"

"Ja, admiral, we agree." Satisfied, Egil returned to his jarl's flank. Dag pulled Karl farther into the room, leading his crew to a less crowded section of the hall to find abandoned stools and a bench.

"Come shieldmaiden, sit by me," Dag offered, scooting on his bench to clear the seat next to him. Martine charmed him with a smile, slipping the shield from her back. Havar propped his knee on the end of the seat and leaned cross-armed over her shoulder in a protective manner. Karl and Jormander settled onto stools, discreetly scanning the room.

"You know how this all began, don't you?" Dag leaned conspiratorially and placed his hand on Martine's arm. She cocked her head, glancing at his hand touching her. "Tis a love story for the ages."

"A love story?" Martine grinned at Jormander. "These north men avoid love poetry. I need a tender tale of the heart... tell me a good love story." To Karl, she lingered on the word 'good,' enough to taunt him with hidden meaning. Out of the corner of his eye, Karl watched Dag try to flirt with her, wondering if she would break his fingers for being too forward—she was no barroom wench or bed thrall.

"Harald's father, Halfdan the Black unified the lands of Vestfold, pulling together scattered kingdoms through inheritance and strength of arms. A mighty conqueror, Halfdan intended to establish a dynasty in his family name, the Gudrodar. When Harald was a lad, his father died, a tragic and unexpected death, and the boy's mother had a brother named Guthorm who took control of the kingdoms as regent in Harald's name. A good administrator, Guthorm commanded no respect from his armies. Soon the jarls in his kingdom revolted. The kingdom Halfdan the Black had fought so hard to unify splintered and broke. T'was a decade ago.

"While Guthorm frittered away Harald's inheritance, the youth traveled the neighboring kingdoms, seeking adventure." Martine acted enthralled with the story, leaning closer to Dag to listen, smiling into his eyes. Karl wondered what she played at....

"On his travels, Harald made his way to Hordaland and presented himself at the court of Eirik the King. Eirik had a beautiful daughter, Gyda, tall, strong, and fair. For Harald, elsk overcame him, a love sickness so deep it threatened to drown him. He begged Eirik for her hand, but the sly king who wanted to avoid a connection to a minor, backwater principality, told his daughter to reject the boy. Gyda refused to marry Harald until he reigned 'King over all the Northern Way.'

"Now, hot-blooded and tempestuous, Harald vowed to never cut nor comb his hair until crowned sole king of all Norway, and that is how he came to be the Tanglehair, or, as they call him in Hordaland, 'shock-head.'"

"What a lovely tale." Martine batted her eyes at Dag. "Tell me, is it true?"

"Of course, true love drives Tanglehair and Gyda waits for him to claim her. And Eirik still stands in his way...." Dag leaned closer to the warrior maid, stroking her arm with his fingers. Much to Karl's dismay, she allowed him to continue his familiar advances. She leaned close and whispered to him, placing her hand on his chest.

Blood flushed Karl's cheeks. Havar gave him a stern glare and taking his foot off the bench, rose to his full height.

Karl snorted and stood, his stool scraping the floor planks and tipping over with a clatter. "I, uh... I need to...." Avoiding Martine and Dag, he grunted and turned on his heel. Jormander followed.

Outside the hall, the poet stepped quietly to his side. He held his tongue as they watched the late afternoon scurry of preparations.

"You know," Jormander spoke softly, not meeting Karl's eyes. "You've been a bear out of his cave for moons...."

"I had to bed that girl."

"Ja, Captain."

"It cemented the alliance with Hamund and his family."

"Ja, Captain."

"I had to do what I had to do. Duty, you know."

"Ja, Captain."

"It's true. ... I've been avoiding her."

"We're not talking about the girl anymore, are we?"

"... No."

"Funny, we joke about elsk, but one should never trifle with such matters...."

"Hmm." Karl scuffed his boots in the courtyard gravel.

"You understand now why skalds are forbidden to sing love poetry?"

Karl grunted. "She's angry."

"Ja, Captain."

"I did not expect...."

"Nor did she, but 'the eyes of a maid tell true....'"

"Was it so obvious?"

Jormander chuckled. "Ja, old friend, long before you knew yourself, we saw it growing."

"Truly?"

"Aye, Captain. Save maybe your nephew...."

"How long...?"

"We suspected when she rushed to your aid against the bear-man—she never left your side that night."

"And...." Karl lifted his hand to his chest.

"After the news of Agne's death when she consoled you. Since that day, the way you turn to her and include her in our plans...."

"And... I broke it."

"Ja. You broke it."

"I cannot fix this, can I?"

Jormander clapped him on the shoulder. "Oh, brother, 'twas never in your hands."

"Have I made a mistake?"

"As the song says, 'Long shall a man be tried.' We must wait and see."

CHAPTER 5
THIS WILL NOT END WELL

CUB

The man next to him snored—tis true, some can sleep in any situation. Cub sniffed. Rain drizzled a chill mist over the warriors lying in wait.

After he chased the Vikings from the town, Robert of Breton March had installed a garrison in the center of Rouen. A stone barracks housed his men, and Rolf's spies had counted a score of soldiers and a stable of warhorses. The Bretons protected the rickety Rouen monastery, its wooden church and steeple tower, and a clutch of decrepit wattle-and-daub houses and a few pit homes, insulated with turf in the northern way. All the houses languished in various stages of repair, recovering from the last battle for Rouen—half the town had burned to rafter beams and ashes. The village lay undefended, no palisade curtain erected to fortify the town, the required trees long harvested by farmers and carted to market by lumber mongers. Yet, after their first defeat at the hands of Rolf's raiders, the Franks had set a series of gates and checkpoints on the main arteries into the town center, establishing defensive redoubts against further incursions.

Designed to test the resolve of the Franks to hold their re-conquered town, the sortie coordinated Rolf's warriors in a three-pronged attack. Colden and his force snuck across the fields before dawn and lay in a drainage ditch on the north side of the village. Hagrold and his troop marched from the west along the river Seine, and Rolf personally led a group of elite fighters to circle and enter the village from the southeastern fields. Rolf would trigger the attack by initiating a battle with the garrison, and an agreed signal would draw their reinforcements.

Cub wiped the damp from his beard. He twiddled his thumbs, stretched, and made handprints in the grass, watching the weeds spring back after his pressure.

What could be taking them so long? he wondered, rubbing his eyes.

Robert of Breton March—Rolf grudgingly admitted his opponent a worthy adversary, outmaneuvering him on the field and forcing his Danes to winter in small fishing villages along the coast. The two had directed bitter campaigns against each other and contested the lush valleys and trading towns west of Rouen. This Breton had fought Rolf's conquest plans to a stalemate.

Cub rolled on his back and examined the sky. *Where was the signal?*

Hold the warhorses in the stables Colden explained as their first task—men on horseback became deadly and difficult to unseat, despite the close confines of narrow streets. Cub could see the stables across the field, a few stallions circling a fenced yard with tattered blankets warming their backs. The smell of morning cookfires drifted across the pasture. As he watched the mounts canter around the pen, he had an idea. Anything to break the monotony of delay.

"Colden." He pointed at the barn across the field. "See the gate on this side of the horse run?"

Colden harumphed in response.

"Why don't I take a wander over and open the gate? Those chargers are full of piss, ready to bolt...."

"You know horses?"

"Farm born and raised. Bet I could free them all, get them out of the way."

"Take Bjorn with you." He motioned for a lanky blond to join him. Taking Cub by the arm, he warned, "Don't get caught." Cub smiled, rose from the ditch, and brushed off his wet tunic and breeches.

"Act natural," Cub advised Bjorn.

Steel-gray clouds obscured the morning sun, the remnants of winter making for a dreary day. Planted with winter wheat, the field greened as the weather warmed, and Cub carefully led Bjorn around the rows of tender stalks. Mud clung in clumps to their boots. They reached the paddock, the gate secured with a well-handled hempen loop. Swinging the gate aside, a few clicks from his tongue and the three steeds bucked past them into the field—and immediately dropped their heads to munch the new sprouts.

"So much for that plan." Cub glanced at Colden hiding at the edge of the field. They continued across the pen to the barn door. No one challenged them—Cub could hear sounds of the waking town, splashes of dumped night water, a rooster crowing and hens cackling. Sliding the door aside, Cub loosened his iron sword at his belt, and motioned to Bjorn, indicating he should ready his hand-ax and the Lindenwood shield on his back.

Movement in the barn drew his attention—a boy carried a bucket of oats with both hands. He halted in their path, his mouth agape. Cub held a finger to his lips.

"Hush." He pointed at the bucket and signaled the boy should continue with his chore, gesturing with his arm to the line of stalls, the beasts snorting, impatient to be fed. The boy hesitated and Cub spoke to him in a low voice, using his broken Cornish to approximate the Breton's tongue. "Feed horses—don't mind us."

Skittish and keeping his eyes on the strangers, the boy hedged around the two warriors to dump oats in the stall troughs, happy horses dipping their heads to breakfast. Cub moved to the stable door.

The gate cracked to allow fresh air to enter, he could glimpse the street beyond. Two Breton warriors leaned against a movable blockade, one munching a shriveled apple. He stepped back into the shadows and quietly drew his sword. With hand motions, he gave Bjorn an account of what he could see through the crack in the door and pointed to a spot near the entrance where a single fighter could hold off any who attempted to enter.

Quaking with fear, the boy fed each stall a scoop in turn —Cub stopped him and pointed to the rafters. "Go, hide." Not needing to be told twice, the boy darted for a ladder and climbed into the hayloft. Cub opened the stalls. Unfed horses stamped and nosed from their stable, easily guided by Cub into the paddock. Beasts mid meal lagged, munching their grain and ignoring opened gates. Cub gave a few a smack with the flat side of his weapon to prompt action. Their whickers gave him pause, glancing to Bjorn at guard by the door. Bjorn lifted his hand to mark a pause— the Bretons loitered, unfazed by the barn noises. Once given an all-clear hand signal, Cub emptied the stalls and the animals wandered through the open pen into the fields.

With a crowd of horses milling about the wheat, Colden climbed to his feet—little likelihood his warrior troop would be recognized, as an immediate fear would be animals foraging freshly-planted crops. He directed his team towards the barn.

A loud whistle sounded, once, twice. Bjorn grinned at Cub and arched one brow—the whistles, the signal they awaited. A commotion began at a distance, shouts, thumps, and the clatter of steel against steel. Peeking through the barndoor, they watched the two Breton soldiers crane their necks to glimpse the cause of the ruckus. Behind them, shouts, cheers—the soldiers turned from the town center and jockeyed for a better view of the fields beyond their gate. As they moved past the doorway and out of Cub's view, Cub gripped the door and prepared to launch his attack. With as much surprise as he could muster swinging a heavy, oaken door aside, Cub jumped into the lane, and Bjorn pushed past him, shield forward, ax held high.

The two guards had seen the horses running free in the fields, men among them. They must have assumed the villagers rushed to capture the wayward animals, and they waved and ran to help, swords sheathed at their belts. Cub glanced at Bjorn—the men dashed nearly to the field's edge before they appreciated their error—not townspeople chasing their livestock but attacking raiders who stole through their defenses. One drew his sword and planted his feet in defiance, the other turned to run toward his post, finding Bjorn in his path. As the sounds of combat grew louder, Cub grabbed the makeshift gate and dragged it from the lane, jamming an end into a narrow alley. Sheer numbers overran the guards behind him, and with a salute to Colden, he turned to follow the road into the village.

Before he reached the banks of the Seine, two Bretons rounded a corner, recovered from the surprise of finding a Dane blocking their way and screamed as they attacked. Each wore a round, iron helm and carried a heavy, short spear with a hammered-iron tip.

The larger of the two, a big-bellied warrior with stumpy legs, swung his spear like an ax and leaped in close to hamper Cub's swing. Ducking under his awkward slice, Cub jabbed at his round middle and raised his sword to parry the spear's return. Expecting to overpower Cub, the man continued his charge, his spear missing Cub's shoulder, his blubber smothering Cub in a bearhug. The other warrior circled warily, watching his mate grapple with the young Dane. Wrestling, the heavier opponent had a distinct advantage and pressed Cub's sword arm and his weapon against his chest in a crushing squeeze. Cub banged his forehead into the man's laughing mouth, bloodying the oaf's lips. He continued to squash Cub's chest in his grip. Cub knew the other warrior behind him would move to strike if he didn't take action to break the hold. Desperate, Cub thrust up on his toes and lifted the heavy man enough to tip their balance. The two toppled, the big man landing on top. His grip loosened in the tumble and Cub jerked an elbow free, jabbed his arm down and ran his blade through the man's boot. Howling, the guard released Cub and rolled aside.

As Cub scrambled from the pile, the other Breton struck with his spear, the blow scraping across Cub's ribs and piercing his tunic. Cub grabbed the staff and clung tight. Rearing to strike a second time, the warrior yanked Cub from the fat wrestler. Shouting, the warrior jerked at his weapon, and Cub, his sword lost underneath his first opponent, rode the heavy staff whipping him back and forth. Like a dog worries a rat, the warrior tried to shake Cub free, Cub refusing to release the spear tangled in his shirt.

Climbing to his feet, the hulk who had initially pinned Cub pulled the iron sword from his foot. Blood welled out of his wound at each step. With a growl, he lumbered towards Cub, the sword in one hand and his spear in the other. Caught between the two, Cub dropped the spear he held and rolled across the roadway. His weapon freed in an awkward hold, the guard whacked at the foe before him, Cub dodging strikes, taking a few smacks on his legs and torso, bruising blows that did little to slow him. The portly guard limped closer and stabbed with Cub's own sword, the blade missing its target, and unaccustomed to the weight of the blade, the fighter drove the tip deep into the dirt and jammed it for a moment, providing Cub an opening.

Cub landed an uppercut in his corpulent face, breaking his nose with a snap. He kicked the flat of his blade, knocking it spinning. Before the big man could react, Cub stomped on his bleeding foot and dove for his own weapon. The spearman behind him rushed to attack, poking his iron-tipped staff at the rolling Dane. Retrieving his weapon, Cub parried the spear and swung to parry again. Growling, blood flowing from his crushed nose, the stout man retrieved his spear and moved to join his companion.

As both Breton warriors lifted their spears, Colden and his squad rounded the corner. Recognizing Cub, they dashed to join his fight. Everyone shouted battle cries. Distracted by the arrival of more raiders, one Breton twisted to address the new threat while one of the warriors followed through on his attack. Cub parried for a third time. As the spear struck next to him, he grabbed it with his free arm and gripping tight, he dropped to his knees, lodging the iron tip under his weight. As the Breton yanked at his stuck weapon, Cub pricked the tip of his sword into his opponent's legs, first one, then the other. Screaming, the soldier heaved himself at Cub to grapple with his smaller foe. This time ready for a wrestling move, Cub bolstered his sword against the dirt and aimed the tip at his chest, letting the man's own weight carry the blade through his lung. Spitting blood, he collapsed next to Cub, wheezing and choking.

Cub climbed to his feet, pulled his blade free and brushed the road dirt off his clothes.

"Been waiting for you."

Colden smirked. "I can see."

His men quickly dispatched the remaining Breton.

"Wait." Cub jerked the iron helmet from one of the dying men. "He won't be needing this."

Fitting the helm over his ears, Cub gave Colden a broad, goofy smile.

"You know, you've cut your forehead."

Cub wiped the blood with the back of his hand. "Hadn't time to notice."

"Be more careful next time, eh?"

"Good idea."

They both chuckled.

Colden raised his shield. "Come, rally to the Ganger!" With a shout, the team marched north along the riverbank.

Someone had fired the wooden buildings. At least two buildings vented flames, smoke trailing across the road. Scared old crones led small children scurrying to safety. *Why does fire always erupt?* Cub wondered as smoke smarted his eyes. They strode the avenue, two abreast, wary of an ambush. The sound of steel striking steel grew louder. They marched past a smashed and bloodied gate. A toppled cart straddled the lane and a group of women clutched each other knee-deep in the river, laundry hanging limp in their hands, wavering over which way to turn. And beyond the hobbled cart, forces converged in combat.

Colden's men surged forward, shouting insults, and attacking any Rouennais soldier before them. Cub threw himself into the fray. He swung his sword at targets to his left and right, drove it deep into an enemy's side and kicked the blade free. He slashed at a spear thrust in his direction, jumped near to his attacker, and punched his jaw. Feeling battle lust surge in his chest, Cub sliced left to a foe's arm and swung right to strike another's torso. The stench of offal and blood overcame the river damp. His blade became notched, soft iron parrying steel did not hold its edge—*no matter,* Cub thought, *I will be done with this tool and collect a better one after we win this battle.*

His vision clouded as his passion increased. He grabbed a dropped shield with a notch in its frame—a broken strap made it flop haphazardly. He didn't care—a damaged buckler afforded a degree of protection for his left side. He stepped between two combatants in a heated contest, overwhelming the foe with the shield, bashing into his surprised face, and finishing him with a swipe across his midriff. A man grabbed him from behind—Cub headbutted him, the chin blow from his iron helm knocking the man to the ground. He swung the shattered shield like a banner, smacking his adversaries in a crazed, unpredictable way, dealing in confused confrontations and rapid counterattacks. His vision tinged red, his blood pounding in his ears. Hack, parry, stab—Cub slogged through the crowd, parting the Rouen from his troops. He tackled a standoff of three guards defending back-to-back, bowling them over in a chaotic charge. His first real battle since Ethandun, he remembered the surrender to the berserk, the raw emotion, the rampage, the killing; he reveled in the All-Father holy blood lust. Fighting with abandon, he cut a swath through the enemy ranks. Blood splattered and laughing maniacally, the conflict ended too soon.

A cheer lifted from the Danes. His inflamed sight faded, returning to normal, and he leaned on his damaged sword, panting heavily. The shield in his left hand a clutch of ruined staves, his iron sword had lost its tip and notches serrated the knife edge, probably damaged beyond repair. Somewhere he had lost the iron helmet. The dead and dying lay scattered in the square, a pile of bodies with the stench of warfare lingering in the morning chill. Their tactic of a surprise attack with overwhelming odds had won the day—the Bretons lay defeated, while few of the Danish forces had succumbed to wounds.

Colden and Rolf crossed to him, Hagrold behind them, barking commands to search the garrison. Unsteady, Cub stood sustained by his damaged weapon like an ancient propped by a cane.

"The All-Father watches you, boy." Rolf smacked him on the back.

Colden crossed his arms and beamed at his leader. "I told you Agneson is a fighter."

"The Valkyries protect this one. Keep him near me!" Warriors laughed along—all had witnessed Cub plunge wildly into the skirmish and harvest his rivals like a crofter with a scythe.

Cub grinned at the compliment. Gaining his composure, he straightened and held his sword to examine the damage.

"Throw that pig-sticker aside, Agne." Rolf dismissed the damaged weapon with a wave. "I'll get you a better one." He stood on his toes, surveying the square, the church, and the shuttered abbey, locked against their invasion. Rolf, a barrel-chested man with blue eyes and brown hair, hulked too big to ride the local ponies—hence his nickname, the Ganger, the 'walker.' A blocky, square jaw clean shaved and blued with stubble, strong teeth and full lips, he stood a head taller than most men. Like the men and women in his army, Cub too turned to the well-spoken warrior for his strategic mind, his great humor, and his compelling manner of speech. *My father was a man like this*, Cub thought, *a born leader. This is one to follow*.

"Come, let's see what the monks have collected for us in the moons since we last called." A few of the warriors banged on the church door.

"Let us in, little monks."

All the victorious joined the call. "Let us in."

Rolf stepped to the door, banging with the back of his hand ax. "Tis I, the one you call 'Rollo.' Back to claim my Rouen prize. Open this door or we shall tear it from its hinges!"

Cheers lifted from the ranks around Cub, and he joined in the shouting.

A clatter sounded as a bolt slowly drew from its tray, and with a high-pitched creak, the door swung open, enough for a tonsured head to poke through. An old friar pleaded in the Breton tongue. Barely controlled tears wet his cheeks.

"Oh, unholy heathens, we entreat you. This is a house of the one true God. Please spare us and this holy place."

"He babbles in the local tongue," Hagrold grumbled. "Make him speak proper words."

"He says tis a house of their god."

Eyes turned to Cub.

"You understand his gibberish?" Hagrold squinted at Cub.

"Mostly. Tis like the Cornwallis I learned in Devon."

Colden agreed. "Ja, Agne speaks their words."

"Ho, Agneson, you are full of surprises." Rolf put his arm around Cub's shoulders and pushed the door wide with his other arm, letting his men enter the church hall. "Come, let's see what these priests have for us."

The church hall had been stripped in a former foray, the long benches and an empty, wood altar remaining. Monks, heads shaved in their peculiar way, trembled behind the table. Cub recognized most ranged younger than he, mere boys. One elder stood defiantly in the middle of the hall, his arms crossed over his chest. Rolf strode forward to the old man, as his commander Hagrold knocked pews aside with angry kicks.

"Priest." Rolf took ahold of the man's homespun robe and dragged him to the altar. "You remember me, don't you?"

"You are Rollo the walker."

"Told you I would return, nay?"

"Robert chased you from Rouen once, he will chase you again."

Rolf spat his laugh. "Fool, I am counting on it." He glanced at his men filing into the room, a few disappearing into a corridor to the heart of the monastery building. "Let him waste his energies and men, throwing them against my shields." Hagrold let an evil chuckle slip. Colden loitered against a pillar. Cub saw the boys whispered and clung to each other.

"Do your worst, spawn of Satan, I shall be a martyr for my God."

"Not today, old man." Rolf regarded the cowering boys behind the altar. "We are here to collect our bounty...."

"You stole everything last time! Our golden cross of Saint Eustadiola, our chalice and communion platter."

Cub worked his way along the wall, stepping next to the wide-eyed boys. One translated Danish for the others, a freckle-faced lad about the age of his younger brother Sorven.

"We took all left for us to find. There is more, I can smell it." The old man thrust out his jaw in a defiant stance. Rolf jerked the man by his robe. "Tell us where you have hidden your treasures."

"I implore you there is no more. Do what you may to me, tis God's will."

"Oh, little man, I'll not hurt you, but I'll make you watch—" he waved to Cub—"as we send those boys to meet your god."

Cub motioned the translator to step forward. The neophyte juddered back from his outstretched hand. Covered in battle gore, he could see his appearance terrified the boy.

"Listen," he spoke Cornish in a low, penetrating tone. "Your master gambles your life. Rolf kills you all. Treasure, only things, nay?" His lower lip trembling, the boy cringed as Cub took ahold of his brown robe and pulled him closer. "We no want kill you. Tell me where silver hides?" Cub leaned close and locked eyes with the child. "I swear, no kill you."

Behind him, the elder protested. A slap from Rolf quieted him.

"I promise, all live." The boy's eyes swept around the

room, the church crowded with warriors and the smell of war.

"You won't kill us?"

"My word." Cub put his hand on his chest.

Fearful, the boy glanced at his elder.

"No, eyes to me," Cub insisted. "Tell me."

The boy dropped his head, and whispered, "You will leave?"

"My word," Cub repeated.

Rolf watched the dialogue, not needing the words to grasp the meaning of the exchange. As the old priest spouted complaints, he hustled the man to Hagrold and with a hand signal indicated his men should drag him to the square. The young priests behind the altar scattered and the Vikings cleared the room, leaving Rolf and Cub facing the young acolyte.

The boy, cut loose from his supportive brothers, quailed as Rolf stepped behind Cub, glaring at him.

Cub kept the boy focused. "You show."

"You leave and stop the murders?"

Exasperated, Cub sighed. "My word. No more kill, no more 'murders.'" Pleased to have learned a new word, he patted the boy's head like a frightened dog.

"Follow." The boy took Cub's forearm and pulled him to the back of the church. They stopped at a hewn-plank wall. He pointed at a knot hole.

Cub bent to inspect the cavity. Fitting his forefinger into the gap, he tugged and popped the plank forward, a small door swinging open on well-greased hinges. Beyond a narrow corridor led to stairs. He gave Rolf a wink and prompted the boy to lead the way, Rolf leaning into the tiny space to watch.

Dim light in the hallway grew shaded in the stairwell,

rough, wooden steps creaking as he put his weight on them. The path led him into a pit, and they paused as his eyes adjusted to the darkness.

A root cellar. Racks and shelves lined the narrow space, the cool earth maintaining a lingering winter chill. Blindly feeling along the shelves, he announced each find in his native tongue as he recognized the object, calling to Rolf.

"Carrots... Cabbages...." He sniffed at a small ball. "Apples... dried apples." He stubbed his toe in the darkness. "Casks, a number of them, by their size, hogsheads I'd guess." He stopped to sniff. "Smells yeasty, like ale...."

Ahead of him in the dark, the boy snapped open a hatch. The small circular window had been cut in the church floor to illuminate the cellar—suddenly, the space brightened. Revealed, the room met Cub's expectations, a long narrow pit outfitted to store provisions, vegetables, dried fruits, hanging onions and garlic, a shelf of flat-bottomed bottles, a long line of casks, racks of strange rolls and small wooden caskets.

"What is this?" Cub plucked a parchment from its cubby.

Startled, the boy gently pulled the scroll from his hands, unrolling it with tender care. "A sacred text." He displayed a sheet of squiggles for Cub to view. Small images and gold leaf marked the page. Curious, Cub peered close in the dim light—seemed like tiny runes arranged in lines across the parchment.

He pushed past the boy and lifted a black glass bottle.

"What?"

"Cognac."

"Humm?" Cub wrinkled his nose at the word. Biting the plug with his teeth, he pulled the plug free and took a whiff. "Ah, aquavit! We take this."

He opened a wooden box—inside lay a white bone on a velvet pad.

The boy jabbered; Cub didn't understand.

"What?"

"Blessed saint relic." The boy touched his own arm.

"Oh, I ken." Cub shut the lid and opened the next. And smiled.

Inside this box lay a stack of silver platters and four matching goblets. The next box held a leather sack of coins and more of the scrolls, more than a few pressed with wax seals and decked with fancy ribbons. Choosing an empty grain sack, Cub placed the objects in his makeshift pack. The boy hung his head as he watched. Holding the rolled parchments, Cub weighed whether to take them and decided to add them to the bag—he didn't know their value but whoever had stored them had decided they merited protection like coins and silver.

He turned to the boy. "Carry," he pointed to the shelf of bottles and kicked one of the casks. The boy glumly complied. Returning to the altar, he handed Rolf the sack and returned to help the youth manhandle barrels up the narrow stair. Cub decided to leave the food for the monks.

Once he completed carting the barrels upstairs, he found Colden had his men gather the loose horses—they had eaten their fill in the field and wandered back to their paddock, seeking a water trough. The men saddled a few, while they yoked the rest to a cart stacked with the ale kegs, black bottles, and spoils from the garrison larder.

Rolf and Colden met him as he finished his last trip, and Rolf handed him a steel sword in the Roman fashion, a heavy, blunt-tipped stub. "Agneson, this will hold its edge better.

"Good work getting the boy to show their hideaway.

Understanding the local words, tis a skill I need by my side. Let's ride together and you can tell me of your lineage and how you came to be in Britany."

SORVEN

Pilloried.

People will swear it is hard to sleep pilloried. With your neck and hands cuffed and rotted vegetables in your nose and hair, crouching uncomfortably, sleep should be near impossible. After two days stooped in the stocks, plastered with stinking garbage and standing in their own filth, both Sorven and Dundle drifted in and out of sleep. Groggy when awake, fitful when asleep, they endured the occasional slaps and strikes from a rod left convenient for any passersby, the indecencies and exposure, and the utter embarrassment of the stocks.

On the first day of their imprisonment, they measured the village square and whispered plans to escape. After hours of struggles, apparent attempts to getaway became futile dreams. Their arms ached, their backs ached, and Sorven wondered if he would ever be able to stand straight again. Neither understood the Welsh around them, and one sadistic guard informed them in broken Danish while they caused a distraction, a companion had stolen a bag of meal and a few chickens and run back into the forest leaving them to suffer. Or at least that is what Sorven thought he said, his thick accent garbling the words.

On the evening of the third day, shivering from cold, damp snow and delirious from the punishment, they awoke to hands fumbling at their bonds. Released from the cuffs, they collapsed and willingly submitted to those who half-dragged, half-carried them and tossed them in a shed, barring the door from the outside. Full of last season's straw, the boys burrowed into the compost-warm pile and dropped into a deep stupor.

Fever dreams haunted Sorven.

Blood on his hands, the shocked face of Magnusson dying in slushy snow.

A horse-faced creature with great wings straddling his chest. An ancient crone chanting over a flickering fire.

His father lying grim and pale on a stubbled field.

He thrashed and struggled against the terrors, barely aware of a cooing voice coaxing him back to sleep.

When he woke, he found himself wrapped in a linen sheet, a soothing cloth across his forehead. He lay on a straw-filled pallet, a bearskin pulled to his chest. A wooden bowl of broth sat near his head on the floor. Attempting to sit, he quickly realized he remained too weak and slumped back on the bed. He smelled of stale sweat and faint vomit, yet his sheet smelled fresh and his hands lay clean on the smooth bedding.

A small room, walls built from stacked field stones mitered with mud, and a thatched roof. A second, straw-stuffed mattress lay next to his—as he examined his surroundings, the entry door squeaked open. A girl entered.

Round faced with apple cheeks naturally blushed, she grinned at him, carrying a small plate of food. Smells made his mouth water—famished, his empty stomach gurgled. He propped himself on his elbow. The girl smiled and spoke, her language full of hard consonants, lip bursts and tongue rolls, completely unintelligible to Sorven. No matter he could not understand—she chattered as she bustled about, dragging a stool to sit at his side and spoon the minced meat and boiled cabbage into his open mouth like a baby. He swallowed every bite and accepted a tilt of her cold broth bowl to wash the hash down.

Near his age, his hostess dressed in a homespun gown with no ornament. Her brown eyes protruded slightly, her nose an upturned button. From his prone position she appeared short, her exposed arms plump and pink, her legs cocked and pigeon-toed. Her curly black hair trimmed in bangs, she radiated satisfaction as she delivered her long speech, reaching to pat his chest as she recounted an important fact. She pressed the remaining food to his mouth, a giggle at a private joke, and continuing to talk to him, she rose and left the room, closing the door behind her.

Fortified from the meal, he made better progress at sitting, and gathered he had been stripped naked and swaddled in his sheet—thankfully someone had cleaned the pillory filth from his hair and torso. He browsed the small room—no breeches, no tunic, nothing. *How did I get this way?* he wondered.

The door jamb popped and Dundle swung in on a blast of cool air.

"Awake a'last, Sorvie?" He wore a faded, blue jacket, generous around his waist and shoulders, a hand-me-down from someone much larger, and a scarred, stained leather apron tied high on his waist.

"Dun, where are we?"

"Saved! Farmer pulled us from the stocks. Paid our debt. Far as I ken, needs hands t'a work, no menfolk 'round."

"Have I been sick?"

"Ja, near gone t' Hel. Out nigh five days...." Dundle puckered to give Sorven his practiced compassionate gaze. "Warms me heart 'ere." He touched his chest, and continued, "to see ya sit n' speak."

"How?" Sorven motioned to his sheet and lack of clothing.

"Thank yer little nursemaid." Dun gave him a lopsided grin. "Cleaned, dressed n' tended, like a prize pullet."

"I can't, without pants..."

"I's fix, getting' good with the lingo." He winked and slipped back out of the room.

Sorven listened to a discussion beyond the door, a wispy voice answering Dundle, and titters of laughter—sounded like more than one girl. The door swung wide, and his nursemaid reentered, his clothing across her arms. Another maiden followed her, a bigger version of the first and an older woman with strong family resemblance—all three had chubby chins and rosy cheeks, hair chopped to high bangs on their foreheads, and the older girl had a full, womanly bosom, while childbearing had spread her mother's hips and padded her paunch. The young girl stepped forward and kneeling, presented Sorven with his cleaned tunic and pants, rips stitched and repaired. Commenting among themselves, the three left him to dress.

With a gulp, Sorven drew aside the sheet and pulled the breeches on in a swift move. He tied the rope belt, and standing, he used the wall to steady himself as he opened the door and stepped out of his makeshift hospital.

A massive hearth dominated the room, iron rods mounted to swing pots over the open flames, cast iron skillets and a cutlery set mounted in a wooden block hung over the mantle. The ceiling opened to the rafters, the roof thatch underside black with soot. Rugs, mostly skins and pelts, draped over the benches, and a rough, carved table sat square and solid in the center of the chamber. A few stuffed pillows close to the fire provided more comfortable seats.

Warming himself by the coals, an ancient man hunched on a padded stool, a rug pulled over his lap. A hunting dog stretched at his feet, drowsy in the heat. Dundle stood next to him and gestured at Sorven.

"Sorven." He moved his arm to indicate the old farmer. "Gethin." The old man wobbled his head in acknowledgment. The women settled Sorven on a bench at the table.

"Gethin save us'n the stocks. We're his 'til he says we can go." The old man peered at Sorven with one bleary eye, the other milky from a cataract. He moved his arm and Sorven recognized what he had mistaken for a shirt was creped, sagging skin—this Gethin had once been a big man, a huge man—sickness or age had leeched his strength and girth away, leaving him a shell of his former self. *That's where the baggy clothes on Dundle come from*, Sorven thought, *they would fall off the old man, so they have been passed along.* His hair and beard cropped short, Gethin had a wool cap in his lap. His hand quivered with palsy.

The old man muttered in Welsh.

"What?"

"Say yer a good boy."

The girls settled on the pouffes, pulling rugs over their laps, while their mother sat at the table across from Sorven.

"An' this 'ere is Heledd." Dun indicated the woman at the table with him.

"Heledd." Sorven repeated.

"Far's I tell, Heledd is wife two for ol' Gethin. Firs' wife dead n' gone. His boys kilt in a Saxon war, now jus' Gwenan." He pointed to each girl in turn. "an' Nia." When introduced, Gwenan blinked her eyes at him and Nia wiggled on her cushion. While the women prattled to each other, the old farmer turned to stare at the coals.

"Are we staying with them?"

"Na, we sleep n'a barn.' Dundle pointed to a darkened doorway. "They sleep back there, where ya were." The old man glowered at Sorven, mumbling words he could not understand. "Gethin wants ya in the barn, nows ya wake." Dundle crossed to the table and sat.

"These 'ere do the farm work. Old man don' lift no more." He pulled skins from the pile on the table.

"'ere, take this." He threw one around his shoulders, and bowed to the old man, speaking disjointed, single words. The old man gave him a curt and stiff bow.

"Come Sorvie, let's get some rest—we gots work a'morrow."

Unsteady, Sorven followed Dundle into the chilly night. Heledd wrapped herself in a skin and followed them out to the barn, and once they stepped into the barn, she bolted the door in place. Dundle called words to her, and she answered in kind—*probably good night*, Sorven thought. Barn smells, heady scents of manure, straw and fresh-sawn lumber and the odor of animals.

"'ere, step this'a way." Dundle reached for Sorven's hand and dragged him across a space to a hump of straw—shuffles and snorts revealed beasts housed in the shed with them. *The barn feels animal warm*, Sorven thought, settling into the fresh straw. Dundle pushed a blanket of the hay over him, insisting "keep ya warm all night." Tired by his minimal exertion and confused by the Welsh tongue and the strange farm folk, he swaddled the skin around his shoulders and drifted to sleep.

At dawn, Heledd came to release them and handed each a seed cake and a strip of jerky. She pointed to a rain barrel where a ladle hung from a string, and Dundle rushed to be first to drink. Taking a length of rope, the farmer's wife tied their legs together, a rough hobble to keep them from running away. Heledd directed them to the farm work with hand signals and claps to grab their attention. Sorven spent the day in silence, learning his chores and attempting to understand Welsh commands. Feed the hens, collect their eggs in a basket, muck an old nag's stall, milk the goats, slop the pigs, spread new hay for the sheep and water all the troughs—the work reminded him of home. His stamina waned by midmorning, and he sat and rested between jobs. Heledd understood, passing heavier chores to Dundle. Nia joined him in the afternoon, churning butter at the stoop and chattering at him as if he comprehended, and when the afternoon sun warmed the stone, farmhouse wall, old Gethin trundled out to sit on a stool. Gwenan sat at his side, carding wool with a wooden comb.

For most of the day Dundle worked to repair a stone wall—frost heave had toppled a section, rendering the field impractical for livestock, and the farmer had marked a new area of pasture to ring. By the afternoon Heledd worked beside him—he carried the heavy rocks and she set them in place, shifting and reseating the weight to steady the wall. They joked with each other—she laughed at Dundle and occasionally gave him a playful shove. Sorven could not understand a word.

In the evening, Heledd gave them a bucket of cold water to clean. Dundle washed his hands and wiped his face, Sorven dunked his head and let the water soak the smell of sick and sweat from his hair. The farmer invited them to sup at his table, brown bread, butter, porridge and goat milk cheese, and a slice of jerky. Plentiful if not flavorful, the food filled them, and if they brewed ale, they kept it hidden and unmentioned. Nia scootched along the bench next to Sorven, and Gwenan served, her mother and father first, turned to Dundle and Nia and finally Sorven. Gwenan made a point of sitting across from Dundle, smiling at him, batting her eyes. Blessed with sturdy appetites, the girls carried a running conversation through their mouthfuls, a banter including a few broken words from Dun and an occasional sentence from their mother, while their father sat morose through the meal, ignoring the exchange. Noticing the laborious way he chewed, Sorven gathered his mouth had barely a few remaining teeth. After the meal, they sat around the fire, the girls continuing their chatter while Gwenan spun her wool in a hand loom, Nia practiced embroidery and Heledd sewed. Dundle stirred the coal bed and Sorven found himself drowsing in the stifling heat thrown from the wide fireplace. Shaken awake, Heledd led him and Dundle back to the barn and bolted them in for another night. *At least,* Sorven thought, *we are warm and dry, not wandering on a snowy mountainside.*

The next day they rose to an identical schedule, and by the following day, Sorven found they settled into a routine—and, as time passed, days of farm labor blended one into the next, and Sorven found his strength returned. Steady meals, clean air and exercise helped him heal. After a week his health improved. As his strength returned, Heledd noticed and gave him more difficult chores and he resolved to dedicate himself to earning his keep. *It's true, we are thralls, but good food and a safe place to sleep, this life is better than living as an outlaw in a miserable forest.* Heledd grew lax about their hobbles, sometimes leaving the ropes off for a morning or afternoon.

Their language escaped him, learning tongues not his skill. He could recognize a few words and learned 'good night' and 'good morning' and 'please' and 'thank you.' The first time he thanked Nia for passing him a plate, she blushed and hid her eyes, her sister jumping in with a string of commentary drawing laughter from the entire table, including the old man, while leaving Sorven glancing from face-to-face in confusion. Later Dundle explained he had used the words correctly, but a familiar usage as between family or lovers. Mortified, Sorven decided to keep his attempts at the local dialect to himself until he knew it better.

Their third week on the farm, Heledd woke them before sunrise and immediately roped their ankles together, checking her knots to ensure all tied tight. She directed them to stand in front of the barn and tied the dog to a post in the yard. Up the hill came a pony carting a flatbed piled high with thatch straw. While the thatch monger lounged against his horse and watched, Heledd directed Sorven and Dundle to unload the bundles and stack them before the homestead. She paid the man from a finger-worn and greasy leather pouch.

As soon as the merchant departed, Heledd freed their legs and showed them ladders to set against the farmhouse. Inside the house they could hear the girls moving the furniture—they dragged the blankets and rugs out into the yard, making a neat stack, and moved the tables, benches and stools, and straw pallets. Sorven guessed they moved the household goods to protect them from straw dust, dirt and insects dislodged by the roof replacement. Heledd gathered her skirt between her legs and knotted it to climb the ladders and direct the roof repair. Sorven noticed no sign of the old farmer this morning.

While Gwenan and Nia unpacked the bedding and refilled it with fresh straw, Heledd directed Dundle to patches of the roof where a leak had sprung. She handed him a stubby hook knife, explaining carefully what she expected. Newly delivered bales replaced each of the old bundles—Dundle climbed the roof and cut loose big swatches of thatch, passing them to Sorven below. He stood under the eaves to catch the wads as they fell, dragging them aside. Hard work, Sorven found himself sweating and coughing in the mold flaking off the old bunches. A few of the bundles burst as they rolled from the roof, leaving Sorven with an unruly pile to manhandle from under their worksite. He shuffled it aside, arms and legs working to push the heap sideways. Working beside Dun, Heledd 'sewed' new thatch bundles in place with heavy twine and a long spike. The sun beat on them, the day growing hot.

Heledd called a break. Gwenan served them dippers of water—Sorven dripped with sweat, Dundle's face and arms dirt blackened, and Heledd not much cleaner. Sorven imagined he fared worse, as he stood underneath the old reeds when they dropped from the roof. Dundle helped him move the last new bundles under the eaves to stage the final repairs and Heledd climbed the ladder to inspect the work.

Heledd yelped—under her the ladder skidded loose and clattered to the ground. She grabbed a bundle of thatch and dangled off the edge of the roof, shouting for help. Gwenan shrieked and dropped her ladle.

Dundle and Sorven scrambled to aid Heledd, Dundle grabbing her kicking legs in an attempt to catch her, Sorven holding out his arms, unsure how to help. The stitching holding her bundle in place snapped, the straw shifted under her, and with a yip, she tumbled onto the waiting boys, landing hard on Dundle's chest with Sorven tangled underneath him. Dust puffed into the air.

Heledd struggled to her feet. Dundle coughed, sprawled on his backside.

"Is she hurt?" Sorven climbed to his knees. "Is she hurt?"

Gwenan rushed to embrace her mother. Sorven pulled Dun to his feet.

Heledd sighed heavily and turned to the boys. Seeing the cloud of dust and anxious faces peering at her, she chuckled and brushed at the dirt on their tunics. Her attempt to clear the dirt made puffs of dust, and she laughed at her own futile efforts. She quipped and pointed at Dundle, and her daughter joined in her laughter. She grabbed both boys in an arm and gave them a hug, spouting a string of words Sorven assumed were thanks for saving her from a broken neck. In her happy enthusiasm, she gave Dundle a kiss on his dirty cheek.

For the remainder of the afternoon, Heledd had her eldest hold the ladder before she climbed and as the final bundles were sewn in place, she called her youngest daughter. Gwenan had gotten grime in her hair and dirt on her arms and face, not as much as her mother and their farm hands, but enough—they all needed a bath. While Sorven and Dundle carried the rotten roofing to an outlying field for a bonfire, at their mother's direction Nia and Gwenan rigged two ropes from the house to fence posts, and hung blankets around a wooden tub, arranging a makeshift bath in the yard. The curtains hung from shoulder height to their knees. The two girls carried buckets from the rain barrels and filled the bathtub.

Returning from the field, Sorven and Dundle slumped by the barn, across the yard from the curtained tub, hot, tired, and filthy. Nia ran for fresh gowns as the women stripped and tossed their grimy dresses over the curtains. From their seat, they could see Heledd and Gwenan's shoulders over the top of the curtains.

Sorven brushed at the dirt on his tunic, worrying at the

grime under his nails until Dundle leaned close and whispered, "Do ya see?"

A breeze blew through the valley, rustling the drapes the girls had made. The blankets shifted in the wind and revealed glimpses of Heledd and her girls.

At home, women bathed in separate bathhouses and custom permitted no men near on bath day. Sorven had never seen fully unclothed women. His few tumbles with the Jorvik barmaid had never required undressing, mostly in dark corners where not much could have been seen.

Heledd bathed first, washing her hair, her youngest using a leather pitcher to pour the water over her head. And while the mother lathered, her daughters disrobed to take their turns in the tub. For modesty's sake, Sorven knew he should turn away... he found he couldn't—Heledd, unwrapped from her usual pinched homespun was... a revelation. Instead of expected rolls of pudge, she stood solid and smooth—he had not suspected her figure would be so... womanly! Next to her, the disrobed Gwenan emerged magnificent, her breasts round and full, her stomach flat in contrast to her mother's gut, her hips and legs firm and shapely. Nia stood helping them both, her tunic lowered to her waist, small breasts high and firm.

Sorven glanced at Dundle and watched him rearrange himself. They watched in silence, Sorven breathing shallowly and checking the door to the farmhouse, wondering where the old farmer hid. *What will he do if he catches us?* he wondered. As Gwenan climbed into the tub and her mother toweled her hair, Sorven forgot about the old man and became lost in the vision of the eldest daughter, chill water pouring over her hair, her face, coursing down her shoulders, her chest....

The girls pulled fresh gowns over their heads and gathered their dirty clothes into a pile by the door. Heledd walked to the blanket and called to Dun.

"Our turn, Sorvie." Dundle jumped to his feet and strolled to the tub. Sorven sheepishly followed, embarrassed by his reaction to the stolen glimpses. Dundle spoke to Heledd and related to Sorven, "Told'er we needs a change, these too dirty." He picked at his tunic.

Once behind the curtains, Dundle stripped. He dropped his dirty clothes in a pile and tugged off his boots. Sorven noticed spying on the girls had had a similar effect on Dundle. He didn't seem to be embarrassed. He splashed water to test the temperature and as he climbed in, Heledd popped her head above the makeshift screen, carrying a pile of towels and castoff clothing. She stepped to the roped blankets and peeked over the curtain.

Sorven gulped—Dundle didn't hide himself! She spoke a few Welsh words and passed the clean clothes over the ropes to Sorven.

"What did she say?"

Dundle fumbled for the chunk of soap and lathered his hair and arms. "Dinner, soon as we done."

Sorven waited his turn and quickly jumped into the tepid water. He rinsed the dirt off his arms, soaped his chest and between his legs, and squatted into the tub to wash off the suds. Dun handed him a towel and he dried a bit, preferring to dress rather than stand and dry in the evening air. His hair damp, he combed it with fingers, pulled a baggy jersey over his head and cinched a pair of voluminous leggings with a leather strap.

Before they dumped the tub, both dunked their boots in the soapy water and scrubbed the caked dirt away. Dundle left his boots on the doorstep. Sorven folded the blankets and untied the ropes before he entered the homestead.

Gethin crouched at the hearth in his usual place. Changing the roof had dislodged soot and dirt from the ceiling and support beams, and Nia had swept a pile next to the door. All furniture had been returned and reset in its original arrangement. Gwenan bustled about serving the evening meal on wooden plates. Sorven slipped quietly to his place. Nia sat next to him, her hair in two braids over her shoulders, each with an early summer flower at the tip. She smelled fresh, her skin glowing from the cold rubdown, her freckles more prominent across her nose.

As Dun moved to sit, Heledd held out her hand to stop him, and laying a gentle touch on his arm, spoke to her husband. The old man waved Nia into the back room. Sorven gave Dundle a questioning glance.

Dundle tipped his head, a glint in his eye. "Heledd names us heroes, bein' we catch her fall. Gethin sent Nia for a special drink. Saves it for festivals n'such." Gwenan brought out carved, wooden cups about one finger deep. A scrape sounded, and something heavy banged before Nia returned carrying an finger stained earthenware jug plugged with a rag. Gethin took the crock from his youngest and placed it within his reach on the tabletop. Bread passed from hand to hand, and each tucked into their supper, eating their fill after the long day on the roof. Sorven noticed Heledd had pulled her hair back with a thong, lifting it off her shoulders, her low-strung gown tied across her bosom with a velvet ribbon. Gwenan had also fixed her hair while they bathed, her single braid wrapped in a bun at the back of her head, her narrow waist accentuated with a wide embroidered belt to highlight her ample chest.

Gethin had Heledd hold each cup as he tilted the jug and poured a clear liquid in each, filling them to the brim. Gwenan and Nia set the cups before each guest, and the old farmer lifted his glass, offering a toast. Sorven had no idea what he said. When Dundle said, "Skal," he knew to drink. The brew burned his throat and Sorven choked, spilling the liquid on the table. The girls tittered and sipped theirs, while Dundle and Gethin gulped and held out their empty glass for another. The old man chuckled at Dun's enthusiasm, and Heledd stepped back from the table, sipping at her drink.

"Gods above, Dun." Sorven took another sip—this time it burned less, and a warm flower bloomed in his chest. "What is this?"

"No idea, but I like." Heledd helped refill their cups. The old man sucked his dry in a single quaff, prompted Dundle to do the same, and offered his empty cup for another round.

An impromptu party began. Sorven finished his first drink and set his wooden cup by Nia and Gwenan. Dundle nursed his second pour, and Gwenan nudged the empty cups across the table for a refill. Gwenan laughed and spoke to everyone, pointing at the drink—Sorven smiled at her as if he understood.

Heledd helped the old man pour another cupful for his daughters and Sorven, the old fellow becoming animated and laughing at Heledd, poking her in her side. He spoke entire sentences, more than Sorven had heard in all the weeks they had stayed at the farm. As Heledd moved past him, he gave her a pinch and raised a squeal, which triggered more giggles from the girls.

Gethin slurped another cupful and waved to Dundle to join him. Gregarious for the first time in weeks, the ancient farmer spoke to the room, waved his arms, and growled throaty laughter. Everyone joined him, including Sorven who had little idea what transpired. Dundle held out his cup for another refill. Heledd filled Dun's cup for a third time and refilled her husband's. Holding it above his head, she led him to his seat by the hearth, wrapping a rug across his lap and pressing his mug in his hand. Heledd spoke earnestly to Dundle and Sorven, waving her finger at each in admonishment. Next to Sorven, Nia giggled. Gwenan finished her second drink and stood to dance, singing tunelessly, and tugging first Dun to his feet followed by Sorven. The three stomped about the room, the old dog growling and shuffling nearer to the hearth. Heledd laughed along and clapped her hands in rhythm. The drink went right to Sorven's head—he remembered this feeling and knew too much would make him sick. He sat next to the tittering Nia and set aside his empty mug. Two servings were enough for him. Heledd joined Dundle and Gwenan in a circle dance, each bowing to each other and carefully holding their cups and the precious liquor.

The dancers stumbled to the table and Heledd poured them another round. Dundle sang an old Jorvik rowing song, loud and off key. *Probably the lone song for mixed company he can remember,* Sorven thought. By the fire, old Gethin had finished his fourth glassful and dozed, his eyes drooping. Sorven watched Dun and the two ladies hold a spirited argument, his broken Welsh making them both laugh. Heledd and her daughters grew flushed from the strong drink, cheeks like ripe berries and the tips of their ears beet red. Nia continued to twitter next to Sorven—she scooted right next to him and lightly touched his arm under the table. To his surprise, she held his left hand with her left under the table and with her right, pointed to the empty glasses and smiled at her mother. Slightly potty, Heledd tipped the jug and partially refilled both Sorven and Nia's cups. She pressed another cupful on Dundle and poured one for herself. Everyone spoke at once, Sorven talking in his native tongue and Nia following along as if she understood every word.

Gethin choked and snorted, surprising everyone into silence.

As they held their breath, he stuttered a long, guttural snore making the hound whimper. His sudden wheeze triggered gales of laughter from those at the table, and Heledd plopped next to Dundle, squeezing him between herself and her eldest daughter. They continued their long discussion with Dundle spouting an occasional word or phrase, triggering more laughter. Sorven sipped. Nia gulped her cup and pushed Sorven to drink his—he hesitated, his head spinning. The girl reached with her free hand and took his glass, swigging the remains and grinning at him, her eyelids droopy. Nia snuggled into Sorven, stroking her hand along his arm—she pulled his hand into her lap and pushed her face close to his. She wet her upper lip with the tip of her pink tongue.

Across the table, Heledd cleared her throat—she spoke to Dun and gazed at Sorven. While her countenance appeared jolly, at her words Nia slumped, protesting to her mother. Gwenan pouted silently at Dun's side. Sorven didn't need words to understand—Heledd called the night over for her daughters. Nia let go of his hand under the table and he pushed back on the bench. Standing too quickly, he nearly fainted and toppled forward, palms on the table. Dundle came to his rescue, wrapping his arm around his shoulder and the two propped each other standing. *Take a deep breath*, he cautioned himself. Nia and Gwenan hunched their shoulders and hung their heads, reluctantly moving to their room. They both glanced back at Sorven and Dun.

"Ya ready?" Dun grinned and gave him a squeeze. Heledd opened the door. They crossed the room in a rush, through the door, across the yard to their barn, the chill night air clearing their heads. Heledd followed them with arms full of blankets and stopped at the barn door, grabbing Dundle by the arm. She handed Sorven a rug and patted his head.

"Go inside, Sorvie, be right in," he mumbled. Heledd pulled his head to hers and spoke quietly.

Sorven stumbled to the haystack and burrowed in, the room reeling every time he shut his eyes. He lay there with his eyes open, staring at the rafters, worried sleep may bring that spinning drink sickness. He had fought hangovers before. Needing more air, he swam to the top of the pile and lay still, his eyes adjusting to the moonlight shining through slats in the walls. Lying quietly with his eyes on the ceiling helped. Deep breaths.

Dundle and Heledd whispered. The night grew quiet—an owl screeched, hunting on the mountainside.

Dun tiptoed in, the door closing softly, the bolt sliding into place. He listened to Dun spread his blanket over the pile of straw, jostling Sorven.

Dun settled on the pile.

"Sorvie," Dun whispered. "Ya awake?"

Sorven lay in the dark, comfortable on the soft hay, tipsy and not yet sleepy.

"Sorvie?"

As he opened his mouth to answer, a scratching at the door made him pause, and the bolt drew back, the barn door swinging open enough for a shape to slink out of the moonlight.

"Dun?" A woman's voice.

Heledd slid the heavy door closed.

The farmer's wife—like the bad joke his Uncle Karl told at Willa's wedding, an old chestnut told in taverns and around campfires.

Dundle and Heledd whispered for a moment, and his name in the jumble of syllables—again, Sorven didn't need words to understand Dundle insisted he slept. In the dim moonlight, he could see their shapes.

As he watched, Heledd grabbed at Dundle, pulling him into her arms with force. They kissed, hands roaming over each other. After a moment, she pushed him back, panting like a dog in the hot sun. She undid the ties at the neck of her gown, and it slipped to the ground, her pale skin glistening in the moonlight. Dundle sighed and kissed her again, her face, her chest. She tore at his loose clothes, pulling them off and casting them aside. They flowed as one to the hayrick.

Sorven lay rigid, listening to their noises. The haystack trembled. Heledd began to pant and mewl.

This is trouble, he thought. *This will not end well....*

KNETTI

Mud season.

Melting snow and fresh rain on last year's rotted leaves.

On the pony she had stolen, the ride took days to reach the high mountain pass. Forced to stop every few leagues to scrape mud and gravel from the pony's hooves, she detoured around partially frozen ponds. The nights remained cold and icy, she huddled under her rags and nestled into the animal for warmth. Despite her fingers and toes having healed, she suffered from aches in her joints and phantom pains in the lost digits. Knetti stooped in a hunch when she walked and knew the pony remained the solitary way she could reach her coven.

Holjan had magicked a beetle to guide her, an enamel-green creature with sharp, black mandibles. A tiny mare, she had kept the insect in a leather sack until the time to leave. She tied a thread to its carapace and let it fly in front of her mount. Once she left the tiny seaside village where Karl Alfenson had been installed as chieftain, she assumed the cape of a wandering volva, a Siedr witch available to bless flocks and households, newborns, and fields, and chase hidden folk from a barn or rafter. Her precautions unnecessary, not a single person crossed her path despite occasional muddy tracks indicating hunters recently passed.

The fluttering green bug led her to a narrow causeway between sharp cliff faces, a rushing alpine stream surging down its center—snowmelt released a torrent. The pony bucked and fought her, fearful of the narrow way, dangerous footing and raging water spilling over rapids. Tucking her scarf tight around her mouth and throat, she raised her crop and beat the beast, driving the hazardous course. Brush scratched their sides. Angry with the balking animal, she smacked and cursed it forward.

Topping the flue, Knetti pushed her pony through winter-denuded brush and scrub pines onto an alpine field.

Recently budded crocus purpled the swath of winter-grayed grass. Circled on all sides by craggy, snow-covered peaks, the bowl lifted the meadow too high for trees to root. The pasture rolled across the plateau and ended in a rocky crag. A wide curtain of ice, a frozen waterfall cloaked the far cliff face and sparkled in the setting sun. The stream bisected the field and terminated at the bottom of the frozen falls. Clouds of newly hatched gnats swarmed to her pony, and she grumbled as she shooed them from the beast's eyes.

A thin line of smoke lifted from near the base of the waterfall. Insistent, the beetle tugged on the string. Clicking her tongue, she urged the pony forward.

Holjan waited for her before a small tent. He stood wrapped in a seal-fur cape, with a matching cap and gloves keeping him warm. His owl perched on the peak tent pole, hunched and miserable in the bitter chill. On a spit over the campfire a rabbit roasted, the smell making Knetti's mouth water. By the flames, Rind sat on her haunches watching the pony meander across the green sward.

"Well met, trickster."

"Well met, son of Garm." She bowed to Rind. "Sister."

"Set the horse free."

"Plenty of grass and fresh water."

Knetti dismounted, careful to place her weight properly on her tender feet.

She hobbled to the warlock, and they embraced. Releasing him, she slowly eased into a squat next to Rind, holding her palms to warm by the coals.

"Holjan, the time to strike is now. The vardoger has been abandoned, and save for his guardian lindworm, there are none can stop us."

"The wyrm gives me pause."

"Three of us could overcome the beast. Poison me thinks, or a concentrated attack when the serpent sleeps... and then, to steal the boy's lich while his hug roams between realms, and torture...."

"Nay, my banner is called. Sulke, the king of Rogaland, and his brother Jarl Sote have declared against Harald the tangle-haired usurper, and we, pledged to their service, must rally to their cause. They expect my Siedr powers to aid their designs. Rind and I must travel south to answer their call."

"What of our revenge?" Knetti hissed and spat between spread fingers. "We must avenge the death of our sister..."

Holjan lifted his hand to quiet her. "We have a plan. Do you not recognize this place?"

Knetti glanced around. The setting sun reflected crimson from the tall, frozen waterfall, and she could see the immense span, a sheer icy face, milky and murky. She waved her hands in bewilderment.

"These are the Falls of Alufoss."

"Alufoss?" Knetti quirked her eyebrows in surprise. "Where Starkad the Jotun lies?"

"His grave, and yes, the very spot where the Lord of Thunder struck him down." Holjan pointed to the icy surface. "There, behind the ice wall lies the eight-armed giant slain by Thor."

"But... he's dead?"

Rind hissed from across the fire. "Can a Jotun ever die?"

Knetti paused, Holjan peering at her with a sly grin. "Dyr Nisse has given us the spell to wake him."

"Trust the Vanir."

"What is our plot?"

"We will work together to raise the giant from his slumber."

"You, trickster, will guide the Jotun to capture the vardoger's sleeping lich."

"And what of the dragon?"

"What lindworm can stand against the legendary Starkad the Old?"

"He will break the dragon into pieces and suck the marrow from its bones!"

Knetti worried her lower lip with her teeth. "And you are certain I can control the Jotun?"

"Dyr Nisse has sworn the one who calls the creature forth shall hold sway until dawn of the second day."

"And when control ends?"

"The dark elf says once the spell is broken, the Jotun will return to its rest. Here at Alufoss Falls, or on to Jotunheim, not clear."

Taking her dagger, Rind sliced from the haunch and offered it to Knetti.

"Eat and rest, tonight at moon rise we shall follow the prescriptions and raise the frost giant. We will chant, there, before the icy wall. While you prepare yourself, I will ready the spot."

Knetti and Rind chewed the greasy meat and watched Holjan move through the twilight. He gathered a sack from the tent, removed a hand sickle and cleared the grass from his chosen location before the sheer cliff face. On the ground he spread salt in cryptic symbols, marking the nine realms and the points of the compass. He chanted Siedr magic to open a conduit from Midgard to Vanaheim and draw on the source of their dark power. This preparation took hours, Rind feeding the flames to keep them warm, while Knetti ate her fill and rested in the fire warmth. Stars flickered in the night sky and Holjan called his witches to his side.

"Knetti, trickster dedicated to Loki, sit here, in the prime location. You shall form the words of power to call and control the giant." Taking her hand, he helped her settle in the correct spot. "I will tell you the words the dark elf entrusted to me—you only need to repeat them. Rind, you here, beside me." Holjan planted her behind Knetti, placing her hand on the witch's shoulder. "We will funnel strength through her, and as one we will call forth the Jotun."

The sky grew brighter as the moon crested over the mountains, its light creeping down the icefall towards them.

"Prepare yourselves, the time is nigh."

Her master's hand took firm hold of her other shoulder. He intoned a Siedr enchantment to join their strengths, Rind and Knetti joining his intonation. An electric prickle surged from the base of her spine, her hairs lifting on her neck and arms—she held her arms out over the mystic marks traced on the ground. As the moonlight reached them, the symbols glowed eerily, and Knetti sensed the flood as the channel to Vanaheim unsealed to pour magic through her. Her chest swelled with power, a heady rush. Her face split in a manic grin, and she hissed through her teeth. Behind her, she could hear Holjan whispering the spell.

She spoke the incantation as she had been taught, loud, clear, and with forceful intent. The thrill of Vanir Siedr poured through her, her hairs lifting from her head, sparks and crackles dancing at their tips. A strange wind whipped and howled, shuddering past and swirling as it gained momentum. As she spoke the final command, the wind slammed into the waterfall and the ice shattered, chunks careening into the pasture and splashing in the stream at its foot. The strange radiance lifted from the symbols before her and settled on her, a shimmering cloak that faded into her torso. Pitch black, a great slash stood open in the face of the frozen cliff.

A low rumbling voice echoed from the crack.

"Alfhildr...?"

A nudge from Holjan drew her attention and Knetti

turned to question him. His hair as well as Rind's had bleached a surprising white.

"Speak to him."

"Starkad! Tis I, Knetti of Loki. I have called you from your slumber."

"Where is Alfhildr?"

"Your elven princess is not here. Tis I, Knetti, call you forth."

A grumble. A snort and movement—the ground trembled as more ice sheared from the cliff face and tumbled to the plateau. The stench of rotting flesh flowed from the crypt in a wave.

The pasture grew silent and the three Siedr volva strained to listen. The voice from the darkness sighed, a long, deep rattle.

Knetti swallowed and called again.

"Starkad, I call you. You are mine."

"I hear...

"I obey."

CHAPTER 6
A VARDOGER IN THE SEELIE COURT

KARA

After the disaster on the road to Clondalkin, Kara and Kaelan snuck through the forest, parallel to the road to the fortress. Four others had survived the ambush. They caught them near the fortress gate, their arrival welcomed, the stronghold guard tired and spread thin by a lack of relief. The captain of the guard decided the six who survived must return to duty, considerably safer behind palisade walls than patrolling forest roads. Kaelan kept close to Kara the entire night, touching hands, and talking in hushed tones.

Kara couldn't have slept in any event—whenever she thought of holding him in the forest glade, her heart beat faster and her lips tingled from the lingering thought of his mouth on hers.

Kisses! Who knew they were so nice? Her thoughts swam with the idea of Kaelan, her 'Kay,' memorizing the curls at the ends of his hair, tracing the whorls in his ears. He persisted, happy to be by her side, and they sat watch all night, never joining in the complaints of the other soldiers manning the station. The way he stared at her made her happy, igniting a warm throb in her chest. When the morning sun lightened the skies, Kara sighed to herself, wishing the night with Kay would never end.

With the dawn, the captain rose and called a day crew to relieve the night watch. After a breakfast in a small, drafty hall, their leader directed each to their appropriate unwed barracks, where Kara found an unoccupied pallet, untied her armor and scabbard, rolled in a homespun blanket, and quickly fell asleep.

Woken after the noon bell, Kara stumbled from the darkened billet into a bright afternoon. Milling about the square facing the open gate, a large contingent of warriors had arrived from Dublinn led by Gunna. Tordis recognized Kara and waved her over.

"Heard ye danced with the Eire lads last night."

"Ja, we were surprised." Kara kept her eyes on her scuffed boots. "You told me true, they fight with madness and a stink of drink..."

"Glad ye survived yer first scuffle."

"What's going on?

"King Ausle wants more silver in his coffers. Gunna leads a slaving run."

"A slaving run...?"

"Aye, lassie, we march the Green Isle and pluck a few from their beds."

"Do you think..."

"Nay, Kara, yer assigned the guardhouse." Tordis gave her a playful poke. "Ye can't slip yer obligation so easy. Gunna takes the seasoned fighters on her run. That'd be me, a' course."

Kara relaxed her clenched fist and glanced around, scanning for Kay. Thanking Tordis, she moved through the crowd and checked in at the guard house. Kaelan met her at the door—they had been given assignments, he to patrol the walls, she to man the guard station at the main gate. They shared an evening meal together, surreptitiously touching hands on the tabletop, her leg against his on the bench.

Duties became a chore without Kaelan at her side. She occasionally glimpsed him marching past on his circle around the fortress walls. The night lingered unnaturally long, a collection of stifled yawns, stretching and pacing to stay awake. She fought the boredom by sharpening her sword, practicing parries and thrusts with other guards. Assignments swapped every few nights to not become routine, and the next night her patrol leader assigned her to walk the walls—not much excitement, save the garrison found a naked man with a bloodied nose complaining of ghosts, probably a drunk. A few nights passed in the same way, pining for the few off-duty hours when she could sit with Kaelan and hold his hand, and sometimes when no one watched, steal a kiss. In her thoughts Kara imagined the entire fortress conspired to keep them from being alone together—they separated for tasks, separated for guard duties, separated for sleep. *Oh, if only we could slip away, find a private spot.* She sighed and rubbed her damp palms against her smock.

On the fourth night in Clondalkin, after they had barred the gate, a loud clatter and calls for help sounded outside. Kara and her mates rushed to the paling wall, peeking out through spy holes, a guardsman climbing a ladder for better observation of the commotion.

"Tis Gunna. Let them in."

With drawn swords in hand, the guards unbarred the gate—Gunna and her warriors drove a group of disheveled women and children into the courtyard. Roped together, neck to neck, prisoners showed evidence of rough treatment, sporting bruises and bloody stained clothes. A few men thralls stumbled in next, their legs hobbled, and their hands tied behind their backs. Kara caught sight of Tordis, her sword unsheathed—as she watched, her friend encouraged one of the prisoners with a smack from the flat of her blade. The man scowled at her, dragging his foot—a dark stain oozed from his leg. Gunna led the remaining Dublinn force, a few with arms in makeshift slings, others with head bandages. Kara estimated more than a handful of Dublinn warriors did not return. Covered in mud and dried blood, the crew hurried their charges into the compound and rushed to bar the gate. Gunna, dragging her hand through her loose hair, marched directly through the bystanders and called for the guard captain. Finding the man in his cups, she pulled him into the guard house and slammed the door shut. The warriors collected the captives and shuffled them into a large barn, calling for fresh water and food.

Kara returned to her assigned duties, this night walking the perimeter inside the stake wall. On her rounds, she found Tordis waiting for her. Her hair wet from a recent wash, she carried a roasted chicken leg in one hand and a wooden mug of ale in the other.

"Fancy a bit o'company?"

"Sure." Kara sniffed. "This watch is dull as needle-binding."

The shieldmaiden chuckled. "Not much for girlie work meself."

"What happened on the sortie?"

"Fought like stone trolls, stupid Eire. We near had 'em surrounded and definitely outnumbered, but, crazy bastards, they threw children at us and fought to the death with their hands and nails. Most of the village succumbed in the battle. Gunna lost seven and four more are wounded. Puts her patrol down eleven hands, too short to continue the round-up."

"Continue?"

"Aye, lass, Ausle told her to bring back two score, and we are short twelve, or more if you count them young'uns as a half."

"Is that why she's angry?"

"Aye, and the fact she must raid this garrison for more hands. She and the captain never stand together—they're rivals, see? And she's not liking the idea of using ya greenhorns."

"Us?"

"Ja, Kara, she needs to replace her dead and wounded and nay risk a loss o' face by begging Dublinn for more warriors."

Kara tried to read Tordis's expression. "I suspect she remains in the garrison, conferring, making a deal." Her bite pulled a chunk of bird from the bone.

"Are you sure she wants to take us on a raid?"

Tordis mumbled through her mouthful, "Aye, old Gunna will take yer entire garrison and leave a skeleton crew to watch Clondalkin. Done it afore, she has."

"Is that safe?"

"Safe enough." She slurped her ale. "Most Eire leave Clondalkin alone. Ya best get lots of sleep when yer relieved —we head out after noon, and Gunna likes to march double step. Expect to put a few leagues behind us by nightfall."

Wishing her a good night, she urged Kara to continue her rounds. Wandering her circle, Kara wondered at what Tordis had shared with her—feasibly, and with luck she could prove herself sooner than she expected. But, risking her life to collect thralls... this was not the honorable service she had intended.

Relieved before sunrise, she ate a hurried breakfast, found Kaelan to warn him of their impending reassignment, and rushed to catch a nap—try as she might, she found sleep difficult, and tossed and turned until she finally dozed.

Someone banged on the door to the unwed women's barrack, waking the sleeping night watch. Bleary eyed, Kara stumbled to the courtyard with the other soldiers. Gunna had everyone stand in a line, the captain standing aside, face pinched in a frown.

"House guard of King Ausle. We have a need for... volunteers." Gunna sneered at the word and glanced at the captain who studied his boots and refused to raise his eyes. "We are going raiding, and we need to bolster our troop. A chance to make an extra coin or two. A chance to show me what you're made of." Gunna strode along the line of guards. "Who's with me?"

A few brash fellows stepped forward immediately—Kara glanced at Kaelan. He watched her, waiting for her to move—*should she step forward?* She wondered. Watching the line, she noticed Tordis, hands clasped behind her back, carefully measuring the volunteers. She winked at her.

Kara decided—she would go. She stepped forward, followed immediately by Kaelan. Gunna dipped her chin, a sharp note of approval, her face inscrutable. Sent to collect their weapons, shields, and armor, Kara helped Kaelan ready himself for a battle. She wrapped his arms in bunting and tied the padding in place. He had been loaned a sax sword, short and sharp pointed, and a small, buckler shield, battered and recently repainted to cover its scrapes and nicks. Once they completed his arm protection, he helped her lace her leather armor and fit Wolftongue on her back. As they mustered in the courtyard, a soldier handed each a rolled, homespun blanket tied with twine.

Tordis had told her true—Gunna expected a forced march at double time, and the squad headed west toward the village Cluain Dolcain, along the border of Southern Ui Neill and the lands of Lagin. Moderately safe, Mael Sechnaill, the King of Mide controlled these lands. As they marched, Kara learned this king had allied with the king of Dublinn and had sealed the deal with the hand of his daughter Muirgel. *Muirgel*, she thought, *the redhead she had spied in the wood in the embrace of a strange Eire man.*

The rushed march led the troop across the hills, skirted around thickets and brambles, and followed cow paths and meandering roads. Gunna, Tordis and the other seasoned veterans knew the way—Kara and the new recruits did their best to maintain the pace. As the sun set, Gunna called a halt and ordered a few small fires and a watch. As each warrior rolled out a rough homespun cloak for sleep, she made a round and explained the next day they would turn south into Lagin territory, contested by the King of Brega. Rich farmland, the hills about the road to Nas Na Rig offered small towns where they could collect the 'prisoners' Mac Ausle had commanded they procure. Kaelan moved to sit by her side, pulled his blanket over his lap and sat quietly staring into the campfire, his knee bouncing and his fingers fidgeting with the coarse weave—she could tell he concealed worries over this venture. She glanced around at their warriors—all together they numbered fifteen, eight veterans of previous excursions, and of those, two nursed slight wounds from encounters earlier in the week. She watched Gunna move from fire to fire, coaching the new guards and ensuring men stood watch while others slept. *She appears confident*, Kara thought, *she knows what she is doing.*

Shaken awake to stand her watch, Kara rubbed her eyes and pulled her father's sword from its sheath to stand ready. She stepped from the fire warmth, the chill helping her overcome drowsiness. Thin clouds striped the starry night, the moon high, a sliver headed to a new moon. Camped against a stand of shaggy pines, the fires had died low to smoldering ashy coals. A few glow worms glittered in the darkness and squeaking bats flit across the sky. She listened to birds begin their morning songs, a few close in the trees. As the sun rose, Gunna flipped dust from her blanket, clapped her hands and roused her crew.

An older warrior with a thick, pink scar across his nose handed each a meal of camp bread and smoked venison. His waterskin tasted musty, and Kaelan declined his offer of a second swig. The wood provided a convenient place to relieve themselves, and once the team gathered ready, Gunna counted off the double-time march again.

Marching at a brisk pace wore the soldiers quickly. A few muttered and complained. Kara kept to herself, Kaelan silent by her side. Gunna and the veterans kept to the grueling pace, and by the midday break, several of the new recruits collapsed to rub sore feet and check blisters. Tordis checked on Kara who reported all well.

By late afternoon, they crossed signs of habitation. Smoke lifted in the distance. A shepherd caught sight of them on the road and abandoned his goats to disappear in a vale where a thicket had choked its stream to a trickle.

Gunna decided not to chase the boy, instead turning southernly and moving off the roadway. She led her team to a hilltop overlooking a small town and its fields, surrounded on two sides by heavy forests thick with old hardwoods. The sun cast long tree shadows across the greenery.

"If we follow this hill to the north, we can stay out of sight until we reach the tree line." Gunna motioned with her hand. "We can slip through the wood undetected and attack at dusk, overcome any farmers and collect our bounty."

"We need to move now, while we have light to see our way." One of the Dublinn warriors pointed at the shadows stretching across the fields. Gunna agreed, clapping to send Tordis to arrange her troops. Tordis placed Kara with the scarred veteran and a group of the recruits.

"Jerrik here is a good fellow, despite his sour temper." She took Kara by her shoulder. "If there's trouble, stay close, he's reliable and will protect ya. I will keep yer boy, Kay, safe with me. Understand?"

"Ja." Kara watched Kaelan move along the line to his place behind Gunna and Tordis.

Jerrick grunted. "Ya lot follow me close. I ain't here to wipe yer noses nor carry yer weight. Come on."

The Dublinn raiders jockeyed for a better position and made a wide circle around the village, moving stealthily in the gloaming. Kara unsheathed her long sword and carried it across her chest. Around her other weapons sighed from their sheaths.

They reached the forest and spread among the trees, tall elms and crooked oaks with scrub pines striving in any open spot. Vines and brush made the course difficult, a few falling behind the others, sticks and brush snapping and cracking with their passage.

"Hush," Jerrik warned.

Gunna signaled for all to hold, Kara stopped, ducking under a heavy branch blocking her view. Creeping forward she saw cookfires and a peculiar group of men milling about a wattle-and-daub shed, probably a livestock cage. Well-dressed, she noticed they wore high leather boots, all identical. Horses trotted in the paddock where they stood, chargers not typical farm ponies. She counted more than ten men —and she noticed most wore swords buckled to their sides. A woman offered a dipper from a pail.

These are not villagers—Kara hissed at Jerrik and scrambled to his side. "Those are not farmers, they act like soldiers... see the swords?"

"Ja, girl, you've got a good eye." Jerrik grabbed a young man from the garrison. "Run and tell Gunna, we got a Bregan contingent. I thought we were in Mide... Ask her what she wants to do, attack or find a softer target?" The wide-eyed, young Dubliner scampered off through the brush. Jerrik motioned for his warriors to hide.

One of the men across the field purposefully strode their way—he fiddled with his belt, undoing his pants as he approached. Kara, like those around her, shuffled back into the mulch and underbrush. The Bregan rushed forward, his bowels demanding he squat as soon as he reached the edge of the wood, merely a few arms lengths from their hiding place.

Oh Freja, she thought, *what death did he eat?* Kara buried her face in the loam. One of the garrison novices stirred, rearing back from the sudden wave of stench. A stick snapped. Alerted, the Bregan jerked around to face the sound. With his breeches around his ankles, he tottered, trying to hold his awkward crouch while peering into the gathering gloom beneath the trees.

Someone moved. Surprise registered on the stooping man's face, and he jerked to his feet, holding his breeches with one hand, and scrabbling at his belt sheath with the other. The hidden warriors scrambled to their feet, exposing their positions. Jerrik called, "No!" Before he could stop them from overreacting, one of the green recruits jumped forward and ran a blade into the fellow's belly.

Mortally wounded, the Eire fighter toppled, gut ropes tumbling from his wound into his open hands. He screamed hysterically. Beside him the Dublinn guard stood, mouth agape, hesitating. Jerrik jumped forward and struck, cutting off the alarm, but the damage was done—the Bregans across the field ran towards them, drawing their swords and shouting.

"Get behind the trees," Jerrik warned his young charges. "Let them come to you."

Kara backed against a tall bole, watching the approaching force—she quickly glanced to her right, trying to see Kaelan and Tordis. She couldn't find them—did they rally to counterattack? Jerrik's team numbered six, and the force charging towards them numbered twelve, two on one, not good odds... and torches rounding the ramshackle buildings implied more headed their way. As she watched, Jerrik rolled out his bedding, wrapping the corner of the blanket around his left hand.

Shouting war cries, the men struck in a savage thrust into the forest. Runners met the ends of prepared swords while others drove their weapons into the Clondalkin force, three of her compatriots falling as the first wave rolled over them. Jerrik leaped from behind a tree, slashing into an assaulting warrior and severing a tendon in his leg. He countered a second attack and swirled his blanket over the head of a third fighter, following with a direct stab into the cloak, a body blow centered on the struggler.

A Bregan warrior jumped at Kara, his arms over his head wielding a two-fisted, downward swing. She ducked aside, his strike chopping deep into the tree trunk behind her, and as he pried the weapon loose, she stepped under his arm and opened his gut with a sideways swipe. Another warrior, a hulking man with bull-like shoulders, shambled across the fallen body of one of her comrades and bellowed at her. She parried his first blow—the power behind his strike numbed her arm. She ducked his second blow and countered, jabbing at his side. As quick as he was large, her opponent parried with a downward swipe. The forest rang with the clangs of metal against metal.

"Fall back!" Jerrik shouted.

A glance showed Jerrik nursed his sword arm, blood streaming its length. He fought defensively, his blanket lost in the scuffle. Before her, the big Irish warrior pulled a knife from his belt. Kara knew this tactic—with a weapon in each hand he could parry her sword and stab her from the other direction. She backed into the brush, and he pressed forward to corner her in the thicket. Around her the wood filled with Bregan fighters, chopping through the brush to surround her and Jerrik.

Someone must have struck her opponent from behind —his face went slack, his eyes rolled back and he collapsed to the ground before her. Not waiting to see who had helped her, she turned and nearly tripped over the body of another fallen enemy. Kara ran pell-mell into the forest. Batting aside sticks and branches, she stumbled and slashed at the brush with her long sword. Sounds of chase followed her, behind her and to each side, the lingering clatter of swordplay, shouts, and calls. A Bregan gave commands, clear, measured words—the crashing around her settled into a methodical search.

Kara ran until her chest burned. A dark wood at night ended in bruised shins, scratched cheeks, and a few solid raps to her forehead by low-hanging branches. Crumpling against a gnarly oak, she labored for her wind. Behind her, the hunt continued to sound, despite the distance she put between herself and her pursuers.

Calm, she told herself, *I must relax and think straight.*

She clasped her bedroll at her back—Jerrik had used his as a diversion, possibly such a ploy would work for her as well. She untied the roll, wrapped it around her left hand, and crept forward through the dark trees. The sounds of her pursuit grew fainter.

Glow worms and insects clouded around her. She pushed through the undergrowth and parting a curtain of vines, she found a glade with a strange hump of earth in its center. Not as dark as she expected, starlight and dim moonlight shined on the glen, and white flowers bloomed on the flanks of the hillock. Tiny flashes of lights followed the insects swirling about the clearing, and as she watched they formed patterns and shapes. The display mesmerized her, a dance with no purpose she understood. A swarm of the Eire night insects buzzed her, and she flipped her blanket loose and swung it around her head. Flipping the homespun like a net, she captured one—the buzzing creature pulled and tugged to escape, and Kara cinched the homespun tight and forced the bug into a bubble where it whirred angrily.

"Stop it." Kara chastised the captured fury and banged her catch against the ground.

An eerie silence fell over the glade.

All the hums and clicks stopped—alerted, she crouched

low, held her sword out in a ready stance and unwrapped her blanket.

As she undid the cloth, a glittering puff of sparkles dazzled her!

The unexpected flash momentarily blinded her, and she toppled from her haunches and landed on her seat.

In the center of the homespun lay a tiny shape.

A little, pink woman with wings like a butterfly.

She rubbed her eyes and checked again.

The little creature moved, shivered all over like a wet dog, and zipped into the starry night.

Kara sat dumbfounded.

She peered into darkness—*what was that?*

What sort of place is this?

The clearing remained ominously silent, and suddenly an uncomfortable prickling tickled the back of her neck—she was not alone. A peculiar feeling of being watched overcame her, her heart banged in her chest, she stumbled to her feet and backed slowly out of the glade, keeping her eyes on the open space, and waving her sword before her, wary of an attack.

Once she backed through the vine screen, Kara turned and ran, plunging through the brush to leave the strange glen behind her. She crashed through the wood like a wounded deer. Panting, she stopped and listened for pursuit. Hearing nothing, Kara crept through the forest, rounding impassable clumps of undergrowth and skirting ponds. She lost sense of time. As the sky lightened before the dawn, she stumbled upon a rough roadway slicing a pathway through the wood, and guessing at north based on the rising sun, she decided to take the road and make better time. Little more than muddy ruts through the turf, the country lane cut through the trees and shrubs, and made her path easier. She jogged, a regular pace like Gunna had forced them to keep. By the time the sun cleared the horizon, she found the way exited the trees and passed into familiar rolling, green hills. She hiked to the top of the first hillock and turned to the east. *This must be the way back to Dublinn,* she surmised, and ducking between the hills she continued her race back to Clondalkin.

THORFINN

After his first night in Eire, Finn decided he must watch over his sister Kara. Notwithstanding she chose to run away, he saw protecting her as his duty to his mother and family. The little village on the coast of the Northern Way remained dull and uninteresting, old Gudrun minding him every moment of the day, forcing him to eat all set before him, to practice his sword forms and recite the poems the skald had taught him, and of course, pushed him to go to bed early, the sole task he did not complain about or shirk. Each night as his vardoger arose from his lich, he took his bullrush, bid Raga and Goorm goodbye, and flew to Kara.

Assigned guard duties, Finn shadowed her around the Clondalkin fortress—she was safest in the garrison around other guards. This crew kept to themselves, a few shared simple convivial moments with her, a hunk of bread or a piece of dried fruit, a loan of a sharpening stone. To his dismay, little fairies flitted about wherever she ventured, and he shooed them continually.

As he prowled about learning the fortress and its defenses and spying on his sister, he discovered two men lurking in a corner of their common hall. One had a burn-scarred hand, and the other a shaggy, black beard and thick, bushy hair, putting his face and especially his eyes, in perpetual shadow. As Finn eaves-

dropped, he learned these two louts had been given coin and promised more by someone called 'Asta.' Hired to hurt or disable Kara, break a leg or arm, these two ruffians carefully measured her. They whispered about a time when she would be alone and an easy target. Finn stood next to them and listened to their crude jokes. They stealthily watched her from their corner. Obvious to Finn, they openly discussed evil deeds, yet his sister remained naively unaware, all moony eyes for her friend Kaelan. He tried to gain her attention, stooping to drawing in the spilled ale on her tabletop, a single arrow to point at the conspirators— nothing worked, she only had eyes for the boy. Exasperated with her infatuation, he became more determined to stay by her side.

The following night the captain assigned Kara the wall watch, spelling Kaelan to sit in the garrison with the other guards. As Kara prepared to join the watch, Finn sauntered over to the two men waiting in the shadows of the hall. They had learned of her new assignment. Thugs, the two hired henchmen feared for their own safety if caught attacking the king's guard. They had searched the town until they found a secluded place, a narrow alley connected with the path the watch followed, an isolated corner where they could set a trap and be assured none would overhear.

Buying an extra horn of ale to fortify their resolve, after a deep swig the two drew hoods over their heads and snuck through the alleys to their ambush site. Finn trailed them, listening to their murmurs.

Armed with wooden clubs, they planned to take Kara from behind, knock her senseless and break a knee or an elbow, having decided a joint would take longer to heal. The burned man made a rude remark about his sister's pretty face, a crude comment about her figure and suggested they should deflower her while they held her.

Deflower my sister? Finn drew Gunhild his magicked sword

and struck the speaker—his attack from the Realm Between did not kill opponents in Midgard, merely caused them to seize and contort in a painful fit. The shaggy-haired fellow bent over his prone companion, shaking him.

"What are you doing? What's come over you?"

Finn gave the hairy one a poke and he tumbled on his mate, shaking with ague.

Kara paced past on her rounds, unaware of the two unconscious in the darkened alley. As he watched her march past, a few of the delicate fae creatures floated along in her wake... now, how had those things found her on her rounds?

Acting upon the physical world from between realms with difficulty, Finn dedicated his efforts and spent the next few hours carefully using the shard of his broken sword that existed in Midgard to slice through the would-be attackers' clothing, leaving them naked with a pile of rags, barely enough to cover themselves. Intent on her duties, Kara marched past their hideaway a few times. As the two men rose from their stupor, they shivered in the night chill, baffled and cross—they grabbed their tattered clothing and ran. Finn tailed them to find their roost, a squalid shanty a few, narrow lanes away. Reaching their door, Finn tripped the burned one with Gunhild's hilt. He smacked his nose on the doorjamb, landed on his back, and whimpered in the dark. The hairy brute stooped over him, trying to help him sit, and Finn decided to give him another dose of Gunhild from the Realm Between, and the hoodlum pitched forward onto his companion, rigid and shuddering. The burned fellow dropped his ruined clothes, climbed from beneath the other fellow, pushed open the door and stooped to drag his fellow inside—Finn shut the door before they crossed the threshold.

Muttering a curse, the man let his friend drop and checked the door carefully, opened it slowly and turned to retrieve his cohort.

Finn shut the door.

The thug rolled his companion aside and slinked carefully to the door, examining the wood in the dim light. He stretched his fingers along the barricade, slid the bar and opened it slowly, holding his hand out in case the door swung back. Convinced it would stay open, he bent and gripped his friend's armpits.

Finn shut the door again.

Fear does funny things to men—all the beer he had drank before they set off to hurt Kara released in a torrent, dowsing his companion beneath him. His face blanched visibly, and he turned and ran as fast as he could muster, his naked bum the last Finn saw as he disappeared around a corner. Finn used Gunhild to scrape aside the pile of tattered clothes, leaving the hairy man naked and exposed. He expected the morning would find him lying listless and prone. Finn wandered the sleeping town and found his sister on her rounds. With a shout, he chased the pestering fairies floating behind her. The night neared its end, dawn pinking the horizon, and he decided Kara would be safe enough on her own—he returned to his hidden bullrush and flew to his own bed.

Upon arriving the next evening, he found the two brutes had fled the fortress town. Kara spent the next few nights manning the garrison or walking the watch. Each night he warned and chased the fae creatures flocking to her—her feelings for the boy Kaelan, he thought, the elf told me love would draw them like bees to honey. Watching her became a chore, each dull night a repeat of the last. At least no recurrence of 'Asta' and her henchmen occurred.

Less than a week passed and Thorfinn arrived to find his sister camped under the stars, Kaelan at her side. He listened to the soldiers talking, meandering his way through each cluster of resting warriors, gleaning bits of their scheme—they marched on a mission to capture slaves for the King—the elder soldiers talked about enemies on all sides.

Finn considered his sister—he could tell she worried about something, the way she arranged and re-arranged her blanket, the way she chewed her bottom lip, her little jump at any noise in the dark, the way she kept her hand near Father's sword hilt, her fingers twitching. Tapped for watch duty midway through the night, he walked alongside her as she patrolled the area, inspected the dark stand of trees at their backs, and squatted by the coals of dying campfires. Finn decided if Kara worried about this trip, he should be extra watchful. Apprehensive about the next day, he wondered how to offer protection should his sister be drawn into a battle while he flew far away. As the sun tinted the eastern sky, knowing well she could not feel him, he touched her hand, took his leave, and sailed back to his sleeping lich.

The next evening, he landed amid a battle. Strange warriors charged a defensive line. Too many attackers! And more rounded a paddock at the end of a nearby village, torches held high. He stumbled through the combatants—Kara! Where was Kara?

After a panicked search, he found her. She had backed into a wood, her sword drawn, her back pressed against a tree. Smaller than her fellows, she loomed less threatening, her pale face shining in the gloom. Her companions scattered in the brush, separate and easy targets. Dropping his bullrush, Finn ran to his sister and drew his sax sword.

Kara parried blows, fighting a direct assault. Finn saw the attackers circle the Dublinn force, surrounding them. Battle noise masked their movements, and one grinned as he snuck behind her—he never saw the vardoger in his way, and Finn laid him out with a quick stab from Gunhild.

Someone shouted for retreat. A great brute of a man hammered at his sister, overwhelming her with his sheer size and weight. Finn rushed past Kara and struck the warrior, leaving him to collapse in a heap. Kara did not pause to investigate her luck; she turned and ran into the forest, chopping at low-hanging branches with her sword. A nearby opponent saw her and moved to chase—Finn collided with his headlong rush and Gunhild paralyzed him.

Thorfinn trailed Kara, mindful of her pursuers, pausing occasionally to turn those who gained on her into a quivering mess in the undergrowth. Much to his disappointment, the wood filled with those little flying pixies and fairies, choking the air in the Realm Between. Soon he had to swat at them to keep them from swarming his sister.

His sister slowed her reckless run through the dense foliage, tired of collecting scratches and bruises on her face, upper arms and calves. Kara untied her bed roll and loosened the blanket, gripping it in her left fist like a fighting net. The homespun snagged on the brambles underfoot, and she jerked and tore it free as she continued to push through the wood. Her hunters fell behind. She moved at a more measured pace and worked to control her breathing. Finn walked at her side. Her flushed cheeks showed exhaustion, and other than cuts and welts, he could find no lasting wounds on her unprotected legs and arms. Her leather armor appeared intact. Relieved, he stopped wringing his hands.

Kara pushed through a curtain of vines and stumbled into a clearing. Finn knew at once they tread in a magical place, no place for his sister to wander. He tried to push her. He tugged at her arm to no avail. She moved forward into the glade.

Finn wasn't certain what Kara saw... here in the Realm Between Realms, this dell hung festooned with hidden folk, in the air, on the ground, and lined on each branch overhead. Glowing, glittering, sparkling, like the parade he had witnessed, fae creatures of different shapes and sizes collected around a central dais built upon a hump of dirt. On the throne a beautiful, elven woman lounged, three tall warrior elves standing behind her, brandishing ornate spears and pointing them threateningly at Kara and Finn. Their platinum hair shone with golden highlights, and their skin reflected a rich, yellow tinge, their silver breastplates worked with golden filigree, their tall helms gracefully tipped with a topknot horsehair mane.

The air filled with winged fairies, as if disturbed dandelion fluff puffed into a swirling breeze. One of the Alfheim guards stepped forward and grumbled, pointing his spear at Thorfinn. "Who are you to interrupt the Seelie Court?"

Glancing around, Thorfinn realized a phalanx of light elves ringed the glade. All turned to stare at him and his sister, who unknowingly continued to stumble forward, creatures before her in a mad scramble to climb from underfoot. The assembled elves knelt before the lady on the throne—unsure, Finn dropped to one knee and bowed his head.

"Forgive us, we did not mean...."

Finn raised his eyes. In Midgard, his sister batted at the creatures swarming her head. Her blows missed the dancing creatures, and on all sides, little twitters of laughter sounded, her angry movement so ungainly and predictable. The Fae found her struggles funny.

The elf on the throne seemed to flow into a sitting position and stretched out her hand in a graceful movement. "A fyreferd," she said, and gestured with elegant fingers at Thorfinn. "Such a thing, to find here in my court."

One of her guards spoke, "True, majesty, we have not seen a vardoger for centuries of seasons...." He waved his spear at Thorfinn. "Why trespass on the Alfheim?"

"I protect my sister." Finn gestured at Kara. Frustrated with the fairies dancing about her head, she began to swing her blanket like a sling—the little creatures thought her actions a

new game, swooping in and around the swirling homespun, their laughter like chimes in the night.

The elven woman spoke, her voice a clear alto cutting through the tinkling laughter. "They smell her elsk, she reeks of love sickness."

With an unexpected snap, Kara flipped her bedroll and captured one of the tiny, hidden folk. She grabbed the loose fabric and tightened her grip. Inside, the little fairy squeaked and thrashed, fighting to escape.

"Stop it!" Kara demanded and smacked her blanket against the ground.

A sudden silence fell over the multitude, most frozen, mouths ajar. The creatures watched Kara, while a few glanced to their elven leader. Finn watched her slowly rise from her seat, her mouth compressed into a severe line, her eyes squinting.

Unaware of the situation beyond Midgard, Kara unwrapped her tiny captive—a glittering puff erupted from her cloth, and Kara stood astounded as she caught a glimpse of the creature lying in her open hand. Finn held his breath—all around Kara the hidden folk buzzed in anger.

With a shudder, the tiny fairy shook itself and shot into the night.

Relief sighed from all sides—Finn watched Kara blink at the creature receding into the starry sky, her mouth agape. Her face paled, and she jerked her head from side to side, suddenly wary and confused. Finn stumbled to rise to his feet, and one of the guards leveled his spear at him, his intent clear. He watched his frightened sister crash through the vines and underbrush, disappearing into the forest.

One of the guards stepped forward. "Bow to our queen." Finn dropped his eyes.

"Please, I must..." Thorfinn pleaded, his eyes on the grass.

"Hush, fyreferd." He peeped at her—Standing on her

mound before her throne, the Elven queen stood taller than the assembly, her hair drifting from her shoulders as she gathered Siedr magic. Like a halo, her golden-white mane crackled with arcane energy. She held out her finger, and the broken fairy dropped from the sky to perch there, its wings twisted and drooping. She gently blew on the tiny Fae, and it glowed red like breath across hot coals. The miniature creature straightened and unfurled gossamer wings. She cast the pixie back into the air to flutter into the trees.

"My sister..."

"Your sister is not your true concern, ghostling."

Around him, the crowd of hidden folk gathered closer. The Alfheim had risen around him, tall, slender, and graceful. While none moved to hold him, he knew they held him trapped. He had fought an elf once... a dark Vanir, similar to these in stature. He remembered how the elf had fought him, so quick and strong... there are so many, he thought. Raga warned me, if I die in the Realm Between, I can never return to my lich... he suppressed a shiver as a multitude of creatures surrounded him.

The queen settled on her throne, her guards moving to posts behind her. Her hair floated back to her shoulders, her charm dissipating. She regained composure, the angry squint fading from her eyes and a slight smile lifting the corners of her mouth.

"Fyreferd, you ward and protect family." She lifted her hand to quiet the throng. "A noble trait among your kind. Not so common, as I recall." Elves around whispered in agreement. "I commune each night with the Norns, the Jotun maidens of Mogprasir, Wyrd, Verdandi and Skuld. Their whispers hint of past, present, and future. All mentioned our paths shall cross, the ghostling who carries the remnants of great sax Gunhild. I see her there at your side. Fear you should, oh child of Midgard, yet, like a hunter's arrow flung into the sea, your dread misses wide its true target."

Thorfinn knelt, confused by her words. My fear misses a true target? He scowled—what could she mean?

"You may depart my presence, vardoger." The Fairy Queen snapped her fingers in a dismissive way. *"We, the Seelie Court of Eire shall not molest you, nor your naïve sibling. Be on your way but carry my warning: You protect the wrong lich this night."*

Relieved, Thorfinn gave an uncertain bow and stumbled to his feet, dashing through the wood to catch his sister. Behind him, he could hear the elves speaking... he ignored their voices and rushed through the trees, following the path he thought his sister had taken. The hilt of his sword, the part of the magicked blade existing in Midgard, caught on twigs and bushes as he forced his way through the underbrush.

He had to find Kara. He had to protect her, alone and lost in enemy territory. And he remembered he had lost his bullrush—he would need another to return home.

Searching took nearly an hour to find her. She surrendered any attempt at passing silently, rushing headlong through the trees. Branches had scratched her face in the dark and he could see her hand bled from a cut. She kept glancing over her shoulder and gripped Father's sword tight to her body. Finn pressed close and remained at her side, comfortable to be near in case anything went wrong. As the predawn faded the stars from the sky above, they stumbled across a roadway through the wood, a path rutted by wagon wheels and horse hooves. Kara ran at a steady pace, and Finn, after following for a while, spotted a marshy wash with cattails and reeds. Leaving his sister to jog away, he searched the pond edge for a bullrush suitable for the Siedr magic to carry him back to his body, sleeping far to the north. With a cutting in hand, he muttered the spell and soared into the early morning sky.

Late, much later than he typically returned home, Finn had tarried too long, watching over his sister. As he flew over the rollicking ocean and the rising sun topped the horizon, his thoughts scattered, light-headed, and a funny pang hollowed out his stomach. His sight darkened, his vision constricted as if he fainted. Suddenly weak, he clung to the reed as it soared through the clouds. He sobbed, his chest heaved, his thoughts became muddled, and he drifted into a deep slumber, the first time he had slept since the witch had torn his hug from his lich and changed him to a vardoger.

RAGA

The night began like any other. After an afternoon of arguments with Finn and the old man, Signy had angrily stomped off to the home of her uncle—she sought the company of her women, and I suspected she was with child. Her departure had been a good development for our peace of mind, as she lorded haughty over Thorfinn and Gudrun as if they were her personal servants.

Worried over his wayward sister, my apprentice, Thorfinn, forced himself to bed late in the afternoon, before the sun had sunk beyond the western sea. Once risen as a vardoger ghost he gathered his broken sword hilt, and bidding farewell to me and the worm, he jumped a ready rush and flew south into the dusk. He had been hurrying to the Isle of Eire for nigh on a week now, returning with tales of how he found his runaway sister and protected her from treachery in Midgard and tricksy fae folk in the Realm Between.

With Karl's young bride absent, I hoped for a quiet night, yet soon after the boy slipped away, his hulking lindworm pet moped about his barn, chafing in his hiding spot, moaning and hissing and knocking the walls with his tail. Lonely and feeling forsaken, the wyrm had not understood Thorfinn's comforting explanations, and it nursed a foul mood, angry to be abandoned once again for a dull and dreary night cooped inside the tight confines of the old horse shed. A confused Gudrun, the last remaining sailor left to guard the boy, hurried from the longhouse with a burlap bag of fresh fish, hoping to quiet the surly beast—the dragon sniffed the bag, turned its nose, and rolled into a tight ball of scales, tucking its head in a crook and hiding its eyes.

A warm wind gusted from the western sea. In the gloaming, the farmers leaving their fieldwork led mud-splattered nags to wash them on the shore. The local fishermen had dragged their flat skiffs from winter storage to ply the waves each morning, dragging netfuls of herring and whitefish back to the short wharf on the bay. With the close of day, they had strung their nets over poles to dry, festooning the small village in a stretch of faintly odorous curtains covering the dockside and hanging from eaves. With Karl and his crew's departure, village life had returned to its routines, at a slower pace as a few of the ablest men joined their lord Hamund to fight in the coming conflict.

Gudrun returned to the empty hall, the shutters propped wide to let in the cool of the night. He checked the sleeping boy, his responsibility to Karl, and poured the fish into a kettle. He tossed a smaller herring to my mare, the raven happy to pick at the morsel on the table near him—the old man chats at the bird, his solitary companion, not realizing I do not ride the mare at night as it rests. Here in the Realm Between Realms, I sat on the bench across from him and listened to his nightly monologue, a collection of superstitions, legends, and snatches of history, much befuddled in the telling or scrambled in his memories. How the giants Fenja and Menja were forced by King Mysing to grind out salt in their magicked hand quern until the salt overwhelmed the sea, how Karl had his fate foretold by a seer on a wayward isle, how Thor and his mighty hammer defeated unruly Jotun time and time again, each story grander in its retelling. As I listened each night, these tales differed, sometimes diverging significantly from the versions recited to Thorfinn by the skald Jormander. The poet remained a more reputable and reliable source than crusty Gudrun, yet, with little else to entertain us, Thorfinn and I had grown accustomed to the old fellow's rambling tales, a veritable font of expertise when explaining the huldre, the hidden folk all around us in the Realm Between. After all, he was the sailor who called a mast troll from the deep to protect and serve Karl and their snekke longship. Wyselhax of the 'Verdandi Smiles' had been a boon companion and protector —I must admit I miss the ruddy kobold, a great font of arcane knowledge and grand conversationalist. The troll had sailed south with Karl and his crew to support their commitment to this Tanglehair and his wars.

Using a bone needle and twine, Gudrun strung fish from their heads as he chattered at my bird. He tied the twine to the barnstoker post next to the fire pit and strung the fish to smoke. The pot he set on the flames to boil and added millet to make a porridge. My raven mare found the operation fascinating and hopped from side to side on the tabletop to watch him prepare the meal for the morrow. The village grew calm, tired laborers falling asleep to wake before dawn and begin their routine again. Finishing his chores, Gudrun stooped to wrap the boy in a blanket, stretched and yawned, and puttered about to ready his own bedroll.

A dull night, with no boy to swap tales and teach magic spells. Centuries ago, when I lived a favored counsel in Constantinople, I never considered my life would degenerate to babysitting a sleeping child on a far-flung, northern coast. Of course, that was long before a dark elf tricked me to Vanaheim where time flowed so differently, where, as the Vanir taught me enchantments and incantations, my real body in the physical world withered, abandoned and cast adrift.

Leaving my raven roosting on the rafters and Gudrun dowsing the torches in the hall, I leaped to the roof peak and settled to watch the night sky—the wide star course overhead calmed my jangled, lonely spirit. Rhythmic surf crashed against the shore. A half-moon rose, dimming the stars and lighting the night. I could see the tilled fields and the nets strung over the village, the low sea wall, and the moonlit bay. A wayward spark scored the heavens, a shooting star drew my eye to the east... and I saw a movement.

Across the newly plowed fields, an outlandish colossus drew near. At first, I discerned a shadow against the sky, a smudge lumbering across the pasture. Tall, taller than the mast upon a ship, the black silhouette loomed a disorderly contortion—I could not ken its shape—could it be more than one approached? Too many arms, difficult to count. The shadow plodded forward, gaining in size as it neared, and as far as I could tell, this creature stalked the lands of Midgard.

What could this be? I decided to ask Gudrun—I dropped through the shingles and took control of my sleeping raven, shaking its wings awake. Riding my mare, I glided from my perch and landed on Gudrun's chest. The old sailor had begun to drift off to sleep and my sudden appearance surprised him. He jerked and sputtered.

"What is it, Raga?" *I clicked and tapped him with my beak, pointing at the door with a single wing. Yawning, the old man climbed out of his bed, wrapping a blanket over his shoulders, his bare legs exposed beneath his bed shirt.* "What are you bothering me for?"

I pecked his ear and flew to the door. He tottered forward, unbarred the door, and stepped into the night air, me astride his shoulder.

Gudrun stepped into the courtyard and cast his eyes left and right at ground level. He grunted and muttered, "Crazy bird."

He did not notice the shape had drawn close, hovering over the shed roofs on the short street to the dock. I used a wing to lift his chin... and he gasped as he saw the monster. For a moment he stood paralyzed, watching the shape step near.

Moonlight illuminated the creature as it closed the distance between us. I had seen Jotun before, passing through the Realm Between... entirely different, this giant stalked Midgard. Hulking over the buildings, the giant lifted a bundle from its shoulders and placed it behind the buildings where we could not see. Freed of its burden, I counted eight arms before Gudrun grabbed me and hopped back inside the longhouse, barring the door behind us. He stood with his back to the door, trembling.

I squawked at Gudrun and poked him with my mare's bill to wake the poor fellow from his stupor, and he shuffled forward in the dim light, glancing side to side and mumbling. What is this beast? I thought. I cawed at him, twisting my head to indicate a query.

"Odin protect us." *He moaned.* "Tis the giant Starkad."

Starkad? I pecked him to prompt his tongue.

"The eight-armed Jotun who stole the Alfheim princess." *The old man rushed through the darkened room, found Thorfinn asleep in his pallet and gathered the boy in his arms.* "Her father begged Thor to save her...." *Gudrun poked the sleeping boy, but I knew his efforts would have no impact as the boy's hug traveled to distant lands in the astral plane. There would be no waking Thorfinn. In a hoarse whisper, Gudrun continued,* "The god of storms caught them in Midgard and drove Starkad far north where he struck him with his mighty hammer Mjolnir...."

An eight-armed giant? Why pass this way? Surely this Jotun had no need for us? I directed my mare to the rafters as Gudrun carried the boy to Karl's empty chamber at the end of the hall.

Leaving my raven disturbed and perplexed on a beam, I darted through the front walls to observe the strange creature pass by.

Dismayed to find the ogre did not move past the insignificant village, I watched as the monster towered over the courtyard before our longhouse, his legs draped in and dragging the loose nets and drying poles—I could no longer assume this was a random event, for the great beast peered at our longhouse rooftop, its hands alternatively clenching and unclenching, forming fists. A noxious odor of rotten flesh assaulted me—rank, the smell had to be overwhelmingly potent in Midgard. A shambling horror, its eyes stared milky and white, bits of rotted flesh hung from its battered jaw, and its fish-belly hide blotched with bruises. From a corner beyond my sight, a whisper and a cackling laugh arose—the Jotun reached forward, gripped the roof peak, and wrenched a great chunk of wood free with four of its arms. The giant punched with its free hands, shattering planks to kindling. Support beams squealed and snapped, and the hall shuddered. Wading forward, the giant demolished the façade.

A voice commanded, "Forward Starkad, forward." A woman, her voice cracking with phlegm.

In the shadows of the village street, I caught sight of a hunched shape, an old crone I moved closer and moonlight lit her face, I could make out her features, her hooked nose and wild, gray hair.

Her! Aged and more decrepit than last I saw her, I recognized the woman from Hamund's hall, the witch we had defeated when Thorfinn released Allinor from her trap. This vengeful volva controlled this undead creature and ignoring the clumsy giant dismantling the hall behind me, I ran to attack her.

Too late, I comprehended this coordinated attack had been well planned. As I flung myself at the enchantress, she flipped her hand and scattered black dust in the air, and to my dismay this powder held a potent Siedr charm that reached across the Realm

Between and struck my ghost like thousands of hornets, burning and biting into me. I fell at her feet writhing in pain.

"Foolish specter! I have waited for this moment—you shall underestimate me no more." *She leered at me, her eyes smeared with a salve, a hexed ointment to allow her to see into the Realm Between Realms—this is how she easily disarmed me, she could see my approach!*

But she could not hold my voice!

"Goorm! Goorm, to Thorfinn!" *I shouted, knowing the dragon would hear me across realms. Standing above my prone shape, the volva continued to press her Jotun to the attack.* "Goorm, come to our aid!"

Wakened by the noise and hearing my pleas, Goorm snapped the bar holding the barn closed and slithered into the courtyard. I shouted at the beast—"The witch, the witch!" The great lindworm saw the giant first and perceiving the ogre comprised the main danger, it attacked. An immobile spectator cast aside, I watched the clash unfold.

The measure of the dragon matched the height of the giant. The wyrm slithered up the giant's leg like a snake, curling and wrapping about its torso and sinking its teeth into one of the creature's arms. Crushing sections of the roof with its uppermost limbs, the Jotun grabbed the dragon by its neck frills with its lower hands and pulled the lindworm from its side. Teeth and claws rent the beast, and a counter strike to its head knocked the wyrm loose, and three arms scrabbled along the dragon's squirming body to clasp at its throat. Goorm snarled and flapped its wings, buffeting the great troll about the chest and face. Using its two fore claws, the lindworm carved deep slashes into the belly and thighs of the giant.

While the Jotun fought the dragon fury, the monster continued to wade and smash its way through the longhouse, the roof collapsing with a tumble and a spout of sparks from the hearth. The witch standing over me continued to chant and call to Starkad, pressing him to find the boy. Laying helpless at her feet I grasped her goal, to steal young Thorfinn's lich! With his body in her possession, she held revenge in her palms. I thrashed against the stinging furies immobilizing me.

My raven mare escaped the hall ruins, winging into the night. Climbing through the wreckage, Gudrun charged the troll brandishing his sword in a brave attack. He struck the giant in its leg, slicing deep through muscle and sinew. As he hacked and chopped at the stony jotun flesh, the monster let go of the dragon with one hand and swung at the old sailor the way one shoos a nuisance fly. Gudrun tumbled aside, flipped head over heels into the debris.

Distracted, the giant let Goorm slip in his grasp, and the wily lindworm snapped on an elbow, his clamping jaw severing the limb at the joint. The dead, white arm tumbled into the rubble of the destroyed hall, while viscous, black sludge drooled from the wound. A momentary victory in the melee, the jotun turned from the longhouse and used its seven remaining arms to clasp and tussle with the wiggling wyrm. Sliding along Goorm's sides, the rotting creature pulled the dragon free and thrashed it. Like a dog with a rat, the hulk slammed the worm against the rubble, smacked it on the ground, and whirling the dragon over its head, it smashed Goorm against the barn, collapsing the building with the force of the blow. The lindworm fell limp in the giant's hands.

Swinging the insensible wyrm over its head, the giant gathered momentum and released the dragon like a trebuchet releases a stone, tossing the flaccid snake far out to sea.

Chuckling to herself, the witch walked right through my motionless form and called to the giant. Dipping its head to her command, the beast tossed aside the rubble. The giant reached into the broken beams and lifted Thorfinn out by his leg. The boy dangled awkwardly in the moonlight. At a word from the witch, the jotun lifted the volva and set her on its shoulder. Gripping Thorfinn by his torso, the ogre kicked aside litter and splintered timbers, stepped over the ruined barn, and turned to the east.

As I helplessly watched, the lumbering shape disappeared into the night.

CHAPTER 7
WHAT HAVE I GOTTEN MYSELF INTO?

R^{AGA}

Dawn broke through the clefts in the eastern mountains.

A mist washed over the breakers on the shore, chilled air over warm currents, and tendrils poured over the dunes and trickled through the village, creeping low to the ground. Raga wandered the debris of the longhouse—the Siedr curse had slowly faded, leaving him numb and shaken. Times like these frustrated him, stuck in the Realm Between Realms, unable to assist in Midgard. The village feigned slumber—while the great calamity had woken all, the crofters cowered in their beds or peered from shuttered windows, fearful the jotun would return.

Raga surveyed the damage. Ripped from their drying poles, the fishing nets scattered in torn clumps and tangles, yet the village itself lay mostly intact. A nearby roof showed damage, missing shingles and a dark tear leaked a trail of cook smoke. The destruction centered on their longhouse compound. The barn tilted askew, its roof hanging precariously over shattered wall supports. What happened to the few horses they had housed with the lindworm? He had no idea—they must have run when the dragon burst through the door, and he had missed their escape during the excitement of the battle. Reduced to a pile of rubble, the hall itself consisted of broken beams, scattered foundation stones and loose cedar shingles.

What a catastrophe, he thought. Poor, poor Thorfinn—what shall we do?

A huge arm severed at the elbow lay discarded in the rubble, mottled gray and oozing black ichor. He avoided the stinking mess. While birds chirped and whistled their morning songs, a different noise drew his attention. A human whimper and groan. The moans drew him to a pile of rafter beams, and there, beneath the wrecked shafts and shards of furniture, he found Gudrun. The old man laid in a pile, his face pale, blood on his vest and his leg twisted in an unnatural position under his hip. Raga could do nothing to help him—he noted he yet breathed, and while his eyes squeezed grimly shut, his arms strained to push the beams from his chest. He repeated a prayer to Mother Freyja and the All-Father Odin, calling on his Asatru, his faith in the gods, the wights of his ancestors and the old customs. "Forn Siedr," he mumbled. "The old ways...."

Raga called for his mare. His raven had scurried to hide when the giant broke through the roof—he could feel the familiar, in the east among the firs. He called, insisting the bird return to him. The beast resisted—it feared the rampaging jotun and the destroyed longhouse. He chanted, insisting the corvid return to his side. Reluctant, the bird circled high in the sky, convincing itself the monster had departed. Raga tapped his foot, his arms crossed. The moment the bird drew close enough, he jumped upon its back and took control, riding it to the nearest house and squawking at the inhabitants.

A shutter creaked aside, and a gnarled fisherman peeked out, a long pole tipped with an ivory hook gripped white-

knuckled tight. Behind him, he could see the shadows of women cringing. Prancing on the windowsill, Raga chittered and pointed with the raven's wing. The man leaned forward and regarded the longhouse wreckage. Raga held motionless, letting the old salt listen to the morning sounds—Gudrun groaned, his cries faint and unmistakable. The fisherman gawked at the bird, turned to whisper to the women and pulled the shutter back in place. Raga screeched and snapped his mare's bill. The fisherman unbarred his door and crept from his house, his fishhook held before him. Raga flew to where Gudrun lay crushed and called to him. Following the bird calls and the sounds of a man in pain, he found Gudrun and attempted to move the rubble pinning him, finding the weight too much for one man. He returned to the village and banged on doors, insisting others come and help him. With his collected neighbors, they lifted the timbers and wreckage from the injured man. They propped shattered beams and leveraged others to immobilize them where they had toppled. Careful of broken limbs, they eased Gudrun from his trap—his leg twisted and with a cry, he swooned. The villagers carried him to the nearest house, and Raga accompanied them, fluttering overhead as they examined and tended his wounds. His leg had snapped mid-femur, a clean break, and the bone had been yanked from its hip socket—As they set the bone and popped it back into its socket, Gudrun screamed in agony, reared in the bed, and thrashed with his arms. The men held him and tied his leg to a stave to hold it rigid. The woman of the house cut his tunic and vest free and used a damp rag to wash the blood from his scrapes and punctures.

Raga hopped back outside. Most of the villagers had seen his raven, a few had fed the bird on occasion. They ignored the animal, their lord's creature, safest to be overlooked. Facing this tragedy, spare thoughts for a pet wasted precious time. As the sky brightened and the fog burned away, the townsfolk stooped and gathered the ruined nets, and dragged them carefully back to the wharf, unwinding the tangles and noting torn sections and broken floats. Women collected dockside, clucking their tongues, and threading their wide bone needles to begin the repairs.

Raga left them to circle the ruined longhouse—a path of wide footprints trudged through the fields where the great ogre had carried Thorfinn. Raga hesitated—should he follow the giant? What could he do, a tiny bird in Midgard? And what if the volva waited for him with another paralyzing curse? And what of the dragon, Goorm? He peered out to the sea where the eight-armed creature had thrown the lindworm. Was Thorfinn's pet dead?

Flapping his wings to gain height, he searched the horizon for a sign of the wyrm.

Scattered shreds of fog striped the surface of the ocean. He swooped closer and systematically searched the swells, combing back and forth seeking a sign of the dragon. The ocean rolled calmly this morning, a good day to sail with a steady breeze offshore. Raga tipped his head, spread his feathers to cup the air, and glided over the waves.

There! He spotted a body in the rollers. A great, white-bellied snake coiled and floated, bobbing at the surface. Raga dropped from his height and landed on the supine form—up close bruises scored the battered Goorm, dark finger marks pressed into its sides and raw, scale-stripped patches of skin. With care, he hopped to the frill at its neck and paused, cocking an eye at the injured beast. The dragon floated with one side of its face in the ocean, its eyes closed. Bubbles rose from its submerged nostril. As Raga examined it, he could see the lindworm drew shallow breaths. He pecked at its frills, clucked in its ear, and tried to wake the beast. He wracked his brain for spells or charms he could use to heal or wake the dragon—he had no such magic. Desperate, he called from the Realm Between.

I entreat you to wake, oh valiant wyrm! We must find our Thorfinn, he's been stolen by those witches, the ones that captured Hamund's daughters, they haunt our lands and dog our steps. I know not the eight-armed giant you fought last night, was it a troll? Gudrun named the thing 'Starkad,' but I know not the name. Goorm, you must wake, for the boy is in mortal danger, his lich has been stolen, oh wake up, wake up!

Raga continued his cries for help until it became apparent nothing he could do would wake the lindworm, and he settled into a crook in the frills and tucked his bird's head under its wing.

The sun rose high overhead. Water sloshed over the beast's back, occasionally splattering the raven. Drying salt made his feathers itch. A group of gulls settled on the lindworm and pecked at its scales. Goorm hissed, and rolled, startling Raga and nearly dipping his mare in the brine. Beating his wings, Raga rose above the waking dragon.

Goorm, Goorm! Are you awake?

The lindworm rolled and twisted. It lifted his head from the waves and pressed his frills tight against its back. The serpent coughed and spat seawater. Its eyelids nictated, the inner lid blinking open and shut.

Goorm, time is wasting, the boy! The giant stole the boy! Do you remember last night? Do you remember the fight? The boy has been kidnapped!

At the mention of Thorfinn, Goorm uttered a low keening, lifted its bulk from the waves and flapped its wings to shiver off the water. The wail grew to a roar and the dragon burst from the waves, writhing into the sky and knocking the raven aside in its wake. Struggling to stay abreast of the dragon, Raga watched the wyrm arc across the sea. He watched the beast for signs of injury—it favored one wing, its membrane torn and shredded.

The lindworm flew low over the village rooftops. Mending

their nets and pulling tarps over ruined roofs, the sudden appearance of the dragon startled the villagers. With yelps and shouts, they scurried to hide, grabbing children and slamming doors behind them—while Raga suspected the fishermen knew the Vikings harbored a strange beast in their barn, none had ever investigated the odd noises or strange prints in the snow, and why should they, as they perceived no threat? The midafternoon arrival of an angry lindworm panicked them, especially after the night of horrors they had witnessed. Their mad scramble ended in an eerie calm, as the village put efforts into concealing themselves from a new terror.

With an ungraceful crash, Goorm landed amid the debris, thrashing and digging at the piles. The lindworm cooed and whimpered, knocking aside the wreckage, searching for its lost master. Raga landed on the peak of the tipped barn roof and called to the dragon.

"He's not there!" The lindworm beat his tail, his head under a pile of beams. "Listen to me, you great buffoon! He's not there!"

Goorm raised its head and howled. Its anguished cry lingered and echoed from the eastern range.

"Here!" Raga fluttered into the courtyard. "This is its track. See here?" He hopped on a great footprint in the mud. The dragon cocked its head and peered at the muddy tracks. Shambling through the piles of shattered timbers, it poked its snout into the print and sniffed, shuffling its head side to side to gain the scent. Goorm reared its head and howled. The beast coiled, crouched low, and launched into the sky, the wind from its wings buffeting and teetering the tipped barn—the destroyed structure tumbled and slid into a new pile—and Goorm flew across the fields. His departing roar rattled the village buildings.

Raga fluttered into the air on the back of his raven mare. He watched the lindworm fly away, winding across the valley headed northeast to follow the trail, the prints a clear path through the green sprouts of fresh plantings. The beast wormed back and forth, tracking the lingering giant stench. As Goorm reached the tree line at the edge of the fields, it flew over the top of the canopy and continued to trail the monster north.

Should I follow? Raga wavered.

Will the beast find the boy? What can I do in Midgard against witches prepared for him? How can I fight them alone...?

We need help, he decided. More than a dragon, a mare and an old ghost—he must find Karl Alfenson and his crew. Martine had a salve to let her see into the Realm Between—he could converse with her, after a fashion, at least pantomime the tale of the kidnapping, and win her understanding. Uncle Karl would know what to do. He could enlist their aid and the crew of the Verdandi Smiles would come to Thorfinn's rescue. Aye, a rescue —they could save Thorfinn.

Soaring high above the village, Raga made his decision— bringing help would be prudent, the best course of action. Turning south, he followed the coastline, seeking the navy of Harald Tanglehair.

KARA

A long, hot day moving stealthily through the grassy hills, the trip did not go as fast as she wanted. Seeing evidence of shepherds and a few wayward sheep, Kara hid in thickets and crept carefully from rise to rise. As the evening fell, she scrambled over the pastures in the gathering gloom.

While her day alone in enemy territory passed uneventfully, Kara remained uncomfortable about spending the night by herself. Her bizarre incident in the forest glade perplexed her, and her fear of Bregan reprisals hurried her forward. As the sun faded, she decided to keep moving, crossing hills and valleys with care, turning to watch her back frequently. Long past midnight, stumbling with fatigue, she came across a copse of stunted cedars on a rocky crest, and, pressed into their grove, fell into a deep sleep.

When she awoke, the sun beat on her, baking her in full armor. Her parched lips chapped. She grumbled, rubbed grit from her eyes, and set a walking pace she could keep. Chancing across a stream, she flung herself face first into a pool to slake her thirst. Weak from a lack of food, her progress slowed to a meandering walk. As much as she tried to find a landmark, Kara recognized she wandered, lost. North and east should be the way to the King of Dublinn's lands. North and east.

Clouds covered the sun, initially easing her trek. Evening gathered in darkness and a drizzle of rain fell. Chilled and miserable, Kara kept moving, one foot in front of the other.

Ahead she saw torches—a roadway.

She crouched to watch the approaching force. A group of men. Moving in a military formation, two by two, their leader upon a horse. As they grew near, she recognized they spoke her tongue. Relieved, she jumped and ran towards them, calling out. The soldiers surrounded her—Dublinners on patrol, their leader recognized her.

"Yer one a Gunna's lot." Kara agreed, resting against his horse's flank. He ordered two of his men to escort her to Clondalkin. "Gunna arrived this morning with five in tow."

Five? Gunna lost two fighters during the battle—Kaelan and Tordis fought with her. Fretting, Kara forgot her fatigue and rushed to the fortress. Surprised, she discovered she had walked to within a league Clondalkin. The return trip took less than an hour.

Through the gate she sprinted to the garrison, finding the captain and Gunna at the table. Stiff necked and squinting, Gunna ordered her report. Kara described the brawl and stressed the fact they were outnumbered from the start. All business, Gunna waved aside the details and demanded to know where the others were.

"I don't know," Kara admitted. "When Jerrik called for us to fall back, I was in the middle of the fight. He ran and I followed...."

"Lucky," Gunna remarked, and she dismissed Kara with a gesture.

As Kara left, Kaelan came dashing across the courtyard and grabbed her in a hug. He lifted her off the ground and spun her. Laughing, she kissed him, not thinking of prying eyes milling about the compound.

"Oh, Kara, I thought I lost you."

She wiggled out of his grasp and stroked his cheek.

"And I, you." She ran her eyes over him. "What happened to your leg?"

"Nothing to worry over." Kaelan ignored her concerned expression, checking her for wounds. "I got stabbed, not deep, a strong salve and bandages will make me right."

Kara stared into his eyes, his smile making a blush rise to her neck, her hands seeking his to hold. More than ever before, she yearned to embrace him—she had been worried he was one of the lost from Gunna's force.

Tordis joined them, giving Kara a smack on her armored back. "I thought ye were a goner!"

"Tordis!"

"Hungry, lass?"

"Oh, ja!" She clung to Kaelan as they led her to the

mess. As Kaelan ran to collect her a bowl of gruel and a chunk of mutton, Kara leaned close to confide in Tordis. The shieldmaiden smiled as Kara related her story in gaps between gulping her meal. She recounted the battle and her escape.

"Strangest thing, after I escaped, wandering in the woods I found this cleared spot. No trees grew within a wide loop. Full of night-blooming flowers and glow worms. In the center was a small hill, an arm's length taller than a man." Listening, Tordis grew contemplative, rubbing her chin. "The bugs and glow worms danced in the sky, making funny patterns and…." Kara motioned with her hand, twirling the air over the table.

"Did yer notice a fairy ring? A circle of big, white mushrooms 'round the hillock?"

"I didn't get a good view, all happened so fast. I had my bedroll in my hand, like I saw Jerrik use his, and the bugs swarmed me, so I swatted them, and… I caught one."

"Only, 't weren't no bug."

"Ja." Kara leaned closer to Tordis and Kaelan. "It was a tiny lady, no bigger than this." She held her forefinger high. "…and, don't think me crazy but… she had wings!"

"Did ya see any elves?"

"No…." Kara glanced from Kaelan's confused face to Tordis' serious frown.

"What happened?"

"I banged it on the ground. Thought I killed it, but it flew off when I let it go. The forest grew quiet, scary, like everything watched me, so I ran away."

"Stay here," Tordis ordered, and bustled out of the hall. Kaelan quirked his eyebrow and held her hand as she finished her dinner.

Tordis returned with a small, wooden box. The carved

lid fitted snug, and she had to work to prise it loose. Inside a sack jingled as if filled with coins, and a scarlet feather lay on top of the contents. She set the feather gently aside on the table.

"Kara, I think ya had a run-in with the Summer Court, the Fae of this green Eire. Lucky ya got away with yer life—mayhap the elves were not there with yer. This time of year, the light elves of Alfheim hold sway. Come winter, they release their court to the Vanir, and the dark elves rule the Winter Court—they're a nasty bunch, will steal yer life in a heartbeat." She continued to rummage through her box and took out a velvet pouch.

"You touched a Fae, captured it, mayhap even hurt it—the Fae may claim ya now. Tis a no-good thing, to be claimed by the Fae. Seldom people who've seen the fairies dance live a year. No good at all. Here, take this talisman." She handed Kara a flat stone as wide as her thumb, with a hole worn through, nearer its edge than its center. Kaelan shrugged when she glanced at him.

"Tis a hag's stone," Tordis explained. "One finds them on the beach after a storm. Old magic. It'll protect you from fae enchantments here in Eire. I know this to be true, saved many a hug from capture by the elves and their kin. Lucky t'was the white elves and not the dark, or ya'd never a come home." Tordis pointed at the holey stone on Kara's palm.

"Tie it around yer neck with a ribbon, lass, and keep with you always. That's yer protection, it will keep your lich and hug safe from the whims o' the Summer Court." She handed Kara a knitted lace ribbon, worn and browned from use. "Here ya go, chile, this will tie'er tight."

Kara found a loop of loose string at the end of the ribbon and threaded it through the hag's stone hole. She tucked her stone and the ribbon under her left arm brace for safe keeping and finished swallowing her porridge. Tordis brought them all a horn of watered-down ale and they shared a drink as Tordis explained how they had escaped the unexpected attack of Bregans. The recount of the tale lost on Kara, she fiddled with Kaelan's hand on the table between them.

"Come, girl, time for you to rest. Kay, you take our Kara and get'er out of her armor." Tordis gathered their empties and carried them over to the barrel as Kaelan helped Kara to her feet and led her out of the hall.

"Kaelan, before bed, I need a bath."

"Should be unused this time of night," Kaelan led Kara to the bathhouse.

The full moon marked the beginning of the month of Skerpla and provided plenty of light to see. They found the door ajar, the wooden tubs stacked upended. Kaelan toppled one over, rolled it to the center of the wooden slat floor and pulled a bench forward for Kara to sit. He moved around the room, closing the shutters for privacy. Returning to her side, he brought her a robe and towels. She untied her bracers, the leather grimy—she set the hag's stone carefully on the bench next to her and tugged her boots free. While Kaelan carried in buckets of water, Kara loosened her tangled braid and combed out the snarls. Once he had filled the shallow tub, Kaelan wet a rag and cleaned the dirt from her leather armor.

Kara finished her hair. "Kaelan, come unlace my chest plate," and she lifted her arms for him. Setting aside his rag, Kaelan moved behind her and untied the strings, carefully removing the back plate to set on the bench. Kara held out her breastplate and he took it from her hands. Her dirty tunic clung sweat stuck to her back, and he carefully stroked her hair aside and lifted it free.

Kara could feel his warmth against her spine. He held her hair gently, its tawny, braided crinkles shining in the moonlight. *This is safety.* Kaelan rubbed her shoulders, his warm hands working her tired muscles, and he bent forward to nuzzle her neck—a gulp caught in her throat as goosebumps lifted along her neck and back. She leaned into him.

"Kara..." he whispered. "I was worried."

She hummed in response. Kaelan massaged her back and sides, running his strong fingers along her torso. His hands moved around her, and he embraced her from behind, a lingering hug making her heart throb. He continued to stroke her and dipping his head to her neck he gave her a prolonged kiss. Goose flesh spread to her loins and Kara arched her back, pressing into his chest. His hands gently stroked her midriff and caressed her ribs, lifting her tunic until he cupped her chest in his strong hands.

Her head swirled. As Kaelan lifted her tunic over her head, she turned to him and pressed her mouth against his. His arms wrapped around her.

A noise of people passing by the bathhouse startled them. They gripped each other tightly, holding unmoving as the night watch marched outside. Kara let a nervous giggle slip. Kaelan took her chin in his hand and gave her a peck on her lips.

"Best not found together... this way."

She leaned closer, unsure he could see her and hesitant to speak. *How natural and calm, to be in his arms, my Kaelan... my man.* With reluctance reflected by slow, uncertain movements, he pulled back from her, stooped to collect her armor and his cleaning rag, and whispered, "I'll bring these to you tomorrow. You wash and head to the dormitory."

"Kaelan."

"Yes?"

"Just one more...." He obliged, squeezing her tight under one arm and bending her back so she clung to him as they embraced.

Kaelan collected the armor and shut the door as he departed. She stood mute, listening to her heart pound, her body tingling from his touch. Kara disrobed, setting her belt and sword on the bench, climbed into the chilly water and sponged the dirt from her body. Kaelan had left her a clean pitcher full for her hair and she dipped in the bath water before she rinsed her curls with fresh water.

Toweling off, she spilled the tub onto the floor, the dirty water drained through floor slats. She wrapped herself in the robe and carried her dirty clothes, the sword and belt, and her two boots across the courtyard to the unmarried women's hall. Carefully threading the center aisle between snoring companions, she found her empty pallet and quietly set her weapon near her head, left her dirty clothes in a pile, and crawled under her homespun blanket.

And lay in the dark, tired, unable to sleep, thinking of Kaelan.

Is this elsk, the love sickness, or is this true love? Should I pray to Var the goddess of oaths between men and women who punishes those who break their vows? Or to Hnoss, daughter of Freya, the master of sensuality and infatuation? All Kara knew was she was happy to be alive, yearning for her Kay, his kisses, and his touch.

Midmorning she awoke—the dorm had emptied. The hag stone lay next to her pillow—she looped the lace ribbon around her neck and tied it securely. The stone hung cold between her breasts. She rummaged through her bag and found clean clothes, gathered her boots and sword belt, and went to break her fast. The courtyard bustled with activity—a party had arrived at the gate on horseback, a few exhilarated stallions snorting and whickering, rousing the steadier geldings and nags to dance and jostle each other. A crowd had gathered, guards tugging the leads and trying to hold the horses in place while a contingent from Dublinn swarmed the garrison door. Kara recognized Gunna's minions, Asta and her crew lounging against the fortress paling wall. A troop of warriors stood before the gate, a quick count indicating more than thirty had been called to this duty.

Gunna exited the garrison followed by redheaded Muirgel, the King's chosen bride. Dressed in a green, velvet gown, Muirgel wore a yellow, doe-leather vest scrawled in fancy embroidery, with matching elbow-length gloves. Gunna wore her standard, gray, warrior tunic—the two contrasted each other, one mousy gray and broad shouldered, the other gay as a strutting pheasant. The garrison captain wandered behind them, sheepishly avoiding their quarrel. From where Kara stood, she could see the discussion grew heated—Muirgel pointed at the horses and soldiers. Gunna gestured dismissively. Muirgel stomped her foot. Kara stood by the food hall door, watching the women argue, not close enough to hear, gaining the gist of the conversation through body language—Muirgel intended to take her men-at-arms and ride, believing the force size protected her. Gunna refused her permission as she wanted to commandeer the fresh forces for the Clondalkin fortress and her slaving runs. Gunna kept pointing at the fortress and dismissing the princess with short, choppy motions.

Kaelan waved to her from across the yard—he had the day watch assignment, a spear in his hand, posted by the gate. Dublinn warriors crowded the open entrance.

Tordis, leaving the dining hall, joined Kara in the doorway. "What goes here?"

"I think Gunna is refusing the demands of our future queen."

Tordis chuckled. "No love lost twixt those two, eh?"

Kara remembered the princess and her secret forest rendezvous. "Tordis, who is Otir?"

"How ya know of Otir?"

Kara thought about telling Tordis all she had seen and decided it might be imprudent to share information when she lacked understanding. "I... ah, I heard the name mentioned...."

"Otir?" Tordis sniffed and squinted at the two arguing women. "Otir be an Irish lord, kind of a jarl. Tis the last son a' Lord Jarnkne. That Jarnkne, we Dubgaill conquered him at the Battle of Carlingford Lough, back in Imar's time and long before I joined his army. Fought like a troll he did, but in the end, we beat his force and sent his head home tied to a horse tail." Tordis turned to face Kara. "Gossips say the redheaded witch was betrothed to Otir, before Ausle carried her off in a settlement with her father, King Mael Sechnaill."

"They were betrothed?" Tordis nodded at the fire-headed woman tramping back to her horse, a black stallion with a white mark on its nose.

"Aye, tis the rumor."

"So, she is a princess of Brega?"

"Nay, lass, I told ya before, there be more kings of Eire than weeds in a field. King Sechnaill lives far to the north, one of Ausle's triumphs from when he rode under Barith's banner. All gold went to Barith. Ausle claimed Muirgel as his personal prize. Took her that very night, so they say, although I hear she fought like a wildcat." She leaned close to whisper conspiratorially. "He likes'em to fight, ya know."

"And she may have been betrothed before King Ausle's claim."

"Aye, lass, that's what they say."

Kara watched Muirgel mount her horse and wave an angry finger at Gunna in a vague threat. Tossing her loose hair back, she motioned for two personal guards to join her and heeled her horse. Her mount slewed sideways in the courtyard, crowded the other horses, and shifted the entire line. Hooves high, her chestnut gelding cantered out the gate headed toward Dublinn.

Kara watched her leave, back stiff and tall in her saddle. Otir, her betrothed, snubbed by her father, Muirgel ransomed to the odious Bradon Mac Ausle, secret assignations deep in the forest at night, fighting not for fame or glory, but to gather thralls to fill a despicable king's coffers, and oddest of all, extraordinary creatures haunting the night woods... This green land of Eire was not what she expected, not at all.

Kara wondered, *what have I gotten myself into?*

KARL

Jarl Aki of Varmland met them at the door to the hall.

"Karl, son of Ironfist, you scallywag! Ever one step ahead of the Valkyries, eh?" The big man grabbed Karl in a bear hug, lifting him off his feet and shaking him from side to side. "How many years have passed?"

Karl laughed along with the good-natured Aki. "Three or four? Put me down, you big oaf!"

"Why? Is little Alfie afraid he'll lose his solemn dignity?" Blowing in his face, Aki dropped Karl on his backside, his guffaws contagious. "Too late, Alf-boy, we all know you here!" He extended his hand to pull Karl from the boards.

Aki stood as tall and wide as Havar, with a prodigious belly and an unkempt brush of beard. Hair everywhere, tufts masked his earlobes and bristled from his nose. With seemingly no effort, he jerked Karl to his feet and waved his crew into the hall, grabbing Jormander as he entered. "Skald, tonight you must sing a saga for Harald and our war council"—he pulled him under his arm and continued in a stage whisper—"once the boring bits are finished, eh?"

"Have you already started drinking?"

"Ja, Karl of Ironfist, but you can catch up...."

Karl introduced his crew, Hamund and his clansmen.

"Well met, Hothlson. Lade speaks well of your swords."

Karl straightened his vest and moved into the great hall. Aki greeted the next as they entered, embracing each as a brother.

The longhouse arched high, the largest Karl had ever seen, each support pillar carved in the Nordic way, depicting ancient stories and legends of the gods. The roof rose two stories high, the tall walls inset with slits to suck out smoke and air the room. A furious fire burned at its center, a spit turning a wide side of boar to crackle, wafting a wonderful odor of roast meat, wood smoke and yeasty ale. Arranged around the room stood tables of varying sizes and shapes, each host to a collection of warriors. Women and boys worked through the crowd, serving slices of pork and bowls of beer. Small, curtained alcoves and niches hid side rooms, and as far as Karl could tell, three rooms lined the back, one with its door propped open, torchlight illuminating the space beyond. A falconer held his red-tailed hawk on his arm, the nervous bird's head hooded.

A few faces around him looked familiar. All wore

armbands and gold rings, gifts from their liege lord. Gryting, the king of Orkdal, and his men, Admiral Uffe and a group of his captains, a group of shieldmaidens in leather, scale armor he had seen at Jarl Lade's farm. And moving about the room, stopping to speak to each in turn, was Tanglehair himself.

Karl had not seen Harald for years. The son of Halfdan the Black, the progeny of the Yngling kings, Harald had vowed to never cut his hair until he had unified the Northern Way under his rule, and his matted, uncombed locks had grown into a disturbing mess. No wonder men had taken to call him 'shockhair.' Karl who had fought beside Harald in past battles stood surprised at the tangled nest drooping over his shoulders and sticking out at odd angles. *He must have worked oil or tar into his scalp*, Karl thought, *to make his hair stand so stiff.*

Havar pushed through the crowd and found a table with room for them. He called them over, telling a server to bring food and drink. Hamund took a seat and Karl stood behind him, searching the gathering, scanning for... there! Dag entered the hall and traded jibes with Aki, and behind him Martine, her hair oil slicked and glistening—he imagined he could smell her scent across the room. She had tied a leather strap around her forehead, three silver studs centered over her eyes, and she held her head and shoulders high, a Lindenwood shield strapped to her back. Dag caught his prying eyes and gave him a wolfish grin. Martine avoided his gaze.

"Sit." Jormander pulled his sleeve. Havar handed him a bowl of ale.

Harald approached their table and called out, "Hamund Hothlson and Karl Alfenson, where have you been hiding?" He hugged each in turn, genuinely happy to see his old men-at-arms. "Remember our battle at Trondelag? You, Hamund, you defeated that ogre-sized fellow and he toppled right on top of you! Boom! Dead heavy! Remember? You cried for help!" Hamund hung his head.

"I remember the man... the size of two horses and stunk of garlic as well. You try being pinned under that load."

"I remember he lost his bowels in death."

"Yeah, 'twas not the only one who smelled that day!" Laughter rose from the table.

"And you spawn of Ironfist, how goes the farm in Northumbria?"

"Well, when I last saw her, a tribute to my father's name." Karl didn't mention his brother's death—why spoil the festive mood?

"And you." Harald pointed at Jormander. "I remember your songs, poet. Mayhap we can entice you to declaim when I am done with our business this night." He didn't frame his request as a question, more as a statement of fact.

"Would be an honor." Jormander bowed his head.

Harald moved to the next group, greeting each he remembered and being introduced to new recruits. A server brought a wooden platter holding a large cut of the roast for the table, each slicing what they wanted. As Karl chewed his pork, Harald clapped his hands and climbed to a tabletop so all assembled could see and hear him.

"The news from the south lands is Hordaland and Rogaland, Agder and Thelemark, all gather to stand against me. They collect ships and weapons, and a great body of men to oppose us. I name them here, our enemies." Somber, he beheld the crowd, focusing on individuals as he counted each foe on a finger. "Eirik the king of Hordaland. Kjotve the Rich, king of Agder and his son Thor Haklang. The king of Rogaland, Sulke, and his brother Jarl Sote. And those two brothers from Thelemark, Hroald Hryg and Had the Hard." As he finished naming his opponents, he raised a fist into the air.

"We call upon the goddess Vor, the careful one, mother of providence and preparing well for the future. This night the goddess blesses us, the prepared, the ever ready, for we shall be victorious. We shall be victorious!"

From the back of the room, Jarl Hakon of Lade shouted, "Victory!" and the room responded with a rousing cheer. Chants of "victory" filled the room. Harald raised his arms to quiet his troops.

"We have our fleet assembled. We travel south, along the coast and gather more fighters as we go, men and women dedicated to our cause. We shall carry this war to Eirik himself and lay defeat like a yule wreath at his door!" A spontaneous cheer erupted from the hall.

As the room quieted, Gryting stood to be recognized and Harald called on him to speak. "The renegade lords intend to draw us into a land battle, where superior numbers will wear and overcome us. What is your plan, my lord?"

"We sail south to lure those craven sea toads to face us on the brine." Harald gazed out at his warriors. "Let their greater numbers swarm the shore—we shall meet their leaders at sea and overwhelm them, every one." Karl noticed men around them agreed with Harald's strategy. A battle at sea—it had not been attempted at this great scale before, an unexpected maneuver—Karl could see the truth in the plan.

A motion caught Karl's eye—Martine rose from her bench and moved toward the door. He had been surreptitiously watching her all night. Karl rose and dipped his head to Harald at his table. Havar gave him a searching review, and Jormander gave his head an imperceptible shake, a cautioning glance between old friends. Karl lifted his palms to indicate his thought—I must try—and he slipped through the room, stepping around the cheering soldiers. He wormed his way to the door.

She stood in the cool evening air, facing the white birch which edged the fir forest.

"Martine."

She turned, her hair shining under the full Skerpla moon. She had used kohl as makeup, a smoldering dark smudge highlighted each blue eye. He crossed the yard to her.

"What do you want?"

"Martine, you should return to sail with us." His words came out dry—he swallowed to wet his throat. "We are... like family."

"Family?" She snorted and rolled her eyes. "Is that what you want? A sister?"

"No." He hesitated. She gave him a slant eye. "We need you, we miss experienced swords, and...."

"We?" Martine poked his chest with her index finger. "*We* need a sword?"

Karl coughed. "Ja, the men, the crew...."

She huffed and turned away. He reached to her shoulder, and she shook him loose and stalked away.

"Wait. Martine...." She stopped and glanced back at him.

"We need, we need." She squinted at him. "What do *you* need, Karl Alfenson?"

"Well, ja, I too. I... need your sword."

"My *sword*?"

He opened his mouth. For all his brash bravado in battle, she left him tongue-tied with not a word to utter. Karl scrutinized his flexing fingers.

"There are swords everywhere, take your pick." She dismissed him with a gesture. "Go find a sword, a shiny, new sword. I am certain you can find a pretty one waiting for you."

"Nay, Martine, I need your sword."

She turned back to him across the yard. "My *sword*? Karl Alfenson, you seek me out to tell me *you* want my sword?"

Karl stumbled, holding out his hands. "If you would only return, back to the way it was...."

He knew she could see his confusion—*Clearly, she knows what I am trying to say, yet... why does she torment me?*

"When you decide what you want, come and tell me." She set her jaw. "I know what I want, and it's not to be another 'sword,' not to be a 'sister.' I know my worth... When you decide, you tell me to my face." And she turned and marched into the dark.

"Martine?" He watched until she was gone.

"Martine...."

Karl slumped to the stoop and rubbed his eyes. *How frustrating,* he thought. He had asked her politely—Jormander had coached him to be polite and not demanding—yet she turned him away. His temper boiled, angry with her, angry with himself... *Why couldn't she see how he felt? Women!*

As he sat before the door to the longhouse, with a noisy celebration underway behind him, a bird dropped from the sky and landed a few feet from him. The beast cawed, flapped its wings, and croaked, a hoarse, annoying chirp.

A raven—it couldn't be—could it?

"Raga?"

The bird snapped its beak and hopped side to side.

"Raga, what are you doing here? I told you to watch over Thorfinn."

The bird cawed loudly, repeated its call, raised one wing, flipped the other, and lifted both in unison. A strange dance ensued, the animal cawed and chortled insistently, clearly upset.

"What? Not you, too!" He swatted at the bird, and it hopped out of reach. "No, I am tired. I am no mind reader, I don't know what to say, I don't know what to do...." He pushed himself to his feet.

"Leave me, bird. I want to be alone." He growled and banged his hilt in its scabbard. And as the raven cocked its head to watch, he stomped into the dark wood.

THORFINN

A sudden sharp pain woke him—a passing branch scored his cheek.

Squeezed tight to his chest, his arms constricted enough to make it difficult to draw a full breath, his every joint ached, especially his hip socket—raw and sore, his side twinged with pain at each swing of his dangling legs.

He gagged—whatever held him reeked of rot and putrescence. He couldn't see properly... he grasped a burlap bag covered his head. Bits of daylight flashed through the weave, and he vaguely discerned shadows as they passed. A low-pitched groan rumbled close to him.

Concentrating, he could hear sounds of branches snapping, and the thump, thump pace of their passage. His body upended and pushed through heavy brush, the scent of pine seeping through the bag on his head.

"Alfhildr," an impossibly low-pitched voice grumbled, the basso rattling his bones. Nearby a woman spoke indistinct words.

All he could do was listen. The sounds of footfall

squelched, a muddy sucking sound, as if their path crossed a marsh. A flock of birds tittered and lifted—he could hear their wings beating as they flew past his head.

Trying to draw a breath, the smell of his captor triggered a fit of coughs. The movement stopped. He upended and jerked, lifted higher. His captor growled and tossed him like a rag, and his aches and pains overcame his senses—he fainted.

Consciousness returned slowly, his head swimming in and out of lucidness, his neck smarting from the recent thrashing. A headache pounded in his ears. He could feel the pace of their passage had increased speed, the thumps falling in rapid succession, each a jar to his aching body.

His body—his lich! Someone had kidnapped his lich! Raga had warned him of this. Know where your lich lies, always protect your lich. This was how Raga had been trapped in the Realm Between, his lich had wasted to death while his hug journeyed the nine Realms. An unconscious moan escaped his throat, and he gasped and held his breath, hoping he had not been heard....

Rhythmic and steady, the quick stride pulsed beneath him. With nothing to gauge an estimate, Thorfinn guessed they traveled leagues, based on the way the sounds changed quickly around him—the sound of rushing water, first distinct and soon gone, the sound of surf crashing quickly fading away. Occasionally he floated, buoyant, as if whatever held him in its grip leaped across a valley or chasm, followed by the noise of scrambles and tumbled rockslides. He slipped out of awareness.

They stopped. Fingers loosened their grip on his sides, and he dropped, landing hard on his side. He struggled to his knees. Upon his release, he realized his hands and feet had been hog-tied. Confusing sounds shuffled around him, the snap of brush, the crunch of gravel. He toppled forward, landing on a crust of snow—astonished, he recognized they had traveled far north to where the summer sun had not yet melted winter away. The woman's voice called, cooing and whispering. Chanting. The cadence rang familiar—she called a Siedr enchantment.

An unexpected kick to his gut disabled him, and while he coughed, face in the snow drift, his captor snatched the sack from his head.

The sun had not fully set, the sky orange and purple at the horizon. Towering over him stood a fierce and outlandish jotun, its head at the treetops, an unnatural cluster of arms on its torso, one set held akimbo, fist to hips, another across its chest, another holding its oversized head and one huge hand poking him, pushing him back against a tree trunk. A crumpled skull from a crushing blow had disfigured the giant, and Thorfinn grasped this shuffling monster was a dead creature reanimated—that accounted for the awful odor, black blood and pus drooling from its wounds. They passed through an arboreal forest, deep in an expanse of shaggy hemlocks and spindly larch crowding a craggy mountainside.

"Alfhildr...." The dead jotun moaned.

"Hush," a woman's voice soothed the giant, and Finn twisted his neck to find her.

Illuminated by the ruddy, setting sun, he saw a hunched-backed crone weaving a Siedr spell, the magic midair sparkles to his vardoger eyes. Draped in matted, white hair, her hook nose poked through the straggly gray mess. She waddled close to him and cast the curse on his prone form. A sickly green aura settled over him. A sudden chill sent shivers along his back.

"Alfhildr."

"Ja, Ja, Son of Storkvid...." She held out her hands, palms facing the jotun. "I release you, Starkad the Jotun, your duty-bound coercion ends. Go seek your elf princess, old troll, or make vengeance on the thunder god who laid you low beneath the falls. I compel you no more!" She clapped her hand three times.

The great beast stretched taller, huffed, and muttered, "Alfhildr" once more. Ignoring Thorfinn and the volva witch, the huge troll turned to the east and lumbered through the forest, its crashing noises fading with the sunlight.

"Now for you, little vardoger." She hunched over Thorfinn and, gripping him by his collar, dragged him back into a kneeling position.

"Who are you?"

The old woman frowned. "Don't recognize me, eh?" She grabbed a loose cloth wrapped around her palm and unwound it. "This jog your memory?"

With a flourish she unveiled her hand, all the fingers chopped off at the knuckle bones. Thorfinn gasped—he knew who hunched before him, the were-vulture he defeated to save Allinor. He had never seen her human face, merely her damaged fingertips left behind after the battle.

"You see what I've done." She gestured to the faint green aura. "I've trapped your hug inside your lich, no escaping to warn your friends where to find you." Her laughter rang in the empty wood. Such a remote place, Thorfinn knew she had stolen him far away. They were alone.

She shuffled closer, pressing a knee into his chest and grabbing his bound hands. Her clothes stank of the giant, her mouth fishy and sour as she leaned to gloat.

"You took from me my wingtips. I shall never feel the

glorious change again—for this you must suffer, suffer as I have suffered." She wrenched his arm to hold tight under her armpit.

From her belt, she drew a short, hooked dagger, the kind used to flay and field dress. She bent and pulled his roped hands to her lap. "You took all my wings at once, but to be quick is too good for the likes of you. No, no, we must not go fast, eh, little vardoger? We must make your pain last, so you suffer like I suffered, eh?"

Realizing her intent, Thorfinn struggled, jerking and pulling at his hand. "No, stop!"

"Let's start with this smallest one, shall we?"

CHAPTER 8
DAUGHTERS

CUB

The people of Bayeux rejoiced.

The marauders had fled! Retreated! Gone!

As their church bell pealed, impromptu celebrations filled every street. Firebrands raised high, wineskins passed from hand to hand, and the harvest bounty shared by all. The happy villagers feasted with food, wine, and dancing in the cobbled avenues. Roast lamb and river perch, fresh bread and apples, ripe grapes, and flagons of wine. Flushed from partaking, the monks joined in the fun, and the local garrison discharged its soldiers to enjoy the festivities, leaving a skeleton crew to watch the walls and the heavy, barred gates. Just as Cub predicted....

Delicious cooking smells drifted across the sluggish river from both sides of the city. Floating on his raft, the smells made his mouth water and his stomach grumble. A raft of lashed timber, skimming the water surface and steered with a long pole, carried four warriors huddled under tarps to the heart of a heedless city lost in their cups.

Despite the treaty Rolf signed with Robert of the Breton March conceding the coastal lands to the Northmen, often cities resisted the Nordic rule. This invasion had been Cub's plot—when Rolf agreed to the strategy, he put Cub in charge of the forward team. The Northmen sought a plan to end the standoff with a minimum of civilian deaths, for, after all, these peasants were Rolf's new subjects. The campaign had been timed well—the neighboring farmland had been harvested, a great summer of plenty, and the people of Bayeux craved their annual festival, recently postponed due to a looming Viking raid. Cub had suggested giving them something to celebrate... after camping within sight of the walls and beyond the protectors' reach for a few days, earlier in the day they mounted an afternoon attack simply as a diversion, a distraction which ended in a preplanned impasse, the villagers barring their gates, and the raiders making a big show of departure. No casualties fell on either side, despite a spate of arrows loosed from the city walls and axes waved for show.

Stealth was the key to this idea and a level of brazen audacity which appealed to both the Ganger and Cub. Hagrold's scouts reported the river bisected the city walls, protected from interlopers by a heavy net dragged across the current each night, anchored to the wall on each bank. Cub suggested a raft on a moonless night could let the current carry them to the net. A small force could cut the mesh free, continue to drift on the river Aure to the city center, enter undetected, and find and open the gates. Rolf and his warriors would quietly return and take their prize with a minimum of mayhem.

Cub handpicked his warriors and dressed them in local, peasant garb, complete with slouchy felted hats and hidden weapons in sacks. His one shield maid dressed in a voluminous skirt with hand axes tied to her thighs. No shields allowed—as he planned it, this sortie required finesse and bravado instead of battle lust and swordplay.

Cutting through the heavy netting, he wondered if they made a mistake... their course set, no way to pole back against the current to their hidden camp upstream.

Sharp knives clipped the net free, and Cub crouched low to pass under the curtain chain—the raft snagged a bit, spun a half-circle and rocked loose to drift on the current.

On all sides the city celebrated, singing accompanied by tambourines and a cranked instrument one of their men called a hurdy-gurdy. Cub liked the strange instrument, droning notes and simple melodies, different from the tagelharpa music of his childhood. Holding his pole level to the waterline, he sought a dark, quiet spot on the banks where they could land undetected. Ahead he spotted a darkened building, its balcony slung precariously over the river.

"Ready...." Tarps pushed aside, his team climbed to their haunches next to him.

"Now!"

Cub jumped and caught the support beams under the overhanging structure. Hand-over-hand the raiders moved under the balcony to the edge of the building and dropped to a stone walkway set in the bank. The footpath ended in stairs to the street level. Taking control, Cub gave commands with hand signals, two to head to the main gate via alleys and back streets, one to follow his lead. Ahead they could see a few women shaking their skirts and dancing around an iron basket filled with flaming kindling. Shedding his black cloak, Cub cast it to the gutter, his companion dropping her similar blanket to display a scarlet, Frankish shawl over her long skirt. She took his elbow

—her name Iona. Cub gave her a toothy grin, sure they would blend with the inhabitants. His hair had grown long enough to trim, and his beard had filled in nicely, a good diet had helped him build back the muscle lost as a slave in the mines, and his back had healed, leaving him self-conscious of the keloids and scars but no longer still or sore. Daily stretches and exercise helped him stay limber, and with a jaunty tilt to his head, he acted another Breton wandering a contented city.

Turning the corner, the street crowded with revelers. Planks had been converted into long, makeshift tables and stacked with food and casks of wine—Cub snagged two empty bowls as they passed, motioning to the matron serving and sharing his happy grin with her as she filled their cups. He handed one to his cohort and led her farther into the city. He had been practicing his language skills with captured thralls, and their clothing had been liberated from the newly captured too, feeding his confidence in his ability to blend into Bayeux. Warily sipping at her bowl, the shieldmaiden clung to his side, her fingers twitching with no weapon in hand. Cub waved to folks around him, laughing and enjoying the party.

Winding their way through the avenues, infectious tunes and happy dancers captured his spirit and taking his warrior by the hand, he swung her around and kicked up his heels. Flummoxed, Iona gave him a withering glance, smoothing her ruffled dress to ensure the weapons stayed hidden on her thighs. He pulled her along into a large courtyard filled with the citizens of the river town.

Noise overwhelmed them. The city gathered in this center square to celebrate. A tall steeple stood at the end of the plaza, its bell ringing incessantly. The throng in the courtyard shouted at each other over the resounding chimes, happily spilling their wine and clapping along to the music of a band playing a lively jig. Women carried tambourines adorned with ribbons and silver bells, adding a jingling beat to the joyous uproar. Cub clapped, smiling with teeth, his eyes studying the crowd, surveying for evidence of the city guard—there, by a small, overcrowded stage, he spotted two dressed in soldier garb, caps pulled back from their faces, cheeks flushed from drink. Not paying attention to the crowd, they lounged beside the raised platform. *This is going to be too easy,* Cub told himself, and he pulled his wary companion along behind him.

Standing on the raised stand, clapping their hands and waving at people in the crowd, a group of young women caught his eye. Lots of late-season flowers adorned their hair, looped in woven necklaces and in gaudy bracelets on their wrists. By their embroidered attire, fancy velvet capes and headdresses, he guessed these were young women of importance, the guards posted to watch over them. Having sampled the fresh, fizzy wine, their cheeks flushed with excitement, and they gripped each other for support, arms about waists or hung lightly over shoulders. As Cub moved closer, he overheard their giggles and laughter.

That's when he saw her.

Raven-haired and taller than the other girls, she stood slightly to the back of the clique, a gleaming diadem affixed to her headband. The gem's sparkle initially caught his eye, but her full lips and heart-shaped face held his attention. Beautiful, laughter lighting her eyes, her embroidered vest highlighting her shapely figure. At ease in the crowd, she pitched her shoulder with a hand on her waist, slightly aloof, apart from the silly girls who gossiped at her side. He watched her bend forward to mention a witticism to her mates, her movements graceful, elegant. Awestruck, Cub stumbled closer for a better glimpse.

"Hey!" The shield woman tugged on his sleeve and pulled his head close to whisper in his ear. "Where are we going?"

Keeping his eyes on the vision before him, Cub whispered back to her. "The corner, there." He pointed. "I will meet you there. I...." He dithered a moment. "I want to check these guards." With a harumph, the woman elbowed her way through the mass of dancers to cross the square. Cub turned and wormed his way to the platform.

He stared at her. She held a hand to her cheek, her slender fingers touching her temple as she listened to a friend. Cub couldn't take his eyes from her, and as he drew closer, she noticed and locked eyes with him, a moment of connection before she demurely dropped her gaze. He pushed between the guards and slyly observed the gaggle of girls who bobbed to the throbbing music. Two of the closest noticed him and leaned forward over a rope balustrade.

"And who are you?"

"Such a handsome lad." Her companion tittered into a kerchief.

Cub recognized his name would give him away, and he beamed and answered, "Your grace, I am your servant. What shall I bring you, ladies?" He gestured across the square in a vague way, his eyes on the tall girl—up close, her ivory skin appeared flawless, her dress expensive. She raised her eyes to his, and he paused, struck by their unique, violet color.

"Oh, I see." The flirty girl turned to the black-haired one and rolled her eyes. "Another falls to your charms, Poppa."

"What an interesting accent you have...." The girl they

called Poppa matched Cub's gaze and leaned nearer to him. He held his breath—her amethyst eyes mesmerized him. "I don't believe I've seen you before...."

"I certainly want to see more of him," one of her more boisterous mates announced, and nearly toppled over the rope, grabbed by the girls around her. They all joined in the laughter.

The guard next to Cub gave him a curt overview and bored by the interloper, mumbled, "Move along now." He gave Cub a shove back into the crowd—Cub appreciated young men surrounded the stage, all near his age and all attempting to chat with the girls on the stand. None of them acted too pleased he had barged into their circle—he ducked his head and wiggled his way back through the dancers. *Poppa*, he thought. *Never in my life have I seen a girl like her.*

The shieldmaiden waited for him at the corner, pressed against the closest building. A drunken man slobbered on her, his slurred questions incomprehensible, his intent clear enough. He kept reaching out to touch her arm, and she pushed his hand aside each time. Cub arrived to rescue her as she prepared to punch the old fool—he could see anger building in her glaring eyes, her hands tightening in fists.

"Come sister, we have appointments," he said in the local tongue, grinned at the doddering codger, and pulled his warrior away. Iona snorted and dipped her head.

"What were you doing?"

"Nothing...." He glanced back at the girls on their raised stage, the one they called Poppa stood with her back turned, her long, black tresses curling past her waist. "Nothing at all."

The number of people thinned as they left the festival

square. They wound through streets and alleys until they reached the stone wall. Finding a ladder, they climbed to the top where a wooden walkway had been mounted waist high from the apex. Wide enough for the defense, they could move two abreast on the catwalk. His companion pulled a hand ax from under her skirt, hiking the dress higher on her waist to free her legs from its tangles. Darkness had settled on the fields beyond the wall—the lights in the city illuminated their path. Ahead a man leaned against his spear—Cub crept forward, ready to spring—the fellow dozed at his post. Upending her weapon, Iona cracked his temple with the hilt and Cub caught him, silently lowering his body to the gangplank.

Circling the city, the next guard they reached challenged them.

"Hey, who are you?" He did not seem alarmed, his spear held slack at his side. "What are you doing here?" Cub held out his open hands and continued his approach.

"Out for a walk...."

"Who are you, and why...?" He never finished—Cub rushed and grabbed him by the waist before he could raise his weapon. Reaching over Cub, Iona smacked the guard with the flat of her ax blade and the two tossed his inert form over the wall, listening to it crash into the underbrush below. They continued along the walkway. The path ended in a ladder next to a stone arch.

To either side stood guard houses, small vestibules for the watch to hide from the weather—from their perch above, they could see a candle glow from one, the other below their feet, out of sight. With hand signals, Cub split the attack: she would lead and take the guard house they could see; he would fall behind her and take the guards immediately below them. She moved quietly to the ladder, hiked her skirt high under her bosom to pull free her second ax and left the skirt riding high, out of the way of her legs—from her expression she did not care for the local fashion.

Iona climbed the ladder, an ax in one hand and the other held between her teeth. Cub pulled a long blade from its hiding place in his shirt and followed. A heavy, oaken door with bands of iron barred the gateway, and an iron portcullis had been dropped behind it.

Cub jumped into the open door of his gatehouse—two men gawped in surprise, both with armor loose around their necks, their spears leaning in a corner, dice scattered on the small table before them. With a lunge, Cub drove his blade into the nearest neck and knocked the first man atop the other. His knife jammed in the man's throat, and the wounded gurgled and clutched at the protruding end. Unharmed, the second guard scrambled over the table to grapple with Cub, shouting for help. Cub led with his forearm, smacking his chin and they tumbled over, smashing the small table, all three tangled in the confined space. Cub lashed out with a knee, connecting with someone, and he found a broken table leg and swung it like a club—the wounded man fell backward out the door. The other continued to shout, flipped the shards of table at Cub and reached for his spear—Cub matched his move, both grabbing the weapon at the same time, wrestling to take control. Older and heavier, the man slammed his head into Cub and wrenched the spear out of his grasp, knocking it against the wall as he tried to right the weapon in the tiny space. Cub smacked him with his improvised club, unable to put weight behind his blow—the bigger man squared his shoulders and rounded on Cub, bringing his spear to bear.

A hand ax came spinning over his shoulder to crease the

guard's forehead, and the warrior slumped to the ground, legs kicking involuntarily. Cub glanced at Iona.

"He was asleep." She answered his unasked question and stooped to retrieve her weapon. Cub had to put his knee on the other's neck to yank loose his blade. Wiping his hands on the body, he turned to the gate.

"How do we...?"

"Tis this." Iona led him to the other gatehouse where she pointed to a wooden wheel attached to ropes and tackle, the ropes hanging taut from a hole in the ceiling. The well-worn handles browned from use, she tentatively gave the wheel a turn—it did not move far before meeting resistance.

"This is heavy, give me a hand."

Cub helped her work the contraption. With a squeal, the iron grate lifted—at the noise, they glanced at each other.

"Let's get this done."

"Ja, mayhap the music will cover."

They cranked the portcullis open, and Cub found a looped rope nailed to the wall which held the wheel in place with the grille lifted high.

"See here, if we pull this loop, the iron grate falls back into place."

"A smart idea."

A long beam barred the gate. Both lifting an end, they boosted it over its iron slots and dropped it, Cub tugging it from the door. The door pulled open from the outside—Hagrold and his men had been waiting.

"Took you long enough." Iona held out her hand. "Got our swords?"

A Viking handed them each a short, sax blade and offered them shields. Iona stepped out of the hated skirt—

she wore leather breeches underneath. She clanged her sword against her shield and joined the men marching to the city center. Their force numbered forty, and Rolf led a similar army—Cub expected the other gate had been opened and they would meet in the center square. Their scouts had reported the village on the other side of the river smaller in size and consisted mostly of residences—this bank held the storehouses, granaries, churches, the garrison, and homes of local nobility. All their intelligence told them this was the side to capture.

Conquering Bayeux was anticlimactic. They marched into the city center to stand unobserved by the carousers drinking and dancing. Colden and a group of raiders arrived opposite the wide courtyard, watching the merrymaking. A few noticed the Norsemen, shrieks leaped from surprised mouths, and the music slowly wound to a stop. A quiet settled over the congregated flock. One of the guards pushed forward through the crowd, threatening Hagrold with his spear.

"Who are you? Why do you come here?" Everyone nearby caught his words. Except Hagrold didn't understand them—with his shield he bashed aside the spear point and ran his sword through the unprepared man.

Chaos broke in the plaza, everyone running at once, women screaming, dogs barking, men scrambling to defend themselves. The Vikings mowed the helpless defenders down—it wasn't a battle to brag about, a complete rout ending as fast as it began. A few drunk men ended chopped into pieces before their mates which stole the fighting spirit from the remainder. Cub focused on the stand of frightened girls—he elbowed his way through the crowd and kicked a few out of his way. A man stepped forward to oppose him—he smacked him in his face with his shield. A second threatened him and he whacked him with the flat of his blade and knocked him aside—nothing stopped Cub from his goal. The girl. He marched straight across the square, his eyes on the young lady, the one with the alluring eyes.

Surrounded by whimpering girls, she stood with her head held high, eyes narrowed, and brows knitted, her arms crossed on her chest.

"Stop crying," Cub barked at them. "No one is going to hurt you." He smirked at the raven-haired beauty. "That's why I am here." And he banged his sword on his shield to emphasize his words. The girls quieted, clutched at each other, and rallied around the one called Poppa.

The raiders forced everyone in the courtyard to their knees—those who didn't comply tasted a sword. Quickly the crowd obeyed. Colden shouted for quiet, and the Vikings banged their shields until the chaos faded to women strangling back sobs. Rolf rolled forward and entered the courtyard, holding his bloodied sword high. He marched through the cowering mob, searched to find Cub and stomped across to him. Finding the stand perfect for his needs, he waved his bloody weapon at the girls to back them up, sliced the rope barrier with a single hack and climbed onto the center stage where everyone could witness his triumph.

"Translate."

Cub hoisted himself onto the platform.

"I am Rolf the Ganger. Bayeux has fallen, Bayeux is mine." He motioned to Hagrold, who pushed through the kneeling people to stand next to Cub. "Hagrold is my man. I leave him here to guard you, to guide you and collect my tax." Cub translated in a loud voice, except he called Rolf by his Frankish name, Rollo the Strider. At this announcement, a collective groan lifted from the assembly and a few women sobbed anew.

"Go to your homes. Bring out your weapons—give to my warriors. None in my Bayeux shall keep a blade or spear without my warrant. The penalty for hiding swords is death." He signaled to Colden and his other lieutenants, and they cleared the crowd from the plaza. Turning to Cub, he asked in a quieter voice, "Who are these?" A toss of his head indicated the cowed girls behind him.

"They are local nobles."

"Nobles? We can ransom them?" He prompted Cub to turn to the girls.

"Who are you?" Cub contemplated the one called Poppa when he asked. While the girls shrank from his question, she did not—she glared at him and spoke clearly.

"I am the daughter of Berenger, the high count of Rennes, member of the Paris court and servant of *your* king. These are my cousins and ladies in waiting—you have no right to keep us here. You shall release us to return to our families immediately." Peering down her nose, she spoke direct to Cub, and glanced at Rolf who watched her carefully. Keeping his eyes on her face, Cub translated her words for Rolf and Hagrold.

"Daughter of a count?" Hagrold chuckled. "She'll make a fine ransom."

"Ja, she will...." Rolf squinted at Cub. "Place them under house arrest and see they have no wants while we define a plan to use them best. Tell them it is for their benefit, their own protection."

Rolf surveyed the emptying square. "Iona, to me." He explained she was to watch over these girls. Violet eyes watched Cub closely, checking for a sign of what was to become of them. Rolf told Cub to tell them to obey Iona.

Cub cleared his throat. "You are under our protection until we can be assured of your safe passage back to your families. None shall harm you. This woman is Iona, she is your guardian—anything you need or want, she will bring to you. I speak your tongue. I will explain if needed." The raven-haired one scowled—she knew 'under our protection' meant captives. Despite her frown, Cub found her enchanting.

"Use that house," Rolf pointed out a large building on the main square, a few steps away. Iona motioned to the girls to follow her.

"Wait," Rolf commanded.

"The count's daughter, what is her name?"

"My lord asks your name...?"

"Poppa," she answered. "Poppa of Rennes."

SORVEN

Welsh Poetry.

Lyrical verses declaimed in serious, sonorous tones to a rapturous, attentive gathering.

Dun had stressed the importance of this art to these mountain people, and how it was an honor to be permitted to join the crowd. Such an invitation reflected their slowly rehabilitated status within the wider community—Heledd had spread the word the outsiders, despite their thrall status, had acted valiantly to save her from her rooftop fall, probably preventing great bruises or broken bones, or a life-changing broken back, or even, gods forbid, a tragic death. Women offered tentative smiles and children no longer hid in fear as they passed on errands for the farm. Somber Welsh farmers acknowledged them with a bow.

Inside the low-roofed, stone-walled edifice which

customarily housed the local council communal hall, benches had been arranged to accommodate as many guests as possible, aligned to face a traveling poet who stood on a wooden box overlooking the crowd of mostly women folk. Two torches on either side of the poet lit the room, casting a dim, smoky light over the spectators. The chill of the evening made the room cold. Starved for entertainment in this remote mountain hamlet, everyone sat attentively hanging on each phrase and politely applauding. While a few men peppered the audience, most of the village farmers and hunters had collected in the low-ceilinged structure across the lane, not a true tavern, the actual home of a local brewer where neighbors and friends all crammed into the narrow space to drink and argue.

Sorven tried his best.

He tried to join in the appreciation clearly evidenced on the faces around them in the standing-room-only hall. A word here and there rang familiar. And yes, the sounds rhymed... to Sorven the recitation sounded like a collection of guttural snarls, half-swallowed coughs, and failed, slobbering mutters.

Nonsense rang in his ears. When those around him cheered, he clapped along and offered Nia a weak smile whenever she turned his way, her eyes glittering with excitement. Uncomfortably pinched between her thigh on one side, where she had purposefully inched as close as possible against him, and a hefty, neighbor woman who smelled of sweat, Sorven distractedly watched the room and tried not to show his boredom.

Beside Nia, Dundle wedged between her mother Heledd, and her older sister Gwenan who scooched tight against the stacked-stone wall. Heledd had shared her shawl with them, the heavy homespun draped over

Dundle's shoulders to cover all three. The narrow confines of the seating satisfied him, allowing Dundle to feign a need to tuck his arms around both women to either side and pull them close. Near the rear of the hall, shadows concealed their familiarity. Gwenan leaned into him while Heledd placed her hand strategically where their legs touched, her fingers tapped his thigh in time with the poetic songs. As the crowd praised the recitation and those on the benches shifted, Gwenan slipped her arm around Dundle and Heledd moved her hand to his knee, both pleased and affectionate. Nia wiggled closer to Sorven and tried to slip her hand into his—Sorven stubbornly crossed his arms and craned his neck, as if he listened carefully to the verses.

Life on the farm had been good for Sorven—in his thirteenth summer, the hard labor and hearty meals filled out his muscles and he grew a hand's breadth taller. Lots of mutton, pork, and porridge. His shoulders broadened like his father, and a first few dark hairs sprung from his chin. Recently old Gethin had begun to share his secreted ale with his thralls, a fine, strong brew which let Sorven, a reluctant witness, sleep through much of Dundle's late-night assignations. Glancing sideways at the three huddled under the heavy wrap, Sorven wondered how long it would take Heledd to grasp Dundle did not cleave to her alone—a week ago Sorven had stumbled across Dundle and Gwenan against the far orchard wall wrestling under a blanket, their clothes and fruit baskets cast aside. It took a moment for him to grasp the situation, and he slipped away before either noticed his inadvertent intrusion. Dundle, who he had respected as older and wiser, and a war veteran as well... in the end Dundle seemed not too clever, he clearly did not understand where this all would lead once the farmer discovered the situation... *best be prepared for the worst,* Sorven decided. After deliberation, he hid a burlap sack with fresh clothes and a carving knife which would not be missed in a cubby in the back of the barn. Each day he added more to his cache, dried apples, a sack of porridge grain, a handful of jerked goat meat, waxed strings for snares, and he marked a heavy raincoat sewn from oiled cloth with a leather hood, hung from a barn peg—used for feeding the animals in inclement weather, he admired its weight and craftsmanship.

On the stage, the poet concluded his spectacle, bowing his head to the instant adulation lifting on all sides. Everyone stood, whistled, and clapped. A dour farmer opened the hall doors, and the crowd shuffled out.

Dundle returned the shawl to Heledd with a gracious flourish. Nia giggled at Sorven's elbow, and they filed into the night. Heledd stopped to greet her neighbors, and Gwenan spoke to a few girls her age, while Dundle stood smiling behind them and Sorven held back, avoiding the people and their chatter. Nia followed him like a stray puppy, underfoot and annoying. They wandered the lanes through the valley, reached the bottom of their hill and climbed to Gethin's farm. Sorven had gotten to know every inch of it—the animal pens and pig slop, the paddock for sheep, the barn with its hayloft, three horse stalls and two small workrooms, the four-room, thatched-roof house and its courtyard, the wheat sown field nearly knee-high, and the orchard bound by field-stone walls. One of the mouser cats crossed their path—he bent to stroke its back and let the others enter the house first.

Gethin slept in his chair before the fire, his old hound, by this time well acquainted with Dundle and Sorven, barely lifted his head from the rug at his feet as they entered. Heledd gathered a blanket and wrapped the old man, while Gwenan found bowls and poured each a share of the ale. Sorven took his and sipped, standing by the warmth of the fire. Heledd raised her bowl and toasted.

"She say, to good friends 'n good poets." Dundle bowed to her and swallowed. Sorven wobbled his head in understanding—Nia followed him to stand by the fire. She beamed when he glanced at her, her pupils wide, stroking her hand along her arm. Brooding, Sorven stared into the coals—she sighed at his disinterest and clung to his side. He finished his bowl and turned to place it on the table, Nia following on his heels.

Heledd made an announcement, and her girls moaned in reaction—clearly, she had told them bedtime had come. She gave Dundle a wink and shooed the boys to the door. In front of everyone, Nia stepped to Sorven and pulled him close to give him a peck on the cheek, blushing furiously at her boldness. While Heledd chastised, Gwenan teased her good-naturedly, their words carrying little meaning to Sorven, who endured their scrutiny, embarrassed by the attention and pressed to escape out the door—Dundle blew a kiss to the room, wished them a Welsh goodnight, and closed the door behind them.

A chill night under the stars, the moon crested the mountain top, a waning sliver—Sorven paused, wondering, *is this the moon of Skerpla or is it Solmanudur?* The weather warmed like the height of summer, and he had lost track of time. Dundle pulled back the hanging barn door and stepped into the shadows.

"Dun, do we head into Solmanudur?" he asked, stepping into the darkened room.

An arm reached out of the gloom and jerked him into

the barn. Cold metal pressed to his throat. The door banged shut.

Dundle grunted. Someone had slugged him—Sorven could discern his shape double over and fall to his knees. With the sound of an impact, Dundle sprawled in the dirt, whining. A voice growled in Welsh—Olof! His unmistakable angry tone quieted Dundle.

Nervous snickers in his ear made him recognize one of the Bumble-Bramble brothers clutched him in the dark. Dundle stuttered, Olof barking single-word questions, demanding answers. Sorven held still, the knife rolled carelessly at his throat.

Dundle wheedled in Welsh—Sorven could hear him pleading. The arms holding him tightened their grip. Dundle shuffled forward in the dark and lifted a shutter, shining a moonlit square on the floor before them.

As his eyes adjusted, Sorven recognized all three of the bandits hid in the barn. Bramble held him, his bandaged arm hung in a dirty rag sling, Olof stood over a cowering Dundle, and Bumble leaned against one of the empty horse stalls, a staff tied to his leg and his boot sliced open from a swollen ankle. In the dim light, he lurched, sallow and sick. Bramble released Sorven, pushing him to the floor next to Dun.

"What?"

"Olof say they watch us long time." Olof snorted at his name. "He want hacksilver, coin."

"We don't have any...."

"Not us." Dundle leaned closer. "Gethin."

Bramble stepped forward, threatening them with his blade. He didn't seem much better than Bumble—his sneer displayed a gap in his teeth, at least two lost, and he had a black, puffy eye. Olof barked again.

"And food... they want food."

Sorven thought, *food, ja, they are starved*. He could see it in the hollows of their cheeks and the dark circles under their eyes. Olof grumbled something else.

"Village gone—they come when all gone." *Of course,* Sorven admitted, *it made sense, they had seen the village all go to the center to hear the poet, leaving empty streets and houses, easier to sneak into town undetected. They watched where Dundle and I slept—they bided, hiding, and waited for an opportunity.*

"Food." Sorven thought fast. "We can get them food." Dundle turned to him, Olof stalked forward and glared at him, muttering in Welsh, and rubbing his hands together. "But... Dundle, they can't stay here, we might have a *visitor.*"

Dundle caught his meaning.

"Ah, ja, that be bad." He blinked at Sorven. "What we say?"

Sorven glanced around the barn, spying the empty stalls. "Tell them a loaned gelding returns this night, sometime after midnight men will bring the horse. Tell them we need to be careful of the angry farmer and his dog."

"What angry farmer and dog?"

"Gethin!"

"Oh, ja, ja." He spoke carefully to Olof. Scowling, the man peered at Sorven. Dundle gestured to the empty stall, and to Sorven, who nodded his head in turn.

"Tell them we can get food, but they need to follow me to the orchard where they will be able to see the entire valley and can escape easier if they are discovered. They don't want to be caught here when the men return the horse...." Dundle translated. Olof tilted his head, squinting and skeptical. Bramble whispered a question, and Dundle agreed, adding more to his explanation, gesturing uphill and downhill, and waving his fists as if he fought a group of attackers. Olof answered, smacking his fist in his palm for emphasis.

"I'll take them to the orchard. You get food from the house and meet me at the back wall. Bring a lot—they seem hungry." Sorven leaned close to Dundle. "I have an idea. You know where Gethin keeps his jug, the celebration drink?"

"Ja...." Dundle raised his eyebrow.

"That drink is strong—and it hits your head fast, eh?"

Dundle thought for a moment. "Oh! We get them drunk."

Sorven sighed.

Dundle spoke to Olof and returned to Sorven.

"They follow ya and I get food." Fast as a snake striking, Olof snatched Sorven by his collar and jerked his face close. He smelled awful. Sorven didn't need Dundle to translate the muttered threat. Sorven pointed to the door.

"I'll show you the way...."

The five crept into the moonlit yard, Olof holding Sorven by the back of his tunic. Dundle tiptoed across the courtyard and Sorven led them around the house and the vegetable plot to the gate in the orchard wall. Taking them right, he followed the wall along the gentle slope and led them to the rear of the fenced orchard.

"See?" he whispered to Olof. "From here you can see the whole valley." He swung his arm wide. Bumble hissed and slumped against the farthest wall, stifling a moan—his swollen ankle a mottled black and gray in the dim light. Bramble cut free a few green apples with his knife, putting them in a pouch at his side. Olof kept his eyes on Sorven. As the wait increased, Olof grumbled and moved closer to Sorven, pointing an accusing finger.

A stick snapped in the darkness. All froze in alarm.

Dundle cautiously crept out from the squat trees, ducking around their low-slung branches. He had a bundle over his shoulder and the jug under his arm.

"What took you so long?"

"Gots a lot." He handed Olof the jug and swung his bag down. Bramble stumbled near to watch him unwrap the food. He had collected the food in the larder—goat cheese in balls, loaves of bread, long strips of jerky, two heads of cabbage, a bunch of carrots, a haunch of cold mutton, a wooden tub of butter, cold porridge, and the jug... which Olof uncorked, sniffed and took a gulp. Sorven held his breath.

"Ahhh." Olof smiled and smacked his lips. Bumble and Bramble fell on the food, snatching handfuls and stuffing their mouths. Olof took another swallow, wiped his mouth with the back of his hand and claimed the hunk of meat as his own, passing the jug to Bramble who took a tentative swig. Dundle whispered something to the three.

"I told Olof ya ready fer horse." He gestured with his thumb and Olof waved Sorven away. Sorven didn't wait, he ducked under the branches and moved quickly through the trees. At the gate, he paused—movements under the house eaves caught his attention. As he watched, Gwenan climbed clumsily out of the window, toppled to land on her backside, the shutter clunking back into place behind her. She froze, afraid the noise had woken the house and Sorven ducked behind the wall, afraid she would spot him. She climbed back to her feet and crept slowly through the yard.

Thinking fast, Sorven bent over and dashed across the hill to the end of the orchard and leaped over the wall. Head down, he ran around the house and crossed the courtyard, reaching the barn door as Gwenan rounded the building—the heavy door stood ajar from their hurried departure, and Sorven tucked in his belly and slipped through the narrow opening.

A soft scratch announced her arrival. "Cariad?"

"Ah, Gwenan." Sorven pushed the door open so she could enter. She glanced around the dark barn.

"Oh, ja, you want Dundle." Sorven glanced around. "He... oh. He had to, you know, nature..." She acted confused. Embarrassed at his own inability to learn the language, he pantomimed relieving himself and she tittered, understanding his meaning. Fumbling at the workbench, Sorven found the shallow oil lamp Heledd had loaned them, and he struck a firestone to chip a spark onto the wick. Tap, tap, tap, and the smoldering lamp caught. A faint flicker lit the barn.

Gwenan slumped her shoulders, a worn blanket wrapped over her sleeping gown, her feet bare and her unbraided hair loose around her shoulders.

Dundle jumped through the open barn door and pulled it shut. Gwenan squeaked and as he turned in surprise she leaped on him, arms around his neck, her weight pushing him off balance against the door.

"Cariad!"

"What she doin' here?"

Gwenan clutched Dundle tightly, kissing his neck and running her hands from his hips to his chest. She pulled his face to her waiting mouth. She dropped the blanket and clung to him—Sorven backed up, feeling self-conscious and aware he intruded on their privacy. He moved past the stalls to a small vestibule filled with tack, horse blankets and hand tools. At least, behind its door, he wouldn't be encroaching. As he turned to motion his intent to Dundle, he noticed Gwenan had dropped her night shirt and tugged at Dundle's clothes, her desire overcoming all modesty. Ducking his head, Sorven stepped into the small room and closed the door.

Sorven listened to the unmistakable sound of bodies settling in the hay. The barn grew hushed, occasional sounds of the passionate couple stirring and crinkling the straw.

A sharp rap sounded on the barn door.

Dundle made a startled noise, and Sorven held his breath—was this Olof returned for more? Dundle scrambled to his feet, and hustled Gwenan out of the pile of hay with a rustle and a few grunts.

Another knock sounded. He shushed the elder daughter and pushed her across the room. *Where to hide, where to hide...?*

Dundle settled on the small closet where Sorven hid.

Yanking the door open, he tucked her in the narrow space.

A naked girl.

Sorven gulped and tried to protest, and Dundle hushed them both and swung the door closed.

The knock sounded again, a more insistent rap.

Not well constructed, gaps between boards let the lamp light filter into the closet. A tight space, designed for a single person to access the shelves, an embarrassed Sorven shut his eyes.

Gwenan giggled. Sorven swallowed and peeped at her.

He stood face-to-face with the nude girl. Her pale skin glowed. So close, he could see the freckles across her nose.

"Sorven." She gave him a sheepish grin, whispering something in Welsh he imagined a type of apology.

"Gwenan..." He struggled in the confined space, trying to keep his eyes on the ceiling.

Outside their hideaway, Dundle pulled the door open to let someone enter. The bar slid into place, locking the door. Peeking through the slats in the door, they could see he had wrapped the blanket around himself and spoke to someone in the shadows. He moved a step backward.

Nia stepped into the lamp-lit space, dressed in her night gown, her braid unbound, and hair puffed around her head. She whispered furiously with Dundle and waved her finger in his face.

Gwenan smiled and using her forefinger, poked Sorven in the chest. "Nia." Sorven understood, Nia had snuck out... to find him!

Gwenan snickered into her hand and whispered to Sorven, a long series of words during which she leaned closer as if she confided in him, pressing her breasts against him in enthusiasm to share her mind.

All of which made Sorven uncomfortable.

Very uncomfortable.

Across the barn, Dundle whispered to Nia, holding the blanket around his waist with one hand and gesturing with the other. Nia answered with a pout, tapping her foot.

Inside the closet, Gwenan continued to whisper to Sorven, sharing a secret in her native tongue. He glanced at her—she held her belly and emphasized her words....

He gave his head a shake, not comprehending.

She crossed her arms and rocked them side to side and patted her belly again.

Slowly it dawned on Sorven.

"Dundle?"

Her grin grew larger, and she bobbed her head, glad he understood.

Sorven slumped back against the horse blankets.

Gwenan was with child, Dundle's child....

Oh, this is not good. Not good at all!

In the barn, Nia grew louder and more insistent.

Gwenan pressed her eye to a crack, trying to watch, wiggling against Sorven, increasing his discomfort and embarrassment. Attempting to ignore her, Sorven held his ear to the slats, listening, when another loud knock on the door made them both jump. Nia and Dundle jumped too.

A voice carried through the door—Heledd called to Dundle, not too brash yet loud enough to announce her arrival, and she rattled the locked door.

Dundle and Nia jostled each other, each turning the opposite way, Nia trying to run to the closet where Sorven and Gwenan hid.

Dundle dropped his blanket in his haste to grab Nia, pulled her back from the closet and pushed her stumbling to the rungs of the hayloft ladder.

A quick glance at Gwenan showed Sorven her face had paled, fear of her mother draining the blood from her cheeks, her mouth agape and hands trembling before her bosom.

Gracelessly, Nia flopped onto the shifting mass of loose straw in the loft, wiggling to find a toe or hand hold. A large clump of hay cascaded from the loft, plummeting to add to the pile on the floor. The barn door rattled, and Dundle jumped to unhook and slide the bar aside.

Heledd stomped through the doorway, her head high and the moonlight highlighting her scowl. She immediately interrogated Dundle, poking a finger in his chest, and while he didn't understand her, Sorven could glean her questions from her forceful tone and demanding demeanor.

"*What is happening here?*" She gestured to the door.

Dundle jerked the door to roll closed, leaving a small gap where it did not pull completely shut.

"*Why was the door locked?*" A stomp of her foot.

A tremor knocked loose straw adrift from the loft.

Dundle whispered in a conciliatory way, holding out his hands palms up, offering a wheedling explanation.

Heledd lowered her voice and stepped farther into the room, gesturing to his privates.

"*Why are you naked?*"

His low-pitched response nearly impossible to hear, his hands moved in a placative wave, calming, comforting, gentle.

Sorven glanced at Gwenan.

Watching her mother and her lover interact in the lamplight, her happy grin melted slowly into a befuddled frown. She tipped her head and peered closer into the gap between the boards.

Heledd stepped forward and placed her hand on Dundle's naked chest. They spoke quietly, Heledd inching closer, he treading carefully back from her advance.

Heledd forced Dundle against a stall gate where he could retreat no farther, and with her head tipped forward and her hair scarcely concealing a lusty sneer, she dropped free her robe and slid against him.

Sorven watched Gwenan.

Her eyes popped wide, and her happy expression faded to a snarl.

Sorven tried to hold her back.

He grappled with her shoulders, unsure where to grip an unclad girl. He wrapped his arms around her in a hug.

Undeterred, Gwenan elbowed him aside and sprang from the closet.

"Mother!"

Sorven knew that word.

More straw tumbled from the loft.

Naked Heledd stared dumbfounded at her naked daughter.

Sorven watched the three naked people in the circle of lamplight. Their hesitation lingered as they stared at each other...

Slowly shock turned to emerging understanding and Heledd turned on Dundle, who covered his privates and shrank back against the stall.

An argument ensued, mother and daughter bickering, their voices rising in volume, suddenly shouting. Sorven imagined the accusations flying about the room, Dundle pleading and wincing, both women barking at him whenever he attempted to speak. Mother and daughter grew redfaced and clenched their fists, tears of anger in their eyes. Sorven reared back to his closet hideaway—he expected a fight to break out any moment.

Gwenan patted her belly and waggled her head in a defiant manner, announcing her big news to her mother and Dundle at the same time.

With her hands on her hips, Heledd shouted back, pointing at Dun and back at her stomach. Both women turned and glared at Dundle...

Dundle's eyes went wide as he comprehended his predicament.

Both of them?!

A tuft of hay tumbled loose, and glancing up for the first time, Sorven saw Nia dangled over the edge, her legs extended into the air past her knees. She barely clung to the slippery hay.

Screaming, Heledd and Gwenan charged each other.

Their shouts and curses rang in the quiet barn. Bravely

Dundle stepped between the mother and daughter, who howled and scratched to reach each other.

The barn door slammed open. A silhouette of a giant stood framed in the opening.

Heledd swallowed a squeal and hopped behind Dundle, suddenly holding out her arm to defend her daughter. Gwenan blundered into her mother and tried to hide her ample bosom behind crossed arms.

Olof staggered into the barn, the empty jug dangling from his finger.

Seeing the dirty bandit lurch toward them, Heledd and Gwenan both emitted an ear-piercing screech. Sorven fumbled around, grasping for something, anything he could use as a weapon.

As surprised as the women were to find Olof stumble into their midst, the drunken goon stumbled flabbergasted to find women in the barn. Naked women! His mouth gaped open, and he waggled his tongue, unable to form words.

Dundle jumped forward in a protective stance, throwing his skinny arms out as if to grapple in defense of the women. Olof snorted and held the jug out like a shield. Gwenan howled again, the sound ringing in the enclosed space. Olof stepped backward and slipped on the freshly dropped hay. Off balance, he tottered, confused and totally unprepared for a girl to fall on him from the hayloft.

The slippery hay pile finally gave way and an avalanche of straw carried Nia off the shelf to land on the unsuspecting outlaw!

As they struggled in a pile, Sorven stepped forward with a horseshoe mallet and gave Olof a sharp whack to his temple. The bandit buckled, spewed a mouthful of poorly chewed mutton and aquavit, and crumpled into the straw.

Torches in the courtyard signaled neighbors rushed to investigate the commotion, to offer aid if they could. All the shouting! All the screaming! Surely, they could help....

Sorven helped Nia climb out of the tangled pile of straw and Olof. She hugged him and cried in Welsh.

"My hero," Dundle explained.

Heledd turned on him and Gwenan—her sharp commands made Dundle scramble to don his breeches. Heledd shook her dusty robe and pulled it back on, and as Gwenan's clothes had been lost in the scuffle, she grabbed a horse blanket and wrapped it around her eldest daughter.

Alerted by the tumult, Gethin and his hound came tottering out of the house, crossing the courtyard and rubbing sleep from his eyes.

Neighbors bearing firebrands charged the hill, and Heledd called them forward to capture the brute lying in their barn. Gwenan flipped away her mother's hand and moved to stand by Dundle while Nia clung to Sorven.

Men pushed forward and took control of the barely conscious Olof, dragging him out of the barn, tying his arms with leather straps and marching him to the stocks. More neighbors gathered to gawk.

Gethin rocked on his heels, glancing from his wife to his daughters in various stages of undress. In his raspy voice, he challenged them. Dundle stepped forward and held out his hand to Gwenan, making a small speech in his broken Welsh. Gwenan took Dun by his hand and stepped in close under his arm.

Gethin grasped the situation quickly and made a pronouncement crafted to protect his daughter from gossip and preserve her honor—a hastily announced betrothal—or at least Sorven would have said something similar if he had been in his position. All the gathered neighbors beamed in agreement, a wise decision to protect his daughter's honor.

Gethin continued by indicating Sorven and Nia at his side, her night shirt exposing much of her legs in an immodest way—he gestured at Sorven and the girl, and she trembled at his side. Glancing at her, he could see the announcement thrilled Nia. She gazed at him, a toothy grin dimpled her cheeks, and she fluttered her eyelashes at him. Around them the villagers spoke in congratulatory tones.

Only Heledd nursed a sour frown.

Sorven inched back to Dun and whispered, "I'm lost. What has happened?"

"Honor bound, I be wed t' Gwenan and ya t' Nia. Old Gethin swore afore his neighbors an' cousins."

Sorven choked.

Glancing at his feet, he struggled for composure. *Wed to Nia? No, that can't be... this is not my destiny.* He glanced to the barn, Nia hugging his ribs.

He remembered Bramble and Bumble, hiding in the orchard.

"Two more!" he raised his voice. "I saw two more." Dundle remembered as well and translated for the crowd. With shouts and torches held high, the well-meaning neighbors surged past Sorven, Dundle leading the way around the house, Gethin and his girls at the head of the pack.

Sorven waited in the courtyard until he stood alone.

He could hear the crowd swing open the gate, its leather hinges creaking and shouts as they found the men collapsed in a drink-induced stupor. Crossing to the open barn door, he stepped to the ready cubby and pulled free his stash.

He lifted the heavy coat from its peg, moved to the

small half-door reserved for livestock, ducked under the beam, and crept out into the animal paddock.

Behind him, he could hear the commotion as the villagers arrested the drunken outlaws. With his head held low, he made a beeline for the corner of the fenced yard, avoiding the ram and his ewes under their byre. He leaped over the split rails and hiked the rocky hillside, moving with speed and determination until he reached the trees.

He glanced back, his view encompassing the small farm, the villagers forcing the two wounded men out of the orchard and the entire valley spread below in the light of the moon.

"Sorry, Dun. This be your life, not mine." Wrapping the heavy coat tight, he plunged into the underbrush.

KARA

"The midsummer festival, two years hence."

"No! Really?" Kara twirled a lock of Kaelan's hair around her forefinger. "Two years?"

"Ja," Kaelan dropped his eyes. "You watched your little brother and sister, one in each hand."

Kara tried to remember—the solstice feast, the crowds and all the stalls. The fire-breather, yes, and the jugglers and those strange volva witches hawking charms and medallions. Wood carvers and coopers and smiths with makeshift tables displaying iron pegs, hooks, and plow blades. The congested display of new Lindenwood shields. Fox pelts and sheep skins. Wandering the stalls with her mother—leatherworks, bolts of homespun in a myriad of colors, imported cloths and those hammered copper bracelets she adored. Mostly she remembered the controlled bedlam of it all—horse traders and cattle men, pens tight with goats and sheep, and people elbowing each other as they passed. Men bartered and swapped stories, showed off their swords and new weapons, women gathered to show embroideries and fancy quilts. Father had bought a ram to sire their ewes, blinders looped over its horns and its back legs hobbled to keep it docile in the press of merrymakers. Yeru had been chaperoning Willa. She had shared a honeyed apple with Hilda, struggling to keep sticky fingers out of her riotous curls. She did remember minding Hildie and Finn. Sorven had run off to find Cub, returning red-faced and sweaty, dirt smudges on his face and hands. Tormod and his father had stopped to speak with her father—the summer when Tormod first met Willa.

"My father spoke with yours." He prompted her memory. "I was with my sister, and you dressed in a green smock, your hair in two braids." She remembered the outfit, and her mother had wound daisies in her hair, she remembered being impatient at her fussy attempts to ready for the festival. A long afternoon in the sun and riding Father's cart back to the homestead.... "I said hello to you."

"Sorry." Kara grinned, gazing in his eyes. "I thought it was last year, when your father let us hide from those murderers...."

"No, we had met before. Well, I remember you, flowers in your hair." Kaelan cupped her chin. "Your forehead pink from sun burn, freckles cross your nose and your goofy smile." She poked out her tongue and tussled his hair.

The afternoon sun settled behind the Clondalkin palisades, casting a shadow over the niche where she leaned against him. Off duty, they lounged on each other in a familiar way. She continued to twist a lock by his temple, gazing into his eyes.

A bountiful Heyannir harvest and good hunting had

stocked the larders, leaving plenty of fresh meat and excess grain for the brewing vats. Smoke houses jammed to capacity with jerky, salted pork belly and ham hocks, a lingering smell of campfire everywhere. Every house collected rainwater for kegs of ale or raided beehives to brew mead. As the moon turned to Tvimanudur the nights grew chill, and leaves faded to bright gold and scarlet.

Clondalkin post had become a welcome routine. Weeks had turned to moons, steady patrols, daily weapons practice, hearty meals, and comfortable, accustomed assignments. And free time to share with Kaelan—when not standing guard, they became inseparable. Her fondness for him increased, and when apart, daydreams of Kaelan filled her thoughts. At first, they stole private moments for furtive embraces. Soon it became apparent none at this outpost cared, in fact, the guards held open liaisons and ignored most dalliances. Nights in the mess hall became bawdy, especially after a long sortie and lots of ale, and once Kara overcame her natural embarrassment, she became comfortable with letting others know she had a relationship with Kaelan. She even let him kiss her in public. An open and familiar affection grew between them. She teased him about his slow spear work. To counter her gentle ribbing, he dedicated efforts and grew skilled at the bow, adding to their table a hare or wild hen each week. In the yard, she braided his hair and shaved his sparse beard with a razor—she liked the smooth feel of his face against hers. No one cared.

For his part, Kaelan teased her about her sudden growth spurt, and indeed, she had not been prepared for such rapid changes. Facing him, they stood nearly eye-to-eye, tall enough she could wear her father's longsword at her belt instead of on her back. In her fourteenth summer,

Kara knew the time had passed when she should purchase a new wardrobe—her dresses hung much too short and pinched tight around her chest. She could barely wriggle into them, and the seams stretched and popped. Her boots fit if she curled her toes. She filled out, her figure resembling her mother more each week, slim-waisted despite the spread of her hips, her shoulders thickening from hard labor. And to her surprise, more blossomed as well—she resorted to binding her bosoms tight under her smock. The good news was her leather armor tightened across her back and no longer gaped at her sides.

Kaelan straightened. "It's time we go."

While this outpost had a few excellent features, it had no real market. If she was to find new clothes and have a cobbler make her a new pair of boots, they would need to head to the bigger town. Yet, certain Dublinners she wished to avoid, including King Ausle, his captain Gunna and her crew. It had been moons since she had last seen any of them—a simple plan, they intended to slip into the city, quickly shop and return to Clondalkin as unnoticed as possible. With the garrison's leave, they followed the road to Dublinn town. The late afternoon sun shone through the thinning leaves and, alone, they held hands and continued their long-running conversation about everything and nothing at all.

Spires of Dublinn rose from the trees, identical to when they had left it. Cook fire smoke drifted in a cloud about the fortress. The shrubs around the paling wall sported yellow leaves, harbingers of the coming winter moons. The gate stood open, a few guards lollygagging in the lengthening evening shadows. One of the men recognized them and waved them inside. Heads lowered, they followed Great Ship Street and turned on Werburgh where Tordis had told her several reputable seamstresses lived. She counted doors and knocked on the fourth, which creaked ajar. A middle-aged woman ushered them inside a tiny vestibule, a curtain closing off the back of the wattle-and-daub house. Two oily tapers lit the small space. Prune faced and standoffish, the Irish woman's expression softened once Kara waggled her purse and the jangle of silver filled the small room.

"I was told you are a seamstress?"

"Aye, tis true." She sniffed and glanced at Kaelan. "Woman clothes and such."

"Do you have any that would fit me?"

She measured Kara with a squint. "Me thinks." She pointed at Kaelan. "He'll have to wait without." Kara handed her sword to Kaelan who slipped back out into the street. The woman disappeared behind the curtain, returning with an armful of homespun in muted colors.

"Try these." She laid a collection of smocks over a wooden bar, holding one in front of Kara to gauge her size.

"Seems a tad big..."

"Girl, ya still be grown'." She huffed as she held the dress to Kara's throat. "Waste ya coin to buy fer t'day, when 'morrow ye'll be a full-grown woman, eh?" She gave Kara a mirthless wink. Kara didn't argue—she squirmed out of the ill-fitting clothes and dropped them in a pile. Seeing Kara, the woman clucked her tongue.

"Why wrap like that? Don' yer ma teach ya? Think it'd be hard to breathe, eh?" She inclined her head and ducked into the back room, returning with a soft, cotton sling. "Here, child," she unwrapped Kara and slipped the sling under her arms. "Turn around." She tied the sling behind her neck, checked the fit in front, adjusting the support with experienced hands. "Here, ya ties it under ya arm 'ere."

She roughly turned Kara to face her. "Don't that feel better?"

"Ja," Kara admitted.

Her mother—Kara thought of her mother, and her little sisters, Hildie and Neeta. *Neeta would have grown over the summer, and Hildie with her blonde curls in constant disarray, her mother struggling with a comb. Aunt Yeru with them...* she thought of her mother's blue eyes, her soft hands, and her cooking—oh, she missed her cooking. She wondered, *do they miss me as I miss them?*

The old woman broke her wistful daydreams with an armful of tunics. She shimmied into a linen underdress, the length reaching to her ankles with ample room at her waist. The woman helped her don a forest green smock, showing her the shoulder straps.

"Lift it here, and pin to hold it." She showed Kara how to raise and lower the straps.

"Needs a sash or a belt." She rummaged in her loose pile and pulled an embroidered, blue band free. "Try this."

Kara wrapped the ribbon around her waist. The woman grunted, tying the strip higher around her middle to accentuate her bosom. Snorting, she ducked behind her curtain and returned with two additional cotton slings and pressed them on Kara.

"Wash'em well and change often." She admonished her. "Nothing smells worse'n stale unders."

They haggled over the price. Kara didn't negotiate too hard—she had plenty of hacksilver, wages saved with nowhere to spend. Kara bought all three slings, two linen dresses, the green smock and a similar red one with white pin flowers embroidered around the neckline, and she left her old clothes behind in exchange for a burlap sack to carry her purchases. While the gruff woman invited her to return any time, her sour gaze belied her kind words.

Kaelan loitered in the avenue, waiting for her return. He admired her new green smock. "You look beautiful."

"Go on...." Kara swished the skirt and grinned at him. "At least these fit better." Taking the sword belt from his hands and fitting it under the blue sash around her midriff, she pointed back to Great Ship Avenue. "The cobbler is there."

They meandered towards the dock and found the leatherworker, his shop an open yard with workbench and tools, and tanning barrels and drying racks. Hides hung stretched from wooden bars, and scraps of leather hung from a low shed roof. An iron brazier held chunks of wood and coals, casting a flickering light. An old man squatted in the half-light, tipped back on a stool and sipping from a bowl. Taciturn but accommodating, the cobbler measured her feet, held two fingers high to indicate his price, and mumbled he would need a week. Kara paid him half to seal the deal and they left him standing in the twilight.

Taking Kaelan by the hand, Kara moved quickly along the avenue, headed for the gate and the road back to their post.

"Shouldn't we sup while we are here?"

"Thinking with your stomach?"

"Well, we are missing dinner..."

Kara glanced around—she had hoped to avoid the King's Hall and all who frequented it. She paused and pulled Kaelan to a halt in the center of the road. "Fine, hungry boy. Let's stop on Wine Tavern Street and find you a meal." She pulled him back into the city.

Several taverns stood open to the roadway, already alive with singing and the shouts of carousing revelers. The songs rang out, words in the native Eire tongue, exotic to Kara's ears and full of emotion and haunting harmonies. The stench of stale beer pervaded the avenue and clots of men moved through the lane, pushing into the louder, more active spaces. She noticed few women on the street—uncomfortable, Kara selected the quietest place, a dark interior glimpsed through the open doorway, the windows shuttered and a single torch burning in a sconce beside the door jamb.

A short, pudgy proprietor met them at the door and steered them to a side table. He wiped his hands on a tattered rag and made a cursory attempt at wiping the table before they sat. Divided into small booths with ramshackle tables and benches in each, the separate walls provided a sense of privacy. Low rafters supported an equally low-slung thatched roof, the reeds bowed overhead. They gave the owner a half coin and he waved over a skinny girl with two bowls of watered-down ale and a freshly baked loaf.

Clearly, they had chosen an unpopular place—all the better to stay out from the watchful eye of Gunna and her mean-spirited mates. The dimly lit public house smelled of burned meats, grease and a sharp, vinegar tang, the sticky table and uneven, planked floor grimy with grit, and bits of straw shuffled under her feet. Kara let Kaelan pick at the bread, and while they waited for the meal, she slyly measured the room. A man sprawled in a corner booth, his head drooping over his bowl. Across the hall in one of the booths, a couple pressed tight together on a single bench, oblivious to anything except each other, wrapped in an embrace with their hoods arranged to hide their countenance from prying eyes. *Serves us well*, Kara thought, *a hideaway for trysts and forlorn drunks, not likely to find the King and his guards here*. With a sigh, she relaxed and crossed her ankles under the table. Kaelan sipped from his bowl and offered her a hunk of the bread. Crusty and chewy, she nibbled at her portion.

The pimply serving girl returned with a bowl of stew, hunks of mutton in peas and gravy. "It's good." Kaelan held out a spoonful for her to try and she tentatively took a bite. Chewing her mouthful slowly, she watched the couple across the room pull apart, their heads close, their hands gripped tightly on the table. White knuckles and whispered words. Opposite them, the drunk snorted and wobbled in his chair.

Taking her wooden spoon, she helped herself to another bite, fishing for the crunchy peas. Kaelan offered her the loaf. She tore free another hunk and sopped the gravy.

Three men entered, all in hooded cloaks, their faces shrouded, their heads nearly touching the low-slung beams. From the way they carried themselves, Kara guessed them experienced warriors—shoulders straight, their stance wide and balanced, and their right hands under their coats as if clasping the hilt of swords. Soldiers. Kara tensed—*what is this?* She placed her hand on Kaelan and gave him a squeeze. He lifted his face from his meal, slowing the pace of his chews as he absorbed the situation. She uncrossed her ankles to sit straighter.

One of the newcomers tossed a purse to the proprietor. He winked at the newcomers, took his girl by the hand, and slipped out a back door. The bolt clicked as it slid home, the noise unexpectedly loud.

Kara gripped Kaelan's hand tighter and released it. Under the table she reached for her hilt, noting Kaelan slide his left hand under the table as well—*he reaches for his knife*, she thought, *he senses something too.*

With merely a glance in their direction, the three crossed the room to where the other couple sat. Benches scraped on the floor. The three leaned close over the table and exchanged hushed words. An angry growl and a pleading woman's voice. The hood slipped aside, and Kara glimpsed a pale face and a wave of red hair.

Muirgel!

What was the princess of Mael Sechnaill doing in this dark tavern? She tensed and shifted in her seat.

"Careful," Kaelan whispered, and drank from his bowl to clear his mouth. "Not here for us...." Kara gave him an imperceptible nod of agreement, swinging her eyes from his to rake the room. The strangers shuffled as they wrapped the cape tighter around the princess to hide her from view. One of the company gripped her shoulders in a protective caress. Kara caught a snatch of her protector's face.

Him! The man from the night in the forest, the one she had called 'Otir.' Here inside Dublinn, an enemy of the King. She shuddered in a deep lungful and held it. Kaelan tipped his head to stir his stew, and Kara dropped her gaze. A clatter and scrape sounded as the warriors exited the low-ceilinged room, shepherding Muirgel out between them. Eyes half-closed, the drunken man at the back table swayed over his empty bowl.

"Quick. We must follow." Kaelan stuffed the last of the bread in his mouth and swigged his remaining beer. Kara slipped her sack of new clothes over her left shoulder, and they scrambled to the doorway, easing around the doorjamb to check the street.

The five stalked towards Great Ship Street, ignoring the clamor of the crowded taverns to either side. Kara took Kaelan by his forearm and led him, trailing the interlopers from a safe distance. At the main avenue, one of the soldiers took Muirgel by the elbow and turned toward the docks, the other three, including Otir, turned south toward the main gate and the King's Hall. Kara paused, indecisive—which to follow? Muirgel and her escort fleeing to the dockside, or....

"The King." Kaelan pulled her in the opposite direction. *Of course*, she thought, *protect our King, we can worry about the princess later*. They stumbled after the cloaked warriors who had faded into the dark avenue. Leaving the brightly lit Wine Tavern Street behind, they rushed to follow.

Reaching the square before the King's Hall, they glimpsed the three strangers enter the longhouse, the brightness of the well-lit room spilling out into the courtyard. The meal completed, the square filled with a swarm of guards, guests and locals who milled about gossiping, gathering to throw dice, sharing a joke. The city gate stood wide, three stout men blocking its opening with crossed spears—Kara recognized they stood unworried and idle, chatting with a group of passing maids. Muttering under her breath, Kara bumped and prodded her way through the throng, Kaelan weaving along behind her. She handed him her sack of new clothes and dodged around a family strolling home after their big meal, pushed aside a gangly youth coming out of the doorway and jumped through the longhouse door.

Kara blinked her eyes, the torches bright after the dark evening outside. The crowd in the hall had thinned, and with alarm, she could see the three cloaked strangers approached the King's table. Unaware of the danger, the king sat with his elderly retinue, waving a brimful horn and gesturing at an alderman. She continued her headlong rush into the room, drawing her sword as she ran... and tumbled headlong, knocking a bench aside and smacking her chin on the floor. Her sword skittered from her grasp.

"Oops."

Laughter erupted behind her. She rolled to her side, flummoxed.

Asta towered over her, Helka laughing at her side—she had tripped her!

"Watch where you are going, little Dubgaill!" Gunna's blonde cronies loomed over her, mocking and laughing.

Asta nudged her with her boot toe. "Clumsy, eh?"

"Trip much, Agnesdatter?"

"The king!" Kaelan shouted from the doorway.

Kara rolled back to face the hall—everything happened in an instant, except to her it seemed like all movement slowed, her body refusing to respond to demands to leap and run to his side, to run to his defense—from her vantage point she could see the three warriors had reached her liege. She opened her mouth to shout, climbing to her feet, her voice welling from her belly.

"Noooo!"

Asta and Helka froze, their mouths open, hands loose at their sides, and Kaelan struggled through the doorway, pushing past gawking locals. Kara fumbled about, scrambling to recover her lost blade, all the while keening her warning cry. The room fell uncommonly quiet, Kara's warning scream piercing the hall.

The attackers cast off their cloaks. In a smooth motion, they drew swords, their leader leaping on the table before the king. His first swing knocked the horn loose, a spray of ale spattering the diners.

"Son of Ausle, tis I." He leaned forward and pressed the tip of his sword to the King's throat. "Otir, son of Jarnkne. He who you Dubgaill so foully murdered at Carlingford

Lough! You stole my father, you stole my betrothed, and I now steal your life!" As Kara and the court watched, Otir slid the blade slowly, meticulously through the King's neck, their eyes locked with one another.

Ausle grimaced back at Otir, his face a mask of hate and rage. He hissed with the sword deep in his neck, burbled and spat blood. His hands gripped the table and he tried to rise, to speak... no words formed. A stream of blood flooded his chest, no way to staunch the wound. Otir growled at him and leaned close to watch him die.

Breaking the spell, Otir kicked the dying king in his chest and knocked his highchair backwards, freeing his sword. He lifted the bloody blade high above his head.

"The tyrant dies!" He shouted—his additional words lost as the room dissolved in a tumult of tossed tables and scrambling guests. In the noise and confusion, his banner men at his side attacked the aldermen at the king's table, hacking indiscriminately at the unarmed elders. The remaining guests surged for the doors, a mad scramble accompanied by screams and shouts. Kara, bending to collect her sword, found herself kicked and punched by people rushing the door. Asta and Helka shuffled from the hastening mob, and armed with simple side arms, they pulled their short blades and tried ineffectually to gain control of the disorganized rush for the exit. Calling for Kara, the crowd carried Kaelan out the door.

Kara found her feet and lifted her sword. She could taste blood in her mouth—whoever had punched her had broken her lip. Across the room, Otir and his two warriors moved back from the longhouse entrance, slashed wildly at any who came near them and headed to the room at the end of the hall. Without thinking, Kara ran toward them.

The three barred the door from the inside. Kara could

hear rough scrapes and bangs inside. She rattled the door and bashed it with her sword. Asta and Helka ran panting to her side.

"Where does this lead?"

Perplexed, Asta worked her jaw, unable to answer. Helka elbowed her aside.

"The King's rooms."

Kara banged the door with her hilt, chipping the wood and doing little damage.

"They must know of an escape."

"Ja." Helka placed her hand on Kara's arm. "Not that way. There must be an exit in the alley." She met Kara's eyes. "Come."

Leaving Asta standing over dead King Ausle, the two dashed to the courtyard.

Kara blinked in the evening dark. Cleared by the screaming, frightened diners, a few disordered soldiers lingered in the square. Kaelan met them at the door, the gate guards shuffling confused behind him.

"Shut the city gate," Helka commanded, taking control of the situation. The men stumbled, asking for the King. "Now, SHUT THE GATE! By Heimdallr, hold your post and shut that damned gate! You there, go find Gunna. Call out the garrison—the murderers, they are still in the city."

"This way." She pointed to a narrow alley next to the longhouse, a tight space where the shingled roof hung low and forced walkers to stoop under the eaves. Ducking, Helka scrambled through the passageway. Bent forward with her sword clasped in her arms, Kara ran after her, Kaelan on her heels.

Rounding the hall, the alley opened into a broader lane, and they quickly found a rear door hanging ajar. As Helka kicked the door wide and peered into the darkened rooms, Kara stood at her back, her sword at the ready.

Kaelan shouted, "There they go!"

They turned in the direction he pointed. Sensing pursuit, the three assassins ran. Without a thought, they chased the fleeing men. Kaelan passed the women with his longer gait and speed. As they crossed Wine Tavern Street, one of the Irish warriors turned to face them as the other two made their escape.

Kaelan came upon him first—his headlong rush carried him to the fighter. Plunging out of the darkened street, he saw the man with his sword ready, his feet planted, his face grim and resolved. Kaelan shouted, leading with his long knife in a thrust to the man's chest. The seasoned warrior merely slapped aside his knife hand and kicked Kaelan, letting his momentum tumble him aside.

Helka and Kara watched him disarm Kaelan's charge as they skidded into the avenue. This was no Irish brawler; his grim squint and ready stance, the way he spun his sword to limber his muscles implied a seasoned mercenary, a king's man experienced in the ways of combat. They slowed their advance, separating to surround their adversary.

Helka clucked her tongue and spoke to the big man in the local tongue. He snorted, sizing her up—Kara figured she cursed or taunted him, to little effect. Kara danced to his opposite side, circling to move behind him—the big man swung his sword at her, his eyes locked on Helka. Kaelan scrambled in the dirt for his lost knife.

With no warning, Helka struck.

The warrior parried. Kara jumped in close, aiming a blow at his chest, surprised to find the strike blocked by a fast return. Helka struck again, battering at him, and Kara jabbed with her long blade. The experienced veteran knew how to hold multiple combatants at bay—his blade arcing, each blow parried or dodged, and through his barrage of strikes, he counterattacked Helka who he perceived to be a stronger enemy. Sword against sword, the blows rang in the night. Kara spat blood from her lip and stepped into his reach to draw his attack, his powerful, downward swing clanging against her parry and knocking her to her knees. She swung her sword in a counter, biting at his knee, and he sidestepped her thrust, and using his hand, grabbed Helka's downward swing and held tight, immobilizing her blade in his grip.

Helka cursed and kicked ineffectually as he lifted her weapon high. He growled and poked his sword at the suspended target she provided. Holding her sword over her head, he dragged her closer, lifting her off her feet where he could skewer her with his blade, heedless of the blood dripping from his wounded hand. Helka wiggled and thrashed as she dangled, narrowly dodging his jabs.

He ignores me, Kara thought, and she swung her sword at his middle. In a graceful and unexpected move, the big man dropped Helka and rolled with Kara's stab, capturing her blade at his side, and bringing his short sword arcing toward her head. A wind from its passage touched her cheek as she toppled over, her trapped blade dragging her off her feet. He stomped on her belly and jerked to pull free her blade. Coughing and gasping for air, Kara clung to her weapon, dragged through the dirt. He bellowed as Helka struck him in the calf, a less than honorable attack, all she could manage against this opponent. The sharp edge of her sword sliced deep along his leg and the tendon at his heel severed with a loud snap. With a grunt, he released Kara's sword and dropped to one knee.

Kaelan shouted, drawing a crowd from the nearby

public houses. Whooping as she struggled to recapture her breath, Kara stumbled and drew back her sword for another run at the warrior. Helka shouted to catch her attention.

"Together."

They approached from opposing sides and struck in concert, each blow timed to strike at the same instant... despite being unable to dodge, his formidable skill helped him parry their joint attack, swinging in tight arcs and deflecting the shieldmaidens' strikes or using his vambraces to deflect blows. Kara gritted her teeth and used two hands to put her weight behind her swings, amazed this opponent maintained his defense with merely a flick and a counter. The battle devolved into a stalemate, Kara and Helka hammering at his short sword, and the wounded Irish deflecting each blow with quick darts of brilliant swordplay. Kara wondered if they could break this masterful resistance. Sweat trickled down her forehead.

In the end, Kaelan broke the battle pattern and opened the warrior's cover. He found his blade and struck from behind, stabbing his knife deep in the man's shoulder along his collar bone.

After the sneak attack, the will to fight drained from the Irishman. His returns slowed, his parries lost their force and Helka struck, followed by Kara who slipped her blade close to nick his torso. The melee continued, Kaelan's knife protruding from his shoulder, the two women hopping around him, chipping at his defenses. His resistance broken, he could parry only one blow while the other struck home. The warriors carved ragged gashes in bloody lines across his chest and back. In a desperate attempt to parry Kara's two-handed swing, he overextended his reach and slumped forward, catching himself on his wounded hand. Helka jumped on his back and plunged her sword into his neck. The sharp tip clipped a chunk of muscle and tendon, leaving a deep gouge. Blood spurted freely. Kara swung with all her power and chopped into his forearm above his wrist. His weapon tumbled from his grasp. He lurched, pitched on to his face and moaned in the dirt.

Kaelan stepped forward, reaching for his knife.

"Careful," Helka cautioned. "He lives." She circled the prone form. "Smart one waits a chance for one final strike, snake that he is." She leered at the small crowd of onlookers who had gathered to watch their fight. "Leave him die. We must find Otir."

She continued along the alley, Kara and Kaelan close behind her. The road led between sheds and hovels, the poorest section inside the Dublinn walls. The stench of sewage swelled to meet them. The passageway opened across from the dockside gate, and Helka found an unconscious guard toppled next to the hatch door.

"All-Father send them to Helheim!" She spat and ducked through the opening. Kara ducked through the door to follow.

They had been delayed too long—a ship floated in the black pool, oars working the Poddle River, thrashing its way downstream to the Liffey, the open sea and escape. On the deck, they could see a lantern and the shapes of four standing by the mast, Muirgel's red hair glistening in the light.

Helka paced the wharf parallel with the sailing fugitives. She reached the end, cursed, and slumped to her haunches with a grunt.

Kara wandered to her side and panted, leaning on her sword.

"You fought well... for a Dubgaill."

"So did you... for a Findgaill."

Helka chuckled.

"Don't get cheeky, girl."

Kara watched the escaping ship's paddles splash. Kaelan rested his hand on her shoulder.

"What happens now?"

"Now?" Helka stared out over the dark waters. "Sichfrith, he's next in line. A son of Imar—Barith's younger brother. They'll be naming him king. A lad, just a boy, full of bluster and ideas of revenge and such. Phew!" She rolled her eyes. "He's a sod, afraid of his own shadow, sees plots and conspiracies in every corner. Loki whispers in his dreams, puts crazed thoughts in his ear. I can't see good come from this... be demanding justice, for Mac Ausle and his elder brother...."

They stood silently watching the vessel fade into the darkness.

"Not so good for you either, I'd wager."

"What do you mean?"

Helka sat quiet for a moment, weighing her words.

"Sichfrith, he's Findgaill through and through, nurses the old grudges. He's no friend of the dark foreign... harkens back to Hingamund and his bloody infighting. Nearly killed us all...

"He hates Dubgaill, Agnesdatter." She hawked and spat. "Our new king, he'll be no friend of yours...."

THORFINN

His head banged. A thud against a hard surface.

A swoon—more darkness.

A pain behind his ear, another quake... he plummeted over a drop, and his head banged again, harder than before... the second thump roused him from his stupor.

Daylight—it's daylight.

A rag stuffed in his parched mouth kept his tongue from reaching his chapped lips. He could taste it, dirty, sweat-salty and coppery from his own blood. He had bit his tongue before she gagged him.

He tried to move—trussed tight. Arms numb at his sides, legs throbbing and wrenched in an awkward position.

The ride jostled and bumped him... he lay tied on an improvised wooden sled.

Finn struggled against the ropes binding him to the sled. Dappled light shining through a tree canopy overhead, the noonday sun flashing in his eyes. His hand pulsated—he could feel a lingering pain, a deep burning....

Blinding flashes, from both glimpses of noon sky through leaves above, and from behind his eyes, triggered by his head battering against the wooden sled.

He remembered.

The witch bound him. She wrapped him in a spell cloak, calling Siedr spells to bind his hug to his lich, and once satisfied she held him captive in both Midgard and the Realm Between, she began with his left hand—her sharp blade honed to a razor edge, it slit each digit fast and deep, the throb of bloodletting revealing his injury. His hands hidden from view, he could only guess at the horror she carved into his skin. As she whittled at his fingers and flayed the skin from the bones and tendons, the pain mounted until he could not hold back his cries.

Finn strived for bravery, to honor his family and ancestors, yet his courageous mien fell as the agony grew all consuming. He screamed, he begged. She hunched over him, smacking him, threatening him, and nicking him with the tip of her hooked blade, until she lopped his smallest finger completely off and plunged his hand in cherry-red coals to burn close his wounds and staunch the blood flow. He fainted.

She woke him, pouring buckets of water over him and shaking him until he recovered, whispering and cajoling him back to lucid thought... and once she had him awake, forced him to connect eye-to-eye, had him fully aware... she commenced on his foot.

He remembered the screaming.

High-pitched, uncontrolled screaming—Finn knew it came from him, the sound ripped from his chest like a beast, fearful, distraught, agonized, ear-piercing. She had gagged him, stuffed rags deep in his throat and wrapped a blanket over his head. Through it all, he screamed.

He screamed and screamed and screamed... until blackness overcame him, and he remembered no more.

He slipped in and out of awareness. Finn lost sense of time.

While he suffered in delirium, the witch decided to move camp. She stopped her torture, packed her meager belongings, checked his bindings, and tightened his straps. His hand and foot ached.

Strapped to a wooden sled she dragged him through the forest. A forced march. They traveled slow—neither strong nor full of vigor, the old crone hauled and juddered her captive through the underbrush, the sled jamming in mounds and catching on roots, making scant progress for all her effort.

He could not see her—he could hear her muttering, calling to her coven. Upset, angry words. Calling to Holjan in pleading words. Holjan, assistance... she needed help.

Occasionally her visage crossed his line of sight. Spittle on her lip, angry teeth gnashing as she demanded he stop

—in his pain, Finn did not understand, could not comply. Something she wanted him to stop, to control. Whimpers tumbled from his mouth, unconscious. She smacked his face, throttled him and pounded her frustration on his damaged foot.

Disturbed, new pains drew a cry from his gasping throat, a croaking wail.

"Hush!" she hissed, clamping her hand over his mouth, and stuffing the rag deeper.

"Damned lindworm...."

A shadow passed overhead, shaking the treetops.

Finn fainted again.

CHAPTER 9
AN AESIR APPEAL

KARL Harald directed the fleet southward along the coast, stopping to gather volunteers at every district, village, and town. A powerful figure, his shock-hair and clear baritone impressed the rural crowds. He spoke with impassioned vigor and clarity, championing the benefits of a unified country, the justice of his rule and the riches to be shared through alliance. His kingly demeanor and the obvious support of the powerful who traveled with him lent credence to his argument. Many, seeing his naval power arrayed along the shores, the strength of his assembled arms and his honest commitment to the jarls and chieftains around him, swore fealty to his cause. Men and women flocked to join his forces, welcome recruits.

Karl found his snekke crammed with willing warriors, a few novices as well as veterans, and a couple of ancients seeking an honorable death and Valkyrie redemption. Elbow to elbow, the overcrowded longship rode low in the rollers.

Havar and Kol hung on the rear gunwale, wedged uncomfortably behind three farmers, husky brothers perched on their shields and sallow faced from the rocking snekke. Karl worked his way through the mob and squeezed himself next to Havar. He fingered the charmed medallion hung around his neck and tucked it inside his tunic. The jostled brothers grumbled, one asking when they could expect lunch.

Rolling his eyes, Havar leaned close to his captain. "Barely enough supplies for the day, the way they eat."

"We stop in the next district, Harald's orders."

"As if we need more volunteers."

"Numbers matter."

"Let's hope they fight as well as they eat...."

They watched Jormander at the bow. He struggled to serve a dipper of water from a bucket to the cramped warriors on the crowded deck. The sail slapped in the breeze. Karl wiped the spindrift from his beard and squinted at the mast.

Thorfinn's bird clung to the cross arm. He knew the bird was a mare for an old ghost named Raga, and the familiar hovered, overly restless and troubled. As if the bird wanted to tell him something—*strange raven,* he thought scratching his beard, *probably a difficulty back north, a hitch between Finn and Signy. Children. I should have left them in better care than old Gudrun... such foolishness we can't deal with now—nothing to be done until this voyage ends, and Harald's quest is resolved, one way or another.* He glanced over his jammed deck, the new recruits a motley troop. A toothless old man, a broadhipped farmer's wife, a few seasoned fighters with their own weapons, the three potbellied brothers, and a collection of eager youths, ready to swear allegiance but untried in the crucible of combat. His eye locked with Jormander amidship and read an uneasy hesitancy in his old friend's expression. Luckily, the *Verdandi Smiles* offered no more room for additional volunteers.

South of Stad, they steered to shore and let the crew disembark for nature's call and a meal. Harald stomped into the town and offered his rousing speech, calling for unity. The locals met him with a tepid reception. The army soon discovered why—rumors spread Eirik, the King of Hordaland gathered his forces to oppose them, armed with all the ships King Kjotve the Rich could outfit. Hordaland and Agder had allied themselves with the chieftains from Sognefjord and the word was the force grew to be 'formidable,' whatever the spies meant by that label. Karl snorted at the 'news,' and corralled his new recruits, keeping them aboard where they would be less influenced by gossip.

Harald understood gathering additional troops would be difficult the farther south they traveled, and since the weather held, he commanded his flotilla to sail with all haste. He decided to confront his enemies in their own territories, either in Hordaland, on the rugged shores of Rogaland or into Agder itself. Karl suspected they would travel no farther than Hordaland.

Spread across the open ocean with a favorable wind, the ships made steady progress and entered the territory claimed by Hordaland by midafternoon. Jormander and Karl stood at the bow of their longship, watching their sister ships lift and sway in the rollicking waves, their sails spread like great wings. On all sides colorful sheets danced over the whitecaps, a flock upon the waters, each fluttering Harald's forest-green banner from their mast.

"A grand sight, eh Captain?"

Karl clapped big Havar on the shoulder and grinned

into the spray. Sailing—how good to be on the sea, the fresh air invigorating. Despite their snug quarters, all around him the crew smiled, thrilled with their rolling course through the waves, enjoying the clear afternoon sunshine and anticipating battle excitement to come. Fish leaped from their bow, and laughing gulls kept pace with the sails, gliding in their sail shadow.

A strange, twirled rainbow illuminated high in the southwestern sky— a multicolored reflection started low over the horizon and swirled into the cerulean blue like a cyclone. The sailors called the sight a good omen, to see the Bifrost Bridge arc across their path. The gods favored them they said, and pointed to the sky.

The steady wind carried them round the coast to Rogaland. Karl had expected resistance as they passed the shores of Hordaland—they spotted residents on the shore, yet no ships sailed to confront them. Harald's navy passed without incident. As the sun set the ships sailed past Kormt Point, and the leading ships turned into the bay beyond Skudenes Island. Sounding the waters with a weighted rope, they found a deep-water bay between the towns of Utsteinn and Soli, at a place their recruits named Hafrsfjord. A quiet place of stony shores, rough tidelines clumped with dune grass and stunted spruce. Karl commanded his crew to drop anchor, aligning his snekke with the other longships, arrayed in a tight row across the bay.

Admiral Egil called a council of his captains on the shore of Hafrsfjord Bay. Karl took Havar and Jormander with him to the council—they jumped into the waist-deep water to wade ashore, gathered on a sandy spit and circled around the admiral. As far as Karl could count, more than one hundred captains and first mates gathered on the shore.

Sun wrinkled and grizzled, a life on the sea had baked Egil nut brown, and he raised a rope scarred hand to call for quiet. He spoke with a lisp, his incisors knocked out in a brawl long ago, and his deep basso cut through the murmuring crowd.

"Harald's spies confirm Eirik assembles his forces in Agder." He nudged the men closest to him aside and cleared rocks and pebbles from the sand with his boot. "We have collected four score and thirteen vessels, several deep-draft knarr or snekke longships, and a few, rigid-deck rafts built for plying ferry ways 'tween near-shore isles and across bays. I have been put in charge of forty vessels, including all our ferries and barges." He traced the outline of the bay and pointed to the rough drawn image of their landing. "Harald has decided we will stand here, in Hafrsfjord. Let Eirik and his ships come to us. The spies expect Hordaland to arrive on the morrow, so we must prepare this evening."

He drew his plans in the sand, explaining his array to his lieutenants, "Our navy will align itself in three rows. The first row will line here, midway across the bay—they will be bait to lure them in." He made x marks on the bay side. "Smoke pyres will be set here and here, as well as behind us here, to obscure the enemy view of our waters."

He drew a second line across his map. "I command our second row. Place the barges in the middle, rope each ship to its neighbor, forming a long wall across the waters. The third row, under Tanglehair's command, will align here, and there..." he pointed to the east and west sides of the bay, near the location of the smoke fires, "perpendicular to our main battle arrays. They will hide their strength. Once Eirik's boys are committed to the battle, Harald will sound the horn to flank the opposing vessels. We'll spring a few surprises on Hordaland. The goal, pinch the enemies to the center where we clear their decks with ax and sword. With the blessings of old Ran the Sea herself, we will tangle our enemies in her nets and send them to her depths." He glanced at the faces of the captains gathered around him. "Questions?"

A few frowned. The sailors voiced no objections.

"Return to your ships—reef your sails and tie the tackle or stow it. Move the ferries and barges, there, to the center...." He pointed out into Hafrsfjord Bay where he wanted the ships.

"Listen close now, this is important: Your ships must be kept tied to each other at all costs. This gives us a field of combat, a reliable platform to defend. We will face these cutthroats like men, hand-to-hand, blade-to-blade. We shan't give ground, there is none to give." He swiveled from face to somber face. "As a last resort, I will command the bindings be cut, and release individual ships to flee." By his countenance, Egil considered any attempt to retreat a matter of despicable cowardice. Their duty lay clear.

Egil offered his captains a drink at his tent, pitched above the high-water mark. Karl and his men hung back from the crowd.

"Did you hear the rumors?"

Karl turned to Jormander. "Tell."

"The rich bastard on Agder's throne commissioned ships from the Danes, more than twice our number." Karl spat and eyed the shoreline. In the gloaming, a second crowd had gathered around Uffe, the other admiral. The crowd shuffled and murmured. He craned his neck to for a better view.

"Agder fights like little girls," Havar reminded the skald.

"As our captain reminds us, 'numbers matter.'"

Karl gazed across the sandy beach, searching the shadowed faces. Firebrands sparked to light the twilight.

"Captain, are you listening?"

"Eh?"

"Karl?"

Havar placed his meaty hand on Karl's arm and gave him a tug, the big man towering over his captain.

"Ja, I listen." Karl waved dismissively.

"No, you sought her."

"Nay...." Karl mumbled.

"She's there with Dag," Jormander informed him. "Hard to see them now, their ship sails in Uffe's wing."

Karl said nothing in reply.

"Means they'll face the brunt of the first attack."

Karl stared into the settling darkness.

"We're done here, Captain."

"Ja, tis probably our last night...."

Karl turned on Havar. "What are you hinting at?"

"Captain." Havar took him by the shoulders. "You know the ways of war. Likely neither you nor her remain alive tomorrow."

Jormander held his shoulders. "Best you go find her and heal this breach before a blade silences one or both, and forever seals this break."

Karl hesitated, tossed his braid over his shoulder, and stared at the ground. *Odin, Tyr and Thor, three triumphant in war and justice, you never forsake me... but where is Bragi's eloquence when I need words? The Bard of the Gods never flies to my aid... what could I say?*

Havar sighed. "Come, poet, let's go lift a horn."

The two wandered back to the crowd, leaving Karl indecisive in the surf.

RAGA

Uncle Karl didn't care.

He didn't attempt to listen or understand what had happened to his nephew. And where was Martine and her Siedr salve to let them see into the Realm Between Realms? With a dab of the ointment, he could have communicated with the Vikingr on the Verdandi Smiles, made them understand! They kidnapped Thorfinn, his lich stolen by a cretinous witch and her monstrous, eight-armed giant. Well, seven-armed now, but still.... His mare squawked in frustration and ruffled its pinfeathers. He nipped at passersby and cawed angrily, continuously, until his voice grew hoarse and croaking.

To no avail. For all his efforts, he could not connect with the men of Midgard, and their preoccupation with the impending war mystified him. Wyselhax, the ship kobold hugged the mast, uncomfortably squeezed between new recruits jammed onto the deck. At least Hax believed him and understood the urgency of Thorfinn's plight, but he had no solutions, bound to the snekke by spells.

When the armada landed in Stad, Raga flew on his mare to listen to Harald's speech. Hearing rumors of an opposing fleet assembled by Tanglehair's enemies, he winged to take a measure of their foe. Easy for him riding his bird, he used the winds to glide far to the south. Crossing the route of the enemy vessels tacking to the north to meet Harald's navy, Raga flapped to a high altitude where he could measure the forces arrayed against his friends.

A vast flotilla spread beneath him. Superior numbers and bigger ships, deep-hulled longships with wide, flat decks, most boasting twice the sailors on the ships in Harald's navy. By his informal count, more than one hundred knarr, and a contingent of twenty, smaller ships filled the bay. The warriors amidships wore iron helms and chain-armor tunics, and the ships bristled with long, iron-tipped spears. More importantly, from his position astride the Realm Between and Midgard, despite the daylight brightness he could see dark flashes and eerie glows indicating Siedr incantations. Volva and warlocks accompanied these forces, more fell wizardry than Harald commanded.

What he saw troubled him, the sheer numbers a strategic and tactical concern, and the dark magic glimmers a subtle, but potent threat. With all the haste he could muster, he winged back to the north to find the longship Verdandi Smiles and his friends. He swooped in on the fleet propelled by strong winds and racing across the waves.

Hax was the only companion who noticed his return—the crew gawked awestruck over an odd celestial phenomenon, a curled, up-welling rainbow, and the men had no time for an exhausted raven. Raga released his mare to rest on the sail crossarm and settled next to the mast troll.

"See there?" Hax grinned, pointing with his clawed hand.

"The weird lights in the sky?"

"Ja, tis the rainbow bridge to Asgard, a good omen if ever there was one."

"Asgard? A good omen?" Raga huffed. "What do we care of far-flung realms? I have seen the opposing force, and these sailors face doom! More than twice the number of ships and near twice the number of soldiers, outfitted with new armaments, heavy helms, and armored jerseys! And they have gathered Siedr witches and those skilled in the arcane arts. They bring superior power in arms and magics, and what do we have...?" He waved his arm in a dramatic fashion at the fleet cutting through the waves on all sides. "They are all destined for a watery grave! See their happy, simple faces—it pains and frightens me! We need to warn Karl, it's time to retreat, step back to fight a different day when the odds are not so leveraged against us."

Hax snuffled and smiled at the twisted rainbow in their path. He reached out and held Raga by the forearm. "I have not seen the Bifrost in years. Does my heart good to see the gateway to Asgard." He pinched the old ghost's arm and licked his lips with his long, lolling tongue.

Despite his qualms, Raga recognized a strange solemnity in his friend. He paused his rant and joined him in contemplating the shimmering rainbow. The refractions danced and swirled in the sunlight. "It is a beautiful sight. Too bad we can't use the bridge to go to Asgard and implore those there for assistance..."

"We could if we wanted."

"Yes, but you can't leave this ship and we do not know any in Asgard."

"Nay..." Hax gazed wistfully into the sky. "I can't leave this mast in Midgard, tis true: I am bound here in this realm, but such incantations hold sway in Midgard—I am free to travel to other realms if I please."

Raga lifted his eyebrows. "Really? Next, you are going to tell me you have friends in this realm Asgard, this place of gods."

Hax chuckled. "Well, not friends... distant relatives, cousins more like."

"Truly?" Raga regarded the ruddy-hued, bowlegged troll with interest. "Could we enlist help from these 'acquaintances' of yours?"

"Well, one can never be sure... I know troll kin there we can call to plead our case before the Aesir. T'would be a shame to lose my precious ship after all these years. It's not good for one's reputation, to lose one's charge...."

"Aren't we at risk?" Raga wrung his hands. "I mean, time flows different in each realm, yes? I lost my true body while spending a few months in Vanaheim, what of Asgard?" The mast troll squinched his eyes. "We could return to a crew long dead, a ship mere rotted ribs beneath the waves."

"Time runs slow in Jotunheim and Svartalfheim, quicker in Alfheim and Vanaheim, and nearly the same as Midgard in the others. In Asgard, time stands nearly still—tis the reason the Aesir chose this realm as their home. With divine fruit for immortal strength and vigor, and a home beyond the river of time, the Aesir gods dwell in eternity, aloof and untouched. At least until Ragnarök. Tis the reason we seldom see the gods themselves in Midgard or any other realms—occasionally, old one-eye roams in disguise. Makes him a tad older each time, stepping from their oasis into the flow of time. He trades unfading godliness for a deeper wisdom, the sly old wanderer." Hax gestured to the rainbow with a claw. *"It's why men, or for that matter elves, dwarves or giants rarely see the gods, and the Aesir seem immune to all pleas and entreaties. The Aesir are loath to leave Asgard, for each moment from this realm ages them, and they abhor the wasting of time's ravages."*

"Time stands frozen in Asgard, you say? We could go to beg assistance and return with no fear of missing events here in Midgard."

"Well, you might have trouble." Hax rubbed his head. *"Many live among the Aesir, elves, dwarves, jotnar and trollkin alike... the hugs of men, you of Midgard, are only permitted in the grand halls, Odin's Valhalla and Freja's Folkvangr. Hugs must be chosen by the Valkyrie, one of the Einherjar, those selected to feast eternally with the gods. We could not cross the great rainbow bridge over the raging Kormt and Ormt rivers. Heimdallr the white would see and bar our way...."*

"What of my mare?" Raga pointed at the roosting raven.

"Mayhap..." Hax wiggled through the crowded decking, stepping over the recruits to lean over the gunwale next to a crewman and his oar. *"I could enchant you <u>inside</u> the bird to carry you, use my arts to hide you... you mustn't make a sound,*

for they swear Heimdallr can hear grass grow and see a thousand miles."

"We should chance it, Hax. We should see if we can find allies to support Karl and his crew."

The troll leaned over the balustrade and dragged his fingers through the water. Raga pressed next to him. "If we want to save your boat and these men in your charge, we need to do something."

Hax licked his damp fingers. "This be dangerous, old ghost. You could be wiped from your half-existence here between realms. Astral travel is fraught with peril."

"I understand the risk. I want to help."

"Call your mare and let me weave you to it. Be warned, this spell will not last long and we must depart for Asgard immediately or it may fail before we step beyond time."

Raga compelled his raven to flutter to the ship's rail. The bird cawed and flicked its feathers, ill-tempered with fatigue. Hax spread his fingers and took Raga by his forearm, whispering an incantation, funny rhyming syllables interspersed with clicks and snorts. Raga experienced a strange pressure, a dizzy, uncontrollable tumbling, as if he flipped frenzied somersaults through the air, never finding equilibrium. Hax reached out and grasped the raven. Raga choked as his consciousness streamed into the bird.

Not at all like riding his familiar, this odd experience was incomparably unique. Raga blinked and snapped his bill—Raga was the bird! He saw through the creature's eyes, he controlled the creature's wings, spread its tailfeathers and hopped on the railing.

"I'm a bird!" his caw burst out, louder than he expected and clearly a tiny voice. Several sailors glanced up.

"Who spoke?" One shifted on his bench and peered over the side into the rushing sea.

"Hush," Hax warned Raga, from the Realm Between Realms. "Inside this animal, you exist in Midgard and between realms now. Do not expose us! Superstitious sailors, these conscripted farmers could break the charm that binds me here." Raga ducked his head.

Hax pointed his clawed finger at the dancing rainbow shape in the sky. "Take me in your claws and fly to the bridge—I will open the way for us." Raga spread his wings and flapped, surprised at the ease of lifting into the sky. Clasped by his muscular shoulder, the troll weighed nothing in his grip. He winged over the waves, the fleet passing below them.

As they approached the rainbow, Hax called out, "Tis I, Wyselhax, Klabautermann of Midgard, seeking passage o'er Bifrost to visit my cousin the bride of Holgi. Oh, great white watcher, hear my plea and permit me provisional visa to the untouched realm."

The air sparkled around them, the rainbow colors reflecting and shimmering—Raga found himself momentarily blinded.

"You can set me down now."

Blinking to clear his sight, Raga dropped Hax unceremoniously and flapped to his side. Behind them, a gaping chasm in midair displayed a panorama of the wide, blue ocean peppered with scattered sails of the fleet moving in unison across the swells. Before them stretched a bridge formed by reflections as if from a crystal in bright sunlight, empty air yet a solid archway.

Raga clucked in awe, glancing at his claws on its surface and stroking the sparkling walkway with an outstretched wing. "Amazing," he muttered.

"Quiet, bird, you'll give us away," Hax spoke, a deep, throaty rumble, different than his normal voice—Raga glanced up... and hopped back in surprise.

"Hax!" He squawked. "What have you done with Wyselhax!?"

On the bridge beside him stood an extremely tall man, much taller than the men of Midgard, his skin a sunburnt glow, his limbs lithe and comely, his luxurious, ebony hair braided and thrown over his shoulder.

"Hush, silly bird." The attractive fellow leaned over and held out his forearm. "Tis I."

Raga fluttered backward, his tail feathers fanned in alarm.

"This is my true appearance beyond Midgard." He smiled and offered his arm again.

Surprised, Raga scuttled farther back, twisting his head to see better.

Aye, he could see now—the eyes held the same knowing sparkle of his troll friend. His pointed ears appeared more rounded, the tips less noticeable, the arcane tattoos that marked the mast troll's body had faded to barely discernible lines, more like faded scars, and his three-fingered claws formed humanlike hands, each digit long and slender, three fingers and a thumb....

"... Hax?"

"Hush, hop to my shoulder and let's move across this bridge before Heimdallr grows suspicious." Raga leaped to his arm and cautiously hopped to his shoulder. This handsome creature, his mast troll friend? Wyselhax towered, muscular and well formed, his stride impressive and his countenance surprisingly... fetching. Raga leaned close to his ear.

"Is it truly you?"

Hax chuckled. "Do you think Odin and Thor would bed so many jotun if we were hideous? Midgard warps our visage into trolls as you know us—here in Asgard, I take my true form. Now, quiet, let's cross into the realm of the Aesir."

With long, graceful strides, Hax commenced crossing the Bifrost Bridge. Raga watched the sky fade to starry night while beneath them roiled a treacherous river full of riotous rapids, surging whirlpools, and violent waterfalls. The unrestrained waters tore through the heavens forming a barrier. Raga scooted closer to Hax, pressing his wing against his temple. An ominous ringing filled the air as the bridge passed over the waters.

Hax strode on. Below them a savannah of tall, golden wheat, ready for harvest and shining as if lit from within, sprung from the banks of the rampant river. This field stretched to the horizon. As Raga watched, the wide pasture grew sparse and deteriorated into a rock-strewn landscape of sandstone cliffs and wind-washed spires—under the dark, star-filled sky, the land lay deserted and empty. A lonely place, Raga thought.

The stony wasteland sprouted skeletal tree shapes and deep crevasses, and soon the spires crumbled into a sea of dust, a desert of undulating mounds and wind-driven dunes. As Raga watched, the sandbanks humped lower and lower, finally sliding into a flat plain of gray which ended on the banks of an expansive river delta, its turgid waters mud-brown and silty.

Mist rose about them, and as it thickened, Raga glimpsed great arms, like tree branches reaching from the clouds below—and as they climbed the bridge, a mountain peeked through the vapors. High and craggy, the peak soared above their pathway—Raga recognized the peak housed their destination, the Realm of Asgard.

Ahead, a gatehouse sat astride the Bifrost Bridge. Raga had never seen the likes of such a magnificent edifice, and he had wandered the halls of the emperor's palace in Constantinople. Two guard towers clad in gold and silver connected walls inlaid with semi-precious stones, and artfully woven trellises lifted fragrant flowering vines over the walkway. As they approached, the foggy sky cleared, and bright sunlight shone on them. Hax strolled forward with a confident attitude, his head high and eyes diverted, his hands clasped behind his back. The small, black bird huddled on his shoulder.

Finely wrought iron gates rolled aside as he approached. The center of the gatehouse consisted of a domed chamber circled by columns of multicolored marble. Inset in the floor an astonishing mosaic of Ygdrasil and the nine realms glittered with gems and abalone shells, the workmanship beyond any skill Raga had witnessed.

Three beings stood in the rotunda, the center one as tall as a giant, robed in white and armed with a massive, two-handed sword, glistening as if rubbed with oil. His pale face, brilliant white hair and ice-pale eyes commanded attention, and his unblinking eyes locked on Hax as he entered the chamber. Raga scrunched aside, attempting to stay as small as possible as this huge being surveyed them.

"Wyselhax," he rumbled.

"Heimdallr." Hax gave a deep bow.

"What calls you to cross Bifrost?"

"To visit my cousin, great white watcher, a short stay, soon to depart back to my charge."

Pulling his eyes from the imposing figure guarding the entrance, Raga quickly glanced at the other two beings in this waiting space—one svelte and willowy, she stood taller than Hax and merely half as tall as Heimdallr. Her jet-black hair, her dark, verdant skin, her long pointed ears and her ruby lips marked her as Vanir, a dark elf. And beside her stood a broad-faced, blubbery fellow with a bird nest of a beard, massive thighs and arms, and a tooled, leather belt which barely held his gut. Shovel-sized teeth bristled from his smile, and he rested his hairy hands on the oaken shaft of a war hammer.

"Passage, I grant you." Heimdallr directed his stare at Raga—he knows, Raga suddenly thought, fear raising his hackles, lifting feathers along his back. "...and your pet, as well."

Hax bowed again, lower this time, and shuffled quickly past the threesome, through another filigree gate which moved aside of its own accord. Raga chanced to peep back—the dark elf watched them depart with a sour, squint-eyed demeanor.

They exited to a grand veranda overlooking the mountainside, from the luxuriant, rolling, green hills below to the rugged peaks aloft. A flock of pastel-colored birds swooped past their patio, dancing in a rhythm of murmuration. Swoop and turn and duck and dance, their aerial schooling mesmerized Raga. A delicate fragrance wafted in the air.

"There," Hax whispered, and gestured to two, massive longhouses far atop the mountainside, a magnificent palace set between them. Glimpsed from this distance, Raga could judge the massive size of the structures, feeling dwarfed in comparison. "To the left is Odin's Valhalla and the right is Freya's hall and between them is the court of the Aesir, where the All-Father reigns."

"Are we headed there?" Raga squeaked, quivering.

"Nay, friend, we are not welcome there." Hax gestured to the hillside, where great, hoary cedars blocked the view. "My cousins live there, with the guests, journeymen and thralls." Below the high castle and the two, immense longhouses, a series of winding lanes led through manicured parks and past reflecting pools and ivory cupolas. Amidst the hedges and trimmed bushes stood shelters, astounding in their variety, shape and size, sprawling open-walled pavilions, pyramids, globes, and odd, stacked boxes, many with bullseye-glass windows reflecting the sunlight or slender spires reaching the treetops. Stained glass, a wonder Raga thought only graced the most hallowed Roman basilicas, seemed commonplace here, wide windows inlaid with crimson, azure and smoky green. Each carved lintel and jamb depicted the myths of the Aesir, Raga recognizing a few of the etched stories. Hax followed the stairs and turned on a path into the wooded hills.

Even the servant quarters approached extravagance,

generous buildings with clinker-fitted siding, slate-shingled roofs and lush gardens filled with flowers and fruit trees. The outer walls decorated with painted patterns, each door a carved masterpiece, Raga found himself lost in the twisting pathway, awestruck by the variety and magnificence. The air smelled clear and fresh, like an alpine valley after a cleansing rain. Enormous bees bumbled across their path, laden with yellow pollen. Despite his unease, Raga enjoyed the tour, the calm serenity of the afternoon sun, the sweet air, and the clear, blue sky.

"We have arrived."

Hax pushed aside a garden gate and stepped into a busy yard. Gravel crunched under his feet, and stone dust lifted and swirled about each step. Mill stones heaped amid piles of chipped rock and granite slabs blocked the entrance to the building, a hall shaped from standing stones with cut turf stacked between each rib. As they wound their way through the confusion Raga noticed each tall monument had a carved rune at its head.

"Torgjerd?"

A voice sounded from within, "Who calls my sister?"

"Irpa, is that you?"

The main door, an iron-banded, hobnailed oaken barrier twice as tall as a man, swung open at a kick, and ducking to pass through the doorway, a blonde giantess leaped out and grabbed Hax in a bearhug, lifting him well off his feet and knocking Raga to flutter aside.

"Wyselhax, you rapscallion! How long has it been?" Dressed in a leather apron and homespun skirt, her thick hair braided and whorled atop her head, her massive hands powdered with granite dust and her cheek smudged with a streak of dirt, the giantess towered over Hax. Raga gawked, smitten—despite her massive size and dun apparel, her figure mirrored perfection, her movements embodied grace, and she exuded an unexpected

womanly charm which enthralled him. He perched on a tipped millstone and gawked.

The two hugged and patted each other, Irpa half-again taller than Hax. He appeared a boy in her arms.

"I thought you called to Midgard, compelled to mind a bark upon the human seas."

"Ja, tis true, cousin. I wait upon the whims of men and protect their tiny raft."

"Wait until Torgjerd arrives, she will give you a pinch—tis been too long since you called."

"Where is Holgi's bride?"

"Soon to return." Irpa leaned close and tugged on his braid. "She's been cavorting with old thunder bones."

"No, I thought he was angered with her. He killed her husband... and no doubt Sif chafes, unhappy you moved to this little cottage." He waved about the crowded yard.

Irpa guffawed in an unladylike way, which seemed endearing to Raga. "Not even Aesir can resist the siren call of Huldatroll when she be transmuted by this mirror Asgard."

Hax laughed, lolling his tongue around his open mouth, reminiscent of his trollface expressions. Raga cocked his head, puzzled, but thrilled to watch the beautiful jotun, hovering on her every word and movement with rapt attention.

"Why all the millstones?

"Idun craves them to grind ambrosia." Irpa pulled a hand hammer and chisel from her apron's front pocket. "A touch of jotun magic in each groove makes them turn and grind with the slightest effort. See these runes of power? Save hours for these Aesir." She pointed to the markings etched into the granite wheels.

"Should we wait, or go seek her?"

"Of late, she brings her amorous companion here to tumble, there beneath the cedar boughs." Irpa clucked her tongue.

"Hidden from Sif's prying eyes. Best he not find you here. What is it you need?"

"Cousin, my ship is conscripted. My captain, Karl, son of Ironfist, is the best of Midgard, surely watched by the Valkyries, a noble and honorable leader. We aid a great man Harald in his drive to unite the northern way. A great naval battle is prepared on all sides, and the scouts tell the force arrayed against us is formidable, conceivably twice our size and armed with Siedr enchanters. We seek assistance to level the field, at least to give a fighting chance."

"Odin has called his court to watch this fight. Bragi has prepared a poem of great eloquence to introduce the warring factions. Your underdog Harald is the subject of many a wager. Many, many a wager. Will he rise triumphant? Will he grace Valhalla? Or will he sink to a watery grave, to be welcomed by warty Surt in Helheim?" She smiled.

"If he fails in his bid, most likely my bark is lost to the depths, and I will carry the shame ever more, never to show my face."

"Such a pretty face, too." She pinched his cheek. "So, you need us to barter with the Aesir on your behalf... what will you offer in return?"

Hax reached into his tunic and drew out the pearl Thorfinn had captured for him in the depths of the Humber Estuary. Here in magnificent Asgard, the gem blazed with a purple fluorescence. He held the globe in his palm, offering the treasure to the summer sun. Raga remembered the gem being as large as a fist back in Midgard.

The grin faded from Irpa's face. She leaned forward, pearlescent flashes glinting in her eyes. "Oh, Wyselhax, where did you find this?"

"A vardoger quested for me and wrest from a tangie 'neath the waves."

"A vardoger, you say?" She turned on Raga. "Not this pet?"

Raga grasped she knew he eavesdropped, and suddenly fearful, scuttled out of reach.

"Nay, not that one. A mere boy, but I smell destiny about him." Hax held out the pearl. "It's charmed and it's yours to share with your sister, should you win support for our side...."

Irpa winked at Hax. "Leave this to me, we'll barter with the Aesir on your behalf." She plucked the gem from his fingers and paused to sniff the air. "Feel the charge in the air, like the freshness after the rain? Torgjerd returns... and she smells of him."

"Thor?"

"Aye, little cousin, take care now. She may be in one of her 'moods.'" The giantess flipped her apron, throwing off a cloud of dust. "Remember when she forced Hakon to sacrifice his youngest son, Erling, before she turned the battle tide in his favor? She yet chuckles about that... one never knows her 'moods.' Grab your pet and hide in the house. I will speak to my sister for you...."

Raga appreciated the danger of surprising an unexpecting demigod. Hax gently captured the raven between cupped palms and slipped into the house, pulling the heavy, oaken door nearly closed, leaving a small crack to spy. He released Raga who settled on his shoulder.

Torgjerd strode into view, carrying a granite boulder under her arm which she casually tossed into the courtyard, as easy as one would toss an empty sack.

"Shinebright! You return early, sister." Irpa held the gate wide for her to enter.

Raga had thought Irpa beautiful... she paled in comparison to Torgjerd Holgabrud. Porcelain-smooth skin, her heart-shaped face and delicate, aquiline nose framed by a mass of fire-red curls, she stood head and shoulders taller than her sister, her silken gown draped over a supple and lissome form. Ruby bangles at her ears, the creamy skin of her neck and arms shined as she reflected the sunlight.

"All's well, Irp." She pointed at the massive rock she had tossed into the yard. *"More stones commissioned."*

"You smell of sparks and lightning...." Irpa hinted.

"Ja, a skosh of canoodling with old thunder britches. Whets one's appetite for more." She wiggled her hips in a lusty way, her belt rustling and jangling. The movement drew Raga's eyes from her captivating face to the wide, tooled belt slung jauntily across her hips....

Skulls.

Severed heads and gory trinkets!

Mostly desiccated human skulls, but also odd, cattle-shaped heads with sharp horns, horse skulls and a few, misshapen troll heads, tatters of flesh clinging to their temples. All bound with fine, silver chains riveted to her patterned belt.

Raga choked, drew back, and tried to hide in Hax's braid.

Torgjerd sniffed the air. "Irpa, who do I smell?"

"Tis our cousin, Wyselhax. He brought us this gift." She lifted the pearl pinched tiny between her finger and thumb. The larger jotun squinted at the gem and cocked her head to peer closer.

"Oh, I see." She grinned, and her face took on a frightening cast as her eyes narrowed and her sharp teeth glinted. *"Tis magicked—of great use is this bauble. Give it me."* Irpa passed the gem to her sister, who held the bead to the sky in admiration. *"Rare, so rare! And what must we do to earn this boon?"*

"Wyselhax is bound to his Midgardian vessel, called by the ancient lore to protect and serve until released. His bark is committed to a grand battle to decide the fate of the northern way."

"Of this I know, tis the gossip of all Asgard. Odin himself has

wagered on the outcome." Torgjerd chortled, "A fool's bet, as he has chosen the weaker claimant. Tis the talk of the palace."

"Wyselhax has asked us to intervene with the Aesir on his behalf. To lose his ship, an eternal shame."

"Ja, but what care we of our cousin's plight?" She winked over Irpa's shoulder at Wyselhax hiding in the darkened house.

"Shinebright, could there be a chore, a task Thor requires, that Wyselhax could swear to finish?"

Torgjerd handed the pearl back to her sister. "Ja, there is a task Thor chafes to complete. It requires he travel to Jotunheim...."

"Jotunheim? He can't go back there. Hate and anger linger since his last visit..."

"Well, he did smash in the head of the king and murdered his wedding guests.... This is why he needs another to take on this quest. It can't be troll nor giant—must be a man."

"A man?"

"Aye, for only a man can touch his trophy..."

"Wyselhax named his Midgard captain, a man called Karl, son of Ironfist. He could take on this duty." Torgjerd leered her dreadful grin.

"Aye, could work. Let's go see our thunder lord, I left him near his home Bilskirnir. Sif was at the palace with Balder and Frey, he should yet be alone." She turned and marched back into the forest.

Irpa held out a single forefinger to indicate Hax and Raga should wait, and she followed her sister.

Raga sighed with relief, glad to see them depart. He glanced around the cabin. The entire back wall opened like a gate... probably to let the giantess Torgjerd in, he recognized. Other than a few strange objects he could not identify, the house appeared humble, a great hearth against one wall and two massive beds against the other, a few, oversized stools and a *butchered sow hanging from the rafters to cure. But... before the fire, a stack of human skulls cured in the radiant heat, and Raga noticed strange skins spread on racks to dry... a subtle smell of death lurked in the darkened room. He suppressed a shudder.*

Wyselhax jumped on a stool, his feet dangling above the floor.

And they waited.

Despite Asgard's position beyond the rivers of time, waiting here was the same as waiting anywhere, a dull pause full of anticipation. Raga fidgeted, hopping from one foot to the other and flitting among the roof beams.

"When will they return?"

"In good time...."

"Must we wait all day? What about this spell?"

"Relax, no time is spent on Midgard. Nothing is lost."

Raga flicked his tail and jumped to the tabletop, examining the odd articles there. He pecked at one, which whirred at him as if alive, and startled, he leaped back to perch on Hax.

"This is boring, sitting in the dark."

"Hush, Raga, you begin to annoy."

"I am saying..."

"Shush!"

They waited in silence. Raga expected the sunny afternoon would fade to evening—despite the hours they waited, the day remained as bright as ever, the sun high in the sky, a fresh breeze blowing through the shutters. Nothing changed here, everything remained constant, identical, a frozen moment.

A commotion occurred beyond the gate and Irpa returned alone. She waved them out into the yard.

"Where is your sister?"

"She spends favors on her beau while his wife is occupied at the palace. No matter, the deal is set." *She offered a sprig of holly to Hax.*

"Take this token from the hand of Thor. He has agreed to save your bark from the follies of Harald you call Tanglehair." Hax hesitated, pulling his hand back from the proffered branch.

"Know this. The captain of your snekke, Karl, son of Ironfist, is bound to this quest by your word and honor, Wyselhax. Your little hug pet is our witness. Thor himself has guaranteed your vessel shall survive the encounter, and its captain as well, for once the battle is over, he must provide a service to the thunder god.

"Thor's chariot is pulled by two goats, Tanngrisnir and Tannfnjostr, those he eats each night and resurrects each morn. One curled horn of Tanngrisnir has gone missing, and sprites of Alfheim tell him the jotnar have stolen his trophy away to Jotunheim. Where? He does not know. These mortal enemies of our thunder god conspire to use the mystic artifact to wound or even cause his fall. Only the descendants of ash and elm, children of men, can touch the mystical horn, and he names this son of Ironfist this quest, to journey to the land of the jotnar and retrieve his goat-steed's antler." Hax stood stiffly listening to her speech—Raga couldn't read his calm expression.

"Thor will side with Harald?"

"No matter what Odin in his battle madness nor Tyr in his justice command, Thor shall stay neutral in this wider affair of Midgard. He has wagers on the outcome. He offers no guarantee of victory for Shockhair, he merely commits your tiny bark shall neither capsize nor sink, and your human captain shall survive to follow his quest."

"And what if Karl does not agree to take this mission? Humans are notoriously strong-willed creatures."

Irpa's mouth quirked in a wry smile. *"Thor indicates there is a second reason your captain will feel compelled to take this quest. Something about a lindworm run amok...."*

"Finn's Goorm," Raga whispered.

Hax bowed his head in thought.

"Agreed."

He plucked the holly from his cousin's fingers.

Glamour shimmered as he took the branch, and the jolt of a Siedr spell rippled over them—they had accepted the god's quest, bound by the spell. "The pearl is yours."

"Thank you, Wyselhax." She rummaged in her apron and drew out a small stone rubbed smooth and dark by the oil of her fingers. "Take this for your captain, a small token to guide them on their quest."

"Thank you, Irpa, and thank your dread sister when she returns. One day I shall repay you both for your aid." She took him by the arm.

"Just... don't fail Thor. Remember his iron gloves, his mighty belt of strength and mountain-crushing hammer. He tends to take his anger out on all concerned...." She hectored them to the gate and waved as they left the yard.

"And may the fates weave skeins of good fortune for your battle yet to come."

SORVEN

Sorven paused on the high Welsh hill above the tree line, the pasture garlanded with summer blooms and wild garlic heads. The typically cloudy Welsh highland sky had broken into tattered puffs racing across the azure. He smelled the fragrant air. Birdsong lifted from the trees.

His wanderings had carried him south and west, near he hoped to the Devon border or west to Cornwallis. His solitary journey seldom passed landmarks, and he avoided the villages he encountered, worried tales of his rapid departure dogged his heels. Provisions running low, he had begun snaring rabbits and picking mushrooms and berries to supplement his diet. Warm days tanned his face, and his stolen coat, slung over his shoulder in the sunny afternoon, served as a blanket during cool, damp nights.

The heat of the late day prickled sweat on his back. He stopped to tie his hair off his neck and he rubbed his chin, straggling hairs sprouting there. He wondered what moon it was... *perhaps my birthday has come? If I were home*, he thought, *would we be celebrating Kara's fifteenth birthday and a wedding arranged for her? Would I be turning fourteen, soon to be a man? If Cub does not return, I will be named my father's heir....*

He adjusted his tight britches—this summer he had grown wider, his clothes tighter, and he suspected he stood as tall as his elder brother Cub—and he knew he would grow to be bigger—he smiled and tugged on the thin stubble sprouting from his chin.

He enjoyed being alone. He did miss his family. Not Dun —he wondered if a different solution would have served him better, conflicted over his abandonment of Dundle, yet on this glorious afternoon he wandered, buoyant and contented. Sorven whistled an old tune his mother had sung when he was a boy, unconcerned any should overhear him. No one wandered this high in the mountains, no one farmed and few shepherded flocks on these steep slopes. His legs rustled through the tall pasture grass.

The pasture ended in a thicket, a game path winding under the brambles and Sorven hunched over to follow the course. He tugged his heavy coat loose from snags and bundled it under his arm to ease his passage.

The underbrush thinned under a canopy of gnarled hardwoods, each wide bole and the path heavy with green moss fostered by the damp Welsh weather. In the dappled sunlight, Sorven found his path a verdant carpet, thick and velvet and unnaturally quiet, absorbing the sounds of his footfalls. Above, the birds grew silent as he wormed his way through the shadowy forest. Hoary vines slung across his path. He wormed his way forward, carefully measuring each step on the spongy layers. As the sun settled behind the hump of the mountain above him, the dusk of the evening crept into the wood. Stumbling across a circle of mossy stones, signs of an old camp, he decided to bed for the night. He scraped at the greenery in its center, finding a flagstone set flat like a hearth.

Gathering wood for a fire became surprisingly difficult. Every downed branch dripped with sodden moss or crumbled with rot at his touch. As the evening gloaming faded into the night darkness, he tore a few branches from an ancient oak and chipped at his flint in a futile attempt to spark the green wood. He could not encourage the tinder to catch. Finally resigned to a chilly night, he gathered his heavy coat around him, chewed a handful of seeds he had collected, and, tucked between two mossy boulders, closed his eyes to rest. The forest rustled in a gentle breeze. Tendrils of fog lifted, coursing the slope like wispy streams flowing through the ancient trees.

As he drifted off, a blue light flared in the darkness.

Sorven opened his eyes.

His attempted fire spontaneously bloomed, a tiny, blue flame crawling along the snapped twigs and stems. The tinder caught in a crackle. With a whoosh, the flames sparked and twirled upward like a flowering vine. That was when he recognized... he wasn't alone.

Sorven jolted. He wiggled to straighten, fumbling at his belt for his knife.

Beyond the fire, two yellow eyes reflected the firelight.

At first, he mistook them for animal eyes but... they

didn't jump or cower. He peered into the shadows, discerning a shape.

A person lurked in the gloom.

Someone had stolen upon him while he rested and lit his fire to warm them both.

"Hello?" He leaned forward to squint over the fire.

No answer.

He slipped his knife from its sheath.

"Hey! What do you want?"

A throaty voice purred. "You have killed a man."

Sorven paused, his blade held close to his side. He couldn't place the strange accent....

"How would you know...?"

"I smell murder on you." A woman's voice— "And so young...."

Sorven scooted aside to peer around the flames.

"Who are you?"

She moved with his movement—she stooped on her haunches and easily shifted to keep the fire between them and herself hidden in the misty dark.

"Why do you hide in my wood?"

"Your wood?" Sorven glanced at the firelight reflecting from the shaggy boughs overhead. "No idea...."

"This is my glen."

Sorven grumbled, not responding to her claim. A white arm reached out of the gloom and set a bundle of branches on the smoldering fire. The flames bloomed and swelled, and the fire illuminated the camp.

She's barely a girl, Sorven surmised, *my age or slightly older.* She wore a homespun robe with a hood thrown back, her jet-black hair glistening in the firelight. Small beads and trinkets woven into her braids added a sparkle about her face and slender neck, at least as far as he could tell from across the fire. Her amber eyes glowed reflecting the flames, her full lips parted to reveal sharp, slightly feral teeth. A fur collar looped around her neck—as he watched, the pelt moved! He rocked back, wary.

A pet ermine, or a stoat.

Sorven twisted his torso from the strange girl. He cautioned himself—don't overreact. He assured himself this was a vagrant wild girl, lost in the forest. Holding his breath, he counted silently and forced himself to relax, sneaking his blade back into its sheath. No need to worry over a girl.

Even bent at the knees in her awkward position, she moved with a languorous grace.

"You should not stay here without my leave."

Sorven decided this claim of ownership was a ruse, a game played by a simple girl. He pushed aside his initial fear of a disembodied voice in an unknown wood. When he spoke, Sorven's voice revealed a barely concealed disdain for her implied ownership, yet his answer came haughtier than intended. "Well, give me leave and be gone, as I intended to sleep and pass beyond your 'glen' by morning."

Tilting her head, she allowed her dark tresses to drape across her face. Reflections from her eyes remained, golden orbs peering at him across the campfire.

"Nay... not stay here...." Her words barely audible over the sound of the burning wood.

"What?" Sorven stifled a yawn.

"This is not a place for rest." She lifted her lily-white hands and wove them in a strange dance over the fire. "Clouds inhabit the night. You wake stiff and sore."

Sorven noted the mist about them thickened, a dense fog rolling off the mountainside, obscuring nearby trees.

With her eyes locked on his, she stood and raised her

arms, lifting her hood over her head, her pet curling around her neck to disappear into the folds. The long cape parted in the front, and Sorven caught a glimpse....

Her daring dress astonished him. A supple, doe leather wrapped her torso like a second skin, its plunging V-neck accentuating the curve of her breasts. Strange, embroidered characters sparkled with inlaid gold and silver threads. A wide belt served as a skirt, scarcely covering her hips, with her long legs beneath free of dress or hose. Her artfully braided hair curled past her slender waist.

He paused. After the buttery round figure of Nia and her sturdy sister Gwenan, the lean, shapely beauty of this young girl struck Sorven dumb. Her grin veiled by glamorous hair, she dropped her eyes demurely and drew her wrap closed, masking her body from his staring eyes.

With a serpentine glide, she stepped around the fire and held out a slender hand.

"Follow me."

Sorven hesitated, his thoughts confused by the sudden, unexpected vision.

In a simple movement, she bent and lifted a firebrand from the campfire, and with its removal the remaining flames extinguished, blinking out as if they had never been burning. Pitch-black and foggy, the night pressed in around them, and a surprised Sorven grabbed for her outstretched hand, gripping her cold fingers in the dark.

He touched her... and his voice caught in his throat, his heart throbbed in his chest, the blood pounded in his temples, and a blush flooded his neck to warm his cheeks. Her tender hand in his, her eyes held him enthralled. He found he could not glance away.... he faltered along after her, tripping and stumbling in the dark. Nothing was unusual, how she floated ahead of him, walking backward in the darkness, her eyes locked to his, her delicate lips encouraging him, glimpses of her figure alluring and tempting him forward.

Sorven did not feel a Siedr charm—the magic was all in her eyes.

KNETTI

"Cursed lindworm!"

Knetti stooped in the shade of the pines at the field edge, holding her hip where the ache had grown to a constant, pounding pain. Her feet and hands throbbed to the same beat, their pain a phantom, a lingering reminder that ruined her sleep, her concentration, her thoughts....

Bent with fatigue and unrelenting pain, the elder volva kneaded the stitch in her side. She smelled of time spent with the rotted jotun, the stench of a week of exertion and rough camps in the wood.

"Oh Surt, I call on you goddess of death, take this bloody jotun spawn! I curse the snake to forever molder in Helheim, to rot at your glorious feet." She squinted at the cloud-smeared sky, searching for signs of pursuit, any notice to indicate where her archenemy lurked. She knew the beast was there—unrelenting, the monster hunted her for days. *Days!* She fought back a dry retch in her throat and scrabbled for a branch to prop her weary stance.

And all had gone so well....

Starkad the jotun, raised from the terrible demise Thor had dealt him, obedient to her commands, he easily defeated the dragon, never a fair contest. She disarmed the pestering ghost which protected the boy. They had stolen the vardoger lich. Their escape had gone exactly as planned, all executed masterfully. She trapped the cursed boy's hug inside his mortal body and once the jotun carried them far afield, she exacted vengeance, her due revenge. Everything as she and Holjan had plotted. Tyr smiled upon her, thank the god of just causes. Exact and perfect.

She glanced into the underbrush where she had left the charmed child bound to a makeshift sledge. Unconscious, his head lolled awkwardly to the side, the entire plank tipped precariously sideways where she had dropped it. His hand wept pus and blood where the coals had not stemmed the flow, his bandages a muddy sanguine.

My vengeance! She grumbled and wiggled her ruined fingers—*my revenge is when my plot went awry. Damn that cursed wyrm!*

Above in the clouds, a rumble... Knetti flinched and pressed into the bracken. *Thunder? Or has that despicable monster found me again? Once the beast harkened to the boy's cries, it tracked his tiniest groans and whimpers* —she had gagged the child to no avail. *Oh, how the trickster god plays with me*—she glanced at the child trussed against his plank —*should I slit his throat and run, leave the body in an open spot to attract the dragon, to bet his mourning gives me time to escape? Damn Loki, damn lindworm, damn this vardoger boy!*

After the beast first found and attacked her, she used her Siedr hexes to hold the creature at bay while she escaped with the boy. She wounded the monster, slowed its charge, but the wound was not mortal, and the combat sapped her reserved magical potency. She dragged the boy through the forest all night, hiding in a shaded ditch during the day, knee deep in sludge, ready to press forward the next night. Like a hound on a scent, the wyrm chased them, circling the skies, keening woefully and hooting for its master. Unwilling to desert her prize, she dragged her prisoner on a makeshift sled for three nights, each night yielding less distance as her fatigue mounted, as her sore ankles swelled and as her hip joint seized.

Overcast with biting gusts, the change in the weather marked the coming end of the summer moons. Knetti knew she had lost more than her way. Her magic derived from inner strength including bodily vigor, and a weakness rode her like the mare of the night rides its victims. A lust for revenge only carried one so far.... She needed to find a solid meal. She needed to rest.

Out of the corner of her eye, she caught sight of a tendril of smoke drifting against the sky. *Smoke? A village, a place where I could steal scraps of food, or find an abandoned place to sleep unmolested...?*

She glanced at Thorfinn. *His bindings will hold,* she assured herself, *he's merely a lad, hurt, starved, unable to escape. I can leave him until I return, and... if he dies while I am gone, tis the gods' will.*

She wrapped her shawl about her head and limped along the meadow edge, grabbing at bushes and saplings for support. Her slow pace dogged by pauses where overwhelming agony forced her to halt, a cold sweat broke across her brow, and she mumbled spells and prayers to protect and hide her. An occasional thunderous howl rang in the air, and she warily eyed the low scudding clouds for signs of her winged nemesis.

Hobbling over a rolling hill, she realized the field was a pasture—reindeer grazed in a portable paddock before her. Well-fed, the herd wandered their enclosure—she hunched low in the tall grass, seeking shepherds—there, a man dressed in black woolens, a dog at his side. She stumbled from the warder, wincing at the pain in her hip. She chewed her lip to stay her tongue. By his dress, she guessed him to be a Skridfinn from the far north, the Sami peoples—and as she crept over another rise in the landscape, the village below confirmed her conjecture.

Below her on a rugged coastline, a Skridfinn summer camp spread along the shore. Round tents made from animal hides, racks to dry hides, strips of jerky and herring strung from long strings, the fumes she had sighted came from a fire purposely smoldering to dry fish and meat. The delicious smell wafted across the field to her, she could taste reindeer jerky on the wind. Seal leather kayaks stacked to dry above the tide line, and a hunting falcon perched on a high staff.

To her dismay, the village massed with people, men, women, and children in their distinctive black and scarlet clothes. Women sat in circles, weaving and embroidering, and at the edge of the settlement, a few men worked salt flats with rakes, collecting salt from evaporating seawater.

Busy, too busy to sneak and steal unnoticed. She would have to wait until nightfall. She crawled back over the low hill, scanning for a spot to hide and bide her time.

Overhead, the lindworm crooned a lonely, drawn-out moan.

Peeking over the grassy knoll, Knetti watched the Skridfinn react to the sounds of the beast. A Skridfinn man with a white fur headdress, probably a shaman she decided, stepped out from the crowd and shouted into the sky. Holding out his arms, he called, and around him, the people echoed his cry.

Unexpected, she noticed a dark shadow traverse the clouds, glimpses of claws and tail dipping through the cover. To her astonishment, the shaman called again, his people chanting with him. With a frightened yelp, Knetti gathered they intended to lure the wyrm from the sky, and she scuttled backward, forgetting her aches in fear of a sudden arrival of her enemy. They called as if they had no dread of the wily monster. As she watched, the wyrm glided through the cloud cover and landed ignominiously on the shore near the shaman. Little children ran to greet the creature and the shaman placed his hands on its nose and spoke in calming sounds, the meaning of which she could not ken.

A shiver gripped her—these people *knew* her tormentor, in fact, they had welcomed the beast before— the way the villagers returned to their duties, this visit was no cause for excitement, nothing novel. As if such a visit were a regular occurrence, the village dogs ignored the beast! Knetti understood her error—this was no place for her at all. She crouched lower in the grass.

The lindworm whistled and hooted, its scales scarred by the damage she had inflicted the last time they had met. The shaman continued to chatter at the beast as if the lindworm understood him, while the dragon hung its head, moping like a berated dog.

Knetti slinked away, crabbing across the pasture, her head held low. She could hear the reindeer snort and whinny nearby. She worked her way over the rise and pushed herself to her feet, preparing to run.

A dog barked.

She pressed panting into the dirt, and the guardian animal barked again, an insistent angry warning.

Turning, she caught sight of the shepherd—he had released his dog to stop her, and the furious animal bounded across the field, yipping as it loped to her.

She turned to run, the grass slippery beneath her feet, her soreness and fatigue forgotten. The dog circled her, baying and growling. She turned to quiet the beast with a hex— warned of her trespass the villagers climbed the ridge and spotted her. Shouting raised the alarm.

The tree line! She ducked her head and ran. She knew she could make the crossing, escape these wanderers, for none followed on her heels....

Landing with a deafening snarl, the lindworm crashed from the sky, blocked her path to the forest and cut off her escape. Thrashing its tail, the monster reared on its haunches and beat its wings, bowling her over to tumble in the weeds. Knetti scrambled to her knees and called on her Siedr powers, chanting and moving her arms in the proscribed manner.

As she clapped to complete the spell, the dragon leaped at her. The crack of the fireball erupting from her hands knocked the wyrm aside, writhing as green flames coursed along his flanks and sparks erupted from his wingtips. The beast threw back his head and howled. A deep shudder twisted her stomach as her limbs twitched from the flow of arcane power.

Woozy, the volva witch stumbled to her feet and skirted the dragon thrashing about in throes of pain. *Run*, she mumbled to herself, *run to the boy—you can hold him hostage, bargain for your life*—these thoughts ran through her head as she stumbled and pitched forward.

Wounded and angry, the lindworm lashed out with his tail. The blow clipped her shoulder, twisting her and tumbling her aside, her face planted in the dirt. She struggled to rise, spitting turf from her mouth and tasting blood. Sniveling, she rolled to her back and began to chant again, molding her hands to call another fell strike of wizard's fire. Strange energy built in her arms and back, a surge along her trembling limbs a faint aura engulfing her digits as she raised her arms to throw the spell.

"Brains always defeat brawn, you foolish...."

An arrow broke her concentration.

It struck her mid-torso, not a fatal blow, but entirely unexpected. The dire power she called for her hex dissipated in a sudden puff.

She gasped and clutched at the fletched staff protruding from her chest. The arrow—*how wrong, how out of place*. She glanced at men chasing across the field toward her, brandishing their rakes and bows. She stumbled to face this new threat.

Another bolt slammed into her, this one low in her gut. She coughed and drew herself straight, a curse forming in her mouth. "Oh, Loki, master of all Vanir, I call on...."

She never finished.

The lindworm, ignored for a moment while she tackled the Skridfinn villagers, shuddered off the remnants of her fiery spell. With his jaws spread wide and an ear-piercing screech, he clamped down on her.

The bite snapped Knetti in half, killing her instantly. The angry dragon slammed and worried the body until only tatters of flesh and a smear of bloody rags remained.

CHAPTER 10
THE BATTLE OF HAFRSFJORD

KARL

No sun rose.

Instead, the dawn seeped into an overcast sky, gradual and plodding, indigo rainclouds reflected in leaden bay water. A threatening dome, storm pregnant and ominous.

Karl stood at the prow of his snekke and watched the fleet rise from the shadows, his Siedr charm a cold lump against his chest. Egil had staggered his ships across the bay, a clot in the center with sweeps of individual vessels curling toward the open sea like arms to welcome the coming forces. They formed the lure, the bait dangled in the center of a trap. The *Verdandi Smiles* moored close to the shore in Uffe's convoy, a disorganized line of ships anchored and awaiting orders. And, camouflaged along the coast to either side, Harald waited to commit his troops.

He could see Dag's knarr out in the bay, in the right arm of the deployed vessels, separated from the centered buildup. Harald's green banner stood stiff from its mast, the ship rocking in the tide, and like his own vessel, overloaded with warriors and crew. The ships crowded too close to discern any individuals.

Word passed from ship to ship, distorted by each who passed it along—Eirik had joined the king of Rogaland, Sulke and Jarl Sote, each commanding five score, more ships than could be counted, karves and snekkes, broad skeid warships, and the royalty on their ornate drakkar longships. The brothers from Thelemark had joined Hordaland as well, fighters of great renown. Rumors spread.

"Here, pass these out." Karl handed the men forest-green arm sashes, the mark of Harald's navy. Each tied them around their left arm. "Make them tight, don't want to lose them in the middle of a fight."

Karl called his seconds forward. "Jormander, organize these recruits and the ropes. When we link the *Verdandi* to the battlefield, ensure the knots are tight, the bonds secure. Once in the fray, we can't worry over riggings." He placed his hand on his old friend's arm and gave it a squeeze. He turned to the big man behind his poet.

"Havar, I see those farmer boys brewing henbane tea."

Havar rolled his eyes. "Indeed, Cap. Poor man's gate to Odin's berserk."

"Keep watch on them—do not let them drink too soon, lest they become enraged long before we face the quarrel."

"No need for crazies aboard with no one to fight," Jorn grumbled.

"Not before we can free them on our enemies."

"Does that... 'brew' work?"

"Why don't you quaff a snort and let us know?"

Karl smiled—his experienced men remained calm, joking with each other. He tipped his head, indicating a small gathering by the mast. A pale-faced boy of fourteen summers sat gripping his wooden club, his mate hugging his knees, watching the horizon. "Jorn, those green boys. Suspect they'll run at first blood." Jorn agreed. "Keep them from under foot—assign them to guard our pilot."

"Captain? Am I a nursemaid?" Kol planted his fists on his hips.

"Keep them out of the way...." Karl gazed over the bay, a field of mast poles pitching with tidal flux. "Egil will draw the enemy into the bay and engage. Uffe will send the *Smiles* where our forces falter."

"A slow start, sure to land us in the thick of it." Havar grinned. Sorli ran his whetstone along his sword's length, a long scrape to make the blade sing.

Jormander winked and poked Jorn in his side. "Miss your lindworm now, eh?"

Jorn chuckled. "Ja, the old wyrm would be a stalwart friend this day...."

"Nay, better the boy and his pet are safe, far from Harald and this challenge." Karl frowned. "If half the gossip is true, we're in for a bitter contest. Best call on the All-Father to send his Valkyries to watch o'er us...." Grins faded at his somber reminder.

RAGA

Tied tight to the main mast with rigging, the cross-spar and tackle had been secured before the battle. Raga stared wistfully at the raven perched on the farthest tip, rocking as the waves exaggerated the post's pitch. He sulks, he thought, the spell binding us for travel to Asgard left the bird muddled and furious. Rather than a guest who rides him like a mount, I had been infused into his tiny spark of a hug, a commanding presence who ruled his existence. How unnerving. His feathers dull, his appetite gone, the bird avoids me—not that I blame him. The difference between a familiar mare willingly called and a possessed lich is vastly unsettling. I tried reasoning, promoting the morsels offered by the crew, to no avail, my corvid continues to brood.

Raga threaded his way through the crowded deck. By this time, he expected to soar over the enemy fleet to gather intelligence, and pass truths from recognizance among the crew... he found himself grounded by a petulant pet.

Wyselhax huddled near the mast, back to his hideously familiar troll self. He had hidden the holly sprig Irpa had passed to him. Raga wondered how they would pass the talisman along to Captain Karl.

The old ghost leaned over the railing, searching the collected fleet from his low vantage point—by his count, thirty ships blocked the bay. Another fifteen complemented Admiral Egil's fleet, seven on one side of the inlet, the others out of sight across the way. And, as for magical assistance, he counted a few mast trolls among the longships and knarrs. Klabautermann such as Hax are not common. It is as Hax had warned him, the old ways forgotten by the youth.

Raga surveyed the snekke and sensed a tension in the Midgard crew—overcrowded with men and boys, the sailors pushing and wiggling through the throng to ready the longship for battle. Too silent, few jokes and none of their usual games of chase the king. Oars had been stowed, ropes coiled by the gunwales, weapons carefully passed to all.

Karl held his solitary watch at the bow, pensive and brooding, peering into the stormy morning.

The tide changed direction and a zephyr rattled the tackle against the main mast. From the Realm Between Realms, Raga sensed a subtle shift, the uncomfortable sensation of being watched.

Hax sensed it, too. He licked his bottom lip with his long, sinuous tongue, a nervous habit Raga recognized.

More than lightning crackles through those menacing clouds overhead, he thought, and wrapped his arms tight across his chest—I smell magic around us....

KARL

Enemy ships gathered.

The fastest arrived first, a few lithe longships rowed into the bay to hesitate in the tidal rush. They reefed their sails and spread across the rollers, separating each from the next in the mouth of the estuary. Karl noted their marks, the red banner of Rogaland: King Sulke and his jarl brother. He had faced their forces years before in a skirmish with Harald, he remembered a hardened fighting force. Rumors hinted Jarl Sote carried a mythical blade of eldritch powers.

The longships treaded in place. He watched them signal with flags.

A surge of ships rounded the promontory, sails unfurled and full of storm draughts. Massed close together they took the bait, rowing furiously to engage with the clump of waiting ships Egil had arranged for them. The Rogaland navy drove across the open waters, oars churning. From his limited vantage point, Karl estimated their amount twice the number of Egil's armada. A chanting-rowers rhythm echoed across the bay.

The Rogaland fleet swooped across the waters and rammed the stationary vessels. Their combined wake sloshed over the stationary boats and battered them deeper into Hafrsfjord Bay, yanking anchors free and tossing unprepared warriors overboard. The initial push crushed hulls and drove knarrs keel over deck, the surge cantilevering vessels into the air to teeter precariously over stunned warriors. Ships capsized. The attackers flung grappling hooks and weighted ropes, and leaped across the narrow gaps, weapons brandished, war cries in their throats.

Karl stretched his neck to glimpse the action, the sounds of combat growing in intensity, a clatter of steel against steel, bellows and shouts.

Havar clucked his tongue. "A thousand or more warriors in the first assault."

Difficult to follow the conflict from their distance, Karl squinted into the cloudy morning. A shower of arrows loosed from the rear fell into the center of the rafts. After the first volley, stray arrows arced over the conflict in a disorganized fashion.

A shrill whistle sounded—Egil unfurled his sail, a signal to command his waiting ships to close on the swarm of committed enemies. The reserved longships rowed forward, gathering speed to strike as Rogaland had. *Put your back into it*, Karl thought, urging his kin forward.

Karl thought he could see Dag's ship, his oarsmen gaining speed with every stroke, faster and faster, frantically rowing to gain speed and slam into the growing bundle. The ship disappeared from view, a loud crunch telling Karl Dag drove his ship like a harpoon into the bulk of enemies.

Each of the remaining warships collided with the Rogaland navy, and sailors scrambled to tie the pitching platform together in a semblance of a combat field. The impact staved holes in the hulls, crushed bows, and shattered spars. Masts toppled. Men and women screamed, and as the platform stabilized and the forces faced each other, the true battle began.

Jormander worked his way forward to join him at the prow. Side-by-side, the two watched the rumble unfold. They lost sight of the main fighting—those warriors in the rear of the conflict cast heavy ropes across their neighbor vessels and climbed from one deck to the next, passing out of sight into the thick of the combat.

"In the center, Karl." Jormander leaned over the bowsprit, gripping the neck of the carved dragonhead. "The battle lines are drawn somewhere in that middle mess, where they can face, each to each."

"Ja, we can't see from here...." Karl slapped the side of the boat. "Time to prepare—Uffe will commit us to the field soon enough." He waved to his man, Sorli, who leaned against the mast. In an exaggerated movement, he pumped his fist in the air.

Sorli understood. Opening a chest by the rower benches, he passed out heavy, leather gloves. Karl and Jormander donned one heavy glove on their left hands, pulled to their elbows. Havar organized the rowers, pulling the long paddles from stowage, setting them in their nocks. Karl considered his men as they prepared, his crew remained relaxed, influencing the new recruits with words and a calm demeanor.

The three burly farmer lads attempted to drink their special brew, and Havar intervened, and shaking one by the collar, forced them to wait for the true call to join the battle. Karl could read unease on the recruits' faces, pale and drawn, eyes blinking rapidly and avoiding their mates, a few sitting on their hands and others bouncing knees in nervous twitches. Karl glanced back at the battle—from their distance, arrows like black flies swarming in high summer arced over the floating vessels to fall amongst the melees.

"Captain, do you want this helm?" A man offered an iron helmet with an earnest smile.

"Nay, nothing to weigh me." Karl motioned to the men splashing in the bay waters. "Nothing to interfere should I need to swim...." Warriors waiting on the deck overheard his comment and reevaluated their leather armor, heavy helms, and mail shirts—they cautiously removed them, setting the heavy protective gear in the bilge slosh along the keel. Karl pulled a shield from its notch in the gunwale. "Best to carry a buckler like this, you can parry and shield, and if you fall in the water, you can float on it."

"But..." Forlorn, one of the farmers held out his trembling palms. "I can't swim."

"Then don't fall in the water!" Havar grinned from over his shoulder and gave him a good-natured clap on his back. Those around him chuckled weakly.

Shouts and cries of pain echoed—the fight had been driven back to the rear ships. Swordplay chased stragglers across the boats. Stricken, a shieldmaiden tumbled into the bay waters where she cried for help, her plaintive calls carrying across the waves.

Karl gauged the battlefield. A confused nest had formed, a muddle of ships roped one to another, side to side and bow to stern, hooks and weights grappling to hold the platform stable. Weapons struck and men fell, the wounded hiding among the half-submerged hulls and jetsam. Shattered oars poked into the sky. The whole raft rocked as another longship collided. Splashes erupted from the sea as men toppled into the whitecaps, a few floundering to swim under the weight of armor, others disappearing instantly under the waves.

Karl sighed. A killing field, he thought.

Few will survive this trial.

RAGA

As the ships entered the bay, signs of Siedr enchantments became apparent to Raga. From the Realm Between he could see powerful auras surrounded a few ships, bile green and electric azure and a strange, crimson-edged black. These ships charged like crazed berserkers into Harald's first defense, plowing through decks and knocking sailors into the brine.

Lightning snaked through the dark clouds. A rumble of thunder rolled overhead, and the clouds released a drenching rain. The torrent tumbled in sheets, curtains washing across the waves. Hax pointed to a fellow troll, perched on a mast post pitching wildly in the middle of the battle.

The hiss of rainfall drowned the moans of the wounded as well as shrieks of battle lust. In the Realm Between Realms, the heavy clouds above parted, dark gaps and deep canyons opened in the sky.

High overhead, Raga recognized the sparkle of the Bifrost and glimpsed shadowy spectators from other realms. Huge jotun and Aesir towered, gazing on Midgard from the safety of their eternal homes. The sky tattered as shadows galloped through the rainclouds... Valkyries, their lustrous hair streaming behind them, their beating wings a glint and shimmer, dropped to hover above the battle, maintaining a careful scrutiny for valor and prowess in death. Amazing and beautiful, Raga thought, watching the death angels dance as the conflict raged below them.

With surprise, Raga appreciated other mystical creatures had entered the Realm Between Realms to contemplate the follies of Midgard. Raga never expected so many denizens of the nine realms would attend this skirmish. A strange, elliptical shell of carved ivory, its hull etched with scrollwork and filigreed to magnificence floated near the shoreline, separate from the combat yet close enough to witness all. This astonishing vehicle held a contingent of tall Vanir, dark elves surrounding a high-backed chair with a silver-crowned ancient observing the combat. In the rough waves, Selkies gathered to tow and steal drowning warriors. A troll, huge, hump-backed and warty, wandered knee-deep in the bay, plucking the dead like oysters from a bed.

The battle roiled and surged across the haphazard field. Masts jabbed like spears into the sky, rocked and pitched on the tide. The Siedr powers swelled and glowed, their auras extended, their purpose unknown. Fascinated, Raga scooted near Wyselhax, the scene unfolding before them, the humans fiercely contesting each scrap of wood. And beneath the waves dark shapes circled to hunt, sharks come to feed on the dead.

Unexpectedly, the sour, green aura detonated, the ship carrying it exploding and bursting into real flames in Midgard. The entire assembled raft shuddered and rocked with the blast, jumbled masts waving against the dark clouds. Screaming in terror, men afire leaped into the sea, and a mad scramble to escape to other vessels began.

A charge of a seemingly overwhelming number floundered, routed by a savage counterattack, while axes hacked the grapples free and the greater platform broke into two smaller islands of fighting. A rush of new troops joined the quarrel, slipping on the blooded planks.

Another wave of sails arrived, the number clogging the mouth to Hafrsfjord Bay. Karl named the symbols on their banners.

"Tis Eirik himself, Hordaland joins the fray!"

Across the bay, Uffe raised his green banner and reefed his sail, damp and tangled in the pouring rain—the signal! The signal for the second fleet to join the combat. Kol and the boys hoisted the anchor.

Karl shouted to his oarsmen and the Verdandi Smiles *lurched forward across the rollers.*

KARL

Karl commanded his pilot with a shout over the splattering rain, "Tack, starboard!"

Gesturing with a chopping motion, he marked a course with a flat palm and guided his longship.

"Now boys." Havar gave the excited crofters a 'thumbs-up' signal. "You can drink your juice." They slurped the tea with gusto, encouraging each other to down the sour draught in a single swallow.

The rowers knocked aside drowned bodies, pushing through shattered spars and tangles of ropes and sailcloth. Oars become mired in flotsam, hampering their efforts. Seeing no need to ram his precious snekke into the friendly ships moored this side of the raft, Kol steered the craft alongside a cohort knarr and called for the crew to cinch to its gunwales. Not abandoned, they found the neighboring ship's deck awash with blood and gore, and a few wounded welcomed them. A limping shieldmaiden offered her hand and pulled Karl across to her ship. His troops assembled on the wet, bloodied deck.

Two of the wounded stepped forward to join them. Their contingent consisted of a score and three men, women and boys, Jorn following the rabble at the rear. A haze from burning vessels trailed across their view. Here at the edge of the floating mat, decks of different-sized vessels had jumbled together to form a humped, confused terrain, a few planks flat and close to the waterline while others canted at an angle difficult to climb, others lifted high, squeezed between ships to ride above a man's head. The raft creaked, wooden hulls scraping and grinding against each other.

Karl gazed over the jumbled vessels. Shapes moved in the haze, too distant to discern for whom they fought. He could not recognize anyone....

"Captain?" Havar touched his arm. He turned to his assembled warriors, recent conscripts, their faces pale, their knuckles white as they gripped their clubs and shields. They milled around him in a disorganized mob, jerky and squirming. Havar frowned, gesturing to the recruits with a side-eyed glance—Karl understood.

"Courage!" Karl barked and lifted his sword. "Harald has called us to defend his claim to the Northern Way. Each of you play a part in this magnificent history." He glanced from eye to eye, all his troops hanging on his words save the three brothers whose sweat-beaded foreheads and shifty, protruding eyes revealed the increasing effects of the henbane.

"This place, this time! This is your battle, your chance to show the gods your true mettle. Valkyries ride this day! They ride for the brave, they ride for you! There is nothing to fear—Harald shall reward us as victors, or our All-Father Odin shall welcome us to his eternal Valhalla feasts. You, each of you, your courage will win this day. It is time to fight!" He pumped his fist high. The men around him shouted and the anxious grinned, lifting their arms in a salute.

"Come!" Turning, Karl and Havar led a march across the shackled decks. They marched around broken corpses and mortally wounded lying in their guts and offal. At each new longboat, they climbed over the rails and crossed to the next—no one hailed or opposed them.

As they pressed forward, the three farmer boys showed signs of a drug-addled zeal in flushed cheeks and a crazy-eyed fervor. One pressed past Karl and Havar, tore his tunic and ran off into the smog, shouting incoherently. The sounds of conflict grew louder, and using ropes, they pulled themselves along a tilted hull onto a merchant knarr. From its canted decking, they viewed the entire raft of combined vessels stretched out below. Harald's forces pressed forward onto the red-banner ships, sailors engaged in hand-to-hand combat. Warriors contested in the melee, more than they could count. The confusion of battle made it difficult to grasp which side held the advantage.

Fresh enemy troops surged across the bay, their ships committing to the conflict, and Karl caught sight of Harald's hidden vessels, his surprise for Eirik, throwing off their brush and sapling concealments, readying their crews.

A curtain of rain sliced across the deck and blew past. With a shout and a point of his sword, Karl commanded his team to climb a rough net and join the battle below. The remaining two farmer boys scrambled away, screeching and swinging their clubs. As his men climbed by turns, Karl indicated a ship to Havar.

"That's Dag's." The vessel nursed a hidden fire, the aft smoldering, the entire ship listing to port.

"Where are they?"

Jormander pointed at the warring factions. "Must be there, Karl, they have driven the Rogaland cowards before them." Flashes of green scarves showed through the miasma.

His men ready, Karl shouted, "Skal!" Scrambling across the slippery planks, Karl initiated a charge, his troops behind him shouting their support. They reached a ship in the midst of the battle crowded with warriors. Having beat each other to a stalemate, the two warring sides faced each other tossing taunts and insults.

Havar jumped the railing in a single bound and with whooping a battle cry, swung his sword at the nearest, red-scarfed antagonist. The unlucky soldier parried his blow, to receive a kick as the huge man's momentum carried him through the standoff. Karl hurdled forward, shoulder lowered, blade point held at chest level across his left forearm. An opponent stepped forward to stop his rush, Karl parried his haphazard jab and slammed into the unsuspecting man, bowling him over. His neighbor attacked, his double-handed swing telegraphing his intentions, and Karl easily dodged the awkward blow, hopped in close and drove his elbow into the man's side, toppling him on his mate. Two of his conscripts fell on the enemies with their clubs. The influx of fresh warriors turned the tide in favor of Harald's forces, and the routed enemies scrambled in all directions.

Karl noticed his newbies jumped to join the chase.

"Hold!" he shouted.

"To me, now! Regroup here!" Karl waved his sword over his head.

"Separate, we are mowed like the Heyannir harvest, together we are strong!" Havar scowled at the sheepish men stumbling back. Their attack had rescued a group of eight and they rallied to Karl.

"The battle lines are there." Karl searched the faces of the warriors—besmirched and bloodied, they anxiously sought guidance.

"Where is your leader? Where is Dagson?"

A shieldmaiden, struggling to catch her breath, blood

seeping from a bruise above her eye, answered, "Dag? Not his crew... we sailed with Fanghard."

Karl craned his neck, surveying the battlefield. "Your ship?"

"There." The woman pointed to the south, six or seven vessels farther apart from Dag's ruined craft.

"Karl...." Jormander pointed to the south where ships of fresh troops strapped their hulls to the floating battlefield. The last of Uffe's command fastened themselves to the floating arena and his troops blustered across the decking, clanging their shields with swords and clubs, skirting swamped rafts and gaps of open water between the haphazardly fettered ships. From the north, a surge of warriors flowed from newly arrived enemy ships, an endless stream of fresh soldiers armed with heavy spears and Lindenwood shields.

The ship before them had been the scene of a heated conflict, ax holes punched through the hull had inundated the decking, railings splintered, broken bodies awash face down in the bilge. Flooded timbers and broken spars blocked direct access to the battle front.

Calming his fighting anger, Karl raised his arms. "Jormander, take command of these and follow our lead. Jorn, Havar, to me!" He scrabbled over the gunwales and dropped knee-deep in the broken neighbor, wading across the floundering vessel to climb aboard the next, Jorn on his right, Havar to his left.

Ahead the battle had devolved into a fracas, a great group of fresh recruits overwhelming the remnants of Egil's forces by sheer numbers. A few small contingents fought savagely against the overwhelming odds. Knee deep, Karl trudged toward the clashing forces, his men behind him. Havar assessed the situation as they closed the gap.

"These are all farm boys." He jabbed with his sword. "See how they coddle their shields, how they clutch their spears, fresh and unscarred?"

"Draftees," Jorn muttered, not bothering to hide his evil grin.

"Ja," Karl agreed. "Paid by the coin of Kjotve—see his banner there."

"And those cowards from Sognefjord, I see their flags as well."

"Easy pickings." Jorn chortled.

"Let's show them real skill, eh?" Karl shouted at the horde, huddled tight together in an attempt at a shield wall formation. Havar bent to grab a short oar and the three jogged forward, growling at the array of fighters spread before them. They leaped the railings and charged across the buckled rafts.

Karl struck first. His sword chopped deep into a wooden spear and wedged in the staff, and he jerked it free of his astonished opponent's grip. With the dangling wood extending his reach, he swung the spear butt against the next warrior in the row, the loose weapon flipping aside uselessly. His action disrupted the man's attack, doing little damage and upsetting the man's practiced approach—confused, he dropped his defense, and Karl jumped forward with an uppercut. His sword sliced across the man's extended arm, and Karl carried the swing through to jab into the side of the man who had lost his spear. Both collapsed, one holding his side, the other desperately attempting to staunch blood spurting from his forearm. Karl parried the next spear thrust with his blade and gripped it with his gloved hand, drawing the surprised fighter close to slide his sword effortlessly into his gut.

"Children."

Havar, a head taller than those who faced him, blocked their bristling spears with his oar. A smack to knock their tips aside and a down slash—he moved along the line and disarmed each in turn, a crack on the skull or a chop to the collarbone and they toppled. "Worse than children...."

"Like wheat before my scythe," Jorn laughed, as he battered an upheld shield, the owner cowering beneath its protection.

Karl disarmed another and sent him stumbling back into the throng. "These are not warriors—these are paid to inflate Hordaland's forces. See how they flee?" A courage based on superior numbers and heavy pockets broke when faced with skill and prowess—struggles commenced between those seeking an escape from Karl, Havar and Jorn, while those behind them pressed forward as commanded. Collapsed fighters knocked each other into a heap of confused rookies—Jorn poked the pile with his sword tip.

Karl shouted, to Jormander and the warriors who followed him, "It's your time! Show the gods your courage!"

"Let's push them into the sea!" Havar shouted, smacking his oar against a warrior's iron helm, pitching him to the deck.

"Care!" Jormander shouted from behind. "Arrows aloft!"

Karl glanced to see a black cloud of bolts whistling their way, and without a thought, dived amongst his routed enemies, his sword tucked to his side. The pile collapsed with him, arms and legs tangled and thrashing. Arrows struck and the wounded grunted.

Kicking and punching, Karl pushed to his knees, shrugging the mound of men aside and yanking his sword free. He blocked a spear thrust—a shield clipped his shoulder—

he chopped at his attacker's foot, slicing into his boot, and ducking his head, rolled clear.

Agonized screams lifted, the random bolts having pierced friend and foe alike.

Havar grabbed Karl by his arm and jerked him to his feet. "Wounded?"

"Nay." Karl checked his ribs where he had banged them in his fall. "You?"

Havar grunted. "Not going to slow me." An arrow had lodged high on his left arm, driven through the muscle a knuckle's depth under the skin.

The confusion of the unexpected volley paused the combat while each side regrouped. Karl glanced at their enemies, several pierced by indiscriminate darts, moaning as they limped to escape the field.

"Jormander, casualties?" He glanced back at his old friend.

His wry smirk replaced by an unusually solemn frown, Jormander pointed with a flick of his eyes.

Jorn sat propped against a shattered cask, a black arrow protruding from his upper chest and a second deep in his thigh. His eyes squeezed tight, his teeth gritted, his sword trembled in his outstretched hand. While Havar began a furious attack to drive the enemy back, Karl dropped to his knee next to Jorn.

"Ja, wyrm-slayer, you caught a few birds."

Jorn grinned, his eyes clamped shut. He drew a ragged breath. "How bad?"

"You'll live." Karl placed his hand on the quivering sword hilt and lowered the blade. "But you are done this day."

Jormander pulled forward two of their younger recruits.

"Carry him back to our ship." They stooped to gather the wounded man under his arms.

Karl grimaced and shouted to rally his team, pointing with his sword at Havar bashing at the pack faltering before them. "Valkyries watch! Charge them, now! Drive these curs into the sea!"

RAGA

Hax clung to his mast, the snekke nearly empty and a distance from the main battlefront. His raven mare, scared by the noise and shouting, flew off to the rocky shore to hide in the tall pines.

Indeed, he thought, the thunder god watches over this ship, holding it safe and far from the struggle. Kol Skegg at the rudder and two boys remained, each with a sharp knife at the ropes fastening the railings to the next ship, prepared to cut the Smiles loose should the pilot command.

In Midgard, Karl had led his troops away, onto the amalgamation of ships and rafts, and their encounters moved beyond his vision. In the Realm Between Realms, Raga watched as glimmering angels swooped into the smoky chaos and plucked dying warriors from the field. The strange black aura tinged with a crimson fire humped and coursed over the hulls, weakening all it touched, an indiscriminate horror silently perverting the war. Raga watched it coil and flow. His eyes on the snaking horror, he moved across the deck to the mast troll.

"Do you see that creeping obscenity?"

"Ja, tis a fell curse, woven by an evil volva in cahoots with the power of Vanir. Whatever it touches crumbles or grows weary. Ships fall into the depths, men topple, unable to defend themselves. Harnessed by Agder it is, brought to Midgard to kill arbitrarily, allowing superior numbers to carry the day."

"We can't let it reach the bulk of our force, it will overcome them."

"What shall we do? I am as ever, bound to this longship...."

Raga paced in a tight circle. "I cannot let them die. I must see if I can help, see if I can find the source and blot it out."

"Take care, old hug. Such arcane mysteries are a danger, even to you."

Raga stomped his foot. "I've decided. You watch over the pilot and prepare to cut free of this floating arena of destruction, and I shall chase this evil to its source and remedy the enchantment before the tide is turned against us."

Raga straightened his turban on his head, pulled his sash tighter around his waist and bounced from the deck to land on the next ship. As he passed over the planks and climbed the hull of the next craft, he paused to watch two youths drag the wounded Jorn back to the Verdandi Smiles.

Wandering across the collected ships, Raga wound his way through the battle grounds, skirting areas of heated conflict. At its height, the battle drew thousands of fighters into the contest. Avoiding active quarrels, he warned himself to stay cautious and watchful. Spirits unclaimed by Valkyries, ghosts of the recently murdered floated in the Realm Between, hugs freed from their corporeal lich, confused in their existence and not yet drawn to Helheim. These fresh specters could capture him, could trap and draw him to Hell, or worse yet, devour his hug in their rapacious grasping for a life so suddenly lost.

In the gaps between the shattered ships, selkies sported in the waves, playing with the bloody carcasses. They hissed at him as he passed, protectively coveting their gory trophies. He hurried on his way, backtracking when necessary to steer clear of dangers.

Overhead the storm clouds roiled, heavy and black. Lightning forked into the sea near his path. Tendrils of smoke from fires drifted and obscured his view. He warily skirted areas where the sinuous black aura seeped and cascaded over the bound ships. The evil cloud split and divided, drawn to the battle front and, like fingers, curled around able warriors and sound boats. Raga bounced from one ship to the next, seeking its font.

Turned about and confused, he stopped to climb a bowsprit canted high over its neighbors. From his perch, he searched the field. Warriors contested on all sides, banners cast aside and trampled underfoot, abandoned for a moment, to be raised aloft to rally a counterattack. He concentrated—where did this evil curse originate? He followed its tracings like feeder streams to a river... the midnight curse could be tracked like a tributary back to its source: on the edge of the great conflict, the enchantment emanated from a knarr under Hordaland's banner.

Raga jumped from his roost and scrabbled across the bloody decks, pushing through a rabble hacking at each other. His path lay across a submerged craft, its floating benches, coils of rigging, and tangled corpses providing him enough stepping points to cross to a more secure mooring. Rising over a hulk of broken spars and crunched clinker planks, he faced the knarr.

Centered on the deck stood an unimposing figure. The volva was scrawny, his hair thin and dank, hanging about his eyes... no doubt here stood the source of the curse. He held an ebony medallion in his outstretched hands, and the eldritch implement sparked and shimmered in the Realm Between Realms, a black essence pouring forth in a steady torrent from the object, spilling across the decking and gushing like a waterfall over the railings. Where he clasped the charm, his fingers had grayed and crisped as if seared in flames. Raga crept aft and climbed aboard. Rising over the till, he paused, realizing the warlock was not alone.

"Holjan. Someone comes...."

Raga recognized her—the witch from Hamund's longhouse, the one who had escaped—she who had transformed into a troll-

cat! She sat cross-legged at the warlock's feet, her eyes milky white with Siedr charms, watching for attacks from beyond Midgard.

The sorcerer growled and turned to face Raga, his font of evil spraying like a hose. Raga leaped into the knarr rigging, scrambling from the black torrent.

Reaching the cross spar, he swung to the mast and surveyed his enemies below. An oily coiling curse too heavy to spout high in the air, the crawling malady fell upon the two of them instead of reaching their intended target. Disgusted, the wizard Holjan turned his evil font back on the warring factions.

"*Rind, defend us! Remove this nuisance before he upends our plan.*"

Raga watched as the milky-eyed woman threw off the spell designed to allow her sight to penetrate the Realm Between. She commenced chanting. Her eerie singsong crackled with power and her shape dissolved and reformed. Oddly compelling, Raga watched intently as the creature warped and malformed.

"*Well,*" *Raga mumbled.* "*One lives long enough, I guess one sees all....*"

Before his eyes, the witch transformed into a cat and entered the Realm Between... with him! Reshaped, the trollcat hunched its back and hissed.

Using its claws, the shaggy feline climbed the mast, inching its way toward the spar where Raga balanced. Unnerved, Raga watched the were-creature crawl towards him. This was not a situation he had planned for—he had thought to disrupt any Siedr spell from the Realm Between Realms, not have to face an enemy on his own. Raga stood unarmed, as he retained his form from the last day he walked the earth, a wide sash belting his belly, his baggy pantaloons gathered at his ankles, his silk slippers and his turban....

His turban!

Over the center of his forehead, a brooch pinned his head wrap, a jeweled ornament affixed by a long, silver pin. As the cat grew closer, he fumbled with his cap and drew out the gem, grasping the pin in his fist like a slender dagger.

The green-eyed cat climbed from the mast to the cross beam and Raga edged from it, easing out over the planks below. The witch crept steadily forward, its mouth split in a hideous grin, needle-sharp teeth around a blood-red tongue. As she reached him, she hissed and spoke, "I remember you." The creature arched its back and stretched out its hooked claws, heavy, thick talons Raga noted. "You lurked there the night Allinor escaped us—you watched when the ghost boy clipped Knetti's wings. You shall die for your interference."

Raga swallowed, biding his time.

She leaped across the narrow space between them. Claws raked his sides, her fangs snapped at his throat. Raga had expected no less—he stabbed his pin into her exposed chest.

His blow surprised the werecat. He landed a second stab before she comprehended he stung her, and she pushed back from the pain, scrambling for a hold on the cross spar. She caught one claw and swung precariously over the deck, spitting at him and grasping with her free limb. In a rush Raga stabbed repeatedly at her padded paw where it clung to the beam, plunging his pin into her forearm... the trollcat wailed, and injured, she lost her grip. She fell with a yowl and landed awkwardly.

Raga checked his sides where the troll cat had scratched him —his clothes ripped and ruined, his hug tottered unaffected, the scratches mere streaks on his ribs. He peered at his adversaries below.

The cat lay motionless, her back legs kicked out at an odd angle, her tail clearly broken.

The necromancer Holjan had moved to the gunwales,

holding the nether medallion over his head and sliding along the balustrade.

He seeks to escape, Raga thought, released his hold on the spar and floated to the ship planks. He runs... from me!

The warlock worked one leg over the railing, attempting to keep his spell focused during his retreat. Raga stepped closer to him, wondering at this cowardice. He held his pin tight in his hands, ready to attack.

This man exists in Midgard and wields an arcane device— Raga realized the device existed in the Realm Between and it operated in the astral plane—*his grip from Midgard tenuous at best, he can barely hold the talisman! His strained expression explains why his hands appear pained, deteriorating from the effort and the fell Siedr magic.*

Without further thought, Raga jumped to jab his pin into the black medallion.

The object shattered.

Holjan flipped over the railing, his hands pulped by the release of unearthly power.

Raga stumbled back, dazed, his jeweled pin melted to slag, his arm numb and useless at his side.

With a thundering crack, the black aura vanished. The great raft rocked in the wake of its disappearance.

Raga slumped to the deck, unconscious.

KARL

Karl and Havar fought in tandem, their fighting experience overwhelming those who stood against them, hacking and chopping their way to the edge of the platform, driving the raw novices into the sea. While most sunk beneath the waves, plummeting with nary a gurgle and drawn into the deep by the weight of armor, others thrashed in an ineffectual attempt to swim. Few of these conscripted farmers had learned to swim, especially not in deep water. During their offensive, no true warriors challenged the pair—King Eirik had swelled his army with inexpensive novices and not enough mercenaries.

A fire had spread across the collected vessels. A thick smoke hampered their vision, especially distant views—they could not judge how the battle ranged nor ken its outcome. From the noise, combat continued unabated. Karl worried his force would be caught and massacred by a new surge from Hordaland. At his command, Jormander fell back with his men, three decks back where they regrouped and rested. While they had lost six during the charge, the rest remained in good spirit.

Havar leaned forward on his hilt and wiped his forehead. They both panted, weary from the exertion. The drive to push back their opponents had taken more than an hour, a solid slog to part the enemy lines. In the heat of the battle, Karl had received a few minor flesh wounds. He inspected two shallow stabs to his sword arm, one over his wrist and one above his armpit, and he favored his left side, battered by a skidding spear blow, sporting a rough bruise with possible broken ribs. A spark from a wayward fire had snagged in his beard, burning a patch to his cheek. Havar had two bloody smudges on his tunic, the one near his belt spreading slowly. Dirtied with soot, a foe's gore splashed his face from hairline to his beard.

Lightning struck the aggregated rafts, thunder booming on its heels.

"Close strike." Havar winced. They both warily combed the sky. "Thor has chosen a side...."

As they rested and caught their breath, a man stumbled out of the smoke and shouted at them. He carried a shield and a sax sword, his shield emblazoned with a Rogaland sigil.

"Usurpers!" he shouted and dashed across the planks. Havar jumped to parry his first blow, his upswing slowed by fatigue. The blood-splattered swordsman screeched and bashed his buckler at Karl, stabbing at Havar's belly. Havar knocked the blade aside and swung his sword in a roundhouse return. The warrior blocked the singing knife-edge and turned to stab at Karl.

"You're a brave one," Karl grumbled. "Facing us both...."

"Whelps! I fear none of you!"

Karl caught Havar's eye. "This one's mine."

With a growl, Karl launched a furious attack, battering the enemy with blows to his shield and sax, one after the other at a quick pace. The unexpected rapidity of the blows checked the Rogalander's charge, his stabs at Karl's chest knocked ineffectually aside and his Lindenwood shield chipping and cracking under the ferocity. Striking high, Karl drew the enemy's counterattack, the short blade angling for his midriff. Karl snarled and caught the blade in his gloved hand. They locked face-to-face as they wrestled, Karl holding the sax blade, his sword pressed against the cracked and scored buckler. Slowly Karl twisted the short sword in his hand, and as the enemy strained to maintain his grip, Karl let his sword skid across the shield to strike the warrior's exposed sword arm. The chop gouged deep, his weapon dropping from a useless hand. Screaming, the warrior threw himself on Karl—he smacked at him with his shield, banging his forehead. Karl grunted and as the fighter swung again, Karl ran his sword through his hip.

Havar stepped in and, gripping the tottering warrior by his collar, tossed him over the railing into the sea. Karl pitched forward, heaving to catch his wind. A cloud of smoke rolled across their deck. Gagging, Havar pulled Karl back from the ocean across the deck to the next ship. The sounds of battle continued on every side.

A rope dangled from the aft of a knarr, its deck waist height over the longship tied to it. Havar climbed aboard and turned to help Karl. Nearby, a moan caught their attention.

"Alfenson."

There, tucked by the tiller, Dag, son of Dag sprawled, a deep slash in his belly welling dark blood. He sat legs splayed, surrounded by a pile of disemboweled enemies. A clatter of swordplay sounded from the bow, a solitary mast visible through the haze.

"No need for onion soup...." Havar murmured, bending over Dag's wound.

"What happened?" Karl checked the death blow.

"We separated, floated...." Dag gestured to the bay. "Took time to return." He coughed, blood in his spittle.

"We rowed... I fought, but... too many, too many...."

"Martine?" Karl fell to his knees before him. "Where is Martine? Has she fallen?"

"Hellcat." Dag pointed into the haze cloaking the bow.

"She fights still. She... fore...."

Karl rushed into the clouds of smoke, skidding on the gory decking. A shape hunched over a figure, a sword raised.

Screaming, "No!" Karl charged the dim shapes and tackled the warrior, knocking them all against the bow.

"Karl?"

Pushing Martine aside, Karl savaged the man with his hilt butt, smashing repeated blows to his face until he crumpled, his weapon tumbling from his hand. He heaved the unconscious man over the bow.

Martine pushed herself to her feet, holding the gunwale to steady her stance. She sported a bruised eye, her lip split and bloody, scratches and scrapes on every limb. Her battered shield lay broken and discarded near her feet.

Relieved, Karl hugged her, swung her in the air and... kissed her.

After a moment of surprise, she melted into his passion, the noise of war, the spray of the ocean and the choking fumes smarting their eyes, all forgotten.

Pausing their embrace to catch a breath, words poured from each, her face buried in his beard, his nose in the crook of her neck.

"Martine, Martine, forgive me... I thought I had lost you. I've been a fool..."

"Oh, Karl! and I you, too...."

Karl closed his eyes and gripped her tight.

The embrace lingered until Havar broke the spell by clearing his throat.

"You two can continue this apology later. Harald has challenged the king of Agder's berserker son Thor Haklang... See, out in the bay."

Karl took Martine by her hand.

"See, there?" Havar gestured to a longship coursing across the bay waters. "If we climb to the ship there, we can watch Harald face his sworn nemesis."

Martine retrieved her sword—its edge chipped and broken. Karl noticed she limped, favoring her right knee, and her breeches soaked with blood. Karl jumped to the next deck and helped her cross. Havar jumped the rails and landed next to them. A few wounded men whimpered between benches and offered no resistance. They crossed the boat and another.

Reaching the longship at the edge of the makeshift

barge, they climbed aboard and moved to the far rail. Ocean breezes here at the verge quickly cleared the haze plaguing the inner vessels. Its hull staved in, water slopped about the bilge, reaching to their knees. The location provided a great vantage point to watch Harald and Hakling as their flagships rowed across the bay. A body floated face-down in the center—Havar pushed the floating corpse aside.

"This bark will never sail again," Havar spoke aloud. Neither Karl nor Martine listened—they held each other and carefully measured each scratch and bruise, eyes roving and searching. Karl could hear his heartbeat in his ears. Martine smiled at him, touching the raw patch where his beard had burned away.

Sea battles engaged slowly, ships maneuvering and jockeying before a frantic paddle to gain ramming speed, plow their opponent and jump into furious conflict. Karl and Martine savored the quiet moment.

"Captain. We're not alone...."

Karl pulled back from Martine.

"More come to witness Harald fight...."

A group of men striding out of the smog, led by two large warriors, red banners tied to their arms and a flag with a two-headed eagle emblem.

"Thelemark."

Karl drew his sword, protectively stepping forward before Martine.

"Alfenson." As tall as Karl, Hroald Hryg leered across the railing at him. "I heard you fought for Tangle-head."

Covered in gore from vanquished foes, his bald head gleamed scarlet, his leather breastplate smeared with blood. His heavy mustaches weighted with silver beads, his grin exposed yellow, file-sharpened teeth. Next to him stood his brother, Had, known as 'the Hard,' a bull-faced brute with a pink scar from his temple to his chin—Had held a double-headed ax, its blades notched from clashes, his belt bristling with knives and hand axes.

"This one's mine." Hroald leveled his iron-pointed spear at Karl. The men accompanying the Thelemark brothers eased back, an unnecessary vanguard, and two stepped forward to occupy Martine. Hroald climbed one leg at a time over the railing into the longship. Karl knew the brothers—they had met years ago in Harald's court, and he had bested Hroald in a wrestling match, a fact the elder brother had never forgotten.

Havar sloshed to the side, squaring off against Had the Hard, his face a mask of grim determination.

"You joined with Eirik after all."

"Nay, Kjotve." Hroald leered at him and splashed in the water, kicking splatters at Karl. "He paid the most."

"Seems he wastes his gold."

Hroald growled. "I've sent thirty-nine to Helheim this day, and you, Son of Ironfist, will make my lucky forty," and he sprang across the submerged deck. With both hands on his sword, he swung a powerful, roundhouse blow.

Karl parried with an upward swing, the blades ringing as they scraped lengths. Both warriors closed quarters, both grabbing with their free hands to grapple a purchase on the other. Karl swung high, his strike blocked by a quick maneuver. Hroald countered and Karl ducked under the whizzing steel.

Had attacked like a berserker.

"Od-iiiin!" he screamed at Havar, and swung his massive ax in a practiced loop, weaving a deadly pattern as he pressed forward through the swamped boat. As Had knocked aside each attempt to block his ax, Havar scrambled back, stumbling, and grabbed a bench from the flotsam. He jammed the wood into the oncoming volley, momentarily halting Had's advance. His big ax blade bit deep into the wood and stuck. Havar jumped close and scored a flesh wound as Had worried free his blade. Had had expected his counter, and as Havar had advanced, a hand shaking the trapped ax covered a dart to his belt where he plucked a ready hand ax. As Havar poked his shoulder with his sword tip, Had threw underhanded, the ax head burying itself in Havar's ribs. With a jerk, Had pummeled Havar with the bench, dislodging the wood from the ax and sending Havar's weapon spinning.

Crazed with blood lust, Had brought his two-handed ax down over his head. Havar stepped into the swing and caught the ax hilt on the downstroke. Both sized similarly, the two warriors grappled face-to-face, shaking with the effort of holding the weapon between them.

Two warriors attempted to surround Martine, leering at her as she fell back against the seaside gunwale. One rushed her, his blade aimed at her chest. She parried his wayward stab and dropped to a kneeling position, his haste carrying him near the boat railing close to her and rearing up, she grabbed his belt and yanked him forward, letting his momentum carry him over her shoulder and into the brine. The other foe barked, surprised at her counter, and swung a roundhouse at her torso. Martine slid along the rail, deflecting each blow, measuring his abilities. As he grew angry with her blocking maneuvers, the man flushed and howled. Attacking with a two-handed, overhead strike, he beat on her defenses, banging his steel against hers in a rapid rhythm. He battered at her upheld sword. He took a deep swallow and reared to put all his weight into his strike. Seeing him prepare, Martine stepped in close. Deflecting his blade to the side, she returned with a backhanded uppercut, and sliced through his leather breastplate, opening a wound across his chest. His return swing winged over her head, his arm extended awkwardly. She drove her sword into his neck, yanked it free and rolled from his flailing arms. His sword slipped from his grasp. Standing at his side, she elbowed him, a rough back punch to his ribs toppling him to join his mate in the bay.

Evenly matched, Karl and Hroald sloshed in the swamped boat, dancing around each other, swinging their weapons in rapid succession, blocking and countering as fast as snakes striking, each seeking advantage. They moved through the dirty water, sail sheets tangling around their legs. The Thelemark staggered, off balance, something in the water rolling underfoot, and Karl stabbed for his midsection. Both tumbled, Hroald toppling backward and Karl stumbling through a hole in the keel, remaining planks crumbling under his weight. He dropped through the hull past his waist, scrambling for a hold, sinking into the briny water to his neck.

Chortling, Hroald recovered his balance and raised his sword.

"Shall I kill you quick, Dane?"

He reared back to strike a two-handed, killing blow.

Hroald forgot the shieldmaiden—Martine struck from his blind side, her sword tip piercing his side under his ribs. Surprised, he gawped, confounded by the unexpected wound.

Forgetting Karl, Hroald bellowed and turned on Martine. Flinging himself at her, he launched an uncompromising attack, pounding at her defenses. Martine frantically parried, trudging backward through the rolling waters, pushed back until his battering pressed her against the aft rail. The Thelemark struck with no pattern, high, low, across her middle, at her head. She thrashed and countered, lodged in her corner, unable to escape.

Heavier than Had, Havar turned the tussle over the ax to his advantage. Superior strength slowly overwhelmed the Thelemark. Havar took control of the hilt, twisting the weapon to weaken his adversary's grip. Had cursed and spat in his face. They both strained, red-faced in exertion, veins popping from Had's forehead.

In a sudden gambit, Had released his ax and dropped to the water.

Unsuspecting Havar toppled forward. A quick knife in each hand, Had plunged his daggers into Havar's gut. Screaming, the Thelemark gave each a vicious twist. Havar dropped the two-headed ax over the edge of the boat and pulled Had the Hard from the water by his shoulders, grasping him around the chest.

Karl floundered, his legs finding no purchase in the deep water. Helplessly struggling, he watched Martine draw Hroald from him, his anger evident in his uncontrolled attack. Spent from a long day of fighting, she would not last long under his barrage....

Composing himself, Karl drew a deep breath and ducked his head under the water. He pushed the shattered planks, slid his hand along the damage until he found a cross-rib. He followed the rib to the keel, where the broken planks ended. Clambering up, he pulled himself from the water. A quick survey—Havar wrestled with one, while the other beat at Martine. Jormander and his crew ran to challenge the other Thelemarks. Grabbing a tumble of rigging and tackle, he skirted around the hull breach and crept towards Hroald and Martine.

Hroald taunted Martine, spitting words at her with each swing. "Think you... can stand... against Hroald and

Had? We chop you... to feed dogs... we rip out eyes... and spit in your skull.... You die... die, worthless bed toy...." Her weariness grew with each counter, each parry slightly slower than the last. With a triumphant sneer, Hroald sliced across her thigh, cutting deep. Her sword tip dropped. Laughing, he drew back to plunge his sword through her torso.

Karl threw the jumble of ropes over Hroald.

The tackle deflected his attack. He whipped around and snarled at Karl, twisting to bring his sword to bear. Martine, seeing an opening, struck, driving her sword into his armpit, and throwing her body into the blow. The blade slid through his shoulder and thrust out his neck.

Hroald choked and wavered. Karl jumped close and grabbed his sword arm, wrenching the hilt from his hand. His bottom lip quivering, Hroald stumbled, propped standing by Martine's sword thrust. With a grunt, she withdrew it.

"Goodbye, Thelemark." Karl shoved Hroald over the railing with his foot. Grabbing a flagging Martine, they watched the body sink under the waves.

In Havar's grip, Had the Hard fought like a badger, stabbing with his knives, kicking and biting, screeching and cursing.

Havar made no sound. Despite the onslaught, his grasp held.

He squeezed.

One of the dagger blades snapped off between his ribs and despite the sharp pain, he squeezed.

Havar hugged the thrashing Had, he crushed until a crack sounded and Had fell limp in his arms. He dropped the broken man over the edge of the boat. Headfirst, the body slipped under the tide.

Karl moved through the swamped boat, holding Martine in his arms, circling where he knew the waves concealed the hole. Havar turned to face him, his chest ripped and savaged by the combat.

"Havar...?"

Blood welled from a deep cut in his chest.

Too much blood.

The big man tottered, unsteady on his feet. Karl and Martine sloshed through the watery deck. Havar crumpled, sitting precariously on the gunwale, and holding his arms out for balance. He gave Karl a wistful grin and gazed into the clouds.

"Think the Valkyries watch me this day?"

Before Karl could reach him, Havar toppled backward, hitting the water with a splash. With no heavy armor, he floated on the tide, his eyes on the storm clouds.

By the time Karl and Martine reached him, he slipped beneath the waves.

Havar was gone.

RAGA

Raga awoke, flat on his back, eyes on the squall overhead.

The sounds of battle raged around him. Smoke drifted through his vision. A fork of lightning branched overhead.

Despite the noise of fighting, he viewed the unobstructed sky, clouds rolling peacefully... he lay unconcerned, removed from the action about him. Slowly he recognized what had occurred, why he had been struck down—He had been knocked unconscious by the powers released when he broke the medallion. Such an occurrence had never happened before... in fact, in all his time as a spirit lost between the realms, Raga had not slept, not closed his eyes, never fainted, or fallen dizzy.

An odd, disturbing experience, to wake after black nothingness.

He attempted to sit and found his right arm would not respond. He struggled to his knees, examining his numbed limb. Shriveled from the energy discharged when he shattered the fell medallion, his hand curled fixed in a cramped half-fist, his arm dangling loose at his side, as if he was a victim of an aneurism—he had seen those symptoms in elders, never in a hug in the Realm Between.

Feeling woozy, he gripped the ship rail with his good hand. Below him, the warlock Holjan lay in a pool of his own blood. Only tatters of flesh and bone remained below his elbows. The trollcat had reverted to her Midgard form, her human back twisted and broken, one leg crushed beneath her. These two no longer posed a danger to anyone. Raga surveyed the makeshift battle grounds.

It was clear to see why the Siedr wizard had chosen this location for his spell weaving—the knarr stood the height of a man over the surrounding ships, affording a wide view of the battlefield. Something happened—the men and woman fighting had stepped back from their opponents; an event of portent had drawn their attention from the fight. Raga decided to investigate.

Bounding across the shackled vessels, Raga found a tall mast on the edge of the open sea. He jumped to the top, clinging to its peak with his good hand. Around him the warriors watched two ships approach each other in the bay. The forest-green banner of Harald Shockhair marked one, the other a red flag of his opponents. Whispers below him helped him understand what he witnessed: Harald drove his ship to face the prince of Agder. Those soldiers named him a berserker, famed for violence and no mercy. Thor Haklang, the son of King Kjotve the Rich.

The two ships rushed forward, their impact shattering oars, momentum scraping the length of the hulls as sailors scrambled to grapple. Iron hooks cast across the gap locked the vessels to each other, and men armed with spears poked and jockeyed, each pushing to gain a foothold on the other longship. The crowd grew quiet, their eyes on the flagships. Raga could discern Harald, his mass of ratty, felted hair standing atop his head. He held a shield emblazoned with his sigil and a longsword. A warrior with a wooden war hammer in one hand and a sax short sword in his other, shouted a challenge across the gap. Harald spoke, his words lost to the surging tides. On both sides, the sailors shuffled aside, permitting the hammer wielder room to climb over the gunwales and face his enemy, man to man.

Even from his distant vantage, Raga could see Haklang rear high in rage, a crazed, red-faced man. His long hair braided and tucked in his belt, his vest sparkled with a bronze glimmer, his tunic made of chainmail. He jumped at the sailors with reckless abandon, smashing with his hammer, striking any who dared oppose him, shoving flailing bodies over the side.

Harald shouted—his words did not carry—from the reaction produced, he goaded the brute. The berserker faced Tanglehair, spitting curses. Harald directed his circle of onlookers to spread and enclose their pitch. These loyal sailors crossed spears and swords to fence the combatants.

With a howl, Haklang attacked. Harald parried and retreated, carefully staying clear of the larger man's reach. The crazed Thor raged at Tanglehair, chasing him about the deck, smashing benches and barrels, hacking at the mast and shattering gunwales. Harald artfully countered, dodged, and deflected the heavy blows. The heavy hammer swung close to Harald and the two joined in a heated struggle—the crowd below Raga murmured in anticipation: Thor Haklang had challenged the would-be King of the Northern Way, this confrontation would settle the day.

The two separated and circled each other, Thor Haklang shaking his shoulders and neck to loosen his muscles. He twirled his hammer to distract his opponent and barked curses and flyting taunts. Raga could see slobber speckled the berserker's beard. Tight-lipped and flushed from exertion, Harald warily evaded the berserker's attempts to close on him. Their initial forays tested each defense, and with determination the two steadily assaulted each other. The pace quickened, blade clanged against blade, hammer blows thumped as the shield blocked. The adversaries molested each other, one scrape followed by a near miss, a quick jab knocked aside, the contest a match of equals.

The Lindenwood shield shattered under Thor's onslaught. Harald dodged the war hammer follow-through and jammed the broken pieces into his rival's chest, his mail shirt deflecting the blow. Wielding his sax like a long knife, the edge sliced Harald along his ribcage. Harald kicked his foe in the belly and stepped under the mallet to score a direct hit to the berserker's chest—while the mail stopped a killing blow, its force halted Thor's advance, and he stumbled, coughing. The people gathered on the ships, as well as Raga, perceived his choking sounds across the waters.

The conflict continued with neither gaining advantage. The throng hung on every strike and counter. Thor threw his weight behind a hammer swing, the blow missed Harald, and the wayward strike smashed into a cask, lodging the head of the mallet in the wooden barrel staves. He struggled to free his weapon. With a two-handed swing, Harald chopped the handle and snapped the hammer head from its shaft. Screaming, Thor slashed at Harald with his sax. Harald flipped his sword to block the upswing and carried through with his hilt, smacking the Agder prince in his cheek and brow. The damage blinded one eye —the warrior roared in anger and grabbed for Harald's tangled locks. With a grip of hair, he jerked Harald to face him and stabbed for his chest. Harald rolled with the attempted blow and as the berserker overextended his reach, Harald dropped to his knees to plunge his sword through the warrior's exposed groin. The wounded prince flopped on top of Harald, trying to grapple and wrestle. His sax smacked the deck planks, banging a furious tattoo. Harald rolled free, rose to one knee and swung his longsword in an arc into Haklang's blind side. The blow connected below his ear and the Agder prince tumbled to his hands and knees.

Harald rose over his enemy and with a single swing, lopped his head from his shoulders. He lifted his gory token over his head, waving triumphantly. A mixture of cheers and defeated groans lifted around Raga. On the Agder ship, their foes stood aghast at the sight of their fallen champion. Harald shouted for action and with his men at his side, he took the Agder ship in a rush. Ruthlessly, they cleared the decks.

Below him, a soldier called out, "Look, Kjotve!" Raga saw where he pointed, a ship, farther back in the mouth of the bay, with the flag of Agder. King Kjotve the Rich had witnessed his son's defeat. As the observers watched, the vessel hoisted sails and tacked away, retreating from the battle.

"Kjotve flies the field!"

"Coward!"

"Agder flees!"

"Eirik has fallen!"

"Harald has won!"

"The battle is ours!"

Shouts rose on all sides. And something else... on the tangled mass of ships about him, Raga sensed a recognition of defeat. Grumbles and whispers... the retreat grew in number and spread rapidly. Men and women dropped weapons and fled. Those who could swim shed their armor and leaped into the sea, making for the Hafrsfjord shores. Others ran to climb aboard a vessel, any raft or punt, cutting them loose... several paddled with their hands, desperate to escape Harald's wrath.

The rain had stopped, and flashes of lightning continued to light the waning day.

As Raga watched, the deserters ran into the Jadar forests.

The battle ended, Raga turned to retrace his steps and return to his berth. Dismayed, he found the ships ablaze behind him, a wildfire spreading from the east to the west, jumping from longship to longship, a conflagration. The burning vessels listed. One collapsed and sunk before him. In sudden fear, he rushed to cross the smoldering waste, worried over Hax and the Smiles fastened to this inferno. Around him, men and women jumped into the sea.

His path was treacherous. Death angels dipped from the clouds to carry the bravest hugs to Valhalla. Confused ghosts, unaware of their recent demise, wandered in his way. The sea churned with great beasts, come to feast on the carrion.

The storm hounding them all day passed. As the clouds overhead shredded and broke, thunder rumbled in its wake, long and low, rattling his chest. Lightning forked through the tattered clouds, a flash so bright it stopped Raga in his flight—it spun and arched, finally snapping loose of its cloudy mooring to slam the fiery vessels before him. Raga bounded over the flaming decks, worry overcoming his good sense.

Reaching the edge of the smoldering boats, Raga found the Verdandi Smiles.

The snekke floated untouched.

The final lightning strike had shattered its neighbors and cast it free of the devastating fires....

The god of thunder had upheld his end of their bargain.

CHAPTER 11
KARA AGNESDATTER GAINS HER FLYING SKILLS

CUB

The Mayor of Bayeux built a sumptuous, two-story building, its foundations crafted from river rocks with stout, oak beams and horsehair-plaster walls. Rolf commandeered the abode and sent the mayor and his family packing—the hall easily held his contingent of lieutenants. The main floor housed a storage room and a kitchen to prepare food as the cooking was completed in the hall's great hearth. Rickety stairs climbed to the second floor, three small rooms under the rafters which Rolf set aside for loot as well as temporary confinement for hostages. The wide fireplace lay cool this late summer night, logs stacked in place to fire in case the night grew chill.

His stomach rumbled, louder than he thought polite. Cub rubbed his belly. A serving girl poured horns of ale and worked her way around. His comrades joked and laughed, pinching the girl to make her spill her brew. Cub held a mug high in anticipation, throwing his leg over the bench.

As Cub settled into his spot at the table, a commotion signaled the entry of the 'hostages,' Poppa chief among them, stomping on each creaky stair. Cub sighed and excused himself to leave his mates around the table.

Whirling across the room with her skirts in her hands, lifting them carefully over the scattered straw on the floor, Poppa cornered him against the sooty mantle. Early she had recognized Cub as their best translator. Her ladies clung to her heels, lending their weight to her pleas and demands.

Haughty and aloof, as the daughter of the Count of Rennes and a member of the Paris Court, a fact she managed to insert in all conversations, Poppa demanded Cub focus his attention on her whenever she found him. Rolf had Cub translate for them, and while Cub suspected she understood more of their tongue than she admitted, the lady enjoyed the sheer adventure of the crass Northmen and their callous treatment of local lords. He caught her grinning when men hand-selected by Rolf replaced the mayor and his aldermen. She didn't exactly flirt like other girls—Cub noticed she knew how to gain an audience in any situation and how she carefully manipulated those around her, both men and women. Cub monitored her every move, learning the nuances of her ways—originally smitten by her beauty, he learned he ranked low in her corps of admirers and the luster of her splendor faded as he perceived the skillful knife hidden in the jeweled sheath. As the skalds warn, 'many a fair skin hides a foul mind.' Cub had lost his infatuation. This beauty was not for him.

"My *lord*," she accosted him, the way she stressed the title subtly indicating her disdain for naming Cub her superior. "Inform your liege I... nay, we cannot stay cooped inside this wretched domicile another day. We need to promenade, to breathe the freshness of air... could he arrange a horse-drawn carriage for my ladies in waiting to tour the countryside?"

Cub chuckled. "No, I not place that ask before Rolf. Why anger him?"

"Why would my most modest request anger the great strider, conqueror of the Breton March and oh-so-dreaded Rollo, warrior king?"

"Now, you are being...." Cub fumbled for the proper word.

"Facetious?" Poppa's eyes twinkled, despite her serious demeanor. Her ladies tittered behind embroidered handkerchiefs and nosegays.

"Ah... ja, you have the word." Cub could tell she teased him, purposefully using big words not in his limited vocabulary.

"Flippant or no, convey to his lordship we are tender youths made waifs by his command, so cruelly contained, nay, pickled in this, his forced captivity." She waved a delicate hand at the room. Rolf sat with Hagrold, drinking from a horn, ignoring the conversation. Cub glanced enviously at his draught.

"I am certain my father has offered gross fortunes to ransom myself and my ladies in waiting from this horrid backwater."

Cub avoided the subject. "You and girls are bored. You want to do something."

"Oui, oui, you truly over-simplify our morose condition, nevertheless, it sums the essence of our predicament."

Cub tried not to roll his eyes. He glanced at Rolf.

"My lord is busy."

"I think not." She scrunched her mouth tight, tipped her head back imperiously and squinted at him.

Cub sighed. "Ja, I tell him you 'wither like a plucked flower.'" He pointed to a smaller table set across the hall. "Ladies, go sit. Dinner. I speak with Rolf."

Poppa sighed and opened her mouth to continue, but Cub interrupted, "Sit... please." He emphasized his gesture toward the table. The ladies-in-waiting scuttled away, Poppa lingering, unused to obeying any command. She turned on her heel and strode purposefully across the room, all eyes in the room following her figure as she swished her skirt side-to-side.

Cub sighed and returned to his place. He climbed over the bench to sit next to Colden, having earned a place to sup at Rolf's table. A roast leg of lamb on a pewter platter had been served, and the food smelled delicious. Foregoing the beer, Cub sliced a hunk of the meat free.

"I have a special task for you, Agneson." Rolf motioned to Cub with a curl of his fingers. Beside him, Hagrold watched Cub coolly, his face stony, his thoughts disguised. Colden stood behind him, interest pursing his lips. Rolf pointed to the door and stood from the table. Leaning across, Cub tore another hunk of mutton before he followed. Poppa watched him leave, tipping her head to indicate expectations for him to ply Rolf on her behalf. As he stepped out the door, he gave into his exasperation and rolled his eyes.

"What is it?" Rolf asked.

"That girl, she vexes me."

"Forget it, I'll handle the willful Poppa of Bayeux." They stepped into the cobbled, center Bayeux square. "There is more than one way to skin a rabbit," he added, with a wink.

Rolf had a long gait matched to his height, and Cub rushed his shorter pace to keep abreast of him. They walked along the river Aure, the water swift and high after rains. In his characteristic straightforward manner, Rolf raised his point.

"Athelstan, King of East Angles, you know him, eh?"

"Athels... I do not know this name.

"You fought under him."

"What?"

"You fought in the Dane army, eh? After defeat, he was goaded by Wessex into the Christian faith, a magic bath they say, and took a new name in the ceremony. Athelstan, you fought for him at Ethandun."

"Guthrum?"

"Ja, that's the one." He reached in his tunic. "He sent me this missive." The roll of parchment crumpled and dirty from handling, Rolf held the roll open, displaying the contents to Cub.

"I make no sense of this scratching."

"Tis an offer of parlay, to consider an alliance."

"Why would Guthrum want an alliance?"

"He chafes under the yoke of Wessex. Seeks a new channel for his ambitions...."

Cub considered the information. "To speak plain, Rolf, why contact us?"

Rolf rolled the paper and tucked it away. He waved his arm, his gesture encompassing the riverside and the shabby, stone houses lined along the reedy shore.

"This place we are granted by Robert of Breton, this tiny strip of Britany... tis too small." A tall man, he leaned to confide in Cub. "I intend to overthrow the Frankish Roi. He is fat and spoiled, and ripe for harvest. We need more men for our armies. Ja, we can squeeze taxes from these lands and build over time... Have I ever been one for patience? To get men fast, we need a benefactor with a loan of silver or trade goods to supply my legions. Your Athelstan of Anglia has silver, and trade goods, and..." he patted his chest where the paper crackled, "he has the desire."

"Why me?"

"Ah, little bear cub, you fight like a seasoned warrior, a trained champion, but more than strength of arms, you can think." He tapped Cub on his forehead. "You think... like a highborn, a courtier even. Tis a credit to your people. You negotiate better than most merchants, and I've trafficked with more than a few. The way you took Bayeux with little bloodshed won us the prize as well as the hearts of the people. The smart ones knew we could have overwhelmed the town our usual, bloody way.

"Don't misunderstand me. Hagrold is dependable, my right hand on the battlefield, a leader the men flock to in times of strife. I can depend on him for strict management of a populace such as this. My Hagrold is a fist—he is not an open palm. He is not a strategist—he is not one to find a middle path so all shall profit. And he knows this to be true—'twas he who recommended you.

"This task requires subtly and cleverness. We all see this quality in you. And you speak the language of both the locals here and our northern tongue. Shrewd, calm thinking is what we will need if we are to forge a partnership with Anglia, and others as well. I have plans, Agneson, and I see you play a part."

"My lord, my family lies in Northumbria. I appreciate everything you have done for me." He touched the gold band on his left arm, a gift for his service. "I always expected to return, I mean, once our campaigns are finished, to claim my rights as heir. Our homestead...."

"Nor would I interfere in such a just claim. As I have rewarded you with bands, with silver and gold coin, I would reward you with a fertile estate here in this Gallic land, a large manor to add to your family holdings. And when we have completed our conquest, I will need to supplant the local gentry with my own loyal men. Smart, capable men. This is a role I see for you, my young friend.

"I intend to siege and secure this Paris. I will take command of this land, and you can help, as your father's father aided in the fall of the old Northumbria before the rule of east men. This is our age, our time—these rotted, old kingdoms crumble before our might and our Asgard gods. We seek allies to strengthen our hands and further our cause. Will you join me?"

Cub paused to watch the river swirl past in the twilight.

"I am honored you would consider me a worthy envoy. I accept your proposal, and ask before I return, I may have your leave to visit my family while in the land of the Angles."

Rolf smiled and offered his hand to shake. "This will secure your place both here and in the Danelaw across the sea. I am certain you will treat with this Athelstan and craft a powerful alliance for us. I shall assign you two footmen, and tomorrow I shall command Colden to sail his *Seawing* across the channel to East Anglia."

They returned to the mayor's house. Poppa gazed expectantly at him as they entered, and Cub avoided her prying, expectant eyes. Rolf threw Hagrold a meaningful glance, and his lieutenant tossed Cub a purse. As he tucked the pouch in his belt, Rolf took his hand in front of his men, and handed Cub a horn, calling the servants over to fill the cups.

"You see before you our new emissary to the East Angles, Agne Agneson! He leaves on the morrow, let's all drink to his farewell."

The men lifted their mugs and shouted, "Skal!"

SORVEN

As Sorven stumbled along the scruffy mountain path, the mist dispersed which made the path easier to traverse. The girl skipped as she led him, hopping over fallen trees, and winding around gorges and landslips. The path wound through a narrow gulch, heavy pines sloped across the way, forcing him to duck under their boughs. As they passed through the thickets, the night peepers and cicadas fell silent in the brush about them. Sorven barely noticed, entranced by her shining, amber orbs.

She pressed forward through a tangle of undergrowth and jerked his hand to follow. Twigs scratched his cheeks. Sorven blinked, confused, and his hair and clothes snarled in the brush. He lifted his head—the willow grove hung draped with moss about him, his boots squished in mire.

A touch on his cheek—it was her, bringing his attention back to her eyes.

Those eyes.

She pulled him, steadied him. They stepped out of the grove.

After the darkness of the trail, the moon cast a pale radiance across the glen, the meadow grass silver in the faint illumination. The girl lifted her firebrand, the dim azure flames jumping higher in open air. Across the hoary turf, a strange structure leaned under the spread arms of an ancient oak.

Constructed between two rocky outcrops, the front wall consisted of a heavy door carved in Celtic symbols and scrolled patterns, surrounded by overlapping planks and a single, round shutter propped open with a wood stake. The shake-shingled roof sloped sharply to a point topped with a tin cap, where a curl of gray smoke lingered, slipping out from slots in the shakes. In the open window Sorven caught a glimpse of countless little eyes reflecting the moonlight. At first glance more pairs than he could count.

Holding his hand, the girl drew him forward and opened the door, settling him on a roughhewn stool. She placed her torch in the ringed, stone hearth in the center of the round room, tinder there immediately catching with a crackly whoosh. Before he could take stock of his surroundings, the darkness faded in the firelight and to his dismay revealed a swarm of small animals surrounding him. The pack flew from the high rafters, wormed across the walls, and leaped to circle him, teeth bared, spitting and hissing. The girl cooed and tsked, shooing the creatures back from Sorven with a sudden clap.

The menagerie astounded him—weasels, stoats, sleek minks and potbellied otters, each fur a different pattern, strange markings around their eyes, gray bearded, bright red stripes, and blonde tufts between their ears. A few rushed to nip at his fingers and tug at his boots, insistent, angry little animals. The majority watched the girl slide around the room, gently relieving Sorven of his burlap sack and his heavy outercoat. The room smelled of a woodsy scent with a tang of animal spoor and a mysterious, cloying perfume.

"What is your name?"

"Ah... Sorven." The fire flickered, casting outlandish shadows on the walls. "Sorven Agneson." Her eyes blazed in the gloom. He found he could not glance away.

"Sorven." She turned her back on him, letting her robe ripple and slide from her shoulders, her long legs and bare back uncovered, her exposed feet dirtied and flecked with forest loam. Her skin gleamed unblemished ivory white, her muscles lean and supple as she moved. Sorven sat bewitched.

The creatures circling him humped their backs, several popped upright on their back paws, paddling the air and squeaking. A few chased their tails. Others chattered and clicked sharp teeth. The girl laughed, amused by her tiny circus, and the ermine at her throat slipped to her arm and jumped into the midst of the gang, causing the mob to scatter and chirp. She hummed, a tuneless melody which enchanted Sorven—*what a lovely tune*, he thought, his fingers wriggling in time with her song.

As he watched, the girl pulled out a wide, flat, copper bowl to set near the fire. Taking a leather pitcher, she poured clear water into the basin, stirring with a slender finger, watching Sorven through the tresses dangled across her face.

"We must bathe," she announced, as if a self-evident truth. Sorven, besotted and full of agreement, tugged off each boot in turn. As she sprinkled scented herbs and crushed flowers into the washbasin, he untied his tunic and loosened his belt. He set aside his knife.

"Will you wash my feet?" Her request hung between them, natural, innocent. Sorven crawled forward on his knees, his belt undone and breeches sagging, his eyes locked on her yellow eyes.

With eyes on her face, he took a rag from her hands and

never noticed her horny callouses, nor the sharp claws which crowned each toe—her mesmerizing eyes and svelte figure seized his attention. As he gently stroked her feet clean, she indolently untied her buckskin halter, one leather thong at a time, slipping it free to toss carelessly aside. She unclasped her leather belt, and held it below her navel with both hands, smiling at the boy happily scrubbing her feet. The downy fur nestled in the curvature between her breasts intrigued him, part of her exotic beauty.

"What is your name?" Sorven begged, gazing rapturously at her.

"Later, my Sorven," she purred. "All in time...."

She dropped the belt and pulled him next to her, wiggling his tunic over his chest and discarding it. His clothes fell away, and she pulled him into the washbowl, pouring a cascade of fresh water over his head and shoulders, brushing him gently with her rag.

Around him, the beasts acted agitated. As the bath continued, Sorven became more muddled—so close to her, he could see tiny wrinkles crinkled around her temples, her youthful vigor and allure hiding something else, something he could not define. She touched and pressed against him as she washed him, teasing him, stroking him. With a firm hand, she drew him to a pallet, and they sank together. The animals surrounded them, eyes reflecting in the dim light.

She pressed Sorven back into silken pillows and stroked his cheek.

"My Sorven."

"Ja ...?"

"You do want me, don't you?"

"Oh, ja, I have never wanted anyone except you." He meant his words, she so enticed him.

"What would you do for me?"

"Anything... Oh, anything! You have but to ask...."

"Tis an easy thing I ask." Stroking his hair back from his forehead, she reached behind him and pulled out an arcane implement. Crafted from silver, the long-tarnished tool was shaped like a tiny animal skull with bulging eyes and a sharp beak ending in a needle-tipped point. As she lifted the device, the ferrets and weasels around them moaned, a mournful cry lost on Sorven who lay across her arm in a stupor, his tongue quivering in his slack mouth, his eyes captivated by hers.

The siren touched the mysterious tool to her arm and drew a fleck of blood. With a gentle kiss, she drew the device in a pattern on his upper chest. She outlined a small Celtic knot, the blood seeping into his chest and leaving a dark stain. The blemish blackened and, as he watched, sprouted tiny hairs....

The strange tattoo made him wince and bow his back. Biting his lip, he could endure the pain, and Sorven found he wanted her to continue, wanted her to draw more, draw all over him. A peculiar ecstasy consumed him, and he didn't notice with every new dab and stroke, her blood leached into him, and his into her, and as he patterned, an abnormal fuzz sprouted where the tracing had passed. Nor did he notice with each sketch she made, the girl shimmered, her hair visibly lengthened, and her limbs grew younger, pinkening with the freshness of youth... only her eyes remained sly and cunning, reflecting an ancient wisdom.

"We must stop, my Sorven...."

Panting, Sorven tottered on the point of tears. "Why? Why must we stop?"

"Many nights will be ours, my love." She set aside the

Siedr implement and ran her finger over the Celtic pattern below his collarbone, brushing the silky fur which sprouted from her symbol. "It will take all winter to mark you, to bind us completely. I must keep you to sustain me these long, cold moons. Once you are mine, my Sorven, you will carry my marks from ears to toes...."

She motioned to the creatures leering at them from the rafters and corners. "And you can join your brothers... to forever be my pet."

KARA

"I know why they call this the Emerald Isle."

"All this rain..."

"Ja. Rain, rain, and more cursed rain!"

"Makes the plants grow, darling." Kaelan pointed to the thick moss carpet caked on the ancient stone wall they traced across the moor.

"Makes me miserable." Better to blame weather than her belly—her time of the moon approached, her cramps more severe than usual. Tired and sore, her weariness had more to do with their forced march than her moon cycle—for weeks in the field on Sichfrith's useless errands, seeking an elusive vengeance for his older brother's murder—forget Mac Ausle, the Vikingr of this land cleave to the will of the sons of Imar. And Helka had told her true: Sichfrith did not trust the Dubgaill. He purposefully set them impossible tasks, including these fortnight-long marches into the Tuatha of competing lordships.

"All hail the Ui Imair!" One of the marchers behind her grumbled, her nose raw from sniffles.

Last moon, Sichfrith had them lay siege on a fortification south of Lock Gabor. Nothing had come from the fiasco save casualties, short rations, and sleepless nights. The Irish refused to face them, lobbing stones and wayward arrows at them for days, and all ended in a poorly executed arson, the entire fortress overcome by flames, scouring the wooden battlements and shacks to ashes, as well as the inhabitants and any treasure they may have hidden. The blaze ended in raw ugliness—the screams of the trapped and dying haunted her dreams—*why had they not surrendered? Why had they not joined us in battle, why not fight honorably, at least with a chance to survive?* She had wandered the ruined fortress after the fire. Charred bodies, dead horses with distended bellies, heaps of coals and slag.

The moon Gormanudur had ridden in with a storm and with it, the last vestiges of summer departed. Carried by sleet and bluster, and framed with frosty mornings, winter settled over Eire. The trees shed their leaves in the storm winds, their boles black fingers stretched against morbid, gray skies. All miserable, a good reflection of how Kara felt.

The joy in her life was Kaelan, her Kaelan. At least, far from Dublinn and prying eyes, they could be together—no one on the march much cared if they spent time in each other's arms.

Their current path wound far west past Cill Dara. Their command, to seek the forces of Cerball Mac Muirecáin of Leinster, thought to be massing for an attack on the seat of power in Dublinn. After days of chasing rumors, they crossed no traces of an army. The small villages they happened across were poorly defended hamlets, no source of rivalry. Unsure what they planned to do if they came across an enemy army, Kara worried over their mission— their squad numbered eight, not what she considered a fighting force. Luckily, their efforts to find an enemy had been fruitless. She anticipated a few more days of tromping across hills and through woods, a fruitless chore overall, and at the end of the fortnight, they would forsake this hopeless undertaking and march back to a warm berth in Clondalkin.

At least she had more time with Kaelan. They worked together on his sword skills. The teaching went slow— like all her brothers and sisters, her father had started her drilling in her eighth summer, and training became a regular routine, every day, sword and shield. Her skills had been practiced for years before she had been apprenticed to Hege in Eddisbury. Kaelan worked a farm for his father, spear practice an occasional pastime when chores and crops permitted. To address the gaps in his skills, they practiced each evening, Kara coaching his stance, his swings and blocks, while he baited her and helped her with her flytings. A good warrior should be able to taunt and anger an enemy, and Kara never acquired the skill. In the uproar proceeding a battle, taunts and insults flew from her thoughts like birds scattered before a hawk. Kaelan teased her, and she found she could mock him back, and he built on their playful relationship.

She peeked at him, marching carefully at her side. His hair long enough to braid now, a short tail hung to his shoulder. His beard boyishly thin, he gave her a side glance with his dopey grin. She loved his silly smile, his blue eyes —she touched his hand. Nice to have him close, at her side.

Finding a glen in a stand of elms, the patrol decided to camp for the night. A drizzle kept them from lighting a fire, each finding a nook between trees or a sheltered niche in the underbrush. Kaelan unrolled his bed roll, and they huddled together under the damp blanket. He murmured in her ear, and she stopped his wandering hands.

"I am filthy from this forced march," she hinted, not

wanting to mention her time of the moon. "Not tonight." Good-natured, he didn't push or press, happy to peck her cheek. She sighed as he wrapped his arm around her.

"Kaelan...." Kara tucked her forehead in the crook of his neck. "This Eire... this Dublinn on the River Liffey is not the place I thought it would be."

"Nor I."

"I have been thinking, and I don't reckon this," she gestured with the blanket, "...is an honorable way to gain skills and renown. When we return to Dublinn, we should consider taking a boat back to Mercia."

"I have coin."

"I saved most of what we've been paid...."

"Your mother would be happy."

"Our reputation...."

Kaelan clucked his tongue. "Nothing to worry about there. You made a name for yourself. Besides, I would return to my father... to have him offer the bride price."

"Kay!" Her heart jumped—this, the first time he had mentioned marriage.

"Tis true, it's how I feel about you, Kara. I love you."

She gazed into his eyes in the twilight. "I feel the same. I... I love you."

They pressed their lips together in a prolonged kiss.

"I will convince my mother to accept your father's offer, no matter the amount."

"Oh, it will be grand."

"You wish!" She giggled and pressed her head into his shoulder.

"I don't get the purse—it all goes to your coffers in case I am a terrible match, and you are forced to divorce me."

"Well, tis our way, and as for divorce, you know I may

have to consider it... piss poor swordsman." She purred, her innuendo obvious.

"Finally, Kara Agnesdatter gains her flyting skills." He laughed. "Too bad she uses savage word play on the one she adores..." He pulled her chin near and kissed her again.

They nestled together for warmth and slept fitfully. Hours before dawn, a soldier poked Kaelan to take his turn at watch.

Broken clouds framed the horizon at sunrise. Geese flapped overhead, honking encouragement as they passed in their V-formation. The patrol broke their fast with tough, dry seed cakes and a gulp from their water sacks. Collecting into the semblance of a line, they hiked west and followed a game trail winding through the damp hills. The final streamers of rainclouds whipped aloft by gusts of chill wind, the morning sky cleared to a faded, winter blue. The squad increased their pace; a brisk march helped ward the biting wind and got their blood pumping after a damp night.

Cresting a rise, the squad happened across a militia in a field below them. They stumbled to a halt.

In a valley bisected by a meandering stream, a group of men had stopped for the night and shuffled about the process of breaking camp. All similarly dressed, the force included cavalry, the two horsemen dismounted to water their steeds, and the footmen holding heavy, iron tipped spears. By their expressions, they had not expected company either. Both sides silently appraised the other.

With a shout, the group challenged them and jogged up the hillside towards them. One of the horsemen vaulted to his saddle. He barked a string of words, probably a warning. Kara did not understand the language or accent.

Einar led their Dublinner patrol, a portly fellow with

bandy legs and a double chin—while not a commanding presence, Kara had fought at his side in the past, a deadly master with his sax. His experience reassured them. Making a quick appraisal of their situation, he pointed back the way they had come.

"To the wood, before those horses ride us down!"

Without a glance behind, Kara and Kaelan ran. Avoiding the gentle slope they recently climbed, they rushed to a sharp drop-off they hoped would be more difficult for horses. Steep and slick with the night's rain, they slid down the hillock into a thicket at the bottom of the gorge. Three of their Dublinn warriors joined them and together they pushed into the undergrowth, closing ranks for protection. Willows clogged this bottom, a dense, overgrown clutch. The sounds of their pursuers surrounded them, a heavy warhorse balking at entering the rough underbrush with stomps and whinnies of complaint. On foot, the opposing force crashed into the thicket, leading with their spears. Kara pushed deeper into the brush, startling roosting birds.

"I count twelve."

"That horse'll never fit in here."

"Fine! Eleven against our five."

"Not enough, they might as well surrender now!"

Kara laughed. The thicket made for tight quarters, difficult to swing her father's longsword.

"Watch my back." Kara pushed Kaelan behind her.

Two adversaries pushed through the dense brush, one brandishing his spear in both hands over his head to avoid tangles. They both caught sight of Kara. Their sneers showed they like others she faced in the past, made quick assumptions about their opponent. Kara enjoyed her foes underestimating her. The first attacker brought his weapon to bear, plunging into the brush near Kara, missing his mark and over-extending his reach. She stumbled forward through the undergrowth, aiming a stab at his torso. Her sword tip bit into his upper arm. The warrior yelped and jerked at his spear, attempting to pull it back for another attack. Kara fell on the staff with her left arm and pinned the pole against her body, swinging her sword to trace a long line from his hip to his knee. The warrior collapsed—she imagined the string of invective he spewed must be curses.

The enemy who had accompanied him was slow to appreciate Kara had disarmed his mate. A boy barely older than she, surprise lifted his brows, and in a credit to his training, he quickly set his spear against the ground and leveled the sharp end in a defensive pose. Kara scrambled to regain her balance and crouched in front of him. She sensed Kaelan at her back.

"To the left," she called, and dodged to her right—the warrior followed her movement with his spear, blocking her blade's swing and leaving his defenses open to Kaelan. With a simple hack from his short sword, Kaelan chopped the boy's hand, breaking his hold on the spear. As his weapon tumbled from his grasp, he turned and fled.

"This way!" Kaelan pulled Kara farther into the grove.

"Take this." Kara handed the dropped spear to Kaelan. Around them the sounds of battle surged, men crying in pain and shouting in anger. Shapes moved through the undergrowth. They ducked through the willows until the brush thinned and they could see a clearing ahead. Steen, another of their patrolmen, stumbled out of the copse, his sword bloody.

"Einar?" Kara asked.

Steen dropped his eyes, the answer obvious.

"There!" Kaelan pointed.

The valley ended in a slanted, shadowed hole, indicating a depression or cave. "We can make our stand there."

"Ja, force them to face us one at a time." The three sprinted to the hollow.

The sounds of battle quieted behind them. Checking over her shoulder, Kara saw a few of their adversaries pushing through the brush, searching for them.

Reaching the dark slash cut into the mossy hillside, Steen entered with no hesitation.

Kara paused at the entrance. "Kaelan, this place...."

"What, Kara?"

"I don't like this... we could get trapped."

Steen poked his head back into the sunlight.

"It's perfect—two abreast can defend the way. Come!" Kaelan jumped into the gloom. Kara inspected the soldiers chasing them—more than five had climbed from the underbrush and regrouped to follow them. She ducked her head and entered the cave.

Kara glanced around her surroundings, her eyes adjusting to the dim light. This was not a water-carved cave—No hanging rocks, spires or columns clung to the ceiling or walls. Chill, dank air, the stagnant space filled with a must of decay. Once through the craggy entrance, the space opened into a dome with a second, darker chamber through an arch in its recesses. Kaelan and Steen blocked the entrance, Kaelan propping his spear butt against his foot as a brace. Any who intended to enter must bend low to clear the overhang—Kara granted the wisdom in hiding here—a defensible position, it would be impossible for a larger force to surround them, and difficult to attack more than two at a time through the entrance. She backed into the semi-darkness, squinting to discern the shapes in the back.

This is a tomb, Kara thought as she examined the rear alcove—*if we are not careful, this grave will be ours....* Despite the shadows, she could see standing stones set in the clay floor, roughhewn tables made of outcrops and stacked stones, and odd pyramids of round rocks. A wide uprooted stump, shaggy protrusions poking from all sides, had been centered in the recess and carved into a massive seat. Over time, the bench had blackened with lichen. Shelf fungus grew from its hoary sides, and corpse-white mushrooms gathered in nooks and ringed the strange, elevated chair, rune-like scratches carved into the wood. Stooping for a better view, Kara disturbed a bat colony, and the frightened creatures flittered and swooped about the hollow, their squeaks and clicks loud and unnerving.

"Kara?" Steen called her back to the main cave. Shaking off her reverie, Kara crept back to the entrance.

Outside, shouts lifted as enemy soldiers called for assistance and gathered forces to rush their concealed bolt hole. Steen bent his knee to peer into the sunlit field.

"They know we hide here. I can see them—they plot an attack."

Kara stooped to case their gathering adversaries.

"They wait for reinforcements. I count five..."

"We cut their numbers more than half."

"Do we know who they are?" Kaelan asked.

"Matters not." Steen hawked and spat. "They want our blood. It's us or them...."

Kara frowned. "There is no exit from this cave."

Steen gave her a grim, mirthless smile. "We go out the way we came in."

A commotion sounded outside the cave. Kara and Steen stood to each side of the opening, Kaelan a few steps back with his javelin wedged against his insole.

"Here they come!"

As expected, their foes rushed the entrance, diving spear first into the gap. Steen and Kara struck the first pair, followed by a second set and a third. While they landed blows on the bevy as they charged, the sheer number of warriors pressed the wounded aside and forced their way into the cave. Kaelan stepped forward and rammed his spear into a man struggling to rise, effectively blocking the entry.

Steen and Kara faced multiple opponents, a few able to fight with minor wounds and others unharmed. Each battled a skillful spearman who used his injured comrades as a distraction. Accustomed to the bright sun outside the cave, the incoming fighters floundered as their vision, unadjusted in the half-light, failed to locate their enemies in the gloom. They stumbled and struck wide of their targets, calling to each other in confusion. Her longsword against spears, Kara dodged the jabs and swung her blade in high slices, clipping her adversaries' upper arms and chests, causing a minimum of damage.

"Worm, join your kin in Surt's domain!" Kaelan barked.

Kara chuckled. Of course, flytings! Beside her, the clang of steel rang as Steen parried an iron tip.

"Toad-licker, your grandmother fights better than you!"

"Dog bride, you smell of whelps and... and garlic!"

"What are you doing?" Steen called.

"Practicing our flytings!" Kara giggled, and knocked a spear up, its thrust carrying over her shoulder and opening her opponent's belly to her counter. The man tumbled to her feet, holding his side.

"But they don't understand you!"

"No matter, she still needs practice." Kaelan grunted, stepping to stop a limping warrior intent on dislodging the body blocking the entry. He drew his long knife and grappled with the man.

Kara danced around two foes, each blinking and stabbing wildly, seeking any purchase on her. She struck with a two-handed thrust, one blow punching into an enemy's belly, the next scraping his fellow's ribs and slicing deep into his armpit. Both collapsed moaning.

Seven bodies lay writhing on the cave floor, one jammed in the arched crawl space. Steen kicked the last to fall, and in a vicious move to ensure no sneak attacks, he worked his way through the wounded and slit their throats. Kara watched the gruesome deed with reluctance—*is this the honor fostered in Eire?*

"Are you hurt?" Steen checked them.

"Nay." Kara waved him off. "Winded."

He checked Kaelan's side. "A scratch, tis all."

Steen bled from a slice high on his forearm. "Looks bad, but not too deep." He stooped to peer under the arch.

"They prepare a second wave, these are warriors of the high kings of Ui Neill."

"We will be ready," Kara announced. "They should know not to cross swords with the forces of the Ui Imair."

"More this time...."

"Let them come...."

Outside the cave, their attackers grabbed the dead man blocking the arch by his legs and dragged his body out of the hole. Kaelan wrenched his spear free. Steen gathered dropped weapons.

"If we had more time, we could block the way in with these bodies...."

The smell of offal hung heavy in the air. Kara and Steen arranged themselves near the entry as before, Kaelan held two spears in a ready pose.

The attack came differently this time. Lying outside the cavern, archers sent bolts into the dark. A flurry of arrows flew into the chamber without warning, one clipping Steen's calf and another sinking into Kaelan's exposed thigh. Steen fell aside as more darts launched into the dark, and Kaelan crawled behind one of the fallen enemies. Multiple volleys pierced their dark hideaway, striking the back walls or sticking into the clay floor.

"Are they done?" Steen whispered. Kara inched forward, closer to the entrance. A spear poked, savagely jabbing through the hole, followed by an iron helm. Kara swung her blade—it bounced off armor. A single warrior crawled through the entry, a huge man outfitted in chainmail tunic and pounded-iron bracers. As he climbed to his feet, she drove her sword into his side. Impossible to tell if she had wounded him... he merely grunted and swung his spear like a club. The iron tip connected with her left side and pitched her to the dirt.

Dazed by bright sunlight, the ogre-sized warrior barked something in his own tongue and a scramble sounded behind him as warriors slithered into the cave on their bellies. Silently Steen attacked the giant, swinging his sword in an arc at his massive legs, and the warrior, warned by hiss of the blade swipe, with a speed belied by his huge size blocked the attack. Spinning his spear in a circle, he cleared the area around him, forcing Steen to back away.

Kara jumped across a fallen body to find Kaelan. The arrow had sunk its head deep in his muscle, and he gripped the shaft, wincing. Taking his shoulders, Kara pulled him farther back into the room. "Stay here," she whispered, and shoved his spear into his hands.

More combatants crawled into the cavern, grouping at the entrance, protecting each other while their eyes adjusted to the dim light. The big fighter in the iron helm took stock of the situation and chose Steen as his target. He advanced, flipping his spear loosely from hand to hand.

Steen attacked, swinging his sword head height, rapidly changing directions in a volley of blows, all of which the brute parried. His weapon had a short reach, while the big warrior had the length of a spear to extend his range. After enduring Steen's initial attack, he dropped to one knee and bashed his staff into Steen, sweeping his legs. Steen fell and raised his sword to counter a pending return stab—the seasoned warrior expected the block and with a round-house strike, he knocked the sax from his hand.

Instead of finishing Steen, the huge man called to his men and pointed, indicating he expected them to kill him. He glanced around the room, quickly judged between Kara and Kaelan and with a flick of his wrist, threw his javelin across the dark cavern.

Kaelan did not have time to dodge. The iron tip hit squarely in his chest and met little resistance as it punched through his lung and out his back.

"KAELAN!"

Surprised, Kaelan moved his mouth to speak, could form no sounds... he gave her his lopsided smile. He dropped his spear and tumbled to his side.

"No, Kaelan, no!" she shrieked.

The big man ignored her—she was merely a girl....

Her vision smeared with tears. She howled and rushed the warrior.

Before he could react, she slashed both his legs across the knees. Deep cuts snapped his tendons. With a whelp of surprise, he spun to grab her, his weapon across the chamber in Kaelan's chest. Wounded legs refused to hold him upright. He stumbled. Unprepared for her fury, he grabbed her shoulders and lifted her from the ground to throttle her... all Kara needed was to close the gap in their height. Snarling, she drove her longsword through his throat. As he dropped her to clutch at his neck, she turned on the others crowded over Steen.

A few enemies had surrounded the Dublinner, a hand dagger his last attempt to hold them at bay. As the shieldmaiden overcame their leader, they paused, astonished.

Blood pounded in her ears. Anger, furious and red hot, surged through her and Kara became a savage, unthinking animal. Her vision ringed with scarlet, she lost herself in Odin's righteous rage—berserk! Like her grandfather Ironfist, she hoisted Wolftongue with no care for her own protection and attacked.

Potent with rage Kara charged the unready warriors, slashed the first on his side, stabbed the second in his gut and stepped on Steen to drive her sword tip into the remaining man hovering over the Dublinner. Ignoring the groan Steen made when she stomped on his chest, she shrieked and carried her battle to the foes arrayed at the entrance.

Kara threw herself at her enemies. Bashing aside spears, she slashed and hacked, all the while emitting an unrelenting banshee screech. Glancing blows bounced from her armor. She grasped a raised spear in her hand and wrenched it from her foe's hands, running him through with her sword. Her blade lodged in one chest, she punched an uppercut past a swordman's block, hammer knuckles cracked into his chin. Spouting blood dowsed her—splattered with gore, she bowled the Irish aside, her wrath overcoming all before her. A coward yelled for help, and more men scrambled into the cavern. Enraged, Kara dispatched them as they ducked through the entrance.

The wounded added their screams to hers, their anguish melting together in the slaughter. Finding Kaelan, she fought over her dead lover. He became her anchor in the melee. Fallen bodies heaped around her.

Blind with the All-Father holy rage, she viciously savaged all who came within her reach, her blade singing in the air.

She took a glancing blow to her temple, and despite a sharp pain, she fought through the agony. A wary warrior thrust into her side, the blade lodging in her breastplate and unfazed, she slashed the man's throat.

A surge of fresh warriors pushed her back into the rear chamber—she lost count of the foes who faced her. Submersed in an all-consuming battle fever, Kara trounced each in turn. She howled in the center of the dark throne room, a blood-drenched Valkyrie.

The last remaining Irish, terrified of her horrible visage, scrambled from her, climbing on a rocky outcrop in a futile attempt to escape. She chased him, yanked his legs to topple him and drove her longsword through his chest, plunging it into the rocky dais underneath. Blinded by her anger, she mutilated the body, pounding and hacking until her savage strikes cracked the underlying stone. Madness pounded in her ears....

No combatants remained. The massacre piled about her.

Kara screamed, frenzied in her wrath and unspent berserk rage. She rushed around the chamber, toppling stacked stones, bashing at the tables with her hilt and kicking the rocks—she dragged the broken bodies onto the strange, black chair and hacked them into bloody pulp.

She stumbled across her beloved.

Falling to her knees, she pulled Kaelan to her lap and sobbed over his body, wretched and grief-stricken....

BEHIND KARA, a shadow moved.

Silent, a dark Vanir elf stepped from the Realm Between Realms into Midgard.

With a sneer of haughty disdain, he struck her with a thin, indigo rod. Kara collapsed over Kaelan, her sword clattering aside.

Shapes arrived in the cavern behind Kara's prone form —more dark elves entered the cave, slender, gaunt, and unnaturally tall.

"See this desecration?"

"This Midgardian has ruined our throne room."

"Did you see her fight? Old One Eye would want this one for his hall."

"You should not have been so quick to dispatch..."

"I sent her to Helheim, nothing in Midgard survives my stroke."

"My throne. See the sacrifice table...."

"She ruined our blood fungus, tended for centuries."

"What shall we do with all these dead Midgardians?"

The elves gathered over her body, surveying the damaged room, the heaps of dead and dying.

"Loki's bane... She lives!"

"What?" One bent to check.

"See here, a lowly hag stone protected her from your all-powerful rod."

Ignoring the sarcasm, the Vanir gestured at Kara's unconscious form. "Pitch this lich out into the fields beyond our chambers."

"And the creature's hug?"

"This *thing* has desecrated my Winter Citadel, the seat of my Unseelie Court here in Midgard. Our Vanir Emperor shall hear of this desecration! Until this damage is repaired, her debt to me is unpaid. I claim this hug as my thrall here, and when our season here ends, she shall face the council of the Unseelie in Vanaheim!"

"So be it, my dark jarl."

EPILOGUE: LAILA

THORFINN

Memory is a funny thing.

He remembered hearing Goorm, the lindworm howling in pain....

Someone gently removed his gag. He floated; no, he was carried. Lifted with care. A slope, a jostle. The smell of the sea.

He awoke in a tent, wrapped in soft furs.

A girl sat next to him.

She fed him spoons of broth, her long, jet black hair pulled back from her face and almond-shaped eyes, a rosy blush to her cheeks. Her black, woolen smock had scarlet ribbons around her neck and cuffs, the decoration a silk brocade with woven lace repeating in complicated, coiling patterns.

He tried to speak. A croak emerged.

"Wait." She set the bowl aside. "My father."

She slipped out the flap.

Thorfinn studied the tent, strange feathers hung from a

string, white furs neatly stacked and seal skin boots. Carved, ivory tusks and a sharp, hooked knife lay by a small, rock-ringed hearth. Intricate, woven patterns adorned the blankets and trimmed the leather tent. A birka-style hat trimmed in fur lay on his blanket.

The girl returned with a tall man dressed in dyed, black skins trimmed in white and scarlet embroidery.

"I know you."

"Aye, child, we have met.

"Where?"

"Upon Sviney, the floating Isle."

Of course, he remembered him... "Ravald."

"You have a good memory for one so young."

"Where...?"

"In my yurt. I am glad you awake—we pack our summer camp and prepare to move for winter. The reindeer strain for the tundra. It is their way."

"How?"

"Your lindworm came to us, seeking you among the mountains."

Alarmed, he struggled to sit. "The witch...?"

"Gone. Your wyrm destroyed her."

"The spell...?" He touched his throat where the threads of Siedr magic had bound him.

"Lifted. I broke the curse when we found you. Once we defeated the enchantress, your dragon followed your scent like a dog on a spoor."

"I remember Goorm crying...."

"Indeed, the great wyrm was sorely hurt. We took him to a sacred linden grove, where he curled around a mighty tree to draw succor from its essence. Over time he shall heal."

"Are you sure?"

"He has already shed his skin and grows stronger every day."

"His skin?"

The girl stepped forward with a bolt of cloth, a shimmering weave like crystalline scales.

"There is much of it. Such skin carries his magic."

"What will you do with it?"

"What?"

"Of course, his skin belongs to you."

Finn eased back into the pillows. "I don't know."

"Possibly we can sew it as a lining into a walrus vest for you, or a cap. You will need warmer clothes for the winter here." The girl smiled and returned the fabric to its place.

"May I...?"

Ravald helped Finn stand. Woozy, his left foot throbbed with each step—he remembered and studied his hand and foot in horror, both bandaged in white muslin.

"My hand?"

Ravald grew somber, holding out a gentle hand. "You have lost a finger and a few toes. Scarring, aye, but they shall heal, none of the wounds are as bad as the black frostbite. Our people suffer from that winter curse."

Light-headed, the words conveyed little meaning to Thorfinn—*lost a finger?* He remembered flashes of memories, the old crone leaning over his face with a hooked knife, waving a bloody finger.

"We found this tied to your skid." He held out an ornamental sword hilt, the blade broken a finger width beyond the crossbar. Finn took the hilt with shaking hands and held it to his chest. *Gunhild....* "There was more, but you can sift through it when you feel better."

With his arm around the boy, Ravald lifted the skin which comprised the door. Outside a pale azure sky brightened the chilly afternoon. The surf rolled in and washed out, a steady rhythm. Ravald wrapped his bear skin tighter around him and arranged it around his neck.

"Careful not to catch a chill, you don't have your strength back."

Villagers eyed him, curious children dashed happily to his side, to be chased back by the raven-haired girl. Ravald walked him slowly around the village, showing him how they break the camp. Dried and prepared food, ready for winter stores, moose, seals, walrus, and whale. Skin kayaks pulled above the tide line, men raked dried salt beds beside them, collecting the sandy white grains in homespun sacks. Snow drifts tucked in corners of the leather shelters, and despite the sunny sky, a few flakes swirled in the cold, afternoon air. At the top of the rise, Finn saw men standing with shepherd crooks, and beyond a herd of reindeer hobbled and roped together. The beasts snorted and bucked, ready for their journey. Exotic smells lifted from the cookfire. His stomach growled.

Ravald sat him on a rock by a smoldering fire of deer moss and driftwood.

Thorfinn paused, watching birds wing over the waves. *Raga*....

The girl returned with a leather cup holding steaming tea. He could smell herbs.

"Drink this." She offered him the mug. He carefully set his broken sword in his lap and accepted the brew.

"Who are you?"

"Me?" She quirked her brow and smiled. "I am Ravald and Njivi's daughter.

"You can call me Laila."

MARAUDERS IN JOTUNHEIM

THE FORERUNNER SERIES
BOOK FIVE

JAY VELOSO BATISTA

COMING SOON...

The fifth book in the Forerunner Series...
Marauders in Jotunheim!

Giants, trolls, monsters & dark elves: Danger in the Halls of the Mountain King!

Cub braves danger in Anglia to return to his Jorvik homestead. In Mercia, impatient Gurid sails to seek her run-away daughter, while in the Unseelie Court Kara struggles to escape magical imprisonment. Across the North Sea, Thorfinn the Forerunner and his Uncle Karl consent to a Thunder God quest.

Cub claims his estate, but when wrongly blamed for murder, he must overcome unjust accusations and his own doubts to lead his clan. Faced with a comatose child, Gurid realizes she needs more than a steady sword arm and mother's love to save her starving daughter—is Gurid willing to accept ghostly clues? In a strange realm where strength of arms fails her, Kara must cultivate new skills and navigate courtly intrigues before her captors carry her to Vanaheim forever. For the crew of the *Verdandi Smiles*, raiding Jotunheim brings perils and riches, but to save his scattered family, young Finn must overcome loss and conspire with a hated enemy.

And who is this Blue Man who fights like a dervish, is he friend or foe?

Described as Cornwall's 'Last Kingdom' meets Martin's GOT and Sapkowski's 'Witcher,' the Forerunner Series marries history, Norse mythology, and oft overlooked mythic creatures with expansive storytelling. If you enjoy fast-paced, multi-character driven fantasy with unexpected plot twists, you'll love 'Marauders in Jotunheim.'

The Agneson Lineage

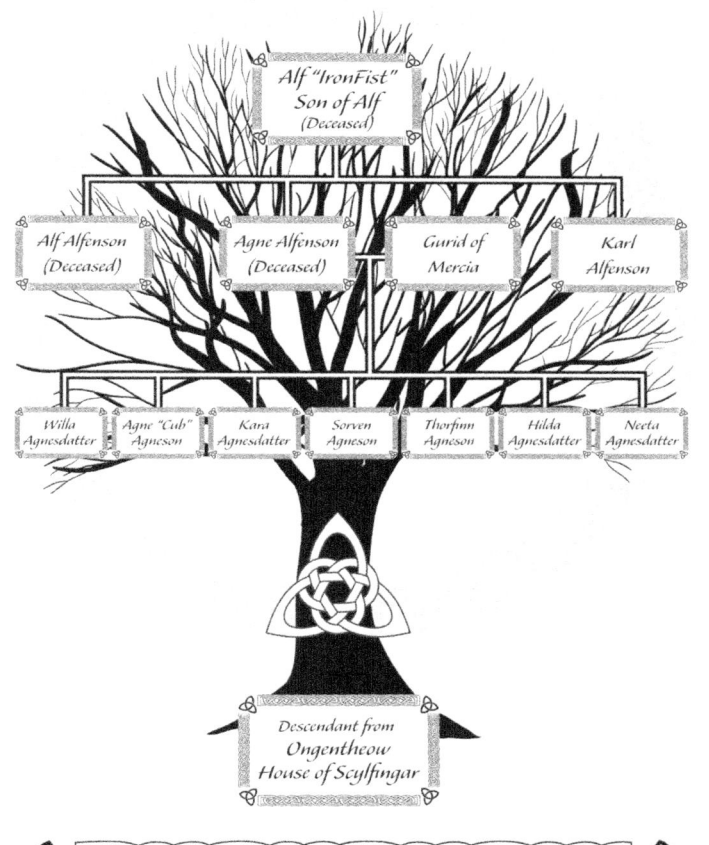

Alf "IronFist" Son of Alf *(Deceased)*

- **Alf Alfenson** *(Deceased)*
- **Agne Alfenson** *(Deceased)*
- **Gurid of Mercia**
- **Karl Alfenson**

- Willa Agnesdatter
- Agne "Cub" Agneson
- Kara Agnesdatter
- Sorven Agneson
- Thorfinn Agneson
- Hilda Agnesdatter
- Neeta Agnesdatter

Descendant from Ongentheow House of Scylfingar

CHAPTER 12
DRAMATIS PERSONAE

--Gurid of Eddisbury, Mercia, known as Blue-eyes, wife of Agne Alfenson, killed at the Battle of Ethandun, age 40

--Agne Agneson, age 19, known as "Cub," first son and heir of Agne Alfenson and Gurid of Eddisbury, a veteran of the Battle of Ethandun

--Kara Agnesdatter, age 14, daughter of Agne Alfenson, carrying their clan's ancestral blade Wolftongue

--Sorven Agneson, age 13, second son of Agne Alfenson and Gurid of Eddisbury

--Thorfinn Agneson, age 12, youngest son of Agne Alfenson and Gurid of Eddisbury

--Hilda Agnesdatter, age 7, daughter of Agne Alfenson and Gurid of Eddisbury

--Neeta Agnesdatter, age 4, daughter of Agne Alfenson and Gurid of Eddisbury

--Yeru, Gurid's widowed cousin and nurse to Agne's children, age 50

--Kaelan Ulbrechtson, age 16

--Dundle, a hired farmhand and veteran of the Battle of Ethandun, age 17

--Ragacheep Nanawan, known as "Raga," a ghost of a 5th Century mage, trapped in the Realm Between

Crew of the *Verdandi Smiles*
--Karl Alfenson, the third son of Alf "Ironfist" Alfenson, age 38, reputed descendant of the House of Scylfingar, Son of Skane, captain of the snekke longboat *Verdandi Smiles,* and younger brother of Agne Alfenson
--Martine La Fontaine—Frankish mercenary, age 24
--Jormander the Skald, age 34
--Jorn, Son of Sven, known as Wyrm Slayer, age 32
--Kol Skegg, shipwright and pilot, age 42
--Rurik the Saarlased, a Letts Sea (Baltic Sea) pirate, age 36
--Hagbard, Smithy, age 44
--Sorli, Son of Gwerd, age 28
--Sven Horseman, age 32
--Ingulf, Son of Osgulf, age 35
--Havar Darkhead, age 37
--Gudrun, a most superstitious sailor, age 52
--Wyselhax, called "Hax," the Klabautermann or Mast Troll of the *Verdandi Smiles*

The Northern Way
Unlahdil Fortress on the Norwegian coast, under the banner of the jarl of Lade
--Chieftain Hamund, Son of Hothl,
--Allinor Hamundsdatter, Hamund's youngest daughter, age 11

--Hamund's kinsmen: cousins Regin and Otr Hothlson, and Alsvid, an uncle by marriage

--Signy, Regin's sister, Hamund's cousin and adopted "niece" of Hamund, age 16

--Holjan, Son of Garm, a Siedr warlock and sworn enemy of Hamund Hothlson; his mare and sigil is an owl

--Rind of the evil eye, a volva shapeshifter witch that takes the form of a trollcat

--Knetti the Trickster, a volva shapeshifter witch that takes the form of a vulture

--Harald Tanglehair, historical figure, the jarl attempting to unify the petty kingdoms of

Allies of Harald:

--Aki of Varmland, historical figure

--Hakon Grjotgardsson, (Hack-on Gree-ot-gard-son) historical figure, jarl of Lade

--Gryting, king of Orkdal, historical figure, the first leader in Trondelag to make a stand against King Harald's ravaging of the country. At the Battle of Orkdal, Gryting's men were defeated and Gryting taken prisoner. After this Gryting swore allegiance to King Harald.

--Dag Dagson, one of Harald's retainers and a battle brother of Karl Alfenson and his men

--Admiral Egil and Admiral Uffe, commanders of naval squads under the Commodore Jarl Hakon in the navy of Harald Tanglehair

Enemies of Harald

--Eirik, King of Hordaland, historical figure

--Sulke, King of Rogaland, and his brother, Earl Sote, historical figures

--Kjotve the Rich, King of Agder and his son, Thor Haklang, historical figures

--Hroald Hryg and Had the Hard, two brothers from Thelemark, historical figures

--The Chieftains from the Sognefjord area, historical figures

Britany

--Rolf the Ganger, the conqueror known to the Franks as "Rollo," historical figure—destined to become Robert the First of Normandy

--Robert of the Breton March, Frankish lord and sworn enemy of Rolf; historical figure

--Poppa of Bayeux, daughter of Berenger, Count of Rennes, and future wife of Rolf; historical figure

--Hagrold the Norseman, Rolf's lieutenant, historical figure

--Colden, captain of the knarr "Seawing," banner man to Rolf

Dublinn, Eire

--Imar, historical figure, supposed son of Ragnar Lodbrok and King of Dublinn, known as 'Ivar the Boneless' in Britain, killed in 875

--Ausle and Olafr (Amlaib in Irish), Imar's companions and co-regents, historical figures

--Cerball, king of Osraige, and Aed Findliath, King of Ailech and northern Ui Neill, Irish lords known to ally with Imar and his co-regents, historical figures

--Barith, eldest son of Imar, King of Dublinn; historical figure; a Findgaill (light foreigner)

--Bradon mac Ausle, son of Ausle, newly crowned King of Dublin, historical figure, a Dubgaill (dark foreigner)

--Otir, son of Jarnkne, historical figure, in love with Muirgel

--Muirgel, the daughter of Mael Sechnaill, Irish king of Mide, historical figure

--Sichfrith, son of Imar, historical figure

--Sitric, son of Imar, Sichfrith's younger brother, historical figure

--Hingamund, historical figure

--Mael Finnia mac Flannacain, king of Brega, enemy of the Dublinn kings, historical figure

--Cerball mac Muirecáin, king of Leinster, enemy of Dublinn kings, historical figure

--Gunna, leader of the Dublinn household guard, a Findgaill

--Asta, Dublinn Shieldmaiden and household guard, a Findgaill

--Helka, Dublinn Shieldmaiden and household guard, a Findgaill

--Tordis, Dublinn Shieldmaiden and household guard, a Dubgaill

--Seelie, Faery of the Summer Court

--Unseelie, Faery of the Winter Court

The Welsh Mountains

--Gethin, the aged farmer

--Heledd, the farmer's second wife

--Gwenan, the eldest daughter of Heledd

--Nia, the younger daughter of Heledd

The Far North

The Skridfinn People
--Ravald, leader and Shaman
--Njivi, Ravald's wife
--Laila, daughter of Ravald and Njivi

THANK YOU FOR READING!

I sincerely hope you enjoyed 'Kara Shieldmaiden of Eire.' I must admit, I love these adventures and you can tell from the last chapter, there's plenty more excitement in store for Thorfinn, his uncle Karl, Kara, Sorven, and Cub. Did you think Cub would be tapped as an ambassador? What's next for our broken-hearted Kara? Stay tuned, because the fantastic journeys of the Agneson clan continue in Book 5.

When I first wrote 'Thorfinn and the Witch's Curse,' I was pleased to receive your notes and letters, and I especially appreciate your opinions about the characters, story and the history. As an author, I love feedback. Candidly, you are the reason I continue with the series, so tell me what you like, what you don't like, what you even hated! I'd love to hear from you. You can write me at jay@jayvelosobatista.com and visit me at http://www.jayvelosobatista.com.

Finally, I need to ask a favor: If you are so inclined, please leave a review of Kara Shieldmaiden of Eire. Loved it, hated it—I'd just enjoy your feedback.

As you may know, reviews can be tough to come by these days. You, the reader, have the power now to make or break a book. If you have time, here's a link to my author page on Amazon. You can find all my books here: http://mybook.to/Forerunnerseries.

Thank you for reading Kara and spending time with me.
In gratitude,

PS. Want to find free books and discounted books in the genres you love? Join Bookbub and follow my author page: https://www.bookbub.com/authors/jay-veloso-batista. Another great place for reviews and information on books is Goodreads, and you can like my author page there at https://www.goodreads.com/JayVelosoBatista

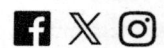

ALSO BY JAY VELOSO BATISTA

Thorfinn and the Witch's Curse
The Forerunner Series, Book 1

The Vardoger Boy
The Forerunner Series, Book 2

On Viking Seas
The Forerunner Series, Book 3